# HAIR OUT OF PLACE

HELEN JULIET

Hair Out of Place
Copyright © 2020 by Helen Juliet

1

# GRIFF

Little did Griff Thompson know on the first day of his new job that the assassins sent to kill his client would be so utterly inept.

Naturally, his Monday morning didn't *start* with flying stars and broken vases. It started with surprisingly good coffee and the short-lived misconception that perhaps this gig would be an easy pay cheque.

"Mr Raphael? Oh, he's no trouble at all," Griff's new co-worker, Winston Smith, said in response to Griff's question about what he was getting himself into. Winston was a grizzly Cockney in a leather bomber jacket over his shirt and tie. Typically, the other guys at the agency were ex-coppers or wannabe MI5 agents, either jaded or full of shit respectively. But Winston had more of a fatherly vibe about him.

The good kind, as opposed to the asshole kind, Griff was happy to say. But it would take more than half an hour to get to know the man, and there were eight of them contracted to the team. So Griff would reserve judgement on this being a simple job just yet.

The two men stood outside the penthouse doors, over sixty floors high in one of the tallest but otherwise nondescript buildings along London's Bishopsgate. This tower didn't have a trendy nickname or interesting architecture that featured in blockbuster movie scenes. Neither did it have a ridiculously expensive sushi restaurant nestled at its base nor a pub with a mini-golf course on its roof. It just blended into the skyline, despite its stature. Probably why Griff's new mysterious top-secret client liked it.

The client he hadn't met yet, not even during his interviews, and knew next to nothing about. Including why he needed round-the-clock protection.

"You've been with him long, then?" Griff asked, probing for information. He hated going in blind on an assignment like this. He always did his research. Except on this occasion, where he couldn't find a single thing about his client or his mother online.

Like that wasn't highly suspicious, at all.

Winston nodded. "Oh, I've been with the family for years. Raphie's a sweet kid, won't give you no trouble."

This was hopefully going to be a pleasant change of pace from the politicians and celebs Griff usually dealt with in the city. He'd become accustomed to ridiculous hospitality riders and clients who resented his presence to the extent they'd throw shoes at his head. He'd tried to convince himself that it didn't bother him, but the truth was, it had gotten tiresome. A babysitting gig for a trust fund brat sounded perfect to keep him occupied for a while. He took another sip of rich coffee from the cardboard cup and almost smiled.

Almost.

He wasn't here to enjoy himself. He was here to protect his client – a young Mr Raphael d'Oro – just like he did any other client. With utmost professionalism and exemplary service. Just because Griff had been saddled with a line of highly strung narcissists from the agency lately didn't make a difference. Every life mattered.

Even a spoiled penthouse baby.

Griff shifted on his feet. To be fair, he hadn't actually met twenty-one-year-old Raphael yet. But anyone who'd grown up in this kind of luxury had to be a proper nightmare. Greedy, selfish, ignorant – the works. Griff had just seen the marble lobby so far with its gold-framed impressionist artwork, and he could tell that this place wasn't real life.

Although it was *damned* nice.

"So what's his deal?" Griff asked, jerking his head to the closed doors he hadn't stepped through yet.

He didn't want to ask outright why the d'Oros needed protection, because that might seem like prying. But he didn't appreciate being kept in the dark. He had very little to be proud of in his life, but his outstanding work record was one thing he held dear. Usually, the agency was better at providing clients' details ahead of time, but they'd insisted that a large part of this job's increased salary was the utmost need for confidentiality.

It made Griff irritable right off the bat. He would hate to make a bad impression, and he felt underprepared. Like he'd had a test sprung on him. Although school had been a long time ago, he still recalled that sinking sensation of dread, of failure before he'd even been given a chance to try.

Still, he would do everything in his power to make this new position a success. He didn't have to like Raphael. But he would *damn* well keep him alive.

His briefing had been as flimsy as a wet paper bag, but from what Griff could tell, Raphael wasn't actually in any immediate danger. He'd just had round-the-clock surveillance his entire life, and one of the regular team had rotated out after two years of deathly boredom. When the agency had approached Griff, he'd almost choked at the wage they were offering, and decided he could do two years of boring for that amount, no problem.

But he had to say he was intrigued. Who *was* this guy?

"Mr Raphael's deal?" said Winston, rubbing his stubble, silver against his dark skin. He glanced back at the doors, where they were still waiting to be invited in by Ms d'Oro. "Honestly? Nothing much, really. He's a sweet kid, does as he's told, and he always remembers everyone's names. A regular ray of sunshine," he added with a fond laugh.

Griff didn't much fancy the sound of a 'ray of sunshine'. That could potentially be annoying. But he sipped the coffee again and made himself promise to reserve judgement until he'd met mother and son. After all, the small, ornate table where the coffee machine stood was also stocked with fresh, buttery pastries and colourful fruit. Griff's stomach growled, but it wouldn't be polite to greet Annabella or Raphael d'Oro with greasy fingers and a shirt covered in crumbs, so he did his best to ignore the temptation. *I've got a cereal bar in my pocket for later,* he reminded himself sternly. *And after my first pay cheque, I can get whatever breakfast I like.*

He almost smiled again at the thought of not having to ration his grocery budget for once in his life. Between London rent rates, bills, and petrol, food that wasn't basic protein or carbs for muscle building was a luxury. But maybe not for much longer.

Whilst he'd been daydreaming about dinners more glamourous than beans on toast, Winston had been happily chatting about the steady stream of people that came through the penthouse on a daily basis. There was a physical visitor logbook that had to be strictly kept, and all appointments were pre-booked. Aside from Ms d'Oro's friends – of which there were only a handful – all other arrangements were generally made months in advance.

Piano, yoga, cooking, flower arranging, ballroom dancing, and several different languages – including British Sign Language: there apparently weren't many things Raphael d'Oro *didn't* have a teacher for. According to Winston, who was still nattering on pleasantly without much encouragement from Griff other than the occasional hum, Raphael had more GSCEs and A-Levels than you could shake a stick at. He had also just completed a combined honours degree in European History and Political Science.

All from this penthouse.

Griff knew he'd have to wait, but his burning question of *why* was growing every minute they were left to linger out in the entrance lobby, opposite the only elevator that reached the top of the building. It required several layers of complex access, and they weren't expecting anyone, so Griff barely paid any attention to it at all. He absorbed everything Winston was telling him, compensating for his lack of a briefing from the agency with any information about the d'Oros he could get.

The more he heard about Raphael – this precious, protected, prodigal son – the clearer the picture he was starting to form in his mind. It was completely unprofessional, but so was the level of mystery he was being forced to endure.

With such a wide skill set, perhaps Griff's client wasn't going to be an insufferable brat. Maybe he would be educated and interesting. He was obviously unfathomably rich, which wasn't exactly a turn-off, and along with the yoga and dance, Raphael also had a PT and swimming coach. Griff licked his lips, picturing a virile, strapping young man, athletic and worldly. Maybe that kind of guy wouldn't be so terrible to babysit.

He mentally slapped himself. So what if this Raphael was sounding more interesting with everything he learned? Griff was a neutral party, here to make sure he and his mum stayed alive and *nothing* else. Boring was the objective here. Maybe the fancy coffee was getting to his brain on an empty stomach. The last thing he'd ever dream of doing was crossing any kind of personal lines with a client.

No matter if he was a young beefcake, down to fuck.

Griff cleared his throat and rolled his eyes at himself as he dropped his now empty cardboard cup in the small, tasteful recycling bin by the refreshments table. Ludicrous. Just because it had been forever since Griff's last hook-up didn't mean it was okay to be thinking with his downstairs brain. Later, he was sure he was going to be very ashamed of himself. But for now, Winston checked his wristwatch and then his phone, nodding and effectively pulling Griff's mind out of the gutter.

"That's a message from Annabella, right on time," Winston said. "Let's get you introduced and show you the grand tour, hey?" He winked, reaching for the door sensor with his key card. "You'll be a part of the family in no time, son."

Before Griff even had time to format a protest in his mind – family had *no* place in business – Winston opened one of the double doors a crack, and a fluffy blur shot out.

Without even thinking, Griff shot his hand out, reflexively grabbing the foreign object. Luckily, he didn't grab too hard, because when he lifted the blur to inspect, it turned out to be a golden-coloured tabby cat with a pink rhinestone-studded collar, squashed face, downward mouth, and strange folded ears. The creature's piercing jade-blue eyes were their most startling feature, though.

Eyes that were very much glaring at Griff, possibly for impeding the cat's escape.

"Sparrow!" a breathless, panicky voice cried as a slim body came crashing into the door that Winston had unlocked, sending it flying open all the way.

And Griff's heart did something very strange.

The young man had to be Raphael d'Oro. He appeared to be the right age, and who else would be chasing a cat around at this time in the morning? But his appearance quite thoroughly shattered the image Griff had been painting in his mind.

He was lightly tanned, barefoot, and in faded blue jeans and a maroon T-shirt that clung to his body. He might have been slim, but Griff's quick glance up and down suggested that the PT and swim instructor had helped develop a solid physique nonetheless. But where he'd been picturing a reserved or brooding young man who'd grown up alone in this tower, it seemed Winston was completely right.

Raphael's big smile and sparkling green eyes were pure sunshine as he saw the cat being cradled in Griff's arms was safe and sound.

And then there was the hair.

In the second or two it had taken for Griff to catalogue his client's other features, his brain now got stuck as he took in the sight of such unusual and quite frankly *astonishing* hair. It was white blond, wavy, and long – but not just regular long. As Raphael bounced off the door frame, then skipped over to where Griff stood, the locks swished and swayed far past his shoulders. In fact, they looked to reach all the way down to his hips. There were several tiny braids around the top of his head that gave an impression almost like a crown, and other plaits of varying widths that trailed down his back, mingling in with the free locks. He looked like he belonged in a fantasy TV series, if it wasn't for the denim jeans.

"Oh, thank you!" Raphael cried, yanking Griff from his trance-like analysis of his new client. He could honestly say he'd never seen a man like this before in his life, and he wasn't sure what to make of it.

His professionalism was hard-wired, though. So he blinked and mentally shook himself as Raphael reached for the confused-looking cat in Griff's hands. "I take it this is yours?" he grunted, offering the small beast over.

Raphael sighed gratefully and took the ball of fluff into his arms. "I know *logically* there's nowhere for her to go up here, but I have this reoccurring nightmare that she'll dash out just as the lift doors open and somehow escape and get lost in the city, and I'd never, *ever* forgive myself." He looked down with such affection at the angry-looking cat, Griff's heart couldn't help but pang. "As much as I appreciate wanting to escape downstairs, that's just not safe, my darling."

For a second, his bright, sunny smile faded into something very sad, but if Griff had blinked, he'd have missed it. Then Raphael took a deep breath, smiled, and smushed his face against the cat's fuzzy cheek.

"But you're safe now, princess, aren't you? Yes, you are, thanks to the nice man." He looked up, flushed and grinning, before he awkwardly stuck a hand out towards Griff. "You must be the new bodyguard, Griffin? I'm Raphie."

Griff had minor whiplash from the whirlwind of chatter that had just been thrown his way, but he managed to nod in what he hoped was a respectful manner. All his thoughts of a simple, easy, *calm* job for the next couple of years were fast evaporating. This guy was a ball of energy.

Griff already felt exhausted, but he gritted his teeth and shook Raphael's hand once, firmly. "I'm Mr Thompson, yes," Griff confirmed. Clients weren't supposed to address him with his first name. It lacked professionalism. "Pleased to meet you, Mr d'Oro."

Raphael blew a raspberry. "Everyone's on a first-name basis around here. We're all family up in the clouds, aren't we, Winston?"

"That we are, Mr Raphael," said Winston, who'd been quietly watching on. He seemed amused by the little scene between Raphael and Griff. "We were just heading inside to greet you and your mother for the tour and then Mr Griffin's briefing. I'm very sorry to have inadvertently aided in Miss Sparrow's escape plans."

Raphael hummed and nuzzled his nose in the cat's fur. "Bad kitty," he said fondly.

Then he flashed that dazzling smile at Griff and Winston, and Griff ignored the strange sensation in his belly. The kid was mildly irritating, but nothing he couldn't handle.

He definitely wasn't cute or adorable. Nuh-uh.

"Let's all head in," Raphael continued cheerfully. "I think Mum is ready for you. We were just getting ready for the day."

He spun on the spot, making his mesmerising white-blond hair twirl out like the skirt of a wedding dress. Again, Griff wasn't sure what to make of his body's reaction to seeing all the cascading hair moving in that way. A shiver flurried over his whole body, and there was a squirming sensation that felt like it wriggled between his stomach and groin. Confusing as his response was, he knew one thing. Anything involving a client and his downstairs brain was the exact opposite of professional.

He just wasn't used to it, was all. The novelty would wear off, he was sure. And once he got something in his stomach other than the rich, strong coffee, he'd start thinking with his upstairs brain again. That was it. No biggie.

Unlike the apartment he'd just stepped into, which was fucking *huge*.

He clamped his jaw shut to stop it from dropping, grinding his teeth as he took in the incredible sight. He'd pretty much guessed that the penthouse would be the entire floor, but that hadn't quite translated in his mind's eye. He walked over marble and looked up at the high ceilings with their contemporary chandeliers. Glancing subtly around, he appreciated the floor-to-ceiling windows in every direction, the marble pillars, the sleek, monochrome furnishings, and the splashes of colour from enormous floral arrangements.

Raphael hadn't been joking when he'd referred to this place as being up in the clouds. Griff had never seen a view of London quite like this. He'd worked in The Shard plenty of times, but that was south of the river, and they were currently opposite Liverpool Street Station. As it was a bright, clear day, he could see all over the East End in one direction, stretching out to the Olympic stadium in Stratford. In the other, the City of London was splayed out with St Paul's Cathedral in the middle, its dome standing proudly in the sunlight.

There was a central column in the penthouse where works of art hung, including one made up of vivid paint splashes that took up one entire side. To the right was a curving staircase leading up to *another* floor. Possibly the bedrooms and bathrooms, Griff guessed. He turned his attention back to his young charge as Raphael skipped over to a breakfast bar by a kitchen island.

A tall, slim woman was sat there, smiling at the men approaching her. She was perhaps a decade older than Griff, well dressed in a trouser suit accessorised with plenty of flashy gold jewellery. She was also wearing a colourful silk headscarf tied in a knot with no visible hair, making Griff wonder if she'd had chemo in the not-too-distant past.

However, her demeanour was cheerful and bright as they approached, and her fluffy cream slippers added a softness to her otherwise business-like appearance.

"Annabella," Winston said fondly, approaching her alongside Raphael. "May I introduce the newest member of our team, Mr Griffin Thompson." He took both of her hands in his briefly before gesturing towards Griff. "Griffin, this is Ms Annabella d'Oro, Mr Raphael's mother."

"Welcome to our home, Griffin," she said warmly, but also with a brisk, formal manner that hinted at her professional status. Her accent sounded Italian or something similar. "It's a pleasure to meet you. I have a conference call now, but it's important to me that everyone is welcomed properly. Perhaps Raphie can show you around, after which we can all have some brunch. Then we can give you your final briefing."

Griff nodded once, not trusting himself to speak. He was pleased that there was at least some plan to illuminate him on the particulars of this assignment, but he was wrestling with some personal demons that he refused to show any hint of.

He had been aware that this new client was going to be wealthy, but it was different seeing it up close and personal. For just a second, he couldn't stop the flare of bitter resentment he felt for that small boy who'd cried himself to sleep many a night from being cold and hungry. He'd been trying to forget that version of himself for years, but when faced with such extravagance, it was difficult not to feel the inequality keenly. With this view, how many other hungry people could they look down on?

"Griffin saved Sparrow, Mum," said Raphael as he twirled barefoot around the kitchen, dragging Griff from his melancholy.

Raphael placed his cat on the counter, then danced over to the couch in the living room area. A pair of socks and some trainers were waiting for him by the sofa arm, and he quickly put them on his feet before returning to the kitchen area. Then he made a beeline for a cupboard which he opened to retrieve a box of frosted rainbow-coloured Pop-Tarts covered in sprinkles that looked like a root canal waiting to happen.

"He's not even been on the job an hour, and he's already earning his keep!" Raphael continued. He grinned and danced his way to the toaster before holding out the box. "Would you like one?" he asked Griff sincerely. "They're my favourite, but I'll share a pack with Sparrow's hero." He bit his lip as he smiled, a blush creeping on his cheeks.

He was the picture of innocence, and Griff stamped down whatever he was feeling in his belly. Probably indigestion. He should take the damn Pop-Tart to soak up the coffee and be done with all these outrageous bodily reactions.

They were creeping dangerously lower than his belly…

But instead, he grunted, "I'm fine, thank you." Of all the things he could accept to eat from a client, a multi-coloured sugar explosion masquerading as a breakfast pastry was probably the least dignified.

The next couple of hours were pretty routine in some ways. Griff catalogued every nook and cranny he could in the vast two-storey penthouse, as well as around the private swimming pool and open-air cinema situated on the roof of the building.

What was not routine was how Raphael chatted non-stop, telling Griff everything imaginable about the penthouse. From the practicalities of the security systems and the history of the various artwork and furniture pieces to little personal anecdotes that he recounted breathlessly as he bounded by Griff's side, his cat curled around his shoulders. With gusto and giggles, he recalled the time Winston had been forced to cover Raphael's arm in garlic butter when he'd got his elbow stuck between the slates of one of the deckchairs, or another time Raphael had slept on the roof to see a particular meteor shower.

His green eyes shone with every little adventure he relayed. He was probably just thrilled to have someone new to talk to, Griff reminded himself. He lived a very isolated life, up in the clouds, so it was most likely that had no particular regard for Griff in particular. Rather a general need for company.

It was very chirpy and annoying having this ray of sunshine bouncing around, Griff told himself. Not charming *or* adorable. Hopefully, Griff's monosyllabic grunting responses made that clear. Although Raphael didn't even seem to notice as he whispered excitedly how he sometimes sent paper airplanes flying from the rooftop with messages written on them for unsuspecting Londoners. When Griff gave in to his curiosity and asked what kind of messages (Raphael's existence was supposed to be a complete secret, after all), Raphael chuckled.

"Oh, just childish things. 'Have a cracking day!' is always nice. 'Watch out for puddles!' if it's been raining. 'Merry Christmas' in summer, just to keep them on their toes."

It was such a simple game and actually kind of sweet if you thought about it. But Griff was suddenly struck with the realisation that was possibly the closest Raphael had come to mingling with the people below. Griff took the tube every day and found himself stuck in traffic more often than he'd like, cursing his fellow commuters.

There was a strong chance Raphael would enjoy something like that as a novelty. How strange.

But the idea of anything dropping off the side of the building – even if they were just paper planes – was physically nauseating, and overrode Griff's pondering over his new client. He had to bite his lip whilst being out at such a staggering height on the open top roof, fighting against his sudden swooping wave of vertigo.

He was much happier once he and Raphie re-entered the main body of the penthouse, and when they did, it was to discover that Ms d'Oro had put on a brunch spread, absolutely insisting he and Winston ate. The d'Oros might have been well off, but at least they didn't appear stingy with it.

Griff tried his best not to come across as hungry or desperate, but it was impossible when mother and son were so happy to accommodate, and he hadn't had a decent or exciting meal in months. As subtly as he could, Griff very carefully helped himself to pastries, fruit, yoghurt, fried eggs, and some sinfully good fried potatoes and onions.

Whilst he ate, Raphael was like a whirlwind, constantly moving through the penthouse as he chatted to his mother, Winston, Sparrow the cat, and even Griff about...well, everything. What he was studying. His cat's antics. Planes that had flown overhead to one of London's various airports. Things he'd seen on TV and read online.

He sounded surprisingly aware of current affairs, considering he never left this building or even went beyond the elevator doors. Griff didn't understand how that hadn't turned Raphael into a raving lunatic, but he didn't come across like a social hermit. Quite the opposite. He talked animatedly, engaging his small audience like he was born to be in front of a crowd.

*He's just a client,* Griff told himself sternly, refusing to be swept up in the storytelling. He had a job to do, and he wanted to impress on his first day. But Raphael was like no one he'd ever met before. It was difficult not to be enthralled as he skipped from musing about French literature to critiquing the cinematography of a TV advert for aftershave he'd seen the day before.

Suddenly, Griff thought he saw something move out of the corner of his eye, pulling his attention away from Raphael. He snapped his head, frowning as he followed his gaze outside the floor-to-ceiling windows. He couldn't have seen anything outside, though, other than perhaps a bird. They were too high for drones to fly legally. Besides, it had kind of looked like something small falling from above. But they hadn't left anyone else on the roof and anyway the only way to access it was through the penthouse.

He must have imagined it.

But still, he brushed his hands clean and washed down any remnants of brunch with a mouthful of orange juice. Then he moved around the breakfast bar, acting casual so as not to alarm his clients. After all, it was probably absolutely nothing. But Griff hadn't survived fifteen years in this business by ignoring his gut instinct.

Right now, it was telling him it would be a nice idea to maybe put himself between Raphael and the window as he continued peering out of it.

If anyone thought his behaviour was suspicious, they didn't say anything. Griff appreciated that. He'd hate to come across as paranoid on his first day because quite frankly, what on earth could possibly be out-?

He didn't even get to finish his thought. In the blink of an eye, something the size of a lunchbox swung on a rope from above. The second it hit the glass, there was an explosion that shattered the entire window, sucking the air from Griff's lungs and forcing him to stumble back towards the kitchen, his arms flung in front of his eyes. Shards ripped through the air, and the *boom* was enough to resonate down to Griff's bones. He was only vaguely aware of that, however, because he was already mid-turn. As debris hit his back, he launched himself at Raphael, seizing him around the waist and hauling him to the ground behind the sofa.

The room was filling with smoke, possibly from the explosion. Or maybe whoever had swung the incendiary device down had followed in with a smoke grenade.

Griff's brain finally caught up with his pounding heart and body, which was pumping with adrenaline.

They were under attack.

## 2

## GRIFF

RAPHAEL SEEMED TO HAVE BEEN IN SHOCK, BECAUSE IN THE few seconds it had taken Griff to tackle him to the ground, he hadn't moved or said anything. But then it was as if he snapped back to life, and he started fighting against Griff's hold on him.

*"Mum!"* he screamed. He shoved his voluminous hair out of his face and began clawing at Griff's arms, but Griff clung on tight. *"Sparrow!"*

"Quiet!" Griff rasped, trying to control Raphael for his own safety. Griff needed more information. "Call out!" he cried to Winston through the air already filling with smoke.

"I've got Beta," his new colleague replied, using their official code names for their clients. Not that Griff needed reminding of his priorities.

Raphael was who they were here to protect above all else.

"I've got Alpha," Griff replied, falling back on his years of training to keep himself calm. But honestly. Of *all* the jobs he'd been on, this was the last one he'd expected a sudden attack on. "Moving to you."

Griff had been in situations before where he'd had to

leave secondary targets unprotected or even abandoned. He wasn't going to let that happen now, though, not on his first bloody day.

"*Mum!*" Raphael screamed again, still scrabbling like a cat in a sack to break free of Griff's hold on him. But that wasn't going to help anyone. There were more sounds coming from out of the window now.

They were being breached.

"Do *exactly* as I say!" Griff barked, squeezing Raphael firmly to make him listen. "We're moving to your mother and Winston. When I say move, you *move.*"

"O-okay," Raphael said breathlessly, instantly halting his struggling.

The room was thick with smoke now, making everyone cough as Griff got himself and Raphael to their feet in a crouch. A couple of loud *thuds* came from the direction of the broken-open window. The breeze at this height was pretty fierce, moving the smoke around like they were in a tornado. It wasn't clearing, making Griff think the gas canister was still spewing out smoke. But even still, there was a *lot.*

It seemed he wasn't the only one who thought so.

"How much fuckin' gas did you think we'd need, Bob?" a woman's low, hoarse voice snapped in a gravelly East End accent.

"Well, I just had to be sure, didn't I, Betty?" replied a man with an accent to match hers. They sounded like they'd just walked off a Guy Richie movie. And throwing around their names like that? Who were these clowns?

Griff could worry about that later. His one and only priority right now was getting the d'Oros to safety.

All of them.

He wrapped his arm around Raphael's slim waist, feeling him trembling. So Griff fumbled until he found Raphael's hand to squeeze as well. "It's okay, Mr d'Oro," he whispered through Raphael's hair into his ear. "I've got you. It's my job to keep you safe. Just stay with me."

Their noses were only inches apart, so despite the smoke, when Raphael turned his forest-green eyes on Griff, Griff could see little flecks of brown in the irises.

If they hadn't been so wide with fear, he would have thought they were beautiful.

"I trust you," Raphael said with a nod.

"Good," Griff replied, ignoring the little flurry those words caused inside him. His body was too overrun with adrenaline to decipher what that could mean anyway.

It didn't matter that Griff had only been in the penthouse a couple of hours. He'd already memorised enough to be able to navigate his way practically blind to the other side of the breakfast bar to where he assumed Winston was keeping Annabella safe. That didn't stop his stomach from lurching at the idea they might accidentally blunder out of the window and plummet sixty floors down onto Bishopsgate below them. They'd be raspberry jam before they knew what hit them.

But that was illogical, so Griff made his vertigo shut up until they stumbled on top of Winston and Annabella. The smoke was so thick they couldn't see each other until they were inches apart.

Annabella looked even paler and frailer than before, and she was shaking in Winston's arms, but as soon as she saw her son, her hand shot out to seize his arm.

"This is it, darling," she said clearly and firmly, all frailty vanished. "We always thought it might come one day. You know what to do. Griffin will get you to safety. You must trust him."

"We should have done the final briefing *before* brunch," Winston said crossly, his eyes darting around.

"What the-?" Griff spluttered. They'd been *expecting*

something like this? Bloody hell, that *might* have been a detail Griff would have benefited from before getting attacked several hundred feet in the air.

Raphael had also been expecting something apparently, because he gritted his teeth and nodded at her once. "Winston, you'll take care of my mum?" he whispered, his voice cracking despite the resolution of his words.

"I'll protect her with my life," Winston said, deadly serious. Then he turned to Griff. "Mr Raphael will have to fill you in. But the agency wouldn't have put you on this job if you weren't capable of it. Get him out of here."

But there had been more thuds whilst they'd been talking, and then the ping of the elevator arriving, suggesting the front doors had been opened.

"Bob?" Betty yelled through the smoke. "Is'at you?"

"Why the bloody hell would it be me?" he shouted back. "Oi! Who's there? This is *our* job. We've been waitin' years! You better-"

A round of bullets cut through the air, their shockingly loud noise making the four people behind the breakfast bar flinch and gasp in shock.

"Well, 'at was rude," Bob grumbled through the smoke.

Who the hell *were* all these people? They clearly weren't working together. It set Griff's teeth on edge, being so in the dark. Literally, with all this smoke.

"If you didn't want people joining the party," a sophisticated English accent declared through the smoke, "perhaps you shouldn't have had so many beers at the Blind Man's Bluff two nights ago. You literally bragged to anyone who might listen about how you'd organised yourselves a helicopter drop-off for this morning." The man laughed. "Honestly, you didn't imagine you were the only one with the d'Oro contract, did you?"

Multiple people had contracts out on this sweet young man? Griff wondered yet again who the *hell* he was.

"I fink we strongly implied we 'ad dibs!" Bob yelled back as the lift doors pinged once more. "Fuckin' rude," he muttered. "Can't a man kill anova man in peace 'ese days?"

Raphael let out a tiny squeak and quivered. But Griff squeezed him closer. "I *won't* let anything happen to you, I swear."

Raphael blinked at him, then jerked his head in a nod.

"There's more of them arriving," Winston said urgently. "We have to move now. Mr Raphael, you have to get the backpack. You'll never get anywhere without it. I'll take your mother down the emergency elevator. You and Griff can follow once you have it."

"And Sparrow," Raphael said stubbornly. His green eyes were wet, but they were also blazing as he looked between Griff and Winston. "I'm *not* leaving her."

Winston didn't reply to that. There were more thumps, bumps, yells, and bursts of gunfire going on all around them. The sound of china smashing mingled with several voices bickering that this was *their* job, they'd been waiting *years*, and everyone else could fuck *off*.

It was carnage.

"Go, now," Winston snapped at Griff. He didn't seem so old and fatherly in that moment. More like a drill sergeant who was not there to piss around. "The backpack is in Raphael's bedroom safe. He has access. Move your arse!"

Griff had seen the safe on their tour earlier, and he didn't hesitate to get going. Raphael was still in his arms, so he made to pull him along with him, but Raphael resisted just long enough to grab his mum's hand.

"I love you," he croaked to her.

"I love you too, darling," she replied, her eyes full of

determination. "Stay strong. We prepared for this. Don't falter."

Raphael nodded stiffly.

Then Annabella and Winston vanished into the smoke as the four of them split into two halves and went their separate ways.

"Do exactly as I say, and you'll be fine," Griff rasped. His eyes were watering, his throat was sore, and his heart was pounding. But he had a job to do, and he wasn't going to fail Raphael.

Because he was a client. That was it. Nothing else.

"We'll go one step at a time," he whispered as they ran in a crouch. "I have-"

Griff gasped in shock, whatever he was going to say forgotten, as an honest-to-god throwing star went whistling in front of their eyes and imbedded itself into the wall, right by Raphael's head. That wasn't something you saw every day, even in Griff's line of work. Raphael squeaked, his breath hitching.

"I've got something!" Bob yelled, making them both snap their heads. *Annabella?* Griff worried immediately. But Bob answered his unspoken question. "Oh, shit, no. It's just a stupid cat."

Raphael jerked like he'd been electrocuted. "Don't you fucking *touch* her!" he screamed. Before Griff could even anticipate anything, Raphael snatched the throwing star from where it was embedded in the wall, and hurtled it through the smoke towards where Bob's voice had emanated from.

*"Fuck!"* Bob howled. "My fuckin' leg!" A hiss cut through the air, followed by the scrabbling of claws.

"Sparrow!" Raphael shrieked. "This way! Come to Daddy!"

Griff had to admit he admired the kid's guts. But a strategist, he was not.

The cat might or might not now know where they were.

But all the assassins in the room had a pretty good idea.

Griff yanked them both to the marble floor just in time to evade another volley of gunfire. The bullets made the smoke curl and shift like a dance before they hit the wall and made paint and plaster rain down on top of them. Then a knife launched through the air and skittered over the marble, about the same time a *boomerang* flew over their heads.

They needed to get that backpack and get the fuck out of there. *Now.*

Griff took a breath, picturing the route to the stairs, then made a dash for it. Raphael moved perfectly by his side, allowing Griff to steer them as one.

"Where the fuck are they?" Betty moaned. "You and your bloody smoke grenades, Bob! I'm so embarrassed right now. And in front of everyone, as well! Oh, my days. What would Mum say?"

"You fink you're embarrassed? I've just been stabbed with a fuckin' throwing star, Betty. That woman never hits *anything.*"

"No, please," said the fancy man. "Keep going. It'll make things simpler for the rest of us if you take yourself out of the picture."

"You dishonour yourself with ease!" a new woman rasped in a tone that suggested an Eastern mysticism. "I will claim this boy's corpse, the money, *and* the glory!"

"Oh, shut up with that stupid voice," Betty scoffed. "You ain't a fuckin' ninja. Everyone knows you're from Putney."

From the sounds of it, another throwing star whizzed through the air, but Griff was too busy getting Raphael up the stairs to determine where it landed. Just so long as it wasn't in either of them, Winston, or Annabella, he didn't care.

"I mean it," Raphael snapped in a trembling voice. "I'm not leaving without Sparrow. Do you hear me?" Griff was focusing on getting them across the smoke-filled landing and into Raphael's bedroom in one piece, so when Raphael pinched him – *hard* – he was ashamed to admit that he yelped. "I *mean* it!" Raphael repeated.

"Okay, okay!" Griff grumbled. "I heard you."

It wasn't like Griff *wanted* to leave the damn cat wandering around here – especially with that big bloody hole in the wall where an entire window panel used to be – but his priority was the human beings in his care.

However, he found himself rolling his eyes as they lunged into the bedroom and relenting. "Fine! But we need to *find* her if we're going to bring her along."

Soft. He was going *soft* in his old age.

Mercifully, this door had been closed, so when they burst into the room, it was mostly smoke-free, enabling Griff to establish that there were no assailants waiting in there for them. Raphael tore himself free of Griff's hold and dashed right for the safe in the walk-in wardrobe, wasting no time in presenting his palm and eye for the recognition software.

Griff closed the door, keeping a lookout as Raphael yanked the safe door open once it beeped and threw the backpack contained within over his shoulders. Without missing a beat, he then sprinted back out into the main body of the huge bedroom, snatching up a packet of something from atop the closest set of drawers by the enormous king-sized bed.

His green eyes met Griff's from across the room. "Open the door," he whispered urgently. "Just a crack."

Griff wanted to argue, but they didn't have time. So he did as his client asked.

Raphael rustled the bag in his hands, and Griff realised belatedly that they were cat treats. Well, he *had* told Raphael that they needed to find Sparrow in order to bring her along, but it sounded like World War Three had erupted in the penthouse with all the gunfire, yelling, and smashing and ripping of things. There was no way the cat was going to hear a bag crinkling over all that, was there?

Obviously, Griff knew bugger all about cats. Because within seconds, a tabby-coloured streak flashed through the door, leaping into Raphael's arms. He gasped. *"Good* kitty!" he cooed, giving her a treat before pocketing the bag, the cat firmly in his arms. Then he gave Griff the same dazzling smile he'd given him at the front door when he'd stopped Sparrow from escaping mere hours ago. "Okay," said Raphael brightly, like there weren't insane people with guns and shuriken running around his home. "We can go now. The emergency elevator is in the central column behind the artwork with big paint splatters. Wow, that's a lot of smoke coming in through the door. Let's get going, shall we?"

He bounced on his feet like he'd just suggested a trip to the beach. Griff blinked, then shook himself. He couldn't be distracted by Raphael's remarkable optimism. "Do you think Winston will have got your mum to it by now?"

Raphael's expression became serious for a second. "If he says he'll protect her with his life, he will. We don't need to worry." He grinned again. "But that smoke is going nuts! So I should follow you, yes? Seeing as you're the bodyguard here."

That was right. Griff was the bodyguard. So he had better start acting like one. He couldn't let this strangely endearing young man confuse him any further. Even a second of distraction at the wrong moment could cost them both their lives.

He cleared his throat and beckoned for Raphael to come to him, which Raphael did without question. He pressed himself to Griff's side, a puff of his breath against Griff's face sweet from the sugary Pop-Tart. Sparrow was clinging to Raphael's front for dear life, which Griff had to say was a reasonable reaction. Another explosion rocked through the penthouse, and Griff wondered if the other residents in the floors below had called the police yet.

Not that it mattered. It would take the authorities an age to get up this high. Griff and Raphael needed to get to the ground and lose these psychos as soon as possible.

Maybe then Raphael could tell Griff just what was in the bag, who was out there trying to kill or kidnap him, *why* they were trying to do that, and where the hell Griff was supposed to take Raphael.

First things first, they needed to reach the elevator. Which meant going through a half a dozen assailants, from the sounds of it, all of which were armed to the teeth and hiding in the still dense grenade smoke.

Griff gritted his jaw. He could do this. He was trained for this. It didn't matter if it happened on his first day or last. This was his job, and he was damn well good at it.

Except when they stepped out in the corridor, it appeared that some genius had started a *fire* in the few minutes they'd been in the bedroom, and it didn't look like the bloody sprinkler system was working for whatever reason. He could see the fire flickering through the smoke over the balcony downstairs, but more than that, he could hear the roar of the flames.

"What the-?" Griff started. But before he could finish expressing his incredulity, a suave, slim man in a black suit emerged from the smoke...swinging a fucking medieval morning star over his head. As he circled the spiked ball on the metal pole, he smirked.

"I've been waiting so very long for this, Mr d'Oro," he said. It was the posh guy who had been taunting Bob and

Betty. Except he was so busy eyeballing Raphael that he didn't see the prone figure lying on the floor between them. As he advanced, he tripped and fell so hard and fast, his handsome face pretty much hit Griff's closed fist all by itself. He crumpled to the floor, but Griff already knew he was out cold, so his attention was back on Raphael already.

"Are you okay?"

Raphael was distraught, his face slack and his eyes brimming with tears. "Our home," he whispered. He looked from the unconscious assassin to the smoke and fire filling the penthouse, and the sounds of more assailants beyond. They'd obviously heard Mr Morning Star's battle cry and were coming to investigate themselves.

The chances of Griff and Raphael reaching the elevator were hurriedly slipping away.

*Fuck.*

Griff looked back down at Mr Morning Star through the smoke tendrils, then realised something that filled him with hope and dread almost equally.

Over his suit, the guy was wearing a parachute pack on his back.

Griff groaned as his vertigo got a head start on its crippling fear. But they had very little choice. They needed to get out of this penthouse right the fuck now. As useless as these would-be assassins appeared to be, they had the simple advantage of numbers and weapons. One of them was bound to get lucky if Griff tried to get Raphael and his beloved cat to either the main or secret lift, and he didn't fancy riding all the way down anyway, knowing that there were several homicidal nutters still up here who could easily fuck about with the elevator cables.

This was the only way.

At least with this plan, there was only about a fifty-fifty

chance they'd end up dead. Griff didn't know what he was complaining about.

Raphael tugged on Griff's suit jacket in the couple of seconds he'd taken to come to this utterly insane course of action. "Griffin?" Raphael asked in a high-pitched squeak.

Griff shrugged him off, although not unkindly. Time was just of the essence. Griff yanked his jacket open so fast the three buttons pinged off and vanished into the smoke, but Griff didn't care. It wasn't like he was going to be wearing the bloody thing again. He ripped the blazer from his arms and flung it to the floor. As he dropped to his knees, he caught Raphael looking at him like he was about to have a seizure.

"What is it?" Griff cried as quietly as he could as he hauled the parachute from the prone man's back.

"N-nothing at all," Raphael said, sounding strangled.

Griff didn't have time to decipher what Raphael's problem was. His shirt was sticking to him from perspiration, making it more difficult to get the damn parachute on. Eventually, though, he managed to shrug it on. He stood and offered his hand to Raphael.

"Do you trust me?" Griff asked.

"Of course," said Raphael with utmost sincerity, slipping the hand not clutching his cat into Griff's. Griff thought that was its own brand of crazy, because Raphael barely knew Griff from Adam. But ultimately, it was the answer he needed to hear as they raced up the stairs, heading for the entrance to the roof.

Bursting through the door, he immediately saw the gear Bob and Betty must have used to rappel down into the penthouse from the outside. They were fearless. He had to give them that. If a helicopter had dropped them onto the roof, Griff realised the glass on the penthouse must have been sound proofed, which was why he hadn't heard them.

That also suggested the siblings (as he assumed they were from their bickering) had some serious funding going on to afford such an entrance. But Griff added that to the list of things he could worry about *if* he and Raphael managed to get off this building alive.

Right now, he had some delightful insanity to be cracking on with.

Thank fuck for his thorough training. He'd never thought in a million years he'd have to double-check that he was wearing a parachute correctly under pressure, but as a spray of bullets and another throwing star chased them up the stairwell, that was exactly what he had to do.

Adrenaline kept his mind focused and stopped him from throwing up all his delicious brunch in pure terror. "We're going to jump," he said to Raphael as they ran to the side of the building that overlooked Bishopsgate. The other three sides had other buildings pressed up against them. Griff just prayed to whoever might be listening that they didn't land on top of a bloody bus.

"W-what?" Raphael asked. His tone was more 'could you repeat that?' rather than 'are you out of your *fucking* mind?' though. "Oh, yes. I suppose that *is* a parachute you took off that man, but are you sure-?"

More bullets. Another throwing star. More sodding smoke from a fresh grenade. The shouting voices told Griff they had seconds at most before they got company.

He spun Raphael and grabbed Sparrow, dumping the poor creature into Raphael's backpack on top of all the other stuff in there, then sealing it closed. Luckily, it was a pretty big bag and only two thirds full. But it showed how terrified she was that she only protested with one angry meow before hunkering down. *Sensible girl,* Griff thought. Raphael needed his hands free if they had a snowball's chance in hell of making this work.

"Whatever you do," Griff said, wrapping his arms around his client and picking him up by his arse, "don't let go."

Raphael flung his arms and legs around Griff like an octopus, locking his hands behind Griff's neck and his feet behind his back. "Okay," he whispered with wide eyes, his plump lips millimetres from Griff's mouth. For a second, they just stared at each other, their breath mingling, making Griff's lips tingle and his insides squirm.

But there wasn't a second to waste. Griff dug his fingers into Raphael's back and stepped up onto the ledge.

And before his brain could protest, he tilted forward and let gravity do its work.

Raphael screamed. Griff couldn't blame him. If he hadn't been completely preoccupied with judging the right moment to pull the release cord, he probably would have been bellowing his lungs out, too. The gut-wrenching sensation as they plummeted down the side of the building was almost too much to bear.

Intellectually, he knew that people base-jumped from heights like this all the time, but he suspected not many of them did so with gunfire zipping around them. He wanted to release the chute right away, but he knew a few seconds extra could give them the distance they needed to ensure that nothing ripped a hole in the precious silk that was going to keep them alive.

But too many seconds more and the chute wouldn't have enough time to deploy and slow them down before they met the pavement. They couldn't go on the run with broken legs.

Or if they were raspberry jam.

It was Griff's job to make the call, though, so he did. The relief as he took a split second to let go of Raphael and tug on the cord was instant. Raphael hugged him for dear life, and then Griff's arm was back around Raphael to join his other one, ensuring that the sudden jolt didn't rip Raphael from him. But as soon as the parachute slowed their descent to a gentle float, Griff took a huge breath, stars dancing in front of his eyes.

They still rushed towards the ground, but slow enough that Griff could tug on the chute's pull cords and clumsily steer them to a gap in the thankfully stationary traffic. With a grunt, his feet hit the ground first, and he rolled with Raphael in his arms outstretched like a cage. His skin got scraped to shit, but he had to preserve enough room so Sparrow wouldn't get crushed beneath them in the backpack.

Then all of a sudden, the two of them were sat upright, blinking as people around them started shouting and pointing their phone cameras at them. Nausea rolled through Griff, but his job was *far* from over. "Raphael," he said hoarsely. "Are you okay?"

Raphael's hair was a curtain around him as he swung his backpack in front of him to check on Sparrow. She popped the top of her head out of the bag through his hair, showing her folded ears, her jade-blue eyes just visible and clearly saying 'what the *fuck* just happened?!'

Raphael swept his long hair back and looked from her up to Griff. Then he broke into his biggest grin yet.

"That was bloody *brilliant!*" he cried.

Griff dragged his hand down his face in disbelief.

That was one word for it.

# 3

# RAPHIE

WHAT.

The.

*Hell?*

Raphie was trembling from head to toe, staring at his new bodyguard with utter disbelief and unparalleled admiration. He'd known the man a couple of hours, and he'd just jumped off a fucking *building* to save Raphie's life. It was the most incredible and also the most terrifying thing that had ever happened to Raphie.

And he'd thought Griffin had been hot when he'd stopped Sparrow from escaping the penthouse.

Whilst he wrestled with the most confusing boner he'd ever experienced, he tore his eyes away from Griffin to look around them. This wasn't how he'd pictured it, but he'd been dreaming about this day for so long. He was *outside*. There were so many people around them! Sure, they were all staring and yelling questions, and drivers of the vehicles in the stationary traffic around them were leaning out of their windows and blaring their horns, but Raphie didn't care.

He was free.

"Did you just jump off a building with a *cat?*" a woman with a toddler in her arms asked incredulously, walking between cars towards Raphie. She looked distinctly unimpressed.

Griffin leaped to his feet, however, and held out a hand the size of a small plate. "Everything's under control, ma'am. I'd ask you to step away, please."

Lucky for them, the toddler didn't take kindly to Griffin. Raphie couldn't blame the tot. Griffin was a *lot* to absorb at once. So when the boy started bawling, the woman immediately became more concerned with him over Sparrow and turned away to soothe the child.

But as Raphie shook his tangled hair back away from his face again, a couple of people about his age with piercings, tattoos, and short, rainbow hair made squeaky noises. "Your cat is *adorable!*" one of them cried, pulling her phone out of her pocket.

"Are you all right, mate?" a man in a high-vis jacket and hard hat asked Raphie.

"Everyone, *please!*" Griffin barked loudly as he unclipped the parachute. Then he held both hands out and glowered at the people closing in. "I'm going to need you to give us some room. No photos. Please stay back!"

Raphie's heart was racing, immediately overwhelmed by so many voices and too much movement after the adrenaline rush of the jump. Sparrow, however, was purring and looking around with interest at all the people cooing at her. Particularly at the rainbow-haired woman who quite possibly took a photo of them anyway with a wistful 'Aww' noise. Sparrow licked her nose, her previous terror apparently forgotten.

Diva.

Okay. Raphie needed to collect his wits. He was sort of free, yes. He hadn't been sure this day would ever come, but now it had and with quite a bang. Several, in fact. As much as he'd been dreading someone finding him, he couldn't say he regretted the fact it had propelled him into the real world after so many years up in the penthouse.

But the danger was far from over, and for the first time in his life, he had no idea what was going on.

Or where his mum was.

"Do you think Mum and Winston got out okay?" Raphie asked Griffin as dread washed through him. He trusted Winston implicitly, but that didn't mean he wasn't still worried sick about his mum.

Griffin was hastily rolling up the parachute as he glanced at Raphie, then at their growing crowd. He was huge – one of the biggest guys Raphie had ever seen in real life. And now that his jacket was gone and his damp white shirt was clinging to his muscular form, Raphie could see even more than before.

He couldn't say it was disappointing.

Raphie shook the thought away. There were killers after him, and his mum was in danger. *He* was in danger. He didn't need to be lusting after some man who was practically a stranger to him.

Even if he had just saved Raphie's life and was the kind of 'tall, dark, and handsome' Raphie had only seen in his dreams.

"Your mum and Winston got several minutes' head start on us," Griffin grunted, finally finishing balling up the chute and sticking it under his arm. Then he offered his free hand out to Raphie to help him stand. Unlike when Raphie had clung to him to make the jump, Raphie could now appreciate Griffin's warm skin and the scratchy callouses on his fingertips. "I'm sure they're fine," Griffin continued in a low rumble once Raphie was on his feet, looking around the busy street, "but we need to move, Mr d'Oro. Now."

Raphie bit his lip and nodded, trembling in excitement, terror, apprehension, and a dozen other emotions he couldn't even identify. Instead, he slipped both his arms through the rucksack so he was wearing it backwards and held Sparrow close through the bag, stroking between her ears. He would never let any harm come to her, but she was still looking at Raphie like he'd…well, like he'd jumped off a sixty-storey skyscraper with her, and she didn't quite trust he wouldn't do it again.

"I'm sorry, sweetie. Daddy will make it up to you with tuna, he promises."

A police siren wailed to life not too far away, and Griffin jerked his head towards it. "Fuck," he snapped, running his hand over his dark stubble.

"Won't they help us?" Raphie asked in confusion. The police were the good guys. The people in the penthouse were the bad guys. Surely they should go towards the siren?

"Oi!" a bus driver yelled from out his window as he blasted his horn. He wasn't the only one. "What the bloody hell do you two think you're playing at? Get a move on!"

Griffin didn't even acknowledge him. He just held his wrist up to his mouth and spoke a little too loudly, like he was speaking into a microphone Raphie knew their security team didn't wear. "Did you get that? Or do we have to do another take?"

"Ohh," said a woman near Raphie. "Are you shooting a film? How exciting!"

"What's it called?" asked another man on a bicycle.

"Uhh," Raphie croaked. Why would these people think he and Griffin were making a movie?

But he was saved again by Griffin, who placed a firm hand on his back and steered him out of the growing throng and away from the towering building where Raphie had spent almost all of his life. "Thank you, everyone! Sorry for the inconvenience!" he called out, nodding at people as they passed but not stopping to answer anything else. Incredibly, they allowed them to leave, no more questions asked.

"I can't believe they bought that," said Raphie, cuddling Sparrow as she moulded to his front, purring aggressively. "Griffin, what-?"

"Quiet, please, Mr d'Oro," Griffin said briskly, shoving what he could of the parachute into a rubbish bin as they passed it. "You're still very much in danger."

"I-I know," Raphie stuttered. "But – okay, well, then we need to go back and talk to the police."

"Negative," said Griffin as they hurried past bars, shops, small grocery stores, and one of the big open entrances to Liverpool Street station. Raphie thought his head might twist off, but after all these years of looking at its roof, he couldn't believe he could actually see *inside*. His view was limited thanks to the stairs that led up to the wide entrance, but what he could see looked shiny and colourful.

He'd always imagined his first moments of freedom being filled with joy, not terror. But he couldn't stop himself from feeling wonder and amazement all the same. For that, he was grateful.

"This way, Mr d'Oro," Griffin instructed, his body brushing against Raphie's as they moved together. His proximity was making Raphie light-headed. He'd never been touched by a man like this before, and Raphie was struggling to concentrate on the running away they were supposed to be doing.

Raphie knew that he liked looking at men this way. He may have lived his life in the penthouse, but he'd still had the internet. He was pretty certain he was gay and had watched every single superhero movie out there not just for the plots, so he was also pretty confident he had a 'type'. But there was a vast difference between ogling the various

Chrisses in their spandex and leather, and having a real-life man whose muscles Raphie could see shifting tantalizingly beneath his white shirt, not to mention the ink of several tattoos.

And the *smell*. Raphie was aware he worked up a sweat after a training session, but this heady man musk was on another level entirely. It was spicy and pungent, and Raphie just wanted to roll around in it, like Sparrow in catnip.

"Hang on – why can't we go to the police?" Raphie asked belatedly, turning his attention back to Griffin.

"I don't think we should trust the police," Griffin said, shaking his head. "We can't trust anyone just yet. That backpack have anything useful in it?"

Raphie frowned as they turned down a narrow alleyway with a few bars with colourful neon signs that weren't very busy-looking. Not surprising, considering it was still mid-morning. "Uh, yes," Raphie said after he'd thought about Griffin's question a second. "Loads. Mum was always vigilant about being ready to flee at the drop of a hat." Raphie bit his lip, reality finally catching up with him like a ton of bricks. After all these years of planning, it had finally happened.

His father had come for him. Raphie had never *really* believed his own dad would be so merciless. Yet here they were.

The assassins were after him specifically, so Mum and Winston should be fine. But going on the run in her condition was far from ideal. She always kept spare medication in her pocket, and now Raphie understood why. So she could manage a day before getting to a pharmacy.

"She's sick," Raphie blurted out. In an instant, panic overwhelmed him, and he stumbled to a halt, crashing his shoulder into the damp brick wall. It was cold through his T-shirt. Thank heavens he'd put trainers on to show Griffin the roof. He usually spent his days barefoot, and normally shoes felt odd to him. Now, on the dirty London Street, they didn't feel strange at all.

Or maybe the shock had caught up with him, and he was just going numb.

"Mr d'Oro, we have to keep moving," Griffin said. His tone wasn't harsh, however, and when he touched his hand to Raphie's elbow, it was gentle.

In fact, the skin-to-skin contact sent a shiver over Raphie's body. His lust wasn't enough to completely shake his fear, though.

"Cancer," he managed to croak. "She had cervical cancer. She's finished her chemo and is on the mend, but she should be resting." The panic was clawing its way up his throat, and hot tears spilled from his eyes. "Griffin, we have to go back for her! She's sick! What if-?"

"Raphael!" Griffin snapped. The use of his first name snapped him out of his rambling. He hiccuped and stared into Griffin's intense brown eyes, and Griffin took hold of Raphie's shoulders. His touch was firm and comforting. "They got straight to the elevator. I'll check soon to see if I've had any word from Winston, but *you* are the top priority. These people are after *you*, and it's my job to get you to safety, understood? Your assailants will be swarming the streets right now." He took a deep breath and rubbed Raphie's shoulders with strong circles of his thumbs. "I know you're afraid. I know this is overwhelming. But we can talk on the move, okay?"

Raphie swallowed and looked over his shoulder. There wasn't anyone following them from the busy main street, but plenty of people were walking past the entrance to the alleyway, and any one of them could be an assassin sent to end Raphie's life.

"Yes, absolutely. Sorry."

Griffin shook his head. "Don't be sorry," he said almost

kindly, which did strange things to Raphie's insides. He knew it was Griffin's job to care about him, but proof of concern was still nice. "It's okay. But we need to get going." He looked down at the still petrified Sparrow in the bag. "Is there any way to secure her? Now we've got her with us, we don't want to lose her."

It was utterly ridiculous, but Griffin's use of 'we' made Raphie stupidly happy, practically melting all his other concerns away. Griffin was concerned for Raphie's precious Sparrow too? Raphie's heart skipped a beat, and his knees went wobbly in a way that had nothing to do with adrenaline.

"Uh, yes," Raphie said excitedly, feeling himself smile. "There's a carabiner and one of her leads in here, so I can attach her and stop her from bolting. Thank you! That's a great idea."

Griffin nodded, his eyes back on the alley entrance. "Okay, hook her up, and then stay glued to my side. We're going to head to Aldgate East station and jump on the tube. That lot didn't seem like the most capable mercenaries I've ever encountered, but I'd rather shake them off by going to a different station and get on a line that doesn't go through Liverpool Street."

Wow, what an exciting life Griffin must lead if half a dozen assassins wasn't that impressive to him. Raphie realised his feet were moving again. They were hurrying down a maze of alleys with Griffin checking every corner before they turned it. Raphie's heart was pounding, and the further they got from the only home he'd ever known – or could at least remember – the more he couldn't stop picturing it on fire.

Everything he owned. Almost every memory he had of his mum, of his whole life, was probably still burning, going up in smoke. They had a sprinkler system, but the fact it hadn't gone off made Raphie think that one of the assassins had tampered with it.

They'd wanted everything destroyed.

"Stay with me, Mr d'Oro," Griffin said firmly as they rushed down a slightly busier street with a sandwich shop, an architect, and a place selling bicycles. The people around them barely gave them a second glance, if they looked at them at all. They were either walking incredibly fast or walking slightly slower but focused on their phones in some capacity. Raphie thought it was odd he and Griffin weren't attracting more attention. It felt to him like they were wearing flashing signs saying they were running for their lives.

"Sorry," he said again, realising he was short of breath and a little dizzy. "I'll keep up better." He pushed his hair away, blinking rapidly and trying not to trip over his feet, which felt clumsy in the unfamiliar shoes. "I just...my home. Everything's gone. I wanted to leave it so badly, but..."

"You didn't choose to leave just now, Mr d'Oro," Griffin muttered, eyeing up another busy road before helping Raphie dash across it. *He didn't even wait for a green light!* Raphie thought in horror. "You were forced," Griffin continued. "There's a big difference." He clamped his jaw, his brown eyes watching another police car go past. This one didn't have his siren on, at least. "Some stuff might be okay when you get back. But really, it's just stuff."

Raphie took a deep breath and nodded as they mingled with the crowd, walking briskly down another street. Griffin never took his hand off Raphie's lower back, and it felt like Raphie was on a lead just as much as Sparrow was, tethered to Griffin for his own safety. Oddly, the thought was comforting.

"You're right," Raphie said emphatically. "Mum and

Winston are almost certainly okay, and Sparrow's okay – the two of us are okay. That's all that matters."

Griffin frowned and pulled Raphie into another alleyway entrance and stopped. It was shadowy and didn't appear to have any businesses down it, purely acting as a thoroughfare between buildings. The people on the street just walked right by the alley without paying it or them any attention.

Wordlessly, Griffin pulled his phone from his pocket and unlocked it with his thumb. "Winston's texted," he grunted, frowning at the screen before nodding. "They made it to a car he had parked at Moorgate, and they're already on the move. Says he can't say where. No one in pursuit as far as he can tell. That was sent a few minutes ago. So they're definitely okay."

"Oh, great!" said Raphie a little too loudly, self-conscious when Griffin shushed him.

But he was so relieved his mum and Winston were all right he quickly let his embarrassment go. More than that, he was experiencing an unfamiliar fuzzy feeling. He'd expressed concern about his mum, and Griffin had stopped immediately to do something about it. Yes, Griffin's job was to look after him, and yes, he'd just told him off, but still…it made Raphie light-headed for whatever reason.

"Okay," he said aloud, attempting to shake off the sensation. "So we're going to get the train, then?"

Griffin licked his lips as he looked back out at the bustling street. "We're going to need cash if we're going to get very far."

"That's no problem!" Raphie said brightly. He dove into the backpack, slipping his hand beside Sparrow and reaching into the interior side pocket. It was easy to find the right one because it was stuffed to the brim with stacks of hundred-pound notes. Raphie pulled out a handful of cash triumphantly, giddy that he could help Griffin.

But Griffin's eyes became comically wide. He let out a strangled noise as he shoved Raphie's hand down, pushing the money back out of sight.

"You can't just flash several grand's worth of cash out on the bloody street!" Griffin hissed. He closed his eyes and gritted his teeth. "You need to be more careful, Mr d'Oro. You'll get yourself mugged," he added in a more restrained voice.

Raphie's stomach dropped, and Sparrow gave a little meow from her perch in his backpack. It felt like she was agreeing with Griffin. Despite all Raphie's studying, he really didn't know anything about the real world, did he?

"Oh," Raphie said, making sure the bound stacks of notes went back in their pouch out of sight. "I'm sorry. I didn't think."

Griffin pinched the bridge of his nose and huffed. "It's okay," he said. He took hold of Raphie's elbow, firmly but not angrily, and steered him back onto the street as they began moving again. "I'm sorry for shouting. Thanks for helping. That'll get us a long way. But I think I really need some answers soon, Mr d'Oro. Perhaps now would be a good time to go through that final briefing that we never got around to. How about you start by telling me *who* you are?"

He sounded kind of pissed off, which was understandable, but it still made Raphie feel small and foolish. Of *course* Griffin deserved an explanation. Normally, Raphie and his mum would make their situation clear to any new hires before they joined the team. But they'd been extra cautious with Griffin, as they were aware the circumstances had changed with Raphie's dad, and an attack could have been imminent.

It turned out they'd been right. But that now meant the person Raphie was relying on to keep him alive was completely in the dark.

"Of course, I'm sorry. It's, uh, kind of a crazy story, really," Raphie said with a nervous laugh as they skirted around a group of tourists taking photos in front of a red telephone box. "What did Winston tell you?"

"That you've had protection all your life and never left that tower until today," Griffin said briskly.

He very rarely looked at Raphie, his eyes always flitting around as they rushed through the streets of London. Raphie hated the idea that Griffin was cross with him, but he had to be careful with how he explained everything. It was such a tall tale, and Raphie had never been the one to tell it. That was his mum's job, and he wasn't sure where was best to start right now.

"Is that all Winston said?" Raphie asked, pushing his hair back as it whipped around his shoulders.

"Yeah, but I also guessed you're obviously incredibly rich. Is that why all those oddballs were trying to kill you – for your money?"

Raphie had to bark out a laugh, causing a young woman walking past them to do a double take. But thankfully, she kept on walking in the other direction. "No, they weren't after my mum's money, although I'm sure they were being paid off."

"By who?" Griffin demanded.

Raphie sighed. "By…by my dad."

Griffin stopped in the middle of the pavement, so Raphie stopped as well, causing a number of people to almost slam into them both. "Shit," Griffin said quietly as the pedestrians shook their heads and muttered, skirting around Raphie and Griffin like a stream around an unexpected boulder. "That's fucked up. Why?" He narrowed his eyes. "You don't seem surprised your dad's trying to have you killed."

"No," Raphie said slowly.

It was odd to talk about someone dying and feel no

remorse at all. But Raphie knew his father hadn't been a very nice man, to put it mildly. Then there was that little matter of him trying to have Raphie murdered, so he had to admit there wasn't much love lost between him and his old man right then.

Sparrow meowed at him, as if warning him to be careful. "Okay...here's the basic version. My dad died last week. Mum and I weren't sure if he even knew about my existence – we never met. But if he did know about me, there was a chance he'd want me dead to make absolutely sure I didn't... inherit anything. He probably organised those assassins long before his death, with instructions to come after me as soon as he was gone."

Griffin narrowed his eyes at him, ignoring everyone else around him. "Inherit what? Like...a company?"

Raphie bit his lip and nodded, wincing as a man pushed past him, knocking shoulders. He was too busy shouting down his phone in a language Raphie didn't speak to even pause, but Griffin immediately shot out his hand to steady Raphie.

The feel of Griffin's hands on Raphie's body was very quickly becoming addictive. Raphie was sure that wasn't appropriate at all, but he couldn't help how his body was reacting one little bit, nor did he want it to stop. It was...kind of delicious, like hot buttered crumpets and strong tea.

"Uh..." he said, blinking and trying to drag his mind back to Griffin's question and away from the rogue thought that had popped into Raphie's brain. If his hand felt that good on him through his T-shirt, how the hell might it feel on *naked* skin?

*Focus!*

"Inheritance! Company!" he blurted, sounding as guilty as he felt. "Yeah. Something like that."

Griffin frowned and dropped his hand again. *Damn.*

"Why wouldn't he just not include you in his will? Why the need for an assassination? And *so* many contracts?"

Raphie fidgeted and glanced down at Sparrow, but she was far more interested in watching the man walking towards them eating a sandwich. "Well, uh, I guess he wanted to make sure the job was definitely done," he said helplessly, not ever having had the opportunity to form an opinion of the man in person. "He was pretty ruthless, by all accounts. A bully. It was why Mum fled when she realised she was pregnant. He always got what he wanted, including my mum. Even though he's dead, it appears he still wanted to get his own way by removing me from the picture."

Griffin shook his head. "None of this makes any sense whatsoever," he said, sounding so confused and frustrated. Despite his size, in that moment he seemed vulnerable, and Raphie's heart ached.

"I'm so sorry for dragging you into all of this," he rasped sincerely, licking his lips and glancing around.

He'd been envious watching the people of London for so many years, but now he was amongst them, he was finding it incredibly hard to concentrate. Griffin picked up on his unease and got them moving again. His hand returned to Raphie's lower back, wonderfully distracting Raphie from feeling so overwhelmed.

"It's okay," Griffin murmured. "'All this' is my job. Let's get on the tube and continue talking there. It should be quiet-ish if we're lucky. We're between rush hour and lunchtime."

Raphie inhaled deeply. "Thanks, I appreciate that."

A particularly strong gust of wind whipped down the street, flicking several locks of hair right into Raphie's mouth. He spat them out and huffed.

"Oh, *enough*," he muttered to himself, not sure if Griffin glanced at him from the corner of his eye or not.

Raphie ignored how much he wanted Griffin to look at him. Or at least, he tried to ignore it.

*Hair, right.* Muscle memory kicked in. He automatically reached into one of the rucksack's outer side pockets to fetch the Tangle Teezer he knew was there. His hair was in knots as well as flying around, and it was driving him bonkers. He had enough distraction from all those would-be assassins and Griffin's intoxicating smell, and he didn't need anything else. So he ran the brush through his mane as they walked, until it was good enough to braid the whole thing down his back and secure it with the hair tie that lived on his wrist, just like he would if he was going out onto the penthouse roof for the afternoon.

That time, Griffin *definitely* glanced at him. "Don't you need a mirror to do that?" Then he looked away again, just as fast, like he regretted asking.

But Raphie's heart didn't get the memo. He *relished* Griffin asking a personal question. This wasn't him doing his job. This was crossing a professional line, and Raphie *loved* it.

"I haven't needed a mirror to do my hair for years, now," he said happily as they passed a pub and a bank…or possibly a pub that *used* to be a bank? London was already fascinating. "My hands know what to do on their own. It should be neat enough. Is it?"

He skipped ahead a few steps and turned his head left and right for Griffin to see his braid. Griffin huffed and reached out, pulling Raphie beside him so he could put his hand on Raphie's back again. "Watch where you're going," he muttered. "And, um, yeah. It looks fine, I guess."

Raphie beamed up at him. "Thanks!"

He was mildly obsessed with his hair and had been growing it his whole life. The little compliment from Griffin sent him into a tizzy that helped him forget his predicament for a minute.

Whilst he was fully aware that most men had short hair, he one hundred per cent didn't care. That had never felt right to Raphie, and even the mere idea of cutting his hair off left him in a cold sweat. It was as if his whole identity was wrapped up in his hair. He hoped that wasn't vain. But he just knew without it, he'd lose a huge part of his identity: one of the things that made him most 'him'. He wondered if that was how Griffin felt about his tattoos or his muscles.

However, it had occurred to him that a lot of men might not find his hair attractive because it was seen as a 'feminine' trait. That was kind of a depressing realisation when Raphie had been painfully lonely his whole life. So Griffin's compliment might have been a half-hearted grunt, but it still gave Raphie a little boost. He needed that if he was going to navigate his first day in the real world *and* stay one step ahead of all the assassins on their tail.

Raphie was soon distracted as the pavement they'd been walking down turned into a crossroads of two main streets with heavy moving traffic. Through the bikes, cars, vans, and bright red buses moving in front of them, Raphie spotted a circular London Underground symbol and an opening under a glass-front building with a blue sign that read 'Aldgate East Station' in white letters. The building was tall – although nowhere *near* the size of Raphie's former home – and the underground opening was dark with buttercup-yellow fluorescent lighting.

A steady stream of people was coming in and out, like it was no big deal. But Raphie realised his feet suddenly stopped walking, his gaze fixated on that opening.

Griffin also stopped immediately, and Raphie could feel him looking down at him. "Everything okay?"

Raphie managed to close his mouth from where it had fallen open. Then he blinked several times before looking up at the top of the huge building standing right above where Raphie was supposed to go *underneath*.

"Uhh..." he croaked, shaking his head. "That's...that's so much weight on top of the station. All those bricks and metal girders and glass and-"

"Hey, hey," Griffin said. His voice was still low and gruff, but it was kind. He placed his hands on Raphie's shoulders and rubbed with his thumbs. "I promise you, it's perfectly safe. Structurally speaking, anyway. If there are any assassins inside, I'll have to deal with them as they come."

He gave Raphie the barest twitch of a smile, and Raphie was relieved that he'd guessed the source of Raphie's anxiety when it had taken him so by surprise. But he figured he'd lived his entire life up in the clouds. The idea of going underground suddenly seemed wholly unnatural to him. But really...it couldn't be that bad, could it? It wasn't like London buildings had a habit of falling down like houses of cards.

"Will, um, Sparrow be okay in there?" he asked.

Griffin's mouth twitched with another brief smile. "She'll be fine so long as she knows her dad is okay. Right, Sparrow?"

He rubbed between her ears, and she purred. Raphie was so surprised that she let him touch her, he forgot about his claustrophobia for a moment. Sparrow *never* let strangers touch her.

Raphie decided to take that as a sign that everything was going to be fine. "Yes, you're right," he said confidently. "I'm not scared, Sparrow, so you shouldn't be either."

He was sure she gave him a withering look that conveyed she'd been fine the whole time, but Raphie wasn't going to lose the spring from his step. He could do this. He had to. There was nothing to worry about.

"Lead the way," he said brightly to Griffin with a nod.

Griffin looked a little amused as they crossed the road. "We'll need to get you a ticket."

Raphie shook his head. "There should be an Oyster card in here," he said, patting the backpack. He was proud to not be totally ignorant in front of Griffin after the snafu he'd made flashing his cash around on the street. He was also pretty keen to move beyond his moment of panic. Of course the underground was safe. Otherwise, why would hundreds of thousands of people use it every day? "Mum made sure it had a good amount on it. I should be fine all the way out to Zone Six."

Griffin nodded down at him. "Good," was all he said as they reached the tube entrance, but Raphie basked as if he'd been bestowed the highest praise.

He wanted to impress Griffin as much as possible.

Somehow, Raphie managed not to trip down the stairs as he rummaged in the backpack for the travel card around a very indignant Sparrow. She batted his nose with her paw and meowed crossly.

"Yes, I know," Raphie said patiently as he fumbled on the other side. "This is your little safe space. But it's also where Daddy's Oyster card is hiding. So if you could just-" She batted his chin, this time with a hiss. But Raphie didn't mind. His fingers had just closed around the slim plastic wallet that held the travel card. "Ah!" he said as he pulled it out triumphantly. "There we go. No more hitting Daddy, okay?"

He was pretty sure the guy manning the barrier laughed at him, but Raphie just winked at him as he proudly tapped his card and entered the London Underground system for the very first time. Griffin had already gone through and watched Raphie like a hawk until he could place his hand on his back again.

Raphie approved of his level of dedication as he put the Oyster card away. For purely professional reasons, of course.

He was suddenly aware that music was floating through the air. Up ahead, a lady with dark skin and a big, beautiful Afro was singing into a microphone along to a backing track being played on a speaker by her feet. She smiled at the people walking by, stepping from side-to-side and clicking her fingers in time to the rhythm. Her husky voice told a story of sunshine and love, and she looked like she was having the best time. Raphie slowed as they neared, transfixed by her happy energy bouncing off the drab walls around her.

"We need to keep moving," Griffin said against Raphie's ear.

Raphie tried not to let his shiver visibly show, but he'd never had a hot guy murmur words against his ear before, and his body was having some strong reactions.

"Can I give her some money?" Raphie whispered, trying to distract himself from Griffin, but also entranced by the woman's song. "That's what people do, right? It's so nice that she's down here, just trying to lighten people's days with her pretty voice."

Griffin sighed. He might have counted backwards from three, but Raphie was too enthralled by the singer to really notice. She realised he'd stopped walking to watch her, and winked at him.

"Fine, if it'll get you moving again," said Griffin. "Hurry." He sounded irritable, but there was that tiny twitch of a smile once more, like he was trying to stop it from escaping. It let Raphie know that he probably didn't mind all that much.

Raphie let out a little squeal and reached inside his bag, earning a headbutt from Sparrow on his jaw. But his fingers found a hundred-pound note in seconds, and he skipped over to drop it in the upside-down sunhat by the singer's feet. He proudly placed the note on top of the scattering of coins, then waved goodbye at her.

They were on the escalator down when he heard her shriek and stop singing. "Did I offend her?" he worriedly asked Griffin, turning back to look up at him and over his shoulder where they'd left the singer. Griffin properly loomed over Raphie from the step above him.

He just sighed. "I think you made her day," he assured him.

Raphie exhaled. "Oh, good. I felt like a proper Londoner doing that!"

Griffin hummed.

Raphie's heart rate was picking up again from the excitement of tipping the busker and yet another overload of his senses. There were so many new things to see with all the posters and people rushing by. The air was warm and humid, and he could smell sweat, perfumes, food, the tang of exhaust fumes, and at one point, urine. When they arrived at their destination, the walls on the train platform were cream with framed posters of the tube network map hanging up.

People kept looking at him, he was sure. Maybe because of his hair. Maybe because he and Griffin looked like they'd escaped an assassination attempt, jumped off a building, then dashed through the streets of London.

Or maybe because he had his backpack on back-to-front and there was a curious kitty poking her head out of it, her squashed face flicking left and right as if surveying her new kingdom.

There wasn't a big crowd on the platform, though. So Raphie and Griff were able to stand by themselves near the very end and wait for the next train, which was only a minute away, according to the digital display hanging from the ceiling. Raphie blinked against the harsh strip lighting, but he was glad as he looked around that even if people were glancing his way, they soon looked away again.

He was going to have to get used to people looking at him.

He was going to have to get used to people full stop.

Griff exhaled loudly, puffing his cheeks out and rubbing the back of his neck, the motion flexing his impressive bicep. Then he leaned his back against the tiles and fixed Raphie with a stare. "So," he said quietly, "it must be some hell of an inheritance to cause all this fuss, Mr d'Oro. Who was your dad?" He looked around to double-check no one was anywhere within earshot. "Are we talking a mafia boss?"

Raphie spluttered in horror. "No!" he cried. Then he made an effort to lower his voice as couple of people glanced their way. "No," he repeated at a much lower volume, but he could hear his defensiveness as well. "My mum would *never* have got involved with anyone like that. He seemed charming and generous when they first met. That's what she always said. It was only later that she found out how much of a bully he could be, and, um…just how married he was."

Griffin raised an eyebrow. "I'm guessing 'very' married."

Raphie nodded as the train squealed to a halt in front of them and the doors *whooshed* open. He moved forward, allowing the couple of passengers who were leaving to disembark before getting into the carriage. He had no idea how long the doors would stay open, but Griffin wasn't in so much of a hurry as he looked up and down the platform. He then stepped aboard, checking out the train's interior just as thoroughly.

There was no one near them, though. The whole train was open with no doors, the carriages connected by rubbery tubes and moving floors, but no other passengers were within twenty feet of them.

Raphie grabbed a seat and breathed his first real sigh of

relief since the penthouse window had exploded. He also felt a kind of daring thrill, knowing he was sort of 'alone' with Griffin. It made him feel giddy.

Which was why his brain probably short-circuited and he answered Griffin's next question with no filter whatsoever.

"So if he wasn't a mafia boss, what was he?" Griffin asked. He was still standing, not even holding on to any of the rails whilst the train doors were still open.

Raphie sat up straighter, wanting to bask in that praise again of being useful and helping Griffin. "Okay, I can finally tell you," he said proudly, just as the doors beeped and began sliding closed. Griffin didn't seem to hear them, though, as his whole focus was on Raphie.

Raphie really liked that.

"Tell me who your dad was?" Griffin asked.

Raphie shrugged. "Tell you everything."

He took a deep breath, mentally running through the most concise explanation. It didn't need to be pretty. They might only have a moment alone, and Griffin needed all the facts.

"Okay!" Raphie said, bracing himself and gripping the bag, hugging Sparrow for support. "My dad was King Tommaso of Campanula, a satellite nation situated within Italy. Their laws recognise children born out of wedlock, so that makes me Raphael d'Oro, Crown Prince of Campanula, first in line to the throne. So now Tommaso is gone, that means I have to get back to Campanula before the official council meeting on Friday night and stake my claim to the throne. Otherwise my twelve-year-old half-sister will be crowned the princess, completely vulnerable to the corrupt palace officials who will continue to run the whole country into the ground to protect the few filthy rich elite. So I need to claim my right as king and try to save my people. Make sense?"

The train finally lurched into motion.

Griffin was knocked off his feet, pinwheeling his arms as he landed flat on his arse. But his startled eyes didn't blink as he stared at Raphie.

"You fucking *what?*" he cried.

# 4

## GRIFF

Did this kid just say he was a fucking *prince*?

He and Raphael stared at each other as the train chugged towards Whitechapel station, and Griff realised he should probably haul himself off the carriage floor before any more passengers got on board. He might have been mortified that he'd fallen on his arse like a bloody tourist, but honestly, they had far, *far* greater concerns right now.

"Are you okay?" Raphael asked in a tiny voice. His green eyes were wide, following Griff as he pulled himself to his feet and hastily dropped into the too-small seat next to his client. He would have rather sat opposite, but clearly they had sensitive matters to discuss, and quietly. If that meant their bodies had to be pressed against one another whilst they talked…well, so be it.

Griff grunted. "I'm fine."

Okay, so maybe he was a little bit embarrassed that he'd lost control like that in front of Raphael. He didn't want his client thinking he was incapable, especially of such a simple feat of *remaining stood up*. But, bloody hell, that had been the last thing Griff had been expecting to come out of Raphael's mouth, and the train's moving had pulled the floor from under him, literally.

Sparrow turned her head as she narrowed her jade-blue eyes at him. Her *'meow!'* sounded more like *'Get it together!'* to his ears in that moment.

Griff opened his mouth, but then they pulled into the next station. Seeing as they were at the very end of the train, most people got on towards the middle, meaning they still had some privacy. Who knew when that could be interrupted, though? The stations were so close together in the city centre. Time was of the essence, so as soon as the doors started beeping, he turned back to Raphael.

"Okay," said Griff with a long exhale. He was trying very hard to keep calm and carry on, and *not* lose his shit somewhere beneath the East End. He was beginning to understand the reason behind his crazy-high salary, but at the same time also questioning if that had even been high enough. *Boring. Dull. Easy.* His day so far had been none of these things. "Do you want to try running that by me again?"

Raphael bit his lip, his gaze flicking over Griff's face. Then he smiled brightly. It didn't quite meet his weary eyes, though. "Surprise?" he said hopefully. Then he cleared his throat, checked that no one was close enough to be listening in, then dropped his gaze down to Sparrow. "Sorry, I know that's a lot to take in, and I was trying to give you the TL;DR."

Griff grunted in annoyance. "And what's that mean?"

Raphael giggled. It was definitely not adorable. "Sorry. I guess you're a bit older than me, aren't you?"

*Try a couple of decades,* Griff thought harshly. He knew he wasn't exactly old, but sitting next to this baby of a man certainly didn't make him feel all that young.

"It means 'Too long; didn't read'," Raphael explained.

Griff arched an eyebrow. "You couldn't have said 'give you the lowdown'?"

Raphael peered at him. "Why would I say that?"

Griff sighed and pinched the bridge of his nose. Of course, by that time they'd reached Stepney Green. An elderly lady in a hijab made her way inside the train a couple of doors along, laden down with several heavy-looking shopping bags, but she sat far enough away that they could continue their conversation whilst they approached Mile End.

"Mr d'Oro," Griff said firmly, holding Raphael's gaze. He was pretty sure his client shuddered as he looked back at him, his mouth slightly open and his gaze rapt.

*That wasn't sexy*, Griff informed his downstairs brain.

He opened his mouth to ask for more details and less youth lingo, but Raphael's expression suddenly changed, and he beat Griff to it.

"Raphie," he said with a nod. "Or at least Raphael. All this 'Mr d'Oro' business is giving me a headache. Please call me by my first name."

Griff's brain stalled for a moment. It was protocol to refer to a client by their title and surname. Plus, he was wary of anything too familiar with this gorgeous young man who was causing strife between his legs. But...this situation was far from by-the-book.

"Will it make you more comfortable?" Griff asked. His client's needs were his top – his *only* – priority.

Raphael's face broke into a sweet, dazzling smile. "Yes, it really will," he assured Griff. Sparrow also squeaked in apparent agreement.

Griff gritted his teeth and exhaled through them. "I think I can cope with 'Raphael' in that case. Although I can't guarantee the odd 'sir' won't slip through."

Was it Griff's imagination, or did Raphael blush? "O-okay,

well, maybe in time you might feel comfortable with 'Raphie'. Until then, 'Raphael' is a big improvement. And, um, am I okay to call you 'Griffin'?"

*No, I'm Mr Thompson,* Griff thought. It was frightening him how fast the walls were coming down between them. But was there really any sense in fighting this? They were in deep trouble. Griff was in *way* over his head. If Raphael wanted more familiar names, Griff guessed he could comply.

"'Griff' is good," he muttered, feeling guilty immediately. Was he really considering his client's needs and wants right now? Or was he simply giving in to the first chance in a long time to hear someone call him by his preferred name?

Whatever the case, the damage was already done. "Griff!" Raphael declared excitedly. "Perfect. Okay, now that's sorted, what do you want to know?"

Giff inhaled slowly. He realised with a jolt that they'd already stopped at Mile End and were going through Bow. He'd been so engrossed in talking to Raphael, he hadn't noticed. That was bad and exactly the reason why he couldn't get too familiar. It didn't matter if having Raphael's full attention made Griff's skin tingle. Griff was here to do a job, which was to keep Raphael *alive.*

"I believe you offered to tell me everything," Griff murmured softly. The old lady in the hijab appeared to be dozing with her shopping bags clutched around her like a dragon guarding its hoard. He doubted very much she'd be able to hear them over the squeal of the train's wheels anyway, but it never hurt to be too careful.

Raphael nodded and exhaled. He was still sort of smiling and looking relieved, which Griff was a little perplexed by. Why wasn't he terrified? He'd lived his entire sheltered life up in that penthouse. But he didn't seem to be freaking out all that much in that moment.

Strange.

"Okay," he said, nodding and petting Sparrow's head. "Umm. So, Campanula is a microstate within Italy. Its population is only about half a million people, but it's had a monarchy since its birth a few hundred years ago. My father is – was – the king."

Of all the crazy scenarios Griff had been trying to imagine as to why Raphael needed protection, this had not been one of them. "Right," he said tersely, rather than keep asking questions. Best to let Raphael explain in his own words and try not to add to bamboozle him.

"When my mum met him, he was so charming." He shook his head, sounding like he was trying not to get bitter. "My mum was traveling from Italy, and she didn't realise he was a *prince.* Just a fun, rich guy." He shrugged. "She was up-and-coming in her field at the time. We've been millionaires most of my life, but back then, she was a woman pioneering her own tech start-up, not used to being taken seriously." He sighed and fussed Sparrow some more. "By the time she realised she was pregnant, she'd discovered the truth. Tommaso was married, and soon to be king. And – more importantly – he was a cruel, manipulative arsehole who always got what he wanted, even if it took some time."

He licked his lips and looked warily around the still deserted carriage.

"Including the *throne.* My grandfather died very suddenly of a heart attack. There have always been rumours it wasn't exactly natural."

Griff tried not to show any emotion on his face. What kind of mess had he got himself into? This was like Hamlet or some other crazy bollocks. "So your mum came to England?"

Raphael shook his head. "No, not at first. She managed to make herself disappear – she's extremely capable with technology, after all. But she had a feeling I should be born in Campanula, just in case."

"In case?"

Raphael studied him for a second. "In case he decided to try and take me out one day. The only way to outrank him and nullify his orders would be to become king myself."

*Fuck.*

*Fuck fuck fuckity fuck.*

He was in so far over his head it was like being at the bottom of a well. This wasn't making sure crazed super fans stayed ten feet back from popstars like Lolita Charisma. This was serious international politics. This was *treason.*

"Why not go to Interpol?" Griff asked.

Raphael smiled at him. "For the same reason you didn't want to go to the police, I think," he said, sounding like he'd just figured something out. "There's no telling who he has in his pockets. Campanula may be tiny, but Tommaso acted like he was king of the world."

Raphael's expression darkened, which looked so wrong on the soft, sunny face Griff had been getting used to. Sure, he'd been scared and confused, but his expression now was pure fury.

"He's had some human rights issues over the past couple of decades. Some of the council try and curtail him, but he's made sure the majority are his sycophants." Raphael puffed out his cheeks and shook his head. "Sorry, this is getting complicated already. Stop me if I'm going too fast."

"No, I'm keeping up," Griff assured him, trying not to grit his teeth.

Filthy rich or dirt poor, Raphael didn't have to explain to him how nice ladies fell for handsome arseholes who seemed okay at first, then turned out to be fucking bullies. Despite all their obvious differences, and the professional distance Griff was trying to keep between them, he felt a deep kinship with his client in that moment.

Raphael puffed out his cheeks and nodded. "Right, so. Once I was born, Mum's company took off within a couple of years. She couldn't stay in Campanula. Her business was gaining too much attention, and we had to stay hidden." He shook his head and gave a rueful laugh. "Of course the best place business-wise to relocate for the company was London, the city with the most CCTV on the planet. She didn't want to commute or trust strangers with my safety, so…that was when she bought the penthouse. We moved in when I was three, and I never left." He took a deep breath, his wide eyes on Griff, telling the gravity of the situation. "Until this morning."

Griff exhaled, looking through the train windows. They were at West Ham and had emerged above ground again. That meant they'd passed under Bow, where he'd spent his childhood. It always made him uneasy passing through there, so he was glad to have it behind them. The train was getting busier, but there still wasn't anyone in their immediate vicinity, so he felt safe enough to keep going with their bizarre conversation.

He wanted to ask Raphael what the hell his life had been like. He must have been so *lonely*. How was it possible that he'd ended up so cheery? But that was crossing a line. He didn't need to know about Raphael's feelings. He needed more facts about the man who had set up this assassination beyond the grave. He had to know what the plan was for their next move.

"So the king had a daughter eventually," Griff prompted.

Raphael nodded. "With his third wife. He got bored of the other two," he added bitterly. "But like I said, she's only twelve. So all my father's cronies will just carry on as they were. Perhaps even worse than before, manipulating her to agree to their laws that will continue to destroy Campanula's welfare state and line their pockets."

"Can't the people vote for a better council?" Griff asked. He'd never even heard of Campanula until just now, let alone have any grasp of its politics.

Raphael chewed his lip. "There have been protests for a fair election, but, uh…certain influential opposition leaders have, well, vanished. Or been shot resisting arrest."

*"Fuck,"* Griff rasped. He dragged his hand over his face, his heart rate still a little elevated and his fingertips tingly. "So they won't be happy if you show up and tell them who you are."

Raphael shook his head as he stroked Sparrow, who gave him a sad, sympathetic chirp.

"We don't know who, but Mum and Winston have long suspected there are certain council members who were in my father's inner circle. They probably authorised the assassins as much as he did. As much as going to Campanula to claim the throne is the best way to neutralise the hit out on me, I'll be walking into a devil's lair. I could quite possibly be presenting my case to the very people I shouldn't be trusting."

It wasn't like Griff hadn't worked with hot cases before. Often security was an offence game. But he'd had to bundle more than one client out of a building and out of a car when things had become too intense.

This was a whole new level, though.

"Winston isn't just a bodyguard, is he?" Griff asked with a raised eyebrow.

Raphael shook his head. "He's so much more than that. He's been preparing for this day for years, trying to anticipate every eventuality." He sighed. "A half-dozen assassins arriving all at once had never been a strong possibility, but, well, here we are." He brightened up. "That's why we hired you!"

Griff blinked, aware they were leaving Plaistow. He wasn't really sure where he was heading for, as his only objective had been to get Raphael away from the assailants and out of the city. But he needed to consider if they were going to ride the tube all the way to the end of the line in Essex, or what.

"Me?"

Raphael nodded. "Winston knew we might need some real muscle, not just guys good at surveillance." He winced and looked guiltily at Griff. "I promise, we had *no* idea you'd be walking into quite this much trouble, *definitely* not on your first day."

Griff shrugged. "Every job has risks," he said out loud, although privately he appreciated the admission that he'd been dropped in the deep end. 'Unprepared' didn't even cover half of it. "So that other guy didn't quit because he was bored?"

Raphael tilted his head. "Oh, no. He was definitely bored. Nothing interesting or even remotely dangerous had previously happened my entire life."

He paused as someone finally walked past them, but thankfully, the guy had his music up so loud Griff could hear the bassline hissing through his earbuds from several seats down. Raphael eyed him as he sat down, then continued in a hushed voice.

"But the other guy was older and wanted to spend more time with his new grandchild, so we thought he'd be perfect to swap out." Raphael licked his lips, his gaze fixed on Griff's. "Then we found you."

He stared just long enough for heat to start creeping onto Griff's neck. Then Raphael snapped his head away.

Uh-oh.

It was bad enough if Griff was arguing with his downstairs brain about his intriguing new client, but he could handle himself. If Raphael was developing a little saviour's crush on Griff just because he'd rescued him, Griff would have to nip that in the bud right the fuck now. Raphael was a young guy who'd had so little real-world experience. This wouldn't be some fling or hook-up to him, and Griff would be a monumental arsehole if he encouraged any kind of lustful inclinations.

So Griff cleared his throat and sat up straighter, staring ahead. "Lucky me," he said flatly. He couldn't help but roll his shoulder again. It was throbbing, and he was starting to think he'd wrenched it jumping off that bloody building.

"Oh, no! Did you get hurt? Do you need to go to a hospital?" Raphael's hands fluttered over Griff's shoulder. He spoke with such earnest sincerity it only went and cut right through Griff's walls two seconds after he'd attempted to put them up. Griff sighed and glanced at Raphael, raising an eyebrow.

"It's fine," he assured him. "What's the point of being a bodyguard if I don't get to actually protect people from time-to-time?"

Raphael barked out a laugh, making Sparrow look up at him. "I like that," he said cheerfully. "That's a good attitude to have. Okay, well, I'm glad I was able to fulfil you today, then."

*Jesus H Christ,* Griff thought as he bit his lip, hard. *I won't think about how else my client could fulfil me. I will not! What is wrong with me?*

He could maybe have understood it if Raphael was his type. But the truth was, Griff didn't really *have* a type, other than male, single, and with no strings attached. He'd dated a nice guy back in his late twenties, almost ten years ago, but in the end, Griff had sabotaged it like he always did.

No. Guys were great for sex, and Griff knew he wasn't

capable of more. He wasn't about to get involved with his sweet, inexperienced client.

No matter what his downstairs brain said.

"What about your hair?" he blurted out as they left another station. Anything to change the subject, and it was something they needed to discuss anyway.

"What about it?" Raphael asked, his hand automatically flying to the back of his neck, running down the white-blond plait.

Griff cleared his throat. "Well, it makes you stick out like a sore thumb," he said bluntly. "The most obvious thing would be to cut it-"

Raphael went very still, his eyes focused outside the windows as the train sped along above ground. Griff thought he saw Raphael's hand tremble as he brought it back down to rest on the rucksack. Sparrow whimpered at him, but he just kept staring forwards.

"Do we have to?" he whispered.

Griff opened his mouth to say of course they did. Raphael's hair was painfully distinctive. He should cut it all off and dye it brown.

But Griff couldn't bring himself to say it. Not only because there were clearly tears pooling in Raphael's eyes, but in Griff's gut, he knew it would just be plain wrong to destroy something that beautiful.

Before he could even get angry at himself for merely thinking that – Raphael was a *job*, for fuck's sake – Griff wasn't here to be his bloody friend or hairdresser! – Griff had an idea.

"Hey," he said, tapping Raphael's knee with the back of his hand. "I'll get you one of those beanie hats. A baggy one. If you make the braid into a bun at the back of your neck, no one will know what's under the hat. Besides, your hair's so fine, I'm sure it doesn't weigh much..."

He trailed off. He'd just admitted that he'd been paying enough attention to Raphael's hair to know its texture. Because how could he imagine running his fingers through all those glorious locks and *not* think about what it would feel like?

*Fucking hell.*

"Acceptable compromise?" he grunted rather than finish his previous sentence.

But it was difficult to stay grumpy when Raphael's face broke into a hugely relieved smile. He wiped at his eyes with the heels of both hands and practically bounced in his seat.

"Oh, yes! Thank you, Griff. You're so kind. That means a lot to me. Thank you!"

Kind. Like that was a fucking word anyone had *ever* used to describe Griffin Thompson. God, this kid was deluded. Griff would do well to remember that. He absolutely should not have taken that one word – *kind* – and wrapped it up in his heart. Well…who knew if anyone would ever say it again? Maybe it would be okay to lock it up and keep it safe. Just this once. No one else would ever know, after all.

Raphael took in a deep breath and nodded at Griff. "Okay, well, I have both my passports in my bag. How easy will it be to go get yours?"

Griff turned in his seat and felt his eyebrows creeping up as he stared at Raphael. "My…what?"

"Your passport," said Raphael cheerfully. "The fastest way to Campanula is to take the Eurostar to Paris, then fly to Milan, then possibly get another flight to Verona, or the train, then-"

"Whoa, whoa, whoa," said Griff, waving his hands. "What are you talking about?"

Raphael blinked. "You taking me back to Campanula," he said, as if that was obvious.

For a second, Griff just stared. Then he frowned and

rubbed his forehead. "Winston just told me to get you out of there. I figured I'd get you to a safe house, then we'd lie low until he contacted us." But thinking about it, that was very short-sighted of Griff. Raphael couldn't go back into hiding, not if his father's hit squad were actively after him now. "You need to go into protective custody. We should contact MI6 or something."

This was *so* far above his pay grade. MI6? Anything he knew about them pretty much came from watching Bond movies.

Raphael bit his lip. "Uh, no. I can't do that. I'll spend the rest of my life in a box." He sat up a little straighter, clutching on to his backpack and Sparrow within, looking Griff dead in the eye. "I was prepared to stay away. Yes, Campanula is corrupt, but there's no guarantee I can save it if I become king. Or that I'll get there alive," he added in a small voice. But he rallied again almost immediately. "Mum and I might have been able to broker an immunity deal to give us back our freedom. But this attack shows Tommaso's hand. My father will have left instructions for them not to stop until I'm dead. And there's a chance that the inner circle of the council might get even *worse* now they don't have an adult monarch to rein them in."

Griff licked his lips. Raphael's eyes were blazing with intensity. Griff didn't want to disappoint him, but Griff was just one man. What did Raphael expect him to do?

"So what, then?" Griff asked in clipped tones. He felt like the more he learned, the less he understood. He never should have taken this job. He'd been seduced by the money. But he ought to have known better than to walk into this so blind.

Raphael took a deep breath. "There's going to be a council meeting on Friday, so in five days. It's basically a formality, but they have to wait until the previous monarch has been dearly departed for two weeks. Then the council meets to officially accept the new monarch. In *theory*, if anyone had a claim to challenge the throne, it would happen then."

"But it never has before?" Griff guessed.

Raphael shook his head. "Only in cheesy TV movies." He inhaled deeply, a determined look in his eye. "But…it's what I have to do. I have to get there before Princess Alessa's coronation – which should be a very small affair. They'll have a big official one when she turns eighteen. Unless I can get there in time and convince either the council or the queen and princess to accept my claim and call off the assassins that will otherwise never stop until I'm dead." He bit his lip. "Then she'll never be crowned. I only need either the council or the royal family to believe me and allow me to ascend to the throne. Piece of cake," he whispered.

What the hell was Griff supposed to say to that? He stared at Raphael for a second, then snapped his jaw shut from where it had fallen open. He turned and focused on the next station they'd just arrived at. It was Barking, which was not only a large station but a National Rail one as well.

"Come on," he said suddenly. He hadn't planned to, but he stood and marched over to the door, holding his arm in front of it in case it started to close. He might have had no clue what they were going to do next, but he wasn't leaving Raphael behind accidentally. "We're getting off," he added when Raphael didn't move.

"Oh!" Raphael jumped to his feet and darted around the passengers who had just boarded the tube. This carriage had just become too busy to continue talking in anyway. "Right, okay, sure." He hopped onto the platform, and Griff stepped beside him just as the doors began to beep and close. They both stood and watched the train depart, leaving them on the open-air platform with the summer air whipping around them. "So you see?" Raphael continued. "You need to take me to Campanula. *That's* what my mum meant just before we left the tower about getting me to safety."

Griff hummed and pulled out his phone.

He couldn't do that. It wasn't in his training. He didn't know how to cross international borders undetected. He had no clue about diplomatic immunity or whether or not he had any rights as a British citizen in the rest of Europe on this matter. And who knew what the hell the Campanulan law was or what rights Raphael had. If he had two passports, then presumably he had dual nationality for the UK and Campanula.

Griff was just some security guard from Bow. His head was hurting from just trying to work out what to do next, and it was time to call in the big guns.

"What are you doing?" Raphael asked as Griff hit the dial button.

"Calling Winston," Griff grunted.

Raphael frowned. "But I thought you said it wasn't safe? That we couldn't trust anyone?"

Griff nodded as the call began to ring. "We can't. But if you trust Winston with your mum, then I trust him to tell me what to do here."

Hopefully, his answer would be to go home and let a team of damned professionals deal with this. Raphael needed the SAS or someone else with real firepower to get him across several international borders and back to his home country in time to prove he was the king's oldest child and rightful heir to the throne.

Not Griff.

No matter how much his heart was screaming at him that he didn't want to leave this sweet young man and throw him to the mercy of a strange team of killing machines. He had to do what was right for Raphael's safety and the future of Campanula. That meant knowing when to step aside.

Right?

Griff ground his teeth, swallowing down the bile in his throat. Winston would tell him what to do, and then he'd do it.

And if that meant walking away from Raphael d'Oro forever...well, that was what he would do.

5

# RAPHIE

"So, what did he say?" Raphie asked.

Griff came wandering back down the platform, his face caught between concentration and a scowl. He hadn't gone far from Raphie, but he'd spoken in such low tones Raphie hadn't caught a single word over the wind rushing through the open platform. Griff had been on the phone to Winston for only a few minutes, but that was long enough for Raphie to get anxious and pet poor Sparrow's fur into a veritable mohawk.

Had he made a mistake by blurting out all his secrets? He was pretty sure he hadn't had any choice, but he'd never made the call to divulge his identity to anyone before. His mum always took care of that in the past. But Raphie was a grown adult now, out in the real world. He'd made a decision, and he had to stick by it.

The truth was that he *had* to get to Campanula, and the clock was ticking with both the deadline to make his claim to the throne and from the threat of the many assassins that had come for him.

But Griff didn't seem thrilled at the idea of travelling to

mainland Europe. Raphie didn't want to be a burden to him, but at the same time, he desperately didn't want Griff to leave. Nerves wriggled in Raphie's belly as he watched the other man come back towards him.

It didn't matter that they'd only met a few hours ago. It was Griff Thompson that Raphie wanted to accompany him on this journey – the mere prospect of which was *terrifying* Raphie, as much as he'd been trying to make himself enjoy his sojourn through London and into Essex. He couldn't even remember going beyond the lift in the penthouse. Now he'd been on the tube and was in a whole new county outside of London.

He'd studied the tube map so much, wondering one day if he would ever get to see the stations for real. He practically knew it all off by heart, and he'd felt a little thrill every time they'd passed into the next zone, knowing exactly when they'd left the city and entered the new county of Essex.

He was feeling okay about that, not too overwhelmed, but only because he trusted Griff with his life. The man had not only jumped off a sixty-storey building for him, but he'd waited to rescue his cat first and fought several assassins to do so.

Raphie trusted Griff. However, more than that, more than tallying his merits as a bodyguard, Raphie couldn't ignore his instincts. Nor his heart. He wanted Griff to stay with him because Raphie *liked* him. Because he had a good feeling about him.

And his cock had reasons for wanting to keep him around as well, but Raphie was trying not to listen to that. Griff was a fully grown man, and Raphie's contracted security detail. There was no way he'd appreciate being crushed on by someone like Raphie, who was practically Bambi, stumbling on wobbly legs out into the real world for the first time in his life. Griff was probably straight, with a wonderful girlfriend. And even if he was neither of those things, he'd never look twice at a silly thing like Raphie.

Except Raphie's heart didn't seem to be getting that memo from his brain, as it raced watching Griff stop in front of him, waiting for the reply to Raphie's question.

"Hm?" Griff asked, glaring at his phone screen.

Raphie licked his lips and made himself smile. If he was happy, then maybe Griff would like him more and stay as his bodyguard.

Wow. He was so pathetic.

"What did Winston say?"

Griff's scowl deepened. "He said to get you to Dover, then wait to hear from him. He said it would be good for us to find a B&B, as he didn't know how long it would take to do… whatever it is he's going to do."

He definitely seemed irritable at that answer, which made Raphie anxious. He knew it was childish, but he didn't want to make Griff upset or annoyed, but he had a question, and he had been taught it was always best to ask when he didn't know or understand something.

"Um, what's a B&B?" he asked tentatively.

Griff blinked as he finally looked up at him from his phone. To Raphie's surprise, his expression softened, just a fraction. "Sorry. A B&B is a bed and breakfast. It's like a small hotel, run out of people's houses usually."

"Oh!" Raphie cried, feeling foolish. "Sorry, of course I know what a bed and breakfast is. It just sounds different, hearing it out loud as 'B&B'. Crikey, that's embarrassing. I'm such a hermit."

He laughed awkwardly and rubbed the back of his neck, feeling his cheeks heating up. He was so sheltered, and worse, he kept babbling at Griff. Raphie understood that a gorgeous guy like him wouldn't look twice that way at

Raphie, but he'd really rather Griff didn't think he was a moron.

But to his surprise, though, that twitch of a smile came back. "S'okay," Griff mumbled. "Nobody knows everything. You're, um, doing just fine, coping with all this change, I mean. You can ask me anything you don't get, all right?"

That warmed Raphie's insides so much his cheeks continued to heat for a different reason. He *loved* that Griff had made that offer to help him. Perhaps he didn't think Raphie was a total wally after all.

"Thanks, Griff," he gushed as they began walking in the direction the station's exit signs were pointing. "I've studied non-stop my whole life, but I swear, sometimes I know nothing at all!"

Griff just grunted, but he didn't seem very annoyed. Raphie bit his lip, pleasure squirming in his belly. It was still probably pathetic of him, but he was quickly realising he'd do anything to earn even just a morsel of Griff's praise or appreciation. Beneath all that gruffness, there really was kindness lurking not-so-far beneath the surface.

"So, how do we get to Dover?" Raphie asked as they used their Oyster cards to get them out of the ticket barriers again.

And just like that, Griff was scowling again. *"Shh!"* he hissed at Raphie, hurrying them out of the busy station. "You need to keep your voice down when other people can hear. We have *no* idea who is working for your father. I didn't see any of those assailants at the penthouse aside from Mr Morning Star. They could be anyone."

Shame washed through Raphie, and hot tears pricked at the back of his eyes. Sparrow looked up at him from the rucksack and gave him a small meow that sounded like 'whoopsie, Daddy', and an extra sad face.

"Sorry," Raphie mumbled as they hurried out onto the street. "I wasn't thinking."

Griff sighed and stopped walking, rubbing his eyes before looking at Raphie again. "It's okay. You're not used to any of this. I do know that. I'm just worried about you. It's my job to do that," he added hastily. "To, um, worry. Keep you safe."

Griff was right. This was all new to Raphie, and he was allowed to make a mistake. Although he'd prefer the ones that were slightly awkward rather than the ones that could get them killed.

"Right," said Raphie. They looked warily at each other before Raphie moved by the station wall, hoping for a little privacy. Griff followed and raised his eyebrows. "So…how do we get to where we need to go and how long will it take?" He bit his lip and looked up at Griff shyly. "I'm kind of hungry, and Sparrow might be too."

For the second time in as many minutes, Griff visibly softened. "That's totally fair enough. I want you to always ask me for what you need, okay? Look. There's a café down the road."

Funny. Raphie had always thought it was pronounced *caf-ay*, but Griff had just said *caff*. Raphie assumed it must be a regional dialect thing. Yet again, Raphie was learning that books and the internet only got you so far.

"What about my hair?" he asked in hushed tones. He'd seriously thought he was going to throw up back there on the train when Griff had suggested he cut it off. But thankfully, he'd apparently seen how much Raphie didn't want to do that and come up with another solution.

How could Raphie's heart not react to that?

"Oh, yeah, right," Griff said, nodding. "Ah, perfect. Let's pop in here."

There was a large clothes store over the road that Griff led

Raphie into. The inside was bright with fluorescent lighting, grubby white walls, and rows and rows of metal clothes rails, but to Raphie…it was glorious. Like a sweet shop. There was so much colour and variety that he felt like his head was going to spin off as he twisted left and right, trying to take everything in.

There were jeans in several shades of denim and T-shirts with all kinds of fun designs. Sparkly, shimmery stuff under a pink sign that read *'Party Time!'* Sleek-looking workout gear in a mixture of dark and neon colours. Raphie glanced longingly at the fluffy slippers and dressing gowns. There was a beachwear section filled with swimsuits, towels, sarongs, and picnic supplies. Raphie had never been to the beach, obviously, but just looking at the photos on the displays filled him with wonder. He had a feeling he'd love it by the sea.

Raphie had always been able to order whatever clothes he'd wanted, and his mum had always been supportive of whatever he wanted to wear. But there was something very different from scrolling through online shops to being in an actual store in person.

"It's *magnificent*," Raphie whispered reverently, blinking back tears.

Griff arched an eyebrow. "It's Primark?"

"I *love* it!"

Griff looked at Raphie with a curious expression. "Fair enough," he said, shaking his head. "All right. Let's try over here."

Griff brought them through to the menswear section. He pulled a grey beanie hat off the rail – the only one available, presumably because it was summer and hats were not in high demand – and fitted it on Raphie's head.

"Okay, how's this?"

Raphie's heart threatened to stop at Griff's touch. He would have expected Griff to hand Raphie the hat to put on himself. Griff seemed to realise what he was doing as he fitted the thing around Raphie's ears, brushing his fingertips against Raphie's neck and making Raphie shiver from head to toe. The skin-on-skin contact felt like little trails of delicious fire.

Griff cleared his throat and stepped away. "Can you get your hair under that?" he grunted.

Raphie shook himself back to reality. It was just a *hat*. He smiled, quickly winding up the braid. The beanie was just loose enough that he could tuck all his hair underneath. "Snug as a bug in a rug!" he announced.

Griff nodded. "Right, okay. Let's pay for that, then, and get the hell out of here."

Raphie wanted to protest. Ideally, he'd love nothing more than to just wander around, touching the glittering sequins and silky fabrics. The price tags didn't look too dear, and he could probably have bought a lot of new and exciting things here. But more than that, he was just relishing the smell of the materials, the tinny music playing overhead, the movement of other people milling around various aisles and the low buzz of their chatter.

But they weren't here to have fun. There would be plenty of time to shop once he was no longer being hounded by assassins.

He hoped.

Griff handled the transaction with a hundred-pound note Raphie gave him. He pulled the tag off the bean rather than getting Raphie to take it off again. The cashier raised an eyebrow at the money for some reason, but otherwise said nothing as he scanned the barcode. Thankfully, they were able to pay quickly and leave without any discussion.

"Thank goodness," Griff muttered as they made their way back to the front entrance. He handed the coins and notes back to Raphie before stepping back out into the sunshine, surveying the street with narrowed eyes. "Now you have some change and won't stick out so much."

Raphie frowned, looking at the plasticky notes and metal coins. "Don't people use hundreds?" he asked.

Griff scoffed, although it wasn't unkind. "Most people haven't even *seen* a hundred-bob note."

Raphie hummed and pocketed the change from the beanie, making a mental note not to even flash *one* of his hundred-pound notes around from now on if he could help it. Of course normal people didn't carry hundreds of pounds around in their wallets. He was aware his mum was rich and the life he'd lived had been saturated in wealth. But it was a cold wake-up call to realise most people probably shopped at places like that Primark place regularly, whereas Raphie had treated it like a novelty.

It was like he was from a different planet. He wondered how many other things he was going to learn about the real world today that seemed obvious to everyone else. Griff must think he was such an idiot. It was difficult not to let shame curl through him like a snake.

"Right, food," said Griff, apparently not noticing Raphie's moment of disappointment in himself and getting them walking again. "Brunch seems forever ago."

That perked Raphie up. He heartily agreed about their last meal as they marched towards the café. He couldn't believe that had been this week, let alone this morning. His entire life had gone up in smoke since then, quite literally.

"I'm excited to try some food that wasn't prepared in my kitchen," he said, petting Sparrow's head and trying to forget his embarrassment. She'd earned herself quite a strange look from the Primark cashier, but luckily they'd been able to leave before he'd asked any questions.

Griff gave a small chuckle that sent thrills tingling down Raphie's spine. "I have no idea if the food will be decent or dodgy, but after all that adrenaline, I think anything in our stomachs will do us good. Didn't you ever get takeaway up in the penthouse?"

Raphie shrugged. "Not that I can remember. We have – had – our own chef, Phillipe, who came in three times a week. So I've definitely been spoiled. But chips on the TV always look so…I don't know, they look yummy."

Griff hummed. "Well, hopefully these ones are okay and not soggy. You deserve a good first impression."

*Do I? Why?* Raphie refrained from asking, though. Instead, he chose to lap up Griff's little nicety. If he thought Raphie deserved decent chips, Raphie was happy to take the small compliment and tuck it away into his pocket.

A guy on a skateboard whizzed past. Instantly, Griff stepped into Raphie's space, placing that hand once again on the small of his back. Raphie loved that Griff was still protecting him, even though it didn't feel like there was any danger. Of course, the point was that there could be danger at any turn, but it was Griff's job to look for that. It was Raphie's job to make it as easy as possible for Griff to take care of him, so he stayed close, leaning into the touch.

Only to make Griff's job easier, naturally.

For some reason, the idea of Griff 'taking care of him' made Raphie shiver and bite his lip to stop himself from grinning so much. He wasn't even sure where his imagination was running off to, but he was pretty sure it involved Griff keeping his hands on Raphie's body, and anything involving that, Raphie was more than okay with.

Naturally, Griff was all business by the time they reached the café. He nodded through the glass front as he surveyed the scene. "Stay close," he said as he opened the door. A little bell tinkled overhead as they walked in side-by-side. The place was mostly full and there was a lot of beige colours on the walls and floors, but it seemed friendly enough. There was a lot of chatter, and the radio was playing pop music overhead. Griff nodded at Raphie. "I – oh, crap."

He hastily pulled his phone out of his pocket as it started ringing and vibrating. Raphie raised his eyebrows, apprehension swimming through his insides.

"It's Winston," said Griff. "Could you get me some fish and chips?" Then he winked, and Raphie's stomach did a gymnastics flip worthy of the Great Britain Olympic team. "I assume you're okay to pay. Just…don't shower the whole café in money, yeah?"

Raphie stuttered. "Gosh, blimey," he cried with a laugh that made Sparrow look up in shock. "You just made a joke! It was funny!"

Griff grunted, his smile wry. "Don't worry. It won't happen again," he said bashfully. "Go on. And, um, thank you. I'll be right behind you, and, uh…I'll sort us dinner tonight." He answered the phone right after that, turning away and murmuring into the receiver.

Raphie thought that was a strange thing to say about dinner. He had a lot of money. He was happy to buy them anything they needed. That was the entire point of having the cash sitting in the backpack all this time, just waiting for this day when he'd need to get to Campanula. But he had to admit he loved the idea of Griff buying him dinner.

It seemed romantic.

Raphie shook his head and laughed at himself as he turned around as well. He was being ridiculous. He'd watched too many sappy movies and TV shows.

There was a small queue inside the café, maybe because it was approaching lunchtime? Raphie always had his lunch at about twelve or one o'clock, but was that what other people did?

Speaking of other people, the customers in front of him all

seemed to know what they wanted pretty quickly. But Raphie looked behind the glass-fronted counter where a couple of dozen sandwiches were on display, past the few people running around serving, to the menu above them. It ran the whole length of the wall, offering more sandwich combinations than he would have thought possible, as well as several hot food options, including baked potatoes with all the toppings you could wish for, and a salad bar that looked delicious.

But anxiety was filling Raphie's veins. Their amazing chef, Phillipe, regularly came in to prepare them all kinds of dishes from around the world, and the rest of the time Raphie and his mum would cook for themselves. But Raphie had never been faced with so much choice in all his life. How did he place an order? What if he got it wrong?

"Next please," a large man with olive skin and thick eyebrows boomed. He looked up from the till and looked down the queue.

The woman behind Raphie nodded to him as he looked around. "That's you," she whispered kindly.

"Oh, um, thanks," Raphie stammered. He leaned closer over the counter, his eyes still skittering over the seemingly never-ending menu. "I, uh…fish and chips?" He'd never had that before, but he'd heard of it. Normally you got it from specific fish and chip shops. He'd seen that on the telly. He wasn't sure if Griff had assumed that they did it here, but got it wrong.

However, the man behind the counter nodded, already tapping on the cash register. "Just one portion?"

Oh! There was his solution! He could just get the same as Griff. "No, two," said Raphie. "Actually, sorry. Make that three. If that's okay?" He looked down at Sparrow, thinking she'd probably appreciate some fish, and Griff could have the extra chips if he wanted.

The guy's eyes narrowed. "Yeah, it's okay," he said. "But that can't stay in here. You want them to go?"

Raphie frowned before he realised by 'that', the guy meant Sparrow.

"Oh," he said, a little hurt. "Why not?"

"Health and safety," the guy said with an impatient shrug. "So you want it to go, yeah?"

Raphie's skin prickled. He assumed 'to go' meant 'takeaway', but Raphie didn't know where they'd eat if they did that. Would it be safe? What would Griff do? The guy was scowling at Sparrow, which was kind of mean. Panic was making Raphie's throat tight, and he didn't know what to do or say. "Uhh…"

"Yes, to go," came Griff's voice from behind him.

Raphie sighed in relief as Griff came to his rescue yet again. Raphie turned and smiled at him. "Thank you," he whispered. He felt completely foolish that he'd fumbled at something as simple as getting them something to eat, but he couldn't deny he was more relieved that Griff had been there to bail him out.

He really, *really* hoped that he'd be there all the way to Campanula to always watch his back.

"Fine," snapped the man. "Cat, out, now. Who's next!"

He'd already moved on to getting the next customer's order. Raphie blinked in confusion. "Aren't I supposed to pay?" he asked Griff.

"Gimme a twenty, and I'll sort it," Griff said, jutting his chin at another guy by the till. "You want a drink, too?"

He placed his hand on Raphie's back, and immediately Raphie relaxed. It was like the best medicine thrown in with a massage. Better than a hot bath and a glass of wine. He never wanted Griff to stop putting his hand there.

"Sure," Raphie stammered. "I'll have whatever you're having. Meet you outside?"

He handed over one of the hundred-pound notes as Griff nodded. "Sure. See you outside." Then his expression suddenly became concerned. *"Don't* go far, though. Stay where I can see you, okay? Right by the door." He caught the eye of the grumpy man. "How fast can you get that order for us?"

"It's coming, it's coming," said the guy scornfully with a dismissive wave of his hand.

Griff glowered and walked with Raphie to stand just outside the door.

Raphie didn't like the feeling that he'd got something wrong. He didn't want to be a freak. He'd spent so long dreaming of going outside and being a regular person, but he was fucking it all up.

"Ah, that was quick," Griff said, looking inside the café through the glass where one of the other members of staff signalled to him with his hand. "Okay, sit on that bench. I'll be thirty seconds."

Raphie nodded. "Thank you," he said, but Griff was already disappearing back inside.

The bench was opposite a pub with pretty hanging baskets decorating the railing that bordered the outdoor seating area. People were eating hot lunches and drinking in the sunshine, talking with each other. Raphie felt a pang. Even though he tried to be grateful for his wonderful life with his mum, there had been many days that he'd just wanted to be normal, free to be anonymous like anyone else. Free to make friends.

Free to fall in love.

He let Sparrow out of the rucksack and onto the pavement to roam on her lead that Raphie looped around his wrist. She sniffed the ground for a second, then hopped up onto the bench and curled herself as close as she could get against Raphie's thigh.

"Yeah," he said with a sigh. "The outside world isn't quite what we were picturing, huh?"

He glanced around at the grey buildings and the fast-food shops that lined the street. He could still see Griff through the glass, and with a lurch Raphie realised Griff was watching him intently. Raphie offered him a small wave, then looked away. It was Griff's *job* to watch him. It wasn't like he was pining for Raphie or anything.

It seemed like there was a bus depot nearby, or at least numerous stops around the station, because red double-decker buses made up most of the traffic. Raphie got a thrill watching through the windows every time one went past, imagining the colourful lives of all the people inside. Every one of them had a story to tell. Yes, it was overwhelming to finally be outside, but it was also exciting and vibrant. Raphie wanted to make the most of this experience. He'd never get his first day out in the real world back again.

"My first cat was called Ruby," he said as Griff came to sit beside him. "After all the red buses I used to watch coming and going on the street below."

Raphie smiled at the memory, wanting to share it with Griff. He'd always had to be so careful with what he shared with his friends online. Nothing too personal in case it could be used to find him. So he wanted to open up to Griff, hoping they could sort of be friends, even though Griff was his bodyguard.

"Oh?" said Griff, sounding a little confused. He probably hadn't been expecting Raphie to say that. He placed the plastic bag with their lunch between them on the bench in. Sparrow immediately sat up, sniffing the hot fish inside with extreme interest. Griff chuckled and scratched between her ears.

Raphie nodded at the bitter-sweet memory. "Ruby was my best friend. I was so incredibly sad when she died. But then a sparrow made her nest up on the roof of the building. I watched every day as the eggs grew, then hatched, and the baby birds grew up until one day they could fly away. It reminded me that life goes on, so when Mum got me a new kitten, I named her after that mummy bird." He stroked Sparrow's fur, even though she was far more interested in sticking her head in the food bag. "The mummy sparrow came back sometimes. I always wondered what adventures she went on whilst she was gone."

Griff hummed, his lips twitching with a slight smile. "Bird stuff. Not as exciting as the day you've had. Here." He removed a rectangular cardboard box from the bag and handed it over to Raphie, along with a wooden knife and fork. "You ever had proper fish and chips before?"

"No," Raphie admitted as he opened the box.

It smelled heavenly, the tang of salt and vinegar filling the air, but he made himself wait to try it. Instead, he cut into the side of white fish that was lying on top of a mountain of chips, stripping back some of the batter so he could dig out a decent amount of fish to cut up in the lid of the box for Sparrow. She wolfed it down like she'd been starved her whole life, making Raphie laugh.

"Winston got us a car," Griff announced as he doused his own box of food with tomato sauce that he squeezed out of several little sachets. "A place nearby. I checked that he'd checked they'd take cash, which they will. Not sure how long we'll need the car for, but I guess we can just start with a couple of days, then take it from there."

It was Raphie's turn to hum as he focused on feeding Sparrow. He'd always thought he'd take the Eurostar over to mainland Europe or fly from one of London's airports. He knew from the hours he'd spent studying a map of the UK on his bedroom wall that Dover was on the coast, near France. What was Winston's plan from there? Would he come and collect Raphie himself to start their journey to Campanula? Or send someone else if Griff refused to go?

"You not hungry?" Griff grunted.

Raphie blinked and looked up. Griff was watching him again. Raphie shrugged and continued to get all the batter off the fish for Sparrow. He regretted getting a third portion now. If he ate anything at all, he'd just pick at the bits he hadn't given his cat. His stomach was churning.

"I spent every day of my life in a routine," he said, concentrating on Sparrow and the food instead of looking Griff in the eyes. "I always knew what lessons I'd be having, who I'd be seeing, what there was to eat or watch on TV. And now…" He poked at the chips with his fork. "I don't know where I'm going or who with. Assassins could be anywhere. I don't know where I'll sleep tonight or where my next meal will come from."

He sighed and squinted in the sunshine at the people wandering past, minding their own business. There weren't any sunglasses in his emergency backpack. Try as they might, he and his mum hadn't been able to prepare for everything. Maybe they could go back and get some from Primark?

"I've spent hours practising how to behave in public," he admitted. It was embarrassing, but for some reason, he had a burning desire to tell Griff this. "Including ordering food at a restaurant. I'd copy scenes from films I saw. And then…" He waved a hand towards the café. "I couldn't even manage fish and chips."

Griff harrumphed. It was such an angry sound that Raphie risked glancing over at him, anxious to know what he was thinking. He jabbed his wooden fork into a particularly long, fat chip. "That guy was a wanker," he growled. "He shouldn't have talked to you like that. You're doing just fine. You'll get better at it. Being around people. You're friendly."

A little thrill filled Raphie's chest. "Yeah?"

Griff nodded. "And don't worry about that stuff. Just deal with one thing at a time. I'll make sure you've got food and a place to sleep, okay?"

Raphie bit his lip as his feelings pulled him in two different directions. His initial thrill at realising *of course* he could trust Griff to provide and take care of him warred with the question that reared its ugly head.

*But for how long?*

Raphie just had to accept that, at least for now, his routine life had been shattered. Even though that had been what he'd wanted, it was a bit different in practice. But for now, he had Griff to help him. One thing at a time. If tomorrow Raphie began travelling with someone else who Griff and Winston considered better qualified, then so be it. But for now, Griff was here, and he was going to make sure nothing bad happened to Raphie.

It was as good as Raphie could get, so he needed to stop fretting and go with the flow.

He smiled and picked up a bit of the batter with his fingers, nibbling at the salty crunchiness with a happy sigh. It was delicious. "Okay," he responded to Griff, licking his lips and then his fingers. "Thank you. I – I trust you. I know you'll look after me. Thank you."

Griff seemed transfixed by Raphie eating, which was strange. Did he have grease on his chin or something? But just as Raphie noticed him staring, Griff cleared his throat and shook himself. "Sure. No problem. Eat up. Then we'll go pick up the car." He nodded and continued to jam his fork into his chips, like each one had personally offended him.

Raphie sighed internally, utterly perplexed by this man. Most of the people Raphie had known in his life had been his mum, staff, and teachers, all of whom pretty much said what they meant. But Griff was a mystery. Perhaps that was one of the things that made him so interesting.

Either way, it looked as if they were stuck together as far as Dover, so Raphie decided to appreciate Griff's company in what little time they *did* have together, and maybe just take in the view.

Because even when he was frowning, Griff was gorgeous, and Raphie would enjoy that for as long as he could.

6

GRIFF

It had been a sort of torture watching Raphael devour his damned fish and chips. Once he'd cheered up, he'd started eating. He'd kept moaning about how salty and yummy it all was, licking his lips and fingers, and fluttering his golden eyelashes like he was on the verge of an orgasm.

Griff had almost bitten his tongue in two trying not to react.

So, okay. There was clearly *something* about Raphael d'Oro that was Griff's type, despite being like no other man Griff had been with in his entire life. But Raphael was one hundred per cent off limits and out of bounds. So Griff tried to keep his mouth shut and not say something incredibly inappropriate.

That worked whilst they discarded their rubbish from lunch, then walked down to the car hire place. It wasn't too surprising that there had been one near the train station as it was such a hub, but Griff was grateful that they didn't ask too many questions or raise an eyebrow at Raphael's stacks of cash.

However, once they drove out of the town centre, it was

pretty much motorways and A roads all the way down to Dover. That was an hour and a half of not much distraction other than each other.

Griff would have been happy (or at least resigned to) keeping his eyes on the road and leaving Raphael to his own devices. But Raphael didn't seem keen on that plan, and for the first twenty minutes of the drive he kept up a constant stream of chatter, apparently trying to get Griff to engage with him.

"It's crazy to me to think all these other cars are full of people, and they're all going somewhere for some reason, and they all have their own worries on their minds or plans they're making. Isn't that kind of amazing?"

Griff grunted. It wasn't that he wasn't interested. In fact, he was probably *too* interested in what Raphael had to say. So it took all his effort to try and remain neutral.

"Is that a kind of sculpture?" Raphael tried again, pointing at a twisty red thing in the middle of a field. It looked incredibly phallic in the half-second that Griff glanced at it, so he *definitely* didn't comment on that one. "Mum's really into art. That's why we had so much of it in the penthouse." He sighed. "She'll be so upset her collection's been destroyed, or at least damaged from the smoke. Personally, I never got why a big square of paint flicks was worth twenty grand, but I'm sad she'll be sad."

*Twenty grand! For that thing?* Griff had to bite the inside of his cheek so he didn't say something he'd regret. He was sympathetic to anyone who was the victim of a fire, especially arson like the d'Oros. But the amount of food twenty thousand pounds could buy was mind-blowing. That money could have gone towards a community centre or a hospital or something *many* people could have shared.

But then Griff had to remind himself that Annabella *did* give a hell of a lot of her money away to charity as well. Was he so bitter that he'd begrudge her buying nice things for her home? Especially when it had been the only place Raphael ever saw?

He decided that he was being a grump and if she'd earned that money fair and square, why shouldn't she indulge in her passion? But by the time he'd swirled those thoughts around, he and Raphael had been stuck in another stretched-out silence.

Luckily, Raphael was ready to try again, despite Griff being useless. "Purfleet?" he commented as they drove past a sign with the town's name on it. "That sounds like where Sparrow should go to become a space cadet. Are you ready to live long and prosper, sweetie?"

Sparrow rolled onto her side and narrowed her eyes at him.

Griff did laugh a little at that one, but it was like the longer he went without speaking, the more weight it would have when he did open his mouth again. He desperately didn't want to cross any more unprofessional boundaries with Raphael, so it was best to just fold in on himself, and try and take up less space by not engaging in conversation.

However, it seemed like the more withdrawn Griff tried to make himself, the perkier Raphael got. Or at least, that was what Raphael was *trying* to do. Griff spent his whole life watching people and paying attention to all their little ticks and cues. Raphael was getting more and more flustered as he talked to himself, with his cheeks getting blotchy and his eyes glassy. Even from where he was driving, Griff couldn't help but notice the change in him.

Griff was pretty sure that for whatever reason, his silence was making Raphael upset. Which made little sense. Why would Raphael care what Griff thought? Yeah, okay, *maybe* Griff was aware that Raphael could be harbouring a little crush. But surely he'd get over it quickly when he realised

Griff might be good at jumping off buildings, but he definitely wasn't someone a nice guy like Raphael wanted to be with for more than one night.

It was a good job Griff would hopefully be handing his responsibility over to someone more qualified in the morning. That had to be Winston's plan. And Griff refused to feel sad about letting Raphael go, or worry that someone else wouldn't actually take care of him well enough. Those were feelings, and feelings didn't belong in work. They just needed to follow protocol and do what was best for the client.

However, it was becoming increasingly obvious that what was best for the client was not Griff's sullen silence.

"Sorry," Raphael blurted, shaking his head and twisting his hands. He turned to look out the window, sniffing and hastily wiping one of his cheeks. *Fuck*. Was he *crying?* "I'm pratting on, talking utter nonsense. I'm probably annoying you."

"No, *I'm* sorry," Griff said with a heavy sigh. Sod protocol. He couldn't take this any longer. "You're not annoying. I know I'm not great company. I've been watching the other cars for funny business." That was true, at least. He didn't think for a second that they'd seen the last of Raphael's would-be assassins, despite how crap they'd been. And it was a convenient excuse for why he'd been tongue-tied that was much better than 'I kind of think I fancy you and am so afraid of saying something inappropriate, I'm saying nothing at all'.

All this worrying and caring about feelings was exhausting.

"Oh, no," said Raphael earnestly. He turned back around with wide, slightly bloodshot eyes. "Have you seen anything? Have I been distracting you? I'm such an idiot. That's *literally* your job to be vigilant, and I've been nattering on like a buffoon."

"No, and no," said Griff truthfully. "There's no one following us as far as I can tell. I think we're safe for now, and, uh, you're not distracting me. I like listening to you talk."

That was also true, even though Griff knew saying so was crossing a line. Raphael knew so much about history, even though he'd spent his whole life locked away in that penthouse. It felt like whenever they passed an exit to a town, Raphael would have something interesting to say about it, like if it was once a Roman camp, or if some X-Factor singer came from there.

His trivia was helping Griff stay awake after all the adrenaline and then heavy food.

Yeah, that was it.

Raphael broke into a smile. "Oh, really? I was starting to think I was getting very irritating."

"No," said Griff quietly. "Not at all."

That was true, too, and perhaps the most surprising revelation of the whole day. When they'd first met, Griff had been convinced that this ball of energy was going to do his head in. But it turned out that Raphael's enthusiastic chatter was actually kind of soothing, like talk radio late at night.

Griff reckoned it would be hard to feel lonely around a guy like Raphael.

"I know it's probably stupid to you," said Raphael bashfully, "but I'm just so enjoying being in a car! I've seen a million of them on TV, but I never knew what it would feel like to be inside one. And, like, you can't explain what it's like to see hills rolling past to someone who's never experienced it. It's something I had to *feel* to really believe."

His whole expression was shining, and he was gazing out the

window at the English countryside as they headed east from London. The vista stretched out with green and yellow patchwork fields, separated with wooden fences and leafy green trees. Griff had never thought it was all that special. Sure, it was different to other countries. The view was quintessentially English, but he'd always thought it was kind of boring.

Raphael made him reconsider.

"Look, Sparrow!" Raphael said to his sleeping cat. "Sheep! Aren't they cute?" Sparrow only yawned and appeared to continue sleeping, but that didn't dampen Raphael's enthusiasm.

Griff was glad his dickhead behaviour hadn't dimmed Raphael's light for too long, either. As much as they were on the run, Griff figured this was also a dream come true for Raphael. He was finally free of that penthouse life, and he deserved to be drinking in all these new sights and experiences.

"We've still got a while to go," Griff said. "When we get closer, I'll stop and look for a B&B. But for now, do you want to put some music on? The car's got a Bluetooth thingy."

He waved his hand at the stereo. Truth be told, he still had a soft spot for his cassette tapes and good old-fashioned radio, so modern music technology was a bit beyond him. But Raphael's face lit up, and Griff only half-tried to squash his delight at that.

He knew there couldn't be anything between them. But he'd rather make Raphael happy than sad, that was for sure.

"Can I, really?" Raphael sat up in his seat. Sparrow was sleeping on his lap, full of fish and probably grateful to be inside and relatively still again after her frightful morning. Raphael looked like he was trying not to disturb her too much as he wriggled to get his phone out of his jeans pocket. "I have a playlist that's all my favourite songs right now. Can we listen to that?" He frowned and nibbled his lip. *Bloody hell.*

The things that did to Griff's crotch area. "Oh, but you might not like my music."

Griff raised his eyebrow as he glanced over at his passenger. Raphael had almost certainly *never* had the chance to share music he loved with anyone before, other than his mum. But that wasn't the same as sharing it with a friend. And now his concern was that Griff might not like it?

Try as he might, Griff couldn't stop his heart from aching a little at that. Also…that Raphael might even consider him a friend, even though that was totally unprofessional.

"I'm not keen on classical," Griff said honestly. "Or anything written before the seventies, actually. But other than that, I'll give anything a go."

Raphael's eyes shone with hope. "Even Lady Gaga?"

Griff could have perhaps been a little more specific about his dislikes, but he wasn't backing down now. He wasn't an arsehole. He could give anything a try for the next hour if it made Raphael happy. "Even Lady Gaga," he agreed solemnly, but he winked to encourage Raphael. Then he pointed at the dashboard and Raphael's phone. "You know how to make those two things talk to each other?"

Raphael blinked. "I already have," he said, mildly confused. "I'm just finding the playlist."

Griff snorted. "Kids these days."

Raphael huffed as he got his music playing. It wasn't something Griff knew, and it sounded like pop, but that didn't mean he immediately disliked it.

"I'm not *that* young," Raphael said. "How old are you anyway?"

This was dangerous. Griff shouldn't engage. But it was like he couldn't stop his mouth from moving, even though they were getting dangerously close to flirting territory. By discussing their ages, it was almost like they were debating their compatibility.

*It's just an innocent question. Answer it, you kettle.*

"Thirty-seven," Griff said.

"Pft, that's nothing!" said Raphael with a laugh, waving his hand dismissively. "I bet we've got loads in common."

Sixteen years older was not nothing. It was totally plausible that Griff could have been Raphael's dad. Plenty of kids on his estate had got themselves in trouble at that age when he'd been growing up.

But the thing was…his feelings were anything but fatherly as he glanced over at Raphael. "You and me?" he grunted, his eyebrow arched again. "Things in common? I don't know." He really didn't think that was likely, but he enjoyed the way Raphael's eyes lit up at the challenge.

"Is that so?" he asked cheekily.

"Go on, then," said Griff.

Okay. So, maybe the age difference wasn't that big of a deal? Just because Griff had been feeling jaded and burnt out for a while didn't actually mean he was that old. Maybe what he needed was someone with a bit more energy to rub off on him. But that still couldn't be Raphael, because he was Griff's client.

*Only until tomorrow morning,* an infuriating voice whispered in the back of his mind. Griff wasn't sure if that made things better or worse.

"Well, we both like fish and chips," said Raphael confidently, ticking off one of his fingers. "Do you like cats?"

Griff felt a smile twitch at the corner of his mouth. "I like *that* cat," he conceded, jutting his chin at Sparrow. She looked him up and down. He didn't have any more fish for her in that moment, so he wasn't sure how much she liked him in return.

"Excellent!" Raphael ticked off another finger. "What else do you like? What are your hobbies? Favourite foods? Oh! Favourite movies! I have *loads* of films I love!"

Heat crept up Griff's neck. He knew Raphael was being totally innocent and was probably just excited to talk to somebody new, but...bloody *hell* this was feeling like a first date.

Normally, Griff didn't date. If he had chemistry with a guy, why bother? All they wanted was to hook up, not go pick out curtains together, so normally it was pretty quick to the down and dirty. But strangely, he didn't mind Raphael asking his questions. Usually, nobody cared about Griff beyond his ability to do his job. It felt quite freeing to have someone genuinely interested in him, even if they were technically a client.

Especially someone as cute as Raphael. Literally nobody else on the planet ever needed to know how much Griff was enjoying this little chat, so why not indulge in it for a few minutes and lift Raphael's spirits?

"Uh, well," he said, changing lanes and thinking for a second. "Okay, um, food. I love meat pie. My mum and nan had this secret recipe for the crust that was off the chain. I haven't had a pie that good since...well, in a long time." He cleared his throat, not wanting to poke that painful hole in his heart. "I work too much to really have hobbies, but I guess I do like taking drives in the countryside when I can. Like this, kind of. And films? Um, well, I watch a lot of those, too, so we *do* have that in common."

"See?" said Raphael gleefully, bouncing in his seat as much as he could without getting bopped by Sparrow. "Like what? I bet you like all those car-chase-spy-type films."

His tone was slightly teasing, but in a friendly way. Griff liked Raphael guessing as to what his tastes might be. Like Raphael really wanted to know him well enough to be able to do that.

Griff nodded, glancing over. "Yeah, yeah. I do love a bit of Fast and Furious, and Mission: Impossible. But, uh..."

He never told anyone this. He never had anyone *to* tell. It was as if talking about himself was a rusty motor he was trying to get working again. Was he really about to confide this silly personal thing to his new client, who he'd only known for a few hours?

Apparently so.

Griff took a deep breath and tightened his grip on the steering wheel. "I also make sure I watch all the Oscar nominations I can. At least for Best Film and Director, but as many of the foreign language films I can find, too."

He swallowed, too afraid to look over at Raphael's reaction. Was he going to think Griff was a massive dork now? Griff knew he shouldn't care so much, but he did. He was torn between wanting Raphael to respect him, and wanting Raphael to see the real Griff. Not some idea of a 'hero'. Just a regular guy.

"That's *such* a cool idea," Raphael said breathlessly, surprising Griff enough for him to glance over for a second. Raphael was beaming at him. "I bet that gives you a really great, quirky selection each year! What made you think to do that?"

Griff shrugged, trying not to feel embarrassed at the praise. "I just got tired of the same action movies over and over. So I set myself a challenge to see how many I could watch. This was *years* ago, back when I was renting DVDs from Blockbuster. Now I stream them. So I tend to wait a couple of years until the films are available, then I work my way through them." He laughed. "Don't get me wrong, some of them are bollocks. But that way I watch political thrillers, historical dramas, coming-of-age stories, even musicals and kids animated films. Then when I go back to the dumb action films, they're more fun, somehow."

And then...he had no one to talk to about them. But maybe...

*Nope. No!* That was insane. Raphael wasn't going to become his movie critic mate.

Except, they spent the entire rest of the drive debating the various Oscar films they'd both seen over the last few years, getting increasingly animated and almost certainly pissing Sparrow off. Well, Raphael got animated. Griff was at least smiling by the time they were approaching Dover.

Griff only had a few more hours with Raphael. Why couldn't he enjoy them, just a little bit? What harm would it really do?

"I love it when a geeky film gets an award and the film snobs don't know what to do," Griff said. "Sure, it's fun to complain about something up its own arse that gets six wins. But I prefer it when Lord of the Rings gets Best Director or whatever, and the Academy gets all embarrassed about it."

Raphael was laughing and smiling at Griff, sending a shiver down his spine. "Right?" he said gleefully. "Like that new animated Spider-Man film, which was *amazing,* by the way-"

"Damn right," Griff interjected.

"-but I think it's good that different kinds of films win," Raphael continued, sounding firm in his conviction. "Just because something is fun doesn't necessarily mean it's of less value than something serious or downright depressing. I want to see the Academy considering more films by and about more diverse people too. People of colour, disabled people, and, um, LGBT people."

Griff didn't miss the way that Raphael squirmed when he said 'LGBT'. If Griff had still held any doubt over Raphael being attracted to men, it vanished in that second.

Once again, he wasn't sure if that was a good or a bad thing.

Griff sighed to himself as he brought them to a halt in a car park by an outdoor sports centre and small lake. He needed to find them a B&B. Before he began his search, he figured they could give Sparrow a little walk to do her business.

He knew *exactly* why he shouldn't get involved with Raphael, client or not. Age gap or not.

Raphael was in an incredibly vulnerable position, and had almost certainly never dated. He was almost certainly still a virgin. He was experiencing the outside world for the first time, and people were trying to *kill* him to stop him from ascending to the throne of a country Griff hadn't even heard of until a few hours ago.

So he was glad they'd had a nice chat about films. But that was as far as it could go. He didn't want to be rude, but he couldn't encourage any crush of Raphael's any more than he already had.

Even if that was the best, most meaningful conversation he'd had in years.

He walked beside Raphael around the grassy area next to the car park, letting Sparrow run as much as she could on her lead to leap and chase blades of grass and tiny insects. Then they got back in the car, and Raphael listened to more of his relentless happy pop music whilst Griff searched for a local B&B that accepted pets. The current song wasn't even in English. He didn't know if Raphael could speak whatever language it was, or if he'd just learned the sounds, but he was singing along to the cheerful beats regardless.

Griff smiled a little to himself, but kept his eyes on his screen. He didn't need to see how cute Raphael was being. It would only make it harder to let him go tomorrow.

"Ah, thank fuck," he said finally.

He'd been starting to get more than a little worried he wouldn't be able to find anything pet-friendly at such short notice. That was their only option. They weren't leaving Sparrow out in the car. It also very specifically needed to be a twin room so they each had their own bed, because Griff needed to keep Raphael close, but with his conflicting thoughts, not *too* close.

"Got one," he told Raphael. "Their last room. It's a bit out of the town, so maybe we should nip to the shops before we drive out?"

Raphael frowned. "For what?"

Griff shrugged. "I'd like a toothbrush and some deodorant. Clean clothes, if I can manage it. Maybe some food so we don't have to risk going back out again?"

"Oh, okay," said Raphael. He nodded and chewed his lip. "So, a big supermarket might have all of those things in one place, yeah?"

Griff smiled at him before he knew what he was doing. "Good idea," he said, already running a new Google search. "See, you're not that sheltered after all."

He could feel Raphael beaming at the praise, even with his gaze firmly on his phone.

<hr>

HALF AN HOUR LATER, they'd found a large Sainsbury's to raid. Raphael had emergency clothing and toiletries in his bag (Griff had never seen so many miniature products in his whole life) but he still joined Griff in clothes shopping. He got positively giddy, like he had in the Primark, and Griff had to admit it was a joy to behold.

He picked out a set of pyjamas with pandas all over so he didn't have to sleep in his underwear (something Griff was logically grateful for and illogically disappointed with), as well as a T-shirt that read 'Avocuddle' underneath a picture of a smiling avocado with its arms outstretched.

Despite it being summer, he also managed to pick up a different beanie hat. This one was sparkly purple and green from the women's section, and Griff had to admit it suited him much better than the drab grey one they'd bought in Primark. But Griff noticed that although Raphael swapped the hats right away, he didn't throw the grey one away. He just put it in the shopping basket with their other new purchases.

Griff wasn't entirely ready to admit to himself why, but he was secretly pleased that Raphael hadn't got rid of the one Griff had bought for him.

Once they'd paid for their new clothes, Griff's toiletries, snacks for them both, and cat food for Sparrow, they hurried back to the car. The most sensible thing had been to convince Sparrow back into the rucksack that Raphael had worn on his front again. But this time with the top closed, so as to keep Sparrow's presence secret from the staff who might kick them out. Griff couldn't let Raphael out of his sight, but they needed these supplies, so they had to hope she wouldn't freak out.

However, as soon as they got back to the car, it was clear Sparrow had just slept the entire time. Raphael sighed deeply and rubbed his eyes. He'd been getting increasingly anxious, worrying for her well-being, but now he was back to his usual happy self. "Good girl, sleepy girl," he cooed as he lifted her limp body out and hugged her on his lap again.

It was another forty-five-minute drive to the little B&B by the coast, so it was approaching late afternoon by the time they finally parked and exited the car with all their bags. Griff groaned as he stretched, his shoulder aching again as he rolled his arms out. He'd picked up some frozen peas and double-bagged them, so hopefully, they'd still be reasonably cold to put on his weary muscles once they got to their room.

"This is *so* adorable," cried Raphael.

He was looking at the solitary thatched house down the lane, the cliff-edge behind it with the blue sea beyond.

Seagulls cawed over the sounds of the waves crashing. Ivy clung to the walls of the house, and there were rose bushes planted either side of the front door.

"Griff, it looks like a fairy tale! And…oh my god, you can actually *taste* the sea salt in the air. That's crazy!"

He touched his fingers to the tip of his tongue, as if to check this was all real. Then he laughed and grabbed his beanie hat to secure it as a particularly strong gust threatened to whip it from his head. Sparrow looked around from the top of the bag with an expression that appeared to be saying 'What fresh hell is this?!' To be fair, that wasn't all that different from her normal face, but she had the added effect of the breeze dramatically blowing her fur around as well.

Raphael shook his head, turning in a circle and looking all around them. "I never knew what people meant by fresh air. Like, London has wildly different weather, but this smells so *clean* here. I can really taste the lack of pollution, even though I didn't know I *could* taste it my whole life. Does that make sense?"

Griff tried not to smile too much at Raphael's unrestrained enthusiasm. "Makes total sense," he agreed. The air quality in London was much better in recent years than it had been, but you could never compare the feeling of taking a deep breath out by the coast to one in the middle of a city.

Raphael was shaking his head against Sparrow, nuzzling against her in disbelief. "I'm sorry. I know this is probably a totally ordinary view to you. But…bloody hell, I'm overwhelmed!"

"It's not ordinary," Griff said simply, attempting to keep his features schooled.

He didn't get out of the city much, so this actually was a pretty novel and lovely view to him. But they could have been looking at Griff's own living room and it would have been remarkable if Raphael was reacting like this. He managed to make everything seem so *wonderful,* and Griff was captivated by his beaming smile and rosy cheeks. A strand of hair had snuck free from the beanie hat, and was whipping in the summer breeze.

He was breathtaking.

And Griff couldn't have him.

He cleared his throat and hoisted up all the shopping bags in his hands. "Come on," he said a little harsher than he'd intended to.

But Raphael didn't seem to notice. "Coming!" he said, practically skipping around the car. He placed Sparrow on the ground, her pink diamanté lead looped around his wrist as she ran beside him. It was such a pure sight, how could anyone not be moved? Griff was only human.

Raphael rushed ahead so he could hold the door open for Griff, which he thought was pretty cute. Griff hadn't met a guy he'd want to hold the door open for until now, but for Raphael, he knew he would.

*Soft.* What was he going to do with himself?

"Oh, hello there!" said the plump, middle-aged lady from behind the check-in desk as they stepped inside the front door.

The entrance hall seemed dark after the bright sunshine outside, but Griff's eyes quickly adjusted. It reminded him of his nan's house, with all the white doilies under china ornaments on dark wooden furniture. Paintings of children hung on the flowery walls, sitting and standing porcelain-faced Victorian dolls were scattered around various surfaces, and Griff felt like he could hear at least twenty clocks all ticking softly over one another.

It was either totally quaint or the perfect setting for a horror movie.

By the joyful look on Raphael's face as he spun around,

taking it all in, it was quaint. Good. If Raphael liked it, then so did Griff.

"It's perfect," Raphael squeaked under his breath at Griff. "Thank you, I love it!"

Griff tried not to let himself warm too much at the praise. It really had been the only twin room available that was pet-friendly. But he wasn't sorry that Raphael liked it.

"Good evening," said Griff as they approached the desk. He placed their many shopping bags down on the swirly-patterned carpet. The woman peered over her bifocals at him, an eager smile on her face. "I booked a room under Peter Jackson," Griff continued." Only a couple of hours ago."

Raphael turned his head sharply, then grinned at Griff. Griff tried his best not to be too chuffed with himself that he'd amused Raphael with his little joke.

"Oh, lovely," said the lady. "Let me check. I'm Bev, and this is my little place. Welcome, welcome," she tittered, absently pulling at the beads around her neck as she looked up their booking on her ancient computer. "Ah! There we go. You got our last double."

Something cold rinsed through Griff. Dread, maybe? Panic? Horror?

"No," he said. "I booked a twin, I'm sure?"

Bev frowned, looking at Griff and then Raphael, who was leaning against the desk and practically vibrating with excitement. Apparently, he hadn't picked up on the problem they were facing.

"It says a double here?" said Bev. She frowned and slapped the side of the ancient computer. "Ah, yes," she cried with a nod. "I think the blasted thing had another glitch. Right. Is the double okay, then?"

"Oh, okay." Griff shifted uncomfortably. "Well, *is* there a twin available for me and my, um, friend?"

But Bev's frown deepened. "Now *really*, dear," she

admonished, peering so hard over her half-moon glasses Griff was amazed they didn't slip right off her nose. "Didn't you see? We've got one of those little rainbow ratings. You don't need to pretend here. I mean, yes, that *is* the only room we have available – last-minute cancellation, you see. But I am *more* than happy to confirm it for you lovely fellows." She clicked her mouse a few more times as Griff's stomach tied itself in knots. *This was a very bad idea!* "There you go. All booked in – *and* it's our honeymoon suite!"

"Honeymoon?" Griff spluttered.

"Oh, we're not married," said Raphael with a nervous giggle.

Bev gave them a look of sincere fondness. "Yes, but you make a lovely couple, if you don't mind my saying. Some people just *look* like they fit together, you know? Besides, it's basically the same as our other rooms. It just has the best view in the house. Maybe you can think of this as a practice honeymoon." She winked at Raphael and began rummaging through a drawer under the desk. "Now! Let me get your keys, and you'll be all set."

"Um, okay," Griff said.

He should have protested and tried to find somewhere else to stay. But causing a scene was a sure-fire way to draw attention to themselves. If anyone was on their tail, they'd be looking for a young man and his bodyguard. Not asking for a couple. And there really hadn't been any other pet-friendly options in the area that he'd seen.

So he slipped his arm around Raphael's waist and mustered up the best smile he could for Bev.

"That's so kind of you," he gushed, doing his best to swallow his nerves. He loathed play-acting, but it would be okay so long as Raphael got it and went along with the charade. "You never really know if people are going to be okay with a gay couple, even in this day and age."

Bev scowled and shook her head. "Honestly, people are such silly sods, aren't they?"

Raphael had gone stiff under Griff's arm, and Griff couldn't blame him. His own body was going haywire at being pressed up against Raphael's side, and he had far more experience of touching people than he was sure Raphael had. But then suddenly, Raphael relaxed and turned his gorgeous smile on for Bev.

"*So* silly," he said breathlessly.

Bev grabbed a sheet of paper that had slowly crawled its way out of the equally ancient printer, then returned his smile warmly. But then her attention dropped to her feet. "Oh! Hello? Who's this?" She looked at the floor by the side of the desk, and Griff realised Sparrow had become curious.

He tensed up. "Ah, yeah," he said. "This place is pet-friendly, right?" He felt oddly protective of Sparrow in that moment, remembered the guy from that café yelling at Raphael to get her out. But he had no need to worry.

"Absolutely," Bev gushed, pushing up her glasses as she leaned down to offer the cat her fingers to sniff. "She's beautiful."

"Thanks," said Raphael, rocking on his toes. "Her name is Sparrow, and she's a Scottish Fold. Say hello, Sparrow!"

To Bev's delight, Sparrow let out a distrustful *'meow'* and narrowed her jade-blue eyes at the B&B owner...then sat on her arse and began licking her tummy fur, her leg sticking gracelessly up in the air.

"How precious," said Bev, clutching her chest. "Oh! Let me get you a bed for her! It doesn't look like you've got one?"

"No, we don't," said Raphael. He turned to Griff and smiled so broadly it made Griff's chest ache. "How kind! Sparrow would love a little bed of her own."

"One second," Bev said, wagging her finger as she bustled

off through a door, presumably to fetch a cat bed for Sparrow.

There was an awkward silence between Griff and Raphael whilst she was gone where Griff was too afraid to even look at Raphael. They kind of had to keep hugging for when she came back, but now it was just the two of them, alone in the entrance hall, holding each other close.

And Sparrow, of course. She fixed Griff with a stare as she stopped grooming herself, looking at him as if to say 'Don't you *dare* mess around with my daddy.'

He tried to stare back and convey that was the last thing he knew he should do. But this bed situation was going to be a bit of a problem. And he had absolutely no idea how Raphael was feeling about it. He didn't seem to have a reaction at all when Griff had been talking with Bev. He just seemed so excited to be somewhere that wasn't his penthouse.

"Here we go!" Bev announced, proudly bustling back into the room with a squishy, fluffy flying saucer in her hands. "A bed fit for a queen!"

Griff wondered if it might fit one flustered, in-over-his-head bodyguard instead.

7

RAPHIE

THIS WAS ONE OF THOSE MOMENTS THAT RAPHIE WAS GETTING used to where he was pretty sure he'd missed something very important but had no idea what. His brain was still stuck on *that hug* and the fact that the B&B owner, Bev, seemed to think that he and Griff were a *couple*.

That made Raphie's knees so weak with giddiness he was amazed he was able to make the climb up the narrow stairs at all. Griff walked in front of him up the two stories, so Raphie was able to take a moment to grin like a loon at the idea that Bev could have possibly thought for a second that they looked like a couple.

Him and Griff. Together.

Raphie's skin was still tingling where he'd been pressed up against Griff's solid, sculpted body. It hadn't been anything at all like when they'd jumped from the penthouse, when Raphie had been made of nothing but adrenaline and fear. But this time, even though he'd been shocked at the sudden charade, Raphie had still been able to appreciate Griff's hard muscles, hot skin, and sturdy arms holding him tight.

Keeping him safe.

*Bloody hell.* That was another good reason for Raphie to be walking behind Griff for a minute or two. Certain areas needed time to adjust and *calm down.* But it was difficult, because Raphie had never been touched by another man in a sensual, or even friendly way. To have someone as gorgeous as Griff hold him was almost too much to cope with. And he now had a pretty good view of his stunning arse as they climbed to the top of the B&B.

Griff had all of the shopping bags in his hands. When they reached the room, he attempted to put them all down and fumble with the key to let them in, but he was having a hard job of it.

"Here, I've got it," said Raphie helpfully. He only had his rucksack on his back and Sparrow's lead looped on his wrist, so his hands were free.

Griff eyed him and licked his lips. *Oh.* Raphie liked when he did that.

"Okay," he grunted. "You unlock it. But then step back. I need to go inside any room first when we're together. Understood?"

Raphie shivered. He also quite liked Griff giving him orders and being all protective. Which was going to get awkward, fast, what with Griff being his bodyguard and all.

"Yep! Sure thing, understood," said Raphie eagerly. He jumped forward to be of use, even if it was only to unlock the door. "There you go. All yours!"

Griff gave him a funny look for a second. Then he shifted the bags to one hand, and opened the door to enter with the other. Raphie waited a few seconds, swallowing anxiously, until Griff called that it was all clear.

The room was cute, like the rest of the B&B they'd seen so far. The bedding, lamps, curtains, and chair coverings were all a delightful periwinkle blue, and lots of sea and nautical-themed ornaments and frames made it all feel like Raphael was under the sea. The carpet was more of the same brown and cream swirl as downstairs, and...

And there was only one bed.

Raphie's stomach rinsed hot and cold as a thrill of excitement was quickly squashed by a realisation that this couldn't possibly be what he thought it was.

Could it?

*Oh. Fuck.* This had been what Griff and Bev had been talking about. This was what he'd missed. Raphie felt his cheeks flush as he realised just how naive he was. "Ah," he said as Griff watched him anxiously. "A twin means two beds. And a double..."

A double meant one bed. To share.

"Yeah," said Griff hesitantly.

Raphie gulped, unsure if he was scared or if he had another trouser problem.

"Oh, okay," he said breathlessly. "That's fine. I'm pretty small, right? We'll fit. And I'll keep very still. After the day we've had, I bet we'll pass out like logs! And, uh, this was the last room, so it's not like we can do anything about it other than make the most of it. It'll be fun!" he added with a mortifying giggle.

He was rambling and mildly hysterical, torn between being utterly thrilled at the prospect of sharing something so intimate with his new friend – bodyguard – whatever – and feeling very small and ridiculous, because Griff would never, *ever* look at him like that. In fact, he was probably cringing at the idea of being forced to share a bed.

"I'll sleep on the floor," Griff grunted, pretty much proving Raphie's point. Griff awkwardly dropped all their bags on the quilted duvet that was stretched over the bed that was slightly smaller than Raphael's one back home, but still big enough for two people. Even someone of Griff's size.

Or not, apparently.

Raphie tried not to feel crushed. "Sure, sorry," he said, rubbing the back of his neck. "I guess you're not actually gay, are you? That lady just assumed. It's weird for guys who don't know each other to bunk up, right? I've certainly never shared a bed with anyone…"

Wow. He should just wear a sign on his forehead that said 'I'm a massive virgin'. For fuck's sake.

"Um, no," said Griff in Raphie's pause. "I *am* gay." He flicked at some of the plastic bags, like he was half-heartedly looking for something, staring determinedly down and definitely not at Raphie. "Not that it matters, about the sleeping thing, but since you asked…look, I feel like I put you in an awkward position just now. It was honestly to maintain our cover. I'm sorry. But if she thinks we're a couple on holiday, rather than a guy with his bodyguard, it might be enough to make any of those arseholes after you overlook this place." He seemed embarrassed at saying so much, scowling and poking at the bags some more. "Like I said, I'll sleep on the floor. S'no problem."

"No," said Raphie hotly. He let Sparrow off her lead, then he stomped over to the bed and Griff by the shopping bags, looking for the peas they'd double bagged. "You're injured!" He slapped the peas into Griff's hand. "Ice your shoulder, now. And *I'll* sleep on the floor."

Griff stared at him for a second. Then his mouth twitched into half a smile, and he raised the wrapped-up peas to his shoulder. He sat on the edge of the bed and sighed. "We'll figure something out," he said, his lips still slightly turned up. "You're a prince. You definitely shouldn't sleep on the floor."

"That's not…" Raphie began, unsure what he wanted to say. "That doesn't mean…"

He'd had years to get his head around the idea that he was actually royalty of some country a hundred miles away, but it still didn't feel real. He was just Raphie, the same man he'd always been. But in that moment, he realised being a prince might just have some perks.

He straightened up and pulled the beanie off his head to let his braid fall down his back. He rolled his shoulders and shook his hair, then fixed Griff with a firm look. "You're right. I *am* Prince Raphael of Campanula. And that means you have to do what I say." He gave Griff an impish grin. "Medical advice beats royal protocol, so I say you're not sleeping on the floor. Okay?"

Griff grunted, but that half-a-smile twitched on his lips. "You're kind of cute when you're bossy," he mumbled, readjusting the wrapped-up peas on his shoulder.

Raphie huffed, blowing away a strand of hair that had broken free from the plait. "Oh, good. *Cute.* That's just what I need to be king." Raphie was pretty sure that despite his extensive education, he didn't know the first thing about how to run a country. But apparently, he was expected to give it a go, anyway.

Griff frowned and looked down at his shoulder. "Didn't say being bossy was a bad thing. And you're good at it." He looked back up, flicking an eyebrow as his eyes met Raphie's, and Raphie's cock throbbed at the sight. "I'm doing what you told me to, aren't I?"

"Hmm," said Raphie, suppressing a whole-body shiver.

He wasn't sure he could form words in that moment, he was so horny and nervous. So he brushed his palms against his thighs and glanced around for Sparrow. She was investigating the wooden furnishings in the room, sniffing everything and prowling around. She was obviously feeling calmer, as she did her trick where she sat back on her hind legs like a meerkat, letting her front paws hang like T-Rex arms, looking around with her big jade-blue eyes and her mouth hanging slightly open.

Raphie was so glad she was here with him, it physically hurt in his chest. He sat down cross-legged on the floor and stroked her back. It felt good to take charge and tell Griff what to do for his own benefit, but there was still tension between the two of them. Something hanging in the air that Raphie didn't know how to defuse.

"May I ask you a question?" Griff asked in a low rumble.

Raphie looked up to find Griff's dark eyes on him. Raphie's mouth went dry under his gaze. They were several feet apart, but Raphie realised that with him sitting on the floor and Griff perched on the bed, Raphie was at the right height to…

He coughed and tried to think of something – *anything* – else to stop the blush from creeping onto his face and his cock stirring more than it already was in his jeans. He may have lived in the penthouse his whole life, but he'd had access to the internet and his own computer since he was a teenager. He'd watched a staggering amount of porn, like any young person with a robust sexual appetite. And it was far too easy in that moment to imagine crawling over to Griff and begging him to let Raphie unzip his trousers.

If Griff was going to be leaving tomorrow and handing Raphie over to a new security team, what did they really have to lose? Raphie hated the idea that he might not see Griff for a while – or ever again – but if that helped Griff to stop seeing Raphie as a client and start seeing him as a man lusting after him, Raphie could be okay with that. At least temporarily. He was more than ready to see his first in-person cock that wasn't his own, and he wanted that cock to be Griff's so badly.

But this was real life, not a fantasy, so he tore his eyes away from Griff and licked his lips to try and moisten his mouth, lest he croaked when he talked. "You can ask anything you like," he assured Griff.

His bodyguard seemed to mull over what he wanted to say. "Are *you* gay?" he eventually asked.

*Shit.* So much for trying to get his mind out of the gutter.

Raphie swallowed and continued looking at Sparrow as he fussed over her. She had dropped back down and was now curled up on the floor next to his crossed legs. This wasn't just about his attraction to Griff.

He'd never come out to anyone before.

Mum had always made it clear to him that she loved him no matter what, and had always talked casually about Raphie one day marrying a woman or a man or someone in between. It had never been a big deal, so he hadn't felt the need to come out. Especially when even the possibility of dating someone had seemed so remote. But Raphie had watched enough film and television, and read plenty of books and articles.

He knew this was a big deal.

Or...was it? He felt safe with Griff after he'd come out himself. Surely Griff would understand.

With that safety net underneath him, Raphie found himself smiling.

"Yes," he said with a thrill. "I mean, it's difficult to know for sure when I've met as few people in real life as I have, but...I'm pretty sure. Yes. I'm gay." His little daydream just now was more than enough proof of that. But he bit his lip, anxiety fluttering around him. Despite his assurances from Griff himself about being gay, Raphie still wasn't entirely sure if he even *liked* Raphie, or if he was simply doing his job and protecting him. "Is that okay?" he felt compelled to ask.

Griff snorted, making Raphie look up. "Yes," he said fiercely. "It's okay. I asked because I figured you might not have met any other gay men. If there's, um, anything you want to know, you can ask. I'll try and help." He rubbed the back of his neck with the hand not holding the bag of peas.

"Although, you've had the internet. Seems you young gays know way more than me lately."

Raphie tutted, feeling slightly relieved. Griff offering to help guide him was relieving, even if it was awkward as hell. "You're not old, remember?" He rolled his eyes with a smile. Some of that tension was dissipating. "But thank you. I really appreciate that."

Except what he wanted to ask, he felt like he couldn't. He needed to *experience* it. Like how it felt to kiss another man. To finally have sex. Raphie felt like the last twenty-one-year-old virgin on the planet. Would he prefer to bottom or top? How would it feel to have his cock in another man's mouth, to be sucked off until he came down his throat?

And that was just the physical stuff. What would it feel like to walk into a gay bar and know everyone there was like him? Maybe not exactly, but queer in some way. Raphie had experienced loneliness to depths most people couldn't dream of. But knowing there were other people out there who were like him and not being able to talk to them face-to-face was especially hard. He knew his mum loved and supported him, no matter what. And he'd been active on plenty of social media sites and chat forums. But it wasn't the same.

"It's just nice to meet another gay man," Raphie said with a shy smile, looking up at Griff through his eyelashes. "What's that, um, been like for you?"

"Being gay?" Griff shrugged and looked away, which made Raphie's heart hurt. There was pain etched on Griff's face, and Raphie suspected that wasn't just from his shoulder bothering him. "S'okay. Mum was always great. Nan never really got it, but she still loved me something fierce." He cleared his throat. "Other people didn't like it. But that's the world. You'll learn that, I'm afraid. Some people are just bellends. Fuck 'em. It's slowly getting better in general, though, I think."

"I think so, too," said Raphie.

He was aware he was probably looking up at Griff with puppy dog eyes, but he couldn't help it. It sounded like Griff had faced tough times in his life for being gay, and Raphie wanted to jump up and kiss the sadness off his face. So the moon eyes were a safer alternative.

"Although I can't imagine what the Campanulan council are going to make of me," he added, trying not to sound bitter or frightened.

"What do you mean?" Griff asked. "What does being gay have to do with them?"

Raphie met his gaze. Was he serious?

"There are no gay kings in the world," he said quietly. "Certainly no one nonbinary, like me. Most royal families are reluctant to even acknowledge queer members."

"Nonbinary?" Griff asked with a raised eyebrow.

Raphie nodded, suddenly anxious. He'd talked a lot about being enby online with loads of other gender nonconforming people. But this was his first time coming out to someone in person about his gender, on top of just coming out about his sexuality.

"Not entirely male or female," he explained, "but something fabulous in between. It's why my hair is so incredibly important to me." He smiled and gave a little flourish with his hand, trying to hide his nerves. But then he sighed. "Which is fine if you're a TV presenter, but I doubt it'll be okay for a monarch. They're all extremely traditional."

Griff scoffed. "Well, that's just not right. You're the heir to the throne no matter what, yeah? The Campanulan law says it's the oldest *child* that ascends to the throne, yeah? Not oldest son?"

Raphie blinked at him, stunned he'd not tripped over the nonbinary issue for a second. "Uh, yes. Oldest child."

"There you go," said Griff. "And hang on a minute. Prince

James right here in the UK is gay – he's full on married to another bloke."

Raphie sighed and offered Griff a half-smile. "But he's not in *line* for the throne, unless something drastic happens to Princes George or Alexander. It's okay for him."

"Then you'll be okay, too, won't you?" Griff said huffily, adjusting the wrapped-up peas on his shoulder. "People just have to get used to it soon enough. That's the way the world is now, thank fuck."

It was kind of horribly naive on Griff's part to think that. However, Raphie couldn't help but love him a little for his optimism. But the truth was, if he was straight, or even more of a macho manly man, like Griff was, then the Campanula council might be less resistant to him.

Who was ever going to accept someone as confusing and challenging as Raphie as their king?

Anyway, that was his problem, not Griff's. So Raphie did his best to shrug it off. "Hey," he added brightly, ticking off his finger. "Being gay is something else we have in common!"

Griff gave a soft chuckle that warmed Raphie's heart. "I guess it is," Griff murmured.

For a second, they held each other's gazes. Raphie couldn't speak for Griff, but the implication of his observation was that they could potentially be attracted to each other, and it hung heavy in the air. Then Griff broke the spell by clearing his throat and lowering the peas. He rolled his shoulder and exhaled.

"That helped a lot, actually. Cheers."

Raphie smirked, feeling emboldened by Griff's praise. "I'm still not letting you sleep on the floor."

Griff snorted. "We'll see."

They didn't really unpack, as Griff insisted that they needed to be ready to flee at a moment's notice. Raphie hoped they wouldn't be jumping out of any more windows any time soon, but he kept all his stuff in his backpack just in case.

They did put the chilled food in the mini-fridge that was in the room. It didn't have alcohol and chocolate bars provided for them, like Raphie had seen in the movies. Just a couple of bottles of water. But that left more room for the food they'd bought at the supermarket. Raphie also found the two small bowls they'd purchased and one of the packets of cat food. At home, Sparrow always had food out, so even though she'd had fish a few hours ago, Raphie wanted to make sure that she had everything she usually did on hand.

But Sparrow didn't seem all that interested in coming out from under the bed, no matter how much Raphie waved her bowl of wet food in front of her. Even her special biscuit treats apparently wouldn't move her, probably because she knew that Raphie would just chuck her a few to crunch on where she was.

Which he did.

"She'll come out when she's ready. Don't worry," Griff said, not unkindly.

He'd basically iced his injury until the peas had turned to mush and he'd had to bin them. Then he'd set about organising their new supplies from Sainsbury's and cataloguing the contents of Raphie's backpack (with his permission, of course). Griff kept rolling his shoulders regularly, as well as his head from side to side, wincing when he'd thought Raphie wasn't looking. He'd been more injured during the penthouse skirmish than Raphie had previously realised.

He definitely wasn't sleeping on the floor.

"I just don't want her to be anxious," Raphie said, chewing

his thumbnail and ruefully wishing he'd packed some of her favourite toys or thought to pick some new ones up from Sainsbury's. He flapped his hands and looked around in case there was miraculously something he could improvise as a toy. "She's lived her whole life in that one space. She has no idea what's going on right now. I need to-"

Griff's hand slid over Raphie's shoulder, making him jump. He was still kneeling from where he'd been peering under the bed. So now he was looking up at Griff, his mouth suddenly dry again thanks to the contact between them.

Griff seemed to notice it as well and, sadly, whipped his hand back. But he managed to give Raphie a small smile. "She's not the only one who spent her whole life there and isn't sure what's going on now. You're wound up tighter than a spring, unsurprisingly. Why don't you lie down on the bed for a while and try to relax?"

Raphie blinked up at him, feeling the heat rising over his neck despite his best efforts to stay calm and collected. Just hearing Griff telling him to get on the bed was short-circuiting his brain.

"Oh, r-right, thanks," he managed to stammer sheepishly. "Yeah, you're right. She's probably feeding off my stress. I guess I could, um, try chilling out. What will, uh, you do?"

Smooth. So smooth.

"Do you mind if I have a shower?" Griff asked. Raphie tried not to immediately picture Griff stark naked and dripping wet.

He didn't really succeed.

"Oh, of course," Raphie blurted. "Help yourself! You've got all the toiletry bits you bought, yeah? And the new clothes?" Raphie could see he did. They were out on the bed. He was babbling, and he tried not to blush.

Griff didn't seem to mind, though. In fact, he reached down and picked up one of the bottles to show Raphie. "I'll leave them in the shower for when you need them," he grunted. "Figured you'd need a lot of conditioner for your hair. My mum always did. These places give you a bottle the size of a thimble, if anything at all. So, uh, yeah. I'll leave it in the shower. Help yourself."

Then he scooped up the products and clothes, and hurriedly locked himself in the bathroom. Raphie tried not to focus too hard on the sound of the running water through the door. Eventually, he sat on the bed like Griff had suggested and turned on the little telly, hoping to distract himself from the image of Griff's hands running all over his bare body that was dancing around in his brain.

When the TV wasn't enough, Raphie fell back on his usual method of meditation and self-care. He got out his Tangle Teezer, and began undoing the braid and shaking out all the little plaits entwined into it. Once all the hair was free, he massaged his scalp for a while, then started brushing all his hair from tip to top, loving the tingling sensation it gave his scalp. Little shivers fluttered over his body as he worked, and by the time Griff finally emerged from the steamy bathroom, Raphie was calm and almost not thinking about Griff naked at all.

Almost.

"I tried not to use all the hot water," said Griff, dumping his dirty clothes on the back of the chair by the counter where the TV was standing. He then rubbed at his hair more with his towel, partially obscuring his face. So Raphie *might* have grabbed the opportunity to look at the way his new plain blue T-shirt clung to his slightly damp body, accentuating all those delicious rippling muscles. "Not sure what the plumbing's like here."

Raphie jerked his eyes up as Griff pulled the towel away to look at him. Raphie smiled at him, trying not to feel guilty for sneaking a peek. He wasn't sure why he was talking about plumbing – why would the hot water run out? It didn't matter anyway, but Raphie liked that Griff seemed concerned.

"Thanks, but I'm okay," he said. "Maybe I'll have one in the morning."

The thought of a shower was nice, but since he'd been sitting on the bed, he'd realised how bone-tired he was, and he couldn't face the prospect of drying his hair for an hour afterwards. In fact, it was getting more and more difficult to keep his eyes open. The temptation to just flop back on top of the blankets and pass out was getting stronger. But it was a little too early to turn in for the night yet. Besides, Raphie didn't want to waste any of his time with Griff. Who knew what would happen in the morning when Winston sent them their new instructions?

Griff nodded at Raphie's reply, then hung his towel over the corner of the bathroom door to let it dry. "Do you think Sparrow needs letting out again?" he asked, looking at the sleeping cat next to Raphie. He'd been right. As soon as Raphie had started to do his hair and relax, she'd come out, fed, then cuddled up next to him.

Raphie nodded. "Probably. She's used to her litter tray."

Griff came over by the bed and stroked her lightly. Sparrow yawned, showing off all her sharp teeth, and wiggled at the attention. "How about we take her for a stroll? Then we can come back here for food. Maybe find something to watch?" He jutted his head at the telly.

Raphie tried not to squirm. That sounded so domesticated and perfect. By himself, it wouldn't be that exciting. It was basically how he'd spent every evening of his life. But with Griff, it sounded like the best evening ever. Except his hesitation possibly said otherwise.

"Sorry I can't offer you something more impressive for

your first night out in the real world," said Griff. "But I think it's safest to lie low."

"Oh, no!" Raphie said hurriedly, suddenly not that tired anymore as he sat bolt upright. The fact that Griff wanted to plan anything at all for them both and not attempt to ignore Raphie like he had in the car was a vast improvement. "That's a great plan. Thanks for, um, thinking of Sparrow. I know you didn't sign on to babysit a cat, but that means a lot to me that you'd think about her."

Griff hummed, then turned to put his shoes on.

They locked their room door and made their way down the narrow staircase again. Raphie waved at Bev as they walked through the reception. "Is everything all right with your room, boys?" she asked happily.

"Wonderful," Raphie said, getting a thrill for simply interacting with another human being he hardly knew. It seemed so exotic. Griff probably thought he was a massive loser, but in that moment, Raphie couldn't bring himself to care. It was so wonderful and normal to engage in chit-chat, Raphie felt like he was *finally* living his life.

The walk along the cliffside path wasn't long, but Sparrow seemed to appreciate it on her lead, jumping and pouncing on every little thing, sniffing it all in interest. Raphie felt like he was addicted to breathing in as deeply as he could, inhaling the crisp coastal air like he could somehow stockpile it for later within his lungs.

He'd thrown his hair back in one simple braid and chucked it back under his green-and-purple beanie, but several tendrils had snuck their way free and were whipping around his face. He loved it, even though he would usually have found that irritating if he'd been on the penthouse roof. Instead, he let the little wisps of hair flick over his skin, leaving the faintest stings. He smiled and licked his lips, tasting the salt that was lingering there.

He'd never quite felt so present in the moment as he did walking along that short, stony path.

Raphie enjoyed strolling beside Griff, even if they didn't talk much. Just being near him was enough, and when anyone passed them, Raphie wondered if they also assumed the two of them were a couple.

Then he'd remember why they were at the B&B in the first place, and wonder if any of them were potential assassins.

But they made it back to their room in one piece, and Raphie was amazed to find he was hungry again even after the fish and chips earlier. He and Griff set themselves up to eat their sandwiches, olives, mini sausages, and pots of pre-prepared fruit on the bed, as there wasn't a table. It felt a little bit weird and intimate, but Griff didn't appear too unsettled by it. Well, he was about as quiet as usual, but there was a calmness to him rather than the brittle tense feeling from the start of the car journey earlier, so Raphie took it as a win.

They flicked between a home makeover show, the news, and some crime drama, before finally settling on an old action film. Raphie wasn't really paying attention to any of it. He was so acutely aware of Griff beside him. So close, yet still so far away.

And then…he wasn't aware of anything. He must have snuggled down at some point and drifted off. Then Griff was gently shaking him, telling him he needed to go brush his teeth. When Raphie mumbled he didn't want to, Griff eased him off the bed with his big strong arms and hands, guiding him to the bathroom, muttering about dental hygiene after all they'd eaten today. Then Raphie realised he had his toothbrush in hand, complete with toothpaste, and his pyjamas were in a neatly folded pile waiting for him on the closed toilet seat.

A part of him realised that worrying about potential cavities wasn't really in Griff's job description as a bodyguard. But that made Raphie want to brush his teeth harder, as if to show Griff how much he appreciated the extra care and attention he was showing.

Somehow, he managed to see to his teeth and get changed. His hair was already braided from the walk, so it wouldn't strangle him in his sleep. When he stumbled back out of the little bathroom, he was so half-asleep that he barely registered that Griff had cleared the bed of food and turned back the sheets on the side Raphie had been sitting on.

"Come on," he said gently as he placed his magical hand on the small of Raphie's back to guide him into bed. "You need to sleep now." Raphie wasn't sure what had caused this change in Griff from stand-offish to caring, but he absolutely wasn't complaining.

Raphie grumbled something about being fine as he face-planted into the mattress. Above him, he was pretty sure that Griff chuckled as he carefully rearranged Raphie until his head was on a pillow and he was under the duvet.

"You, too," Raphie mumbled, mustering enough energy to get bossy. "No floor. Bad shoulder. Bed sleep." He thumped the mattress beside him, causing Sparrow to scarper to the end of the bed to curl up by his feet.

The last thing he remembered was Griff chuckling some more, then feeling the bed dip with his weight as he sat down...

***

Raphie was warm and he was safe. But something was wrong.

He was caught in that precarious balance between sleep

and awake. He kept dreaming that he'd opened his eyes, only to be dragged back under again into unconsciousness.

There was something heavy around him. Maybe the extra heavy duvet Mum got out when he was sick? He hardly ever got ill, though, and he didn't feel bad. In fact, he felt *so* good.

He snuggled against the warmth and hummed to himself. His dreams were getting kind of sexy. His belly and below was tingling as the faceless man ran his hands over Raphie, kissing his neck. A part of Raphie remembered he'd never had anyone do that to him before, but this was a dream and everything was muddled, so he also knew that he loved it. In fact, his neck was definitely one of his favourite places to be kissed, he was sure.

He rolled his hips, chasing friction. In his sleepy, dream-filled state, he wasn't surprised to find it. *Fuck.* That felt *amazing.* He gasped and moaned again, his eyes fluttering open…

And what he saw made no sense.

There was a man holding him in a strange bed, and for a second, Raphie figured it was a dream within a dream.

Until Griff's warm breath ghosted over Raphie's lips, and his strong arms flexed around Raphie's body. Because sometime before dawn, they'd apparently rolled into each other's arms, so now their bodies were pressed together, chest to chest.

And that meant Raphie's morning wood was also rubbing deliciously against Griff's equally hard cock, causing his brain to short-circuit as he rushed back into consciousness.

Just as Griff's eyes also flew open.

For several seconds, Raphie stared into those gorgeous dark pools. Neither of them breathed as their gazes remained locked. Griff's hands were splayed over Raphie's back, holding him perfectly in place. Griff was still wearing his new T-shirt and a pair of boxers, but the cotton did nothing to stop the heat from radiating off him. Raphie had one arm draped over the curvy dip where Griff's hip met his torso, and the other hand placed on his chest. Raphie could feel Griff's heartbeat against his palm. It was thumping almost as fast as Raphie's, which felt like it was going to smash its way out of his chest it was going so crazy.

Raphie's vision swam, and he inhaled. As he did, he threw caution to the wind, and rolled his hips ever so slightly, just to see what might happen.

What happened was that Griff's mouth came crashing against Raphie's as Raphie also rushed towards him, and Griff's fingers dug into Raphie's back so hard it felt like they bruised him instantly. And Raphie fucking *loved* it. His fist bunched around a handful of Griff's T-shirt as he kissed him back. Griff's lips parted and his tongue found Raphie's, and Raphie almost came in his bloody pyjamas as he rutted against Griff's hot, hard cock.

It didn't matter that this was Raphie's first kiss. With Griff guiding him, he felt like he knew exactly what he was doing. Raphie had waited so long for this moment, and now it was finally happening, it was better than he ever could have possibly imagined.

One of Griff's hands moved to cup the back of Raphie's head, tugging deliciously at the braided hair, making Raphie groan. Griff nipped at his bottom lip and kissed down his jaw as he ground his cock against Raphie's with even more fervour.

*"Fuck,"* he growled animalistically. Raphie gasped and held on for dear life as Griff kissed his neck on his pulse point, just like he'd been dreaming about.

It was so good, but Raphie needed more. Or less, actually. Less clothes definitely sounded like a great idea. He began scrabbling, getting his hands under Griff's T-shirt and running them up over the back muscles that were shifting under Raphie's palms as they undulated together. Griff found his mouth again, kissing him desperately and nudging Raphie onto his back as his hand slid down Raphie's side, his fingers running along the waistband of Raphie's pyjama bottoms…

Then there was a knock at the door.

Their mouths sprung apart like they'd been struck by lightning, gasping and staring at each other with their bodies still pressed together. Griff looked stunned, and Raphie felt the same.

Had that really just happened?

The knock came again, followed by Bev's concerned voice. "Mr Jackson? I have an urgent courier delivery for you. Are you awake?"

Griff blinked, his eyes still locked with Raphie's as his chest heaved. "Yeah, coming," he rasped, which made Raphie blush even harder than he knew he already was.

With any luck, they'd both be coming. Soon.

But even as he thought it, something shut down in Griff's expression, and he untangled himself from Raphie. He managed to get out of the bed, but his raging hard-on was totally visible in his tented boxer-briefs. Whilst Raphie drank in the sight, he doubted Bev would feel the same. Griff evidently agreed, and he hastily yanked on the pair of jeans he'd bought the day before, hiding the most obvious evidence of what had just transpired between them.

Raphie's heart sank.

Griff cleared his throat and marched across the room. "Sorry about that," he grunted, opening the door ajar. He blocked most of the gap with his (stunning) body, shielding Raphie from view. Raphie watched his back anxiously as Bev apparently handed something over and apologised for disturbing the two of them so early whilst they were on holiday. "S'okay," Griff assured her. Then he wished her a pleasant morning and firmly closed the door between them.

Raphie's heart was in his mouth. Did Griff regret what had just happened? Or would he come back to bed to pick up where they'd left off? Raphie knew he *absolutely* wanted the latter. Because if that was orders on where to meet Raphie's new security team, and he wasn't ever going to see Griff again, he *desperately* didn't want to part ways before he knew where that epic kiss could have led them.

But something was off in Griff's body language. Raphie might not have been around many people growing up, but he recognised tense shoulders when he saw them.

"Everything okay?" Raphie whispered. He jutted his chin towards the manila envelope, but really, he meant between them. Because holy fucking hell he wanted things to be okay. Better than okay.

His heart banged like a drum as he watched Griff wordlessly tear open the envelope. *Look at me*, Raphie prayed. He just wanted to see those brown eyes again to know everything was all right.

But instead, Griff focused on the items that he'd pulled from inside the envelope, his eyes getting wider.

"Well?" Raphie prompted gently. "What is it?"

Griff blinked, still not looking at him, and Raphie's heart dropped again, all the way down to the floor. Griff licked his lips, plump and wet from kissing, keeping Raphie's cock pulsing despite his reservations.

"Two ferry tickets to Calais," Griff rasped, "my passport, and a very clear note from Winston that I have to get you to Campanula on time, come hell or high water."

Raphie didn't know whether to laugh or cry. Griff wasn't leaving him just yet.

But by the look on his face, he absolutely wasn't getting back into bed now.

*Cry, then,* Raphie thought. Rather than give in to his slowly cracking heart, though, he plastered a grin on his face. "Brilliant!" he croaked, ignoring the burning at the back of his eyes.

He'd cry later in the shower, where Griff couldn't see him.

"So, um, I guess you're stuck with me," Raphie continued babbling with a nervous laugh. "That's great, though. I'd rather not get a new team now. You're the best bodyguard ever! I can tell, even after just a day. No one else has jumped off a building with me before, after all! It'll be fun, right? An adventure. Um…"

*Look at me! Say something!* Raphie's thoughts screamed.

But Griff just swallowed and shook his head slightly. Then he dropped the passport, tickets, and note onto the bedside drawers, and shoved his feet into his shoes.

"I need a minute," he mumbled, slamming the door behind him, and leaving Raphie all alone.

Maybe Raphie could have a little cry now, after all.

8

---

GRIFF

GRIFF ONLY MADE IT AS FAR AS THE FIRST LANDING BEFORE HE stopped, clenching his fists and jaw, and staring out through the window over the cliffside to the ocean. "What the *hell* are you doing, Thompson?" he whispered harshly to himself.

He should never, *ever* have kissed Raphael. But he sure as hell couldn't leave him alone. Griff's one and only purpose was to watch over Raphael. He was his *client.* That meant getting his arse back into that room and not even *thinking* about kissing him again.

All the way to Campanula.

If only Bev had knocked two minutes earlier.

But...then he would never have discovered that Raphael tasted like sunshine, or that his lips were soft and needy, or that his fingers clawed and dug into Griff's skin with an erotic desperation that still had Griff hard in his jeans now.

He angrily rubbed his eyes and sighed heavily. Was it better or worse knowing these perfect, wonderful things about someone he couldn't have?

"Get a grip, you utter prat," he told himself firmly.

Seriously. He'd only met Raphael a day ago. Literally twenty-four hours. How was Griff having this much trouble? Raphael was just a man, just a client. Griff had never even been tempted to cross this line before, no matter what the circumstances.

Until now.

He scrubbed his face and stared out over the vista, trying his best not to picture Raphael's crestfallen face as Griff had fled from the room.

Not only was he getting soft and unprofessional, but he was also becoming a coward. He needed to march back in there and explain to Raphael exactly why what they'd done had been a mistake, then reassert some professional boundaries. Easy. They would just…

Griff frowned. What was that glinting in the morning sunshine by the cliff edge? He stepped closer to the window. It wasn't like he'd been scrutinising the view before, but he was pretty sure that reflective…whatever it was…hadn't been there a minute ago.

In an instant, his training kicked in, completely overriding his previous emotional whirlwind. He took the stairs two at a time as he ran back up to his and Raphael's room, bursting in to find Raphael still curled up in the bed.

He'd obviously been crying. Under his eyes were red, and his cheeks shone in the morning light from the tears that had fallen down them. Of course, he sniffed and wiped his face, attempting to smile as soon as Griff came in, but it wasn't hard to tell.

Wow. For such a big guy, Griff had no idea he could possibly feel so small.

"Griff-" Raphael began, but there was no time. The shiny object could be an empty crisp packet for all Griff knew. But he'd listened to his gut when he'd seen something outside the penthouse window, and he was listening to it now.

"Raphael, I'm sorry, but you've got to pay careful attention to what I'm about to say." He moved over to the bed and took hold of Raphael's shoulders, looking into his wet but still beautiful green eyes. "I might have seen something outside. I want you to lock the door behind me, then lock you and Sparrow in the bathroom. *Only* come out if you hear me knock loudly three times. Do you understand?"

Raphael hiccuped and blinked, then nodded, his eyes wide and fearful. "Yes, Griff. I understand," he whispered.

Griff let go of him to pick up the old-fashioned, heavy metal key, then pressed it into his palm. But then Raphael surprised him by grabbing his wrist. They locked eyes.

"Be careful," Raphael said softly.

Griff nodded. Adrenaline was already pumping through him, and his objective was clear. But he still couldn't seem to stop those words nestling their way into his heart.

"Lock the door," he said firmly as he moved back towards it. "Three knocks, remember. Don't open to anyone but me."

Raphael nodded, standing and following Griff as he stepped out into the hall. They shared a lingering glance, where Raphael bit his lip, a hundred things hung unspoken between them.

Then Griff was gone, running down the stairs as he heard the door bang behind him, not meeting anyone as he sprinted through the front entrance and out into the fresh morning air. As he'd bolted down the stairs, a brief glance through the windows had shown him that the shiny thing was still there. He wasn't imagining it.

Now to go find out what it was.

The cliff was to the back of the bed and breakfast, so Griff hugged the building as he dashed around it. There was a stretch of open grass between the house and cliff edge, so Griff had little choice but to make a break for it with no cover. As long as Raphael was locked behind two doors, Griff had to do what he could to protect him, even if it made him a sitting duck.

Of course, the truth was that if any of those assassins from the penthouse really wanted to break through the doors or windows to get to Raphael, they could. Those little locks wouldn't protect him for long. Griff just had to do everything in his power to ensure that it didn't come to that.

As it transpired, his gut instinct had been bang on. The shiny thing was a goddamned grappling hook.

Griff slowed slightly as he approached the wicked-looking four-pronged hook. There was a thick black rope attached to it that disappeared over the cliff edge, and it was shifting back and forth against the stone. The wind whipped around Griff's ears, tugging at his short hair. He scrubbed his face and wished for once that he'd been issued some sort of weapon by the company. Security guards in the UK basically had the same rights as any citizen. In other words, they just had better training, but didn't carry guns, batons, or even pepper spray. But he kind of wished he'd looked around the B&B for something heavy he could have wielded if this was a real threat.

Hell, it might have even been satisfying to whack someone over the head with one of those creepy-as-fuck dolls, if only to watch it shatter.

But as it was, he peered over the cliff edge with nothing more than his wits and his right hook…

…and came face-to-face with Mr Morning Star.

Griff wasn't sure who was more shocked. Him or the assassin.

It was the hitman that recovered first, however. "Hello again, old chap," said the dashing man. He was hanging from the rope three feet below, dressed all in black, with a bloody *crossbow* attached to his back. On the water beneath them, a dinghy bobbed on the waves. He gave Griff a lopsided smile. "Spiffing day for a climb."

"Hmm," said Griff.

They stared at each other for another two and half seconds before Griff seized the grappling hook, yanked it free from the rock, and sent Mr Morning Star back down towards the beach with a furious howl.

Griff wasn't heartless, despite the fact that the guy was absolutely here to harm Raphael and Griff didn't exactly feel warm and fuzzy about him. But he'd seen the rope was secured at several other points up the cliff's edge, so Mr Morning Star slammed to a sudden halt about ten feet above the sand, jerking like a fish on a line.

"You can't leave me here!" he yelled up at Griff, his words only just travelling over the sound of the waves. "It's just not cricket!"

"Yes, I bloody can," Griff grumbled, already stomping off, back towards the house.

That was too close.

In a way, it was almost a good thing that Griff had been grossly unprofessional and started snogging his client. Otherwise, he never would have stormed off onto the landing and seen the grappling hook out on the cliff edge.

But that line of thinking led to danger. Griff couldn't allow himself to believe that kiss had been a good idea in any way, shape, or form. That perfect, heart-stopping, cock-swelling, kiss that Griff couldn't get out of his head no matter how hard he tried.

"Sort it out," Griff growled to himself just as he barrelled back through the front door of the B&B. The kiss had been a bad idea and would bring him nothing but trouble, and that was all there was to it.

Whatever the case, this was definitely his and Raphael's

cue to leave the bed and breakfast, even if they didn't now have a ferry to catch.

"You out for an early stroll?" Bev asked cheerfully from behind the desk.

"Birdwatching," Griff said with a nod.

He tried not to noticeably sprint through the entrance hall. Instead, he walked briskly until he got to the stairs, then he launched himself up them two at a time, anxious to make sure that Raphael was okay. But his thoughts managed to run rampant as he climbed the stairs.

Griff had almost certainly lunged forward at the same moment as Raphael. He couldn't solely blame his client for what had happened. Not that he should, anyway. Because Griff was the older and supposedly wiser of the two, and more importantly, there was a power imbalance between them that made this totally unethical. Raphael was Griff's client, but he was also young, vulnerable, and in Griff's care.

He had to shove his personal feelings aside. There was a possibility that he might have remembered (vaguely) when he'd been rutting against Raphael's lithe, perfect body that he was shortly supposed to be handing Raphael over to a new team. He'd been convinced that was the plan, so it didn't seem *so* terrible that they'd started making out like horny teenagers, because they'd be parting ways in a matter of hours. But honestly, Griff hadn't been thinking with his upstairs brain. He wasn't sure he could have resisted Raphael throwing himself at him, even if Griff hadn't recalled that detail, and anyway, the point was now moot.

Griff was one hundred per cent Raphael's bodyguard again. He was the only person standing between that sweet, beautiful, intelligent, *dazzling* young man waiting for him on the top floor, and arseholes like that wanker Griff had just sent flying. Griff couldn't afford to get distracted, and that meant absolutely *not* thinking about how delicious Raphael had tasted. Or how perfectly he'd fitted against Griff's body. Or how utterly intoxicating he'd been whilst moaning into Griff's mouth.

If he didn't think about all of that, hopefully he'd be able to stop it from happening again. Because once Raphael's lips had touched his own, it was as if Griff had no choice but to devour Raphael, to run his hands over that gorgeous hair and his toned body. *Fuck.* Griff was in danger of getting hard again thinking about it as he dashed back up the stairs.

Griff had to get Raphael over to France, then drive him across mainland Europe to Campanula without giving in to this explosive chemistry that had obviously been simmering beneath the surface since he and Raphael had locked eyes with one another in the penthouse back in London.

Great.

Because that was the other issue. If Griff had kissed a guy who was about to be *not* his client, that would have been manageable. Sort of. But Raphael was not only still his client, but he was also Griff's client because he was a fucking *prince.*

His royal status hadn't been much of a problem before, because Griff had been stubbornly convincing himself that the client thing would have been barrier enough to stop him from doing something so monumentally stupid as getting off with Raphael. But now that cat was out of the bag, and Griff had to stay strong and make sure it didn't happen again. He couldn't fuck a prince, for the love of god. Griff was just some security guard from the East End. A bit of rough. Good for a night, but no one's idea of a catch.

Certainly not a crown prince, currently in a race against time to claim his throne and save not only his country but his *life*.

Griff stood outside the room door and scrubbed his face,

taking a deep breath and trying to compose himself. He'd made a mistake. That was only human. Many mistakes, actually. He wasn't sure which he was more ashamed of: kissing Raphie or running away from him twenty seconds after opening that bloody envelope.

Time to face the music.

Griff gave three firm knocks. "It's me," he said loudly and clearly through the door, hoping Raphael could hear him. He waited several seconds, holding his breath, but eventually he heard movement beyond the wood.

"What film won the Oscar for best picture in 2015?" Raphael's shaky voice came through the door.

Griff sighed, a smile creeping on his face as relief blossomed through his chest. Raphael was okay, and Griff tried to ignore any other feelings. Like pride at Raphael asking an extra security question, or longing that he'd asked a question about the subject that had cracked Griff's walls down in the first place.

If they hadn't started raving about movies, making Griff feel stupid things like *seen* or *important,* maybe he wouldn't have given in to that kiss.

Whatever. The damage was now done. No use crying over spilled milk.

"The only thing I remember from 2015 was that Fury Road got robbed," he said through the door with a rueful sigh.

There was a click, and Raphael opened it a crack. "Is everything okay?" he asked in a tiny voice. His eyes weren't quite as red as they had been, but he was still pale and frightened-looking.

Griff nodded. "We're all right, but we need to get moving. Am…am I okay to come in?"

Fucking hell. He needed to get his confidence and sense

of authority back, right now. He wouldn't be able to protect Raphael if he was too concerned about upsetting him all the way to Campanula.

Raphael managed a small smile as he stepped back to allow Griff inside. "Only because you answered my question one hundred per cent correctly."

"Thanks," Griff said awkwardly, definitely not pleased that Raphael agreed with him on the Mad Max film. "May I?" He held his hand out for the key, which Raphael gave him. "Cheers."

He cleared his throat and made sure the door was closed and locked with the heavy key. It wouldn't stop any more would-be assassins for long, but it would at least give them a few seconds warning if they tried to force their way in.

"I'm sorry I left you alone," Griff said stiffly, not quite able to meet Raphael's puffy eyes.

"Oh," Raphael squeaked with a dismissive handwave. He was still in his panda pyjamas and looked so delicate. "It's fine. I'm *fine*. Are you okay?"

*No*, thought Griff irritably. In fact, Raphael asking that and showing how kind he was just made him feel even shittier for how badly Griff had failed him.

He huffed. "I'm fine," he answered, lying through his teeth. "But I was right. When I left the room, I saw there was someone outside through the window. The guy with the morning star from the penthouse. He's been dealt with, but we need to head to the ferry port, now. Just in case anyone else has tracked us this far."

Or if Mr Morning Star had made it back up the cliff side already. Griff hoped not, but there was no sense in dawdling.

Raphael didn't bring up why Griff had left the room, but he sensibly latched on to the right detail of Griff's story.

"They've found us?" he cried. His face dropped as he spun

around. "I did wonder when you told us to hide in the bathroom. Sparrow? Sparrow, come here, baby. We have to get going."

The cat was lurking under the bed, but she allowed Raphael to coax her out with more of those magic cat treats so he could put her back on her lead. Then he and Griff danced awkwardly around each other as they packed up their few things, with mumbled 'excuse me's and 'thank you's. Raphael got changed out of his pyjamas in the bathroom.

Griff hated every second of it. All he wanted to do was wrap Raphael up in his arms and tell him everything would be all right. But Griff had already proved to himself that the second he gave in to his downstairs brain with regards to Raphael, his upstairs brain shut down and put them all in danger. The *only* thing that mattered was getting Raphael to Campanula and getting him there in one piece.

Griff reminded himself of that harshly as Raphael stepped out of the bathroom sniffing and rubbing his eyes.

It was just a silly crush. Raphael would get over it when he met nicer blokes. It didn't matter that Griff couldn't remember *ever* feeling this way about anyone. That was because Raphael was one of a kind, whereas a brute like Griff came two-a-penny, and Raphael would surely soon find himself another guy who was more befitting a prince.

Griff ignored how strongly he already wanted to punch any other man who might come anywhere close to Raphael. But that was him not thinking with either brain, and he'd promised himself he'd never become the kind of man who resorted to fixing his personal problems with his fists. He'd only use violence to fend off Raphael's would-be attackers, not suitors.

Probably.

"You got everything?" Griff grunted. He'd already swept

the room, but it was worth asking Raphael to glance over it too.

"Yep," Raphael said briskly. He was back in his jeans and T-shirt along with a soft-looking grey cardigan that made his blond hair really seem to shine. But of course he then had to wind his night-time braid into a bun, securing it with pins he produced from his jeans pocket. Then he slipped the colourful beanie hat on to hide his distinctive hair.

Hair that had been escaping its plait from where Griff had tugged at it whilst they'd been snogging.

*Let it go.*

As they left the room with Sparrow on her lead, it became easier for Griff to switch back to a more professional mindset. He walked ahead of Raphael, checking every corner and doorway for a potential threat. Concentrating on his job helped clear his thoughts and focus him for the first time since he'd woken up.

"Oh, good morning!" chirped Bev as they entered the entrance hall of the B&B. She smiled brightly and gave them a little wave. "I hope I didn't disturb you too early, but the courier wanted to storm up there and break down your door, so I thought at least I'd be more gentle!" She tittered and looked curiously at Griff, probably wondering what was going on.

But Griff just smiled. "It was no problem," he said politely. "Thank you for a very comfortable stay. We wish we could stay longer, but we're heading north and want to get to Maidstone in time for lunch."

Hopefully, if anyone came asking for them, that was what Bev would tell them and send them in the opposite direction. It might not throw any decent assassin off the trail, but these people didn't exactly feel to Griff like they were at the top of their game, so he reckoned it was worth a try.

After all, Mr Morning Star was going to get himself off

that dangling rope at *some* point. Best to try and put as much distance between him and them as possible.

Griff glanced down at Raphael, who appeared to stir from a trance-like state. "Yes, Maidstone, that's right," he said happily, full of sunshine once again.

Griff hated that he'd taken that away from him.

"We'd like to settle our bill," he said, automatically reaching for his wallet. Between the kiss and the assassination attempt, Griff's mind was elsewhere. They were paying everything with cash for a reason. Luckily, Raphael spotted his mistake before he could get his credit card out.

"Honestly, *babe*," he said, emphasising the endearment that made Griff's heart pang. If only it could be real. It snapped him back into the moment, though. "I told you, this holiday is on me. Put that away." Raphael waved Griff off, getting out his own wallet. At some point he must have transferred some of his huge wodge of cash into a regular wallet, which he now pulled from his jeans pocket. "How much will that be, ma'am?"

"Ma'am," Bev repeated in amusement, but her rosy cheeks suggested she quite liked the title. "A hundred and twenty for the night. I won't charge you for breakfast, seeing as you didn't get to have any."

Griff's stomach rumbled, but he ignored it. They still had some leftover food with them from the supermarket, but he was too queasy with guilt over how he was treating Raphael to eat just yet anyway.

"Aww, that's so sweet of you," said Raphael, sorting through the various notes in his wallet. "But I'll add a tip anyway. Sparrow loved her little bed you got her."

Sparrow had spent the entire night either on or underneath the human bed, but Griff thought it was sweet of

Raphael to tip the bed and breakfast owner for her thoughtfulness anyway. It was probably his first chance to tip anyone. Griff wondered if he'd been practising that in the mirror, too, like ordering food from a restaurant. Probably.

Swallowing, Griff made himself focus. It didn't do any good to be pondering over Raphael's past life or thinking he was sweet. Griff needed to keep his gaze laser-focused on the exits and make sure Mr Morning Star or the Wannabe Ninja or the Abseiling Siblings didn't surprise them again.

"Oh, that's so kind of you," gushed Bev, her eyes wide. Probably because Raphael hadn't quite got the hang of tipping yet, and had given her an extra hundred-pound note on top of the hundred and twenty they actually owed. Griff tried not to smile, but that went beyond sweet all the way to adorable.

How the hell was he going to survive the next few days with his heart or his sanity intact?

"Um, here!" Bev cried, proudly producing two lollypops from a selection she had in a mug on the desk. "I usually save these for my youngest guests, but that'll do for breakfast for now, hey?" She winked and Raphael giggled as he took them, and Griff ushered him out of there before Raphael could make his heart hurt any more with his loveliness.

As soon as they got back on the road, though, a terrible awkwardness descended in the car. The silence was heavy between them. Even Sparrow was quietly curled up on Raphael's lap. Griff tried punching a few of the radio station pre-set buttons, but none of them had been programmed in. So they just made the drive to the ferry port saying nothing, the rumble of the car on the road the only sound keeping them from total silence.

The longer it went on, the worse it felt. But Griff had no idea how to break the ice now. He wanted to tell Raphael that their moment together had meant a lot to him, but that would be leading his client on and Griff refused to be so cruel. Keeping his mouth shut wasn't hurting Raphael much less, but at least it wasn't giving him false hope that anything more could happen between them in a personal sense.

Instead, Griff focused on driving the correct way once they reached the port. He'd never done this before, and they couldn't afford to go the wrong way and miss their ferry. The sooner they put the English Channel between them and the assassins, the happier Griff would be.

Lorries were being directed one way and regular traffic another. So Griff joined the queue for cars, vans, and other smaller vehicles, crawling up to several manned booths where they would presumably show their documents before they'd be allowed out of the country. Griff kept his eyes flitting all around them, making sure no one got the drop on them whilst they were in stationary traffic.

"Good morning!" an extremely cheery guy cried once they rolled up to the next available booth. He beamed down at them through the window Griff had lowered on his side. "May I see your passports and tickets please?"

Griff handed over what Winston had sent him, silently cursing the man for the dozenth time that morning for putting him in this awkward position. Then he looked over at Raphael in order to take his passport as well. Except Raphael handed him three different coloured passports – one was the usual UK burgundy, the second a golden, sunny yellow, and the third a bright blue.

Griff was distracted from asking what the extra ones were by Raphael's tentative smile and the way their fingers brushed as he handed the documents over. "Thanks," Raphael whispered.

"You're welcome," Griff mumbled. He so desperately

wanted Raphael not to hate him. But what was more important? Raphael's approval, or Raphael being alive?

Griff knew the answer. It didn't mean he had to like it.

He hastily turned to offer the cheerful man Raphael's passports.

"Aww, and this must be Miss Sparrow!" the guy announced, looking from the blue document to the cat swishing her tail in Raphael's lap. She gave a warning growl that was pretty fierce for how small she was, and the guy in the booth laughed. Griff hadn't even thought about taking Sparrow across an international border, but of course Raphael and his mum had planned for that. "Ohh, she's a spicy one, isn't she?" the guy commented.

"She's protective," Raphael agreed. "Sorry, she growls at people she doesn't trust yet."

It was stupid, but Griff couldn't help but note that Sparrow had never once growled at him.

"Right," Booth Man continued. "I don't need the Campanula one, so here you go." He handed back the blue and yellow passports, keeping both the burgundy ones as he cross-referenced them and the tickets against his computer. "Excellent. You're all set, Mr d'Oro and Mr Thompson."

Once they had their passports back, Griff was directed to the huge ramp that led them up to one of the ferries. There was an archway in front of it that read 'DOVER 3' in letters probably taller than Griff, and a long line of cars was snaking its way into the belly of the boat. As they crawled into the dark interior, Griff became even more hyper-aware of Raphael sitting beside him. It was as if his body was radiating heat, calling out to Griff.

All passengers had to vacate their vehicles for the duration of the hour-and-a-half crossing, so as soon as the doors were securely locked, the signal was given to everyone to get out, lock their cars, and move along the gangways to the upper decks of the ferry. As soon as Griff exited the hire car, he took several deep breaths to try and compose himself away from Raphael's magnetic presence.

Luckily, they'd already thought to coax Sparrow back into the rucksack, and Raphael was wearing it on his front again so she was safe from getting trampled. However, Griff's sense of relief was short-lived. The crowd was bustling and noisy with hundreds of people's voices echoing off the metal chamber where the vehicles were parked bumper to bumper.

Never mind that there was suddenly a huge security risk to Raphael, but his eyes also went wide and Griff would have bet all the money in his backpack that Raphael was completely overwhelmed by being in his first real throng. Sure, the London streets had been busy, but the tube hadn't been that packed and there was always a sense that you could escape if necessary.

Right now, they were trapped on a boat about to venture into the English Channel.

Griff didn't listen to the voices that had been warring in his head all morning. He just paid attention to his gut, which was telling him to wrap his arm around Raphael's waist so they could walk together, side-by-side.

"You're okay," Griff murmured into Raphael's ear. "I've got you. You're safe."

"Okay, Griff," Raphael repeated breathlessly, clinging to him.

It felt so *right* for them to be pressed together like that, it was almost breathtaking.

Sparrow's head twitched left and right as she sunk lower into the bag. Raphael took a breath and felt like he loosened up a fraction. It took all of Griff's self-control not to kiss his head through his beanie hat. Instead, he bit his tongue and kept looking around the crowd as they made their way towards the stairs.

They made it into the public area of the ferry without incident, and as soon as the crowd began to disperse towards the lounge areas, restaurants, and shops, Raphael definitely relaxed. Which probably meant Griff should let him go and throw up the professional wall again. But his gut was screaming to hold on just a little longer, and Griff was too selfish to fight himself on it.

"Come on," he said, leading Raphael towards the open-air deck, where the horde of people was much thinner. As they stepped out into the bracing sea air, the sound of the ferry's engines hit their ears. The boat was starting to slowly chug away from the port and the stretch of white coastal cliffs that Dover was famous for.

"It's stunning," Raphael said, sounding tired as they approached the rails.

Sparrow was still on her lead with the end looped around Raphael's wrist, so Griff wasn't worried about her getting spooked and jumping from Raphael's backpack into the water. But he was anxious about being in a crowd so soon after Mr Morning Star's attempted attack, even if the boat's deck wasn't that packed. Griff was torn between wanting Raphael to have this moment of seeing a stunning natural beauty after a lifetime cooped up in that tower, and getting him to a less exposed location.

Griff figured with his arm still wrapped around him, Raphael was at least partly protected. But then Raphael sighed and leaned his weight more against Griff's side, practically snuggling, and Griff's gut regrettably informed him that now was probably the time to let Raphael go. And then Raphael opened his mouth and absolutely reminded Griff of the reality of their situation.

"About this morning..." Raphael began.

*Nope!* Griff's upstairs brain screeched at him. That was far too dangerous territory. So he immediately released his hold on Raphael and stepped away.

"Was a mistake," he said firmly, ignoring how much it hurt his heart. "I'm your security detail. Your safety is my top priority, and I should never have been…distracted. I apologise profusely, Mr d'Oro."

Raphael stared at him, an expression altering his features with something Griff hadn't previously thought Raphael capable of until that moment.

Rage.

"Mr *d'Oro?*" Raphael hissed incredulously, keeping his voice down so other passengers couldn't hear them over the wind, but still clearly furious. *"Fuck you,* Griffin Thompson. Seriously!"

He spun on his heel and began marching away, down the narrow side aisle where not many passengers were hanging around. There probably wasn't a huge security threat down there, and it looked to be blocked off at the end. Nevertheless, Griff gave chase.

That was his job, after all.

"Wait!" Griff called, not daring to shout Raphael's name.

But Raphael continued stomping away, leaving Griff little choice but to grab his elbow and pull him into an alcove by a 'Staff Only' door that probably led to cleaning supplies.

Raphael snatched his arm away, and Sparrow poked her head further out of the rucksack. Both of them glared at Griff as he awkwardly shuffled into the alcove as well. "Raphael, please-" he tried.

"Oh, it's Raphael again, is it?" he scoffed, green eyes blazing.

Griff sighed dejectedly. "I'm just trying to do my job. Keep things professional," he said heavily.

"No!" Raphael snapped fiercely, his eyes blazing up at

Griff. "You do not get to treat me like I don't matter. You don't get to pretend like that didn't happen between us. You don't get to blow hot and cold with me. What happened between us was *important* to me. That was my first kiss!"

"I know," Griff mumbled miserably. He wished he could take it back for Raphael's sake. So that he could have shared it with someone better.

He already felt like a total arsehole. He didn't need any help. But Raphael had every right to be angry. Griff had been acting completely out of order. The kind of shitty man he'd seen far too much of in his life, and had never wanted to be. But he didn't know how else to handle this *thing* between them, this relationship that had been shifting like tectonic plates ever since the moment they'd laid eyes on one another.

"I'm just trying to protect you." Griff lifted his hands to Raphael's arms, rubbing his thumbs against Raphael's cardigan, attempting to explain what he really meant.

*I want you, but I can't have you.*

"I don't *need* protecting," Raphael snapped, stamping his foot and glaring up at Griff.

The throwing star appeared beside his head as if it had popped up through the wall like a fucking daisy.

There was a split second where Raphael's eyes flicked sideways to look at it as his jaw dropped open. Then Griff threw them both to the floor with Sparrow, just before several more shuriken impaired themselves in the wall Griff and Raphael had just been pressed up against.

"Okay, maybe I need a *little* bit of protecting!" Raphael squeaked, then bit his lip as real fear made his forest-green eyes impossibly wide.

Griff cupped the back of his neck. "I've *got* you," he promised fiercely.

And he meant it.

He reached up and tried the closet door to their backs. By some stroke of luck, it was unlocked, so Griff pushed the handle all the way so he and Raphael could scramble beside the mops and buckets within.

"It's that ninja woman," Raphael hissed, clutching Sparrow to his chest.

Griff nodded. He couldn't work out where she was attacking them from, but he hoped wherever she was, she hadn't hurt any of the other passengers.

Who knew? At close range, her aim might actually be decent.

Griff could mock her all he wanted, but she still had razor-sharp throwing stars and the odds were that she'd probably hit true at least *some* of the time. Griff had to deal with her right now, before she did some real damage.

"Stay here," he ordered Raphael, who nodded earnestly.

Griff grabbed one of the propped-up mops as he stood to venture out onto the gangway again, pulling the door closed behind him to offer Raphael at least a little bit of a shield. The mop head dripped quietly as he peered around the alcove, looking left and right down the gangway. There were no passengers, but someone had placed a 'No Entry' sign up at the walkway entrance, stopping other passengers from wandering down from the open deck.

That was pretty clever, Griff had to admit. It also gave him hope that if this person was making an attempt to keep civilians away, they hadn't left a trail of bodies behind them. Griff didn't want *anyone* to die.

But especially not Raphael.

Griff was so busy looking left and right, as well as over the railing at the churning waves as the ferry rushed over the channel's waters, he didn't think to look up. The black boots swung out of nowhere, smashing Griff in the face and knocking him back into the door, rattling it.

Shaking his head to dispel the stars in his vision, Griff managed to get his mop up just in time to stop the knife flashing through the air from reaching his body. Its owner had dropped to her feet from the ferry's roof. She was perhaps just over five-foot-tall and clad head to toe in black, only her eyes visible. She slashed her curved blade back and forth as she let out a high-pitched wail.

That was, until the knife got lodged in Griff's mop and wouldn't be pulled back out again, no matter how much Wannabe Ninja yanked. Her battle cry died in her throat, but that didn't stop her from shouting after a brief, disbelieving pause.

"Your ancestors will be shamed on this day!" the ninja shrieked in a Japanese accent so bad, it belonged in a Christmas pantomime. She and Griff wrestled back and forth. Every time she pulled the knife, Griff would yank the mop back, splattering water droplets everywhere. "I am the night! You cannot defeat me!"

Griff grunted and allowed her to struggle with the mop some more. He could probably have twisted it and landed several punches on the ninja by now, but he was turning her around to get the angle he wanted.

"You get that out of a fortune cookie?" he asked.

That only seemed to infuriate the pint-sized assassin. She screeched and tried to kick at Griff's shins. "You will rue the day you came between me and my quarry! You may be a mighty oak, but the wind is patient, and the acorn-"

Griff sadly didn't get to hear the end of that proverb, although he was sure it was very deep. Because at that moment, he chose to let go of the mop, just as Wannabe Ninja pulled it. The wooden staff smacked against her head with a sickening crack, causing the ninja to stumble backwards, dropping the mop and the knife still embedded in it. She pinwheeled her arms as her feet slid on the splattered mop water, careening over the railing and landing on the other side with a thud.

Into the bright orange lifeboat Griff had spotted earlier and had been hoping to deposit this menace in. It was ten feet down, and there was no way to climb back out again without being winched. As an added bonus, the bash from the mop combined with the fall seemed to have knocked the assassin clean out. Griff watched for a minute, making sure that her chest was still moving and her head wasn't pouring with blood. Once he was satisfied, he looked around him, but thanks to Wannabe Ninja's sign, no one else seemed to have noticed the disruption. Thank heavens for small mercies.

Griff had plenty of colleagues who would have preferred to terminate any threat permanently, but that wasn't his style. He just hoped it didn't come back to bite him in the arse. With any luck, the authorities would deal with the ninja, especially once Griff picked up the knife (using his T-shirt so as not to get any fingerprints on it) and tossed it down to the other end of the boat next to her.

That taken care of, Griff could now focus on his main priority.

Raphael.

He dashed back over to the broom cupboard, hauling it open to find Raphael sat trembling, his knees pulled up to his chest. Sparrow was curled around his shoulders, the backpack resting on the floor beside him.

Griff dropped down, cupping his hands on either side of Raphael's face, helping him to look Griff in the eyes. "It's all okay," he said soothingly. "They're gone. You're safe. Nothing to worry about. I'm here."

Raphael blinked and licked his lips. His gaze flicked to glance behind Griff, as if checking the coast was clear for himself, then settled back on Griff's face. "Thank you," he rasped. "I – I'm sorry I was shouting at you. It was childish. I know you're my bodyguard. I know people are trying to kill me. That's all that matters. I know…" He gulped. "I know the kiss didn't matter. I should never have put that pressure on you."

And just like that, Griff's resolve melted. He knew it was wrong, but he couldn't bear to hurt Raphael when he was already shaken and scared.

"Raphael – *Raphie*," he corrected himself. That was his preferred name, and Griff was done acting like they could just ignore what was going on between them to make it go away. "That kiss meant *so much*. I'm just terrified of not doing my job right and getting you hurt." He shook his head. "Or worse."

Raphie's eyes widened. "Really?" he whispered.

"Really," Griff assured him.

For a second, they just stared at each other, sitting on the floor of the dusty utility cupboard. Then Raphie clambered into Griff's lap and curled against his side, shivering as he clutched Griff's T-shirt with one pale hand. His knuckles seemed to strain against his skin, as if it was made of paper.

Throwing caution to the wind, Griff gently wrapped his much larger hand over Raphie's, rubbing his thumb against the trembling fingers. Sparrow meowed, probably because the angle that Raphie was now leaning at was threatening to dislodge her from his shoulders.

So she climbed off them and onto Griff's, purring as she settled around his neck instead.

And then it was just a slippery slope before Griff slid his own fingers under the beanie hat and over that glorious, silky hair of Raphie's. He pressed his cheek to the top of Raphie's head and inhaled deeply, holding him closer, as if that might take all his pain away. "I've got you," he murmured. "You're safe."

"I know," Raphie whispered back. He wasn't crying or

screaming at Griff for the fright he'd just had. He was simply clinging to Griff the way Sparrow had to Raphie. Sharp claws digging into clothes like a feeble scream of *'Protect me!'*

Raphie didn't have to worry there. Griff was already tragically committed to this mission. What that meant for their personal relationship, he honestly wasn't sure.

But there was only so much more he could fight these feelings, and even less that he wanted to keep trying.

9

———

RAPHIE

ALL HIS LIFE, RAPHIE HAD BEEN A CHATTER BOX. MUM WAS always saying so, and had the video archives to prove it. It was very rare that he couldn't think of something to talk about, not unless he was lost in a book or something on the TV.

But it had been well over an hour now, and Raphie's tongue was still struggling to come back to life.

It wasn't that he didn't have things to discuss with Griff. That was just it. There was *so much* that it had all become overwhelming, and Raphie's connection between his brain and mouth had faltered.

He wasn't sure how long Griff had held him in the broom cupboard in the end. But the next thing Raphie really remembered was making their way back to the car again with Sparrow, clinging to Griff's side like a life raft. His arm was firm and secure around Raphie's waist, assuring him that nothing else bad was going to happen.

Raphie let himself believe that for the moment. Otherwise he'd never make it off the ferry.

Griff only let him go when he carefully sat Raphie once again in the passenger seat of the car. He buckled Raphie's seat belt for him, placed the rucksack at Raphie's feet, and made sure Sparrow was secure in Raphie's arms before shutting the door and hurrying to the driver's seat.

It was taking forever for all the hundreds of cars to slowly fight their way off the ferry, but no one had attacked them again, so Raphie just watched it all in a daze, not really thinking too much about anything if he could help it.

Sparrow was on his lap, grounding him. But even better than that, Griff had his left hand on Raphie's thigh whenever he didn't need it on the wheel. Which, considering the queue was moving at a snail's pace, was a lot.

Through his haze, what had just happened between Raphie and Griff was finally sinking in.

Something had actually changed between them.

Griff was calling him Raphie now, not the formal Raphael. He'd said that their kiss had *mattered*. He'd held Raphie in a way that went far beyond professional, and now the comforting hand on his thigh was definitely not something any of his other bodyguards had ever done. Raphie was almost too afraid to breathe in case the moment evaporated. But this *was* real, not his imagination, and some of his despair from that morning was starting to melt away.

Griff's comforting hand on his thigh felt like something a lover would do, perhaps in a scene from one of the romance novels Raphie had devoured over the years.

Was Griff his lover now? His boyfriend? Even in his slightly catatonic state, Raphie recognised that was him jumping ahead a *lot*, but he couldn't help it. He'd been on a hell of a roller coaster over the past couple of days, and his only reference for relationships was through media, which he was at least savvy enough to know wasn't reliable.

All he could think as they crawled towards the ferry exit was that he just really *liked* being near Griff, and feeling Griff touch him, and having Griff look after him. With no other experience to fall back on, that was all he could trust. Being around Griff just made him feel floaty and hopeful and so bloody safe.

Maybe that was all that mattered for now, and he could work out the rest later. Especially as Griff seemed to be behaving more like the man who'd kissed the hell out of Raphie first thing this morning, and less like the stiff robot who'd replaced him for the intervening hours between then and the attack.

*Fuck.* That had brought Raphie back to reality with a harsh thump. He'd lulled himself into a false sense of security, despite Griff saying there'd been another attempt from Mr Morning Star at the bed and breakfast. That had been abstract for Raphie, as he hadn't seen the guy. It wasn't that he hadn't believed Griff's account. It was just a *lot* harder for Raphie to pretend everything was fine when he'd felt that throwing star whizzing past his ear on the ferry.

And now...now they were rolling down the ramp, and Raphie was in France.

Another country.

Yesterday morning, Raphie couldn't even remember leaving the penthouse in his life. Now, he'd jumped off a fucking building, gone on the run, ordered food (mostly) by himself, slept in a strange bed – with a hot man, no less – *kissed* that man, had a fight with him, fled from more assassins, been on a boat, made up with the hot man – hopefully – and was now breathing in French air.

So, yes, he was having a little trouble wrapping his head around, well...everything.

All he knew was that Griff's strong hand felt amazing and

solid on Raphie's thigh, with his thumb rubbing soothing circles against the denim of his jeans. Raphie looked around at the industrial port of Calais, and figured there'd be more prettier sights to see of France later. So, for now, he closed his eyes and took one hand off Sparrow to place over Griff's, giving it a little squeeze.

"You okay?" Griff asked in a low rumble.

Raphie nodded, but kept his eyes closed. "It's just...a lot..." he said. "But thank you."

"For what?" Griff said with a rueful chuckle. "Being a bellend to you?"

Raphie shook his head. "Not that part," he agreed with half a grin, cracking one eye to take a peek at Griff. He was concentrating on the road, but he seemed pretty relaxed. "For everything else. Being here."

Griff didn't respond verbally. Instead, he flipped his hand over so he and Raphie could slide their palms together and entwine their fingers. At least, until Griff needed his hand back to drive again. Raphie treasured every moment until he did.

After several minutes of attempted meditation, Raphie cleared his throat and let his eyes flutter open again. He was so far from normal, he wasn't sure when he'd ever truly relax again. But he felt like his mouth and brain were at least reconnected, and his heart wasn't going to slam out of his ribcage. He took a couple of soothing breaths.

"So," he said with a sigh. "We're driving all the way to Campanula?"

Griff nodded and pointed at the SatNav. "Says it'll take about fifteen hours, but we'll need to stop to sleep somewhere. Should still get you there in plenty of time for that council meeting thingy."

Raphie hummed, definitely not ready to think about that yet. Just because he was the rightful heir to the throne didn't mean he was the best person for the job, or that anyone in Campanula would even let him do it.

He might be walking into a public execution.

He shivered, and reminded himself that this was the twenty-first century. He almost certainly wasn't going to get beheaded. But there were leaders of other countries who had been under house arrest for years – *decades.* After experiencing freedom for the first time in his life, Raphie didn't think he could stand going back to being caged up again. Not now that he knew what was out here, in the world.

Not now he'd met Griff.

Who chose that moment to pipe up. "I can hear you worrying from over here," he grumbled, but when Raphie looked at him, a smile was playing on his lips. "What?"

Raphie shrugged, feeling a little light headed. He couldn't quite believe that Griff was concerned about him. And not in the usual bodyguard way, like stopping shuriken from embedding in his head. But in a way like they were real friends.

Maybe more than friends.

Raphie could worry about the enormous political stuff later. Right now, it was just him and Griff in the car (besides Sparrow, of course) and that was what was concerned Raphie more.

"So…where are we right now?" he asked.

Griff frowned at the SatNav, then the main road they were speeding down. "On some autoroute – that's a French motorway – going through a national forest."

"No," Raphie said gently with a laugh. "I, um, meant *us.* You said that kiss this morning meant something. Were you just being nice, or…?"

Griff sighed and glanced over at Raphie before paying

attention to the road again. "Raphie…it's complicated," he said.

"I know," Raphie assured him, even though the brush-off hurt. Although Raphie wasn't giving up, even if he was inexperienced. He knew what he wanted, and now Griff had given him even just a glimmer of hope, he was going to take it. "But just…tell me what you're feeling. Not what *protocol* says. It's just us, in this car. I've never tried to navigate anything with a man I liked before. I've never *met* a man I liked before. Help me out. Am I just some immature brat annoying you? Did I imagine…this?" He waved his hand between them.

Again, Griff sighed. "Have you considered that it's just hormones from meeting the first eligible man to cross your path?"

"Fuck off," said Raphie, but not with real vehemence. "I mean, *yes*, I have wondered that. But I'm not an idiot. I'm actually kind of a boffin."

Griff laughed. "Boffin? Bloody hell, I haven't heard that word for years."

Raphie tried not to blush. "It's Mum's word. She's proud of all my studying and achievements, but she shows it by teasing. Anyway, so, I'm clever. Which means I think I know the difference between throwing myself at the first hot-blooded male to come my way, and having feelings for someone who's nice."

"Nice? Me?" Griff arched an eyebrow and glanced over at Raphie like he was utterly insane. "I think we just established that I've been a complete pillock towards you."

But Raphie wasn't going to be dissuaded. "Yes, nice. Ask Sparrow," he insisted. "Sparrow? Is Griff a nice man?" He put on a silly voice, pretending to be his cat as he bounced her on his lap. *"Yes, he's very nice. He stayed to rescue me and didn't make Daddy cut his hair off and then saved Daddy's life TWICE."*

Raphie grinned at Griff. "See. Sparrow said so, therefore it must be true."

Griff narrowed his eyes at the road. "Raphie," he said gently, almost sadly. "I've been acting like a prick most of the time we've spent together. You don't know me at all."

Raphie shrugged again. "I know you were a bit, um, rude, yes. But you apologised. And it doesn't matter that I haven't known you long." He waved his hand dismissively. "I'll be blunt. I like you. A lot. I was really into that kiss and wanted more. I've spent my whole life waiting for things, and now I'm out in the real world, I don't want to let something good go because I'm too cautious. You said that kiss meant something, so I'd love it if you didn't play games with me and said what that 'something' was."

Griff growled and drummed on the steering wheel. "I don't want to do something that will put you in danger, okay? This isn't some casual hook-up. This is a big deal for you, and I'm pretty sure you deserve a man a hundred times better than me. You're a prince. I'm a commoner. I'm your bodyguard, and both attempts on your life today came close because I took my eye off the ball. I'm older than you. I'm – as we've established – a grumpy twat. I'm trying to do the right thing here."

"Wow…" said Raphie, really dragging the word out. "That was a really long and crappy list of really unfair stuff about you. Which we'll discuss in a sec. But I'm pretty sure I asked you how you felt about *me*, and the longer you avoid the question, the more I'm starting to think you kissed me back because I just happened to be a warm body in your arms."

Griff's immediate snapped response of "What? No!" *did* go a long way in soothing Raphie's fragile, inexperienced ego. "Raphie, how could you – that's just – mate, you're *stunning*. You're a million miles out of my league. I've been forcing myself to keep my hands off you because I've never met a man like you in my life!" He bit his lip. "Or, um, I'm been meaning to ask. Is it okay to say man? You said about being nonbinary before, and I've been wanting to check."

Raphie felt his mouth drop open. Then he smacked Griff's muscular thigh and stared incredulously until Griff at least glanced at him. "How can you be all thoughtful and sweet like that and then tell me you're not nice? Shut up. And, um, thank you. I'll stop being vain now. I believe you like me." He felt himself blushing crimson, but he was grinning too much to care.

Griff grumbled and changed lanes. "Okay, fine," he said begrudgingly. "I like you. You like me. But I'm still very sure that we need to at least attempt to keep things professional so I can do my job. Your life is in danger. You're on your way to try and claim your throne. I need to concentrate."

Raphie blinked at him. "By *not* getting off with each other or having sex?"

Griff made a kind of whining noise, which Raphie couldn't help but gleefully interpret as Griff wanting *exactly* those things, and Raphie took his successful provocation as a small victory.

"Those things are *very distracting*," Griff said firmly.

"And this awful tension between us isn't?" Raphie demanded with a snort. "So you're saying that being angry and miserable with each other is preferable to a post-orgasmic glow?" He shifted slightly in his seat, really giving Griff all his attention. He'd been trained in debate and negotiating. He knew what he wanted, and he was almost certain he knew what Griff wanted, and he wasn't going to let Griff talk them out of it because of some misplaced sense of duty. "I may not know much about the real world, but that sounds like poppycock to me."

Griff's mouth twitched with a smile. "I think you know a little something, boffin," he said with affection that made

Raphie's heart soar. Then he reached over, offering his hand for Raphie to take again, and Raphie had to stop himself from bouncing in his seat he was so giddy. "I'm sorry I upset you and made you worry," Griff muttered, keeping his eyes on the road. Raphie didn't mind if the apology was quiet and awkward, though. What mattered was that Griff was issuing it at all.

"That's okay," Raphie said keenly.

Griff shook his head. "I don't..." he said, sounding like he was struggling for the right words. "I don't really do feelings. It's been a long time since I tried to have a relationship. So...I don't want to promise you something I can't do – certainly not a relationship." He shook his head. "I think you're brilliant. But...let's just take this slow, all right?"

Raphie didn't particularly want to take anything slow after a whole life that felt like it had been on pause. However, he didn't want to push Griff either. And logically, he did know that he'd been jumping ahead by picturing the two of them as boyfriends or something, but it did hurt a little to hear Griff so definitely rule out having a relationship. That being said, he was still holding Raphie's hand and rubbing little circles with his thumb, so that wasn't nothing.

After a lifetime of nothing, Raphie would take what he could get.

"Okay, we can go slowly, sure. Thank you, Griff," he said warmly.

Griff glanced over and chuckled, shaking his head. "Why do I get the feeling you're going to cause trouble anyway?"

Raphie blinked and looked innocently at him. "You mean *more* trouble than the assassins currently chasing us? I wouldn't dream of it."

Griff hummed, sensibly not agreeing with him.

But Raphie didn't want to pressure Griff into anything that made him uncomfortable, so he would actually do his best to be good. Griff knew how he felt now. With that clear between them, the door was open for something more, so Raphie would keep his hopes up.

"It's enby, by the way," Raphie said, picking up the previous conversation. "Short for nonbinary. That's me, so, thank you for asking. Although I like he and him pronouns." He gave Griff's hand a friendly squeeze. "*See.* You're not some old dinosaur gay. That was a really thoughtful question."

Griff shrugged, but Raphie was sure he blushed slightly. "I read and shit."

"Ahh, so you're a boffin, too?" Raphie said, teasing affectionately. He'd never had someone to banter with in real life before. It was like playing tennis with his coach, but in conversation instead of a ball. It was making him feel exhilarated.

"Me? Clever? Hardly," Griff scoffed, but he looked pleased nonetheless.

How circumstances could change in a few hours. Raphie was exhausted from bouncing between hope and disappointment, excitement and fear, but there was no chance he was going to fall asleep, not now he and Griff had talked. They liked each other, and that was all he'd really wanted to hear. The kiss between them had been real.

And there was a possibility it could happen again, if Raphie was very lucky.

Raphie had a fifteen-hour drive – or more likely two days with stops – to make the most of whatever was blossoming between him and Griff. He could spend that time worrying, or he could bask in what they had right now and see where it took them. He might not particularly love being patient, but after a lifetime, he was very good at it.

So when Griff had to let his hand go to use it to drive again, Raphie tried not to miss his touch too keenly. Instead, he reconnected his music to the stereo system, trying to find songs that Griff liked as well, and talking about whatever popped into his head like the chatterbox he was.

Good things come to those who wait, or so the saying promised. And Raphie was willing to wait for something as good as Griff.

Just hopefully not for too long.

# 10

# GRIFF

"See, I knew you'd be fine," said Winston on the other end of the phone.

Griff hummed and looked around the car park of the French service station they'd stopped in. He'd filled up the tank with fuel, then he and Raphie had quickly raced inside the shops to grab some food. Pets weren't technically allowed inside, but that hadn't stopped them in Sainsbury's and it wasn't going to stop them now. So Raphie had sweet-talked her into hiding in his backpack with the top closed once more, and they'd bought what they wanted in record time.

Now Sparrow was free inside the car again. Raphie was sat with her, happily munching on a brie and grape baguette, and talking to his mum on his phone.

Because when they'd come back out of the service station, Griff had realised he'd received a text message from Winston, saying they were both safely hidden away and free to contact. Griff had no idea if his and Raphie's phones were being tracked or anything, but they were both so desperate to check in, he decided to take a risk.

He'd given Raphie the privacy of the car, and Griff had chosen to call Winston back whilst standing outside. The summer sunshine was bright but not too hot, and Griff had picked up a cheap pair of sunglasses from one of the shops, so he could finally stop squinting.

"I don't know if 'fine' is really the right word," Griff grumbled, scuffing his foot on the tarmac. "But we're still in one piece, at least." He sighed heavily and rubbed his forehead. "So…you knew Raphie is a prince, huh?"

Winston hummed. "I'm very sorry for keeping you in the dark, son. We were about to fill you in, but, well…"

"There was a big explosion," said Griff with a sigh, but also an understanding tone.

"Exactly," Winston agreed. "Does knowing it now make much of a difference to your job?"

To Griff's job? Not really. It was pushing him to do more than ever before, but he had no choice and, honestly, once the initial shock had worn off, he'd become pretty confident in his abilities to keep Raphie safe.

But to Griff's feelings for Raphie and his ability to act on them?

Yeah, him being a prince made a pretty big fucking difference.

Bloody hell, that conversation in the car earlier had almost killed him. Raphie was basically *begging* Griff to let them explore their attraction to one another, and Griff was trying so hard not to risk either Raphie's feelings or his life by doing something reckless. But Raphie was gorgeous and sweet and clever as fuck and it was like every minute Griff spent with him, he was sliding further and further into this hopeless longing.

Raphie was going to be the king of Campanula. That did not leave any room for the likes of Griff in the long term. Of all the men Griff was compelled to actually *want* to try and have a relationship with, it felt cruel it was with the guy for whom that just wasn't possible.

And if Raphie had at least *some* experience with men, Griff might have considered a fling. But that also felt unfair. Raphie deserved something special and meaningful for his first relationship.

His first time in bed.

At least they weren't angry with each other anymore. That might be the best Griff could hope for. He didn't really believe that Raphie was all that attracted to him in particular. Griff just happened to be in the right place at the right time to cross Raphie's path. However, it was still nice to hear him say sweet things. Even if Griff was ready to dismiss them all as naive and innocent.

He listened as Winston ran him through his and Annabella d'Oro's movements since the attack on the penthouse. Winston didn't risk saying where they were over the phone, as they wanted to stay there for the next week or so, but it was a safe house somewhere in the UK. Raphie would be pleased to know his mum was all right and comfortable, which made Griff happy.

"As for your accommodation tonight," Winston continued, "I can help you out. I've got a little holiday home that's pretty much on your way. It's just a small fishing lodge, but I figured if it saved you having to book anywhere or pay, it would be preferable."

"Yeah, totally," Griff agreed. "That's a big help. Thanks a lot."

He wanted to ask how many bedrooms the place had, but that would bring attention to his and Raphie's not-so-little issue, and Griff didn't want anyone to know about what had happened that morning after sharing a bed the night before.

Damn, that felt like days ago. Griff was glad he'd bought a

coffee to help keep him focused for the rest of the drive that day. He picked up the disposable cup from where he'd left it on the car roof and took a sip.

They'd find out the sleeping arrangements as soon as they got there, and Griff was confident there would at least be a sofa he could sleep on. It would be safest for both him and Raphie to keep apart and not let their bodies get the wrong idea again.

"Look, you've got this, okay?" Winston said firmly as they began wrapping up the call. "You just need to get Raphie to the palace by Friday afternoon. He's got his birth certificate with him and blood test results – basically all the proof he needs that he's the rightful heir to the Campanulan throne. But none of that will matter if he doesn't get there before Princess Alessa's coronation. Their law is pretty firm about that."

"And the quicker he gets recognised as the heir, the quicker he'll have the power to call the assassins off, right?" Griff said.

However, no matter what Raphie had said to him, he wasn't convinced they would back off. Judging by his pause, neither was Winston. The assassins' orders could hardly have been sanctioned in the first place. But, hopefully, if Raphie got the support of his country's government, it might be enough to dissuade their pursuers that murdering a king was more trouble than it was worth.

The thought of anyone hurting a glorious hair on Raphie's head made Griff so enraged he wanted to punch something. All they saw was a political threat, someone who was after power. No, it was worse than that. That was how his late father had seen him, and perhaps the corrupt members of the council. But these assassins just saw Raphie's cold-blooded murder as a fucking payday.

No one saw the adorable guy who was currently hand-feeding his cat chunks of roast chicken, laughing as he spoke with his mum. Just as Griff was looking down at him, his heart full and aching, Raphie glanced up. As their eyes met, Raphie beamed through the car window and gave Griff a little wave, sending Griff's heart into overdrive.

Those assassins *better* back off once Raphie took his official title. Otherwise, Griff would dedicate his life to tracking them down one by one and stopping them for good.

Next time, he might not be so generous as to leave them breathing.

Just because he couldn't have Raphie didn't mean the world should be denied his shining light. The man was a walking ball of hope and sunshine. Griff knew enough about global politics to appreciate that the world stage needed compassionate leaders sympathetic to minorities. Raphie was the kind of twenty-first-century monarch that could change the world, even if his country was tiny.

Griff closed the call promising to do his very best to see to it that Raphie's arrival in Campanula went as smoothly as possible, and to only call Winston again in an emergency. Once Winston sent through a text with the address of his fishing lodge, Griff took his time to examine the route, giving Raphie the opportunity to wrap up his conversation with his mum in peace. Griff sipped on his coffee – which was good, but not a patch on the stuff he'd had when he'd arrived at the penthouse yesterday morning – and tried not to worry about completely fucking things up with Raphie.

Whatever this was between them was doomed anyway, so Griff shouldn't have cared as much as he did. But there was a part of him that just wished things could be simpler. That Raphie could be an ordinary bloke like Griff was.

But then he might lose all the special things about him that made him *Raphie.*

There was no point in wishing that life was different. Griff had learned that particularly harsh lesson several times throughout his life. He had to accept the hand he'd been dealt, and that meant he was allowed to enjoy Raphie's company to a certain extent, but he had to keep his own hands strictly to himself.

RAPHIE MADE for easy company most of the time (when Griff hadn't pissed him off) but after speaking with his mum for half an hour, he was practically bouncing off the car upholstery. He chattered non-stop, relaying every single thing his mum had said to him. Griff didn't spoil his fun by letting on that Winston had already filled him in on all the details of his and Raphie's mum's escape. Besides, it was better hearing Raphie's version.

He added all kind of silly details that his mum had obviously told him, like how there'd been a randy pigeon that had stayed on the car bonnet during slow traffic through Hammersmith. Or how Winston had obviously tried to impress Annabella with a fancy dinner, but they'd only been able to find a tacky pizza chain to eat at where the waiter had knocked their red wine over the table. It seemed Raphie shared Griff's initial impression that Winston was sweet on his mum, and they both agreed it was pretty adorable.

Privately, Griff wondered if the pair were having their own romantic adventure, cooped up in the safe house together for the next several days at least.

Not that he and Raphie were having a romantic adventure. Not at all. Nope. Griff kept telling himself that the entire drive, until they pulled up to Winston's fishing lodge.

Then Griff realised just how much trouble he was in.

If he was honest, he'd been expecting little more than a one-room wooden shack that smelled of fish bait. He hadn't been thrilled by the prospect – and he'd been pretty worried what Raphie might make of it – but the added security of not making a booking at a hotel or bed and breakfast had made it the more preferable option.

He hadn't been expecting a fairy-tale cottage, covered in ivy, with a red slate roof, and a little dock leading out to a gorgeous aquamarine lake. It was surrounded by pine trees, with lily pads scattered over the surface of the water, and a small sandy beach stretching out by the jetty. The cream stonework of the cottage looked centuries old, and, as they pulled up, Griff spied a small water wheel operating from a brook that ran into the lake.

It was only the fact that the walls weren't made of gingerbread that stopped Griff from picturing Hansel and Gretel from coming out and greeting them. This was one of the most romantic settings he'd seen in his entire life, and he was supposed to get through the whole night without giving in to Raphie's hopeful or flirty looks?

Maybe the inside would be super ugly or rat infested to save him.

Griff gulped as Raphie gasped and pressed his nose up to the car window. Then he held up an unimpressed Sparrow so she could see as well. *"Look at this!"* Raphie squealed breathlessly. "Did you know it was going to be so pretty, Griff?"

"I'd had no idea," he admitted, killing the car engine. Before he'd even secured the handbrake, Raphie had Sparrow securely on her lead, and was jumping out to get a better look at their lodgings for the night.

"Is this seriously Winston's holiday home?" he asked in awe. He slowly spun on the spot and took in the cottage and the stunning scenery. "Does he really not mind us staying the night?"

Griff still wasn't convinced it wasn't going to be a horror show on the inside – largely because he was half-hoping for that – but he didn't want to dampen Raphie's spirits. "Yep, it's all ours for the night."

"I wish we could stay here for a week or two," Raphie said dreamily. "I've always wanted to go on holiday. To see oceans and lakes and mountains and forests. It's…well, I can't really explain what it's like to see something like this for the first time." He inhaled deeply, his eyes shining as he smiled at the French vista. "I can't believe this is real."

Griff's heart contracted. For just a second, he allowed himself to fantasise that he'd brought Raphie out here for his first-ever holiday, and that they could take their time to explore this little corner of France, just the two of them. They could take long walks and sit on the end of the dock, maybe paddle at the edge of the small beach…

*Fuck.* That very quickly led to Griff's downstairs brain asking his upstairs brain to conjure up an image of Raphie in swimming trunks, which was the exact opposite of helpful. Especially when Raphie took off his beanie hat and shook out his hair from the plait. He closed his eyes as he turned his face to the sun, his hair moving in the gentle breeze.

Griff cleared his throat and spun away from the beautiful sight, popping the boot of the car to retrieve their bags. They had their few belongings, but they'd also nipped into a little supermarket when the SatNav had shown they were getting close to the cabin. Winston had informed Griff there was a small kitchen inside, so they could make their own proper dinner and give them a break from eating easy crap.

Winston had also told Griff where the spare key was to the cabin, and sure enough, it was hidden away under the plant pot by the front door. Griff wondered if Winston had people come and maintain the place, because the flower pots weren't overgrown with weeds and the porch was pretty well swept. Griff's hopes for a disastrous interior were already dwindling, but when he unlocked the door, all prayers for a lack of romance flew out the window.

It was gorgeous.

11

GRIFF

Griff let out a slow breath and began raising his guard against this extremely unfair and picturesque attack on his resolve to behave around Raphie.

The walls were the same rough cream stone that could be seen from the outside, but inside there were also roughly hewn wooden beams and doors. It wasn't quite as small as it might have first seemed, with three doors leading off the main kitchen and living room space. A large metal bin of wooden logs sat next to a wrought-iron burner with a long chimney flute stretching up to the ceiling. Griff stepped over rustic wooden floorboards that weren't dusty in the slightest, damn them, as he looked at the shelves, eclectic but well-matched photo frames, and ceramic plates mounted on the walls.

He placed the grocery bags on the kitchen table, ducking a little to avoid the pots, pans, and bushels of dried herbs hanging from the ceiling. A wine rack was filled with bottles of red, and around the counters were jars of different types of dried pasta and lentils, as well as a fully stocked rack of herbs and spices.

When Winston had insisted that they help themselves to anything, Griff had kind of assumed he'd meant teabags and long-life milk. Not a functioning pantry. He bit his lip, trying desperately to remind himself that they *weren't* on holiday and that he was absolutely still working. But it was extremely difficult when Raphie came bounding in with Sparrow and gasped. Then he squealed. Then he did a kind of little dance, and Griff was only human. Who in their right mind could deny how adorable that was?

"I love it, Griff! Please tell Winston thank you so much!" He began running around, inspecting every clock and book and house plant he came across. Then he dashed back to close the front door before letting Sparrow off her lead to explore. "It's amazing! Is this the kind of place you normally go on holiday to?"

Griff thought about the very few times he'd been on holiday in the past several years, and the cheap package deals he usually got to perfectly nice but pretty sterile hotels, and couldn't help but smile. "No," he admitted. "This is pretty great."

*Personal,* a voice in the back of his head whispered. *Intimate. A love nest.*

If Griff's upstairs and downstairs brains were going to keep conspiring against him, luring his battered heart over to the dark side, he was going to be seriously fucked.

*Only if you're lucky,* the voice whispered gleefully.

"For *heaven's* sake," Griff growled under his breath.

But of course Raphie still managed to hear him. "Is everything okay?" he asked hesitantly.

Griff made himself stop and take a breath. He refused to be an arsehole…again. "Sorry," he mumbled contritely with a meek smile. "I'm, um, just tired, and I can't work out where the fridge is." That was true, at least. He kept opening the same three cupboard doors over and over.

"Oh!" said Raphie brightly, skipping through the kitchen, his hair swishing free behind him. "I bet it's concealed behind a cabinet that matches the rest. Ah! There you go," he said proudly, having immediately discovered the right cupboard. Raphie looked bashful at how quickly he'd zoned in on the right place. "I, uh, used to design imaginary homes for fun when I was a teenager. It's amazing what you can do to pass the time when you're desperate."

Griff refused to think about Raphie being lonely, or the fact that he'd only been a teenager *two years ago*. Griff's only concern was looking after Raphie in the here and now as his client. And Griff had learned that if he seemed happy, that made Raphie happy too. So he made himself smile and nod.

"Thanks," he said as pleasantly as he could manage (a sort of not-grunt) and began to put some of their perishables away. "I was thinking about starting making dinner, if you fancy?"

"Actually, um," Raphie said so shyly, it made Griff look up from the shopping bag he was unpacking. "I thought, maybe," Raphie continued, wringing his hands, "that I could c-cook for you? To say thank you for all you've done."

*Danger!* Griff's upstairs brain screeched at him, finally being useful again.

Griff shrugged, wilfully interpreting Raphie's offer in a professional manner. "That's okay," he said sincerely. "I'm just doing my job."

Raphie snorted, his nerves apparently giving him a second off. "Yeah, okay," he said warmly with an eye roll. Perhaps Griff hadn't been as convincing as he'd thought he'd been. "Don't make me pull out the prince card. I'd like to make you dinner, Griff, just because I like you. Please don't be a stuffy grumpy guts and just let me, okay?"

He bit his lip, showing a flicker of nerves again, but his eyes danced mischievously, and Griff found he didn't have the strength to fight this battle. He'd need it to conquer bigger obstacles, he was sure.

"Fine," he said with a long-suffering sigh. "I guess I'll *let* you cook us dinner." He winked at Raphie, which was probably dangerously close to flirting, but Griff just wanted Raphie to know he was only teasing.

Yes, Griff needed to keep his client safe. But they were also in a charming French cottage and on the closest thing to a holiday Raphie had ever had. If he wanted to cook something nice for them, where was the harm, really? It was like letting him play his music in the car. He'd had a lifetime of not being able to share the things he loved with anyone besides his mum and the penthouse staff. Was it really so bad that Griff was honoured that he got to be some of Raphie's firsts? These innocent ones would have to do, because there was no way Griff was going to be Raphie's first in any other sense. It would be unethical.

So Griff was going to do his best to remain professional here, but he also wasn't going to be the bad guy.

Raphie rewarded him by laughing in delight and clapping his hands. "How gracious of you," he teased right back. "Okay. I know we had something in mind in the shop, but having seen this fabulous pantry, I have a few other ideas. Would you like to pick or shall I surprise you?"

"Surprise me," Griff murmured. *Like you've been doing since the moment I set eyes on you.*

Their gazes lingered together until Griff made himself spin around and go exploring through the rest of the cottage. Fucking hell, he was his own worst enemy. He focused on assessing the remainder of the cabin's exit and entry points.

There were indeed two bedrooms, thank fucking god, both with double beds. So there would be no arguing tonight about Griff's dodgy shoulder or Raphie's royal status. They would both get *separate* beds, and be done with it.

Never mind that troublesome voice in the back of his head that whispered that Raphie would be *much* safer sleeping right next to Griff rather than on the other side of the cabin. Griff would just keep his door ajar, and trust that the long drive on top of everything else today wouldn't knock him out cold.

He was so distracted, warring with himself over whether he was being more or less responsible by sleeping in another room to his client, he didn't even realise he'd flung the living room windows wide open. His only thought was to let in some air for a minute. He couldn't leave them open, after all, just in case any pesky assassins snuck in. But he was made aware mere seconds later, with Raphie's strangled cry of *"No!"*

Griff almost tripped himself up, moving so fast to peer out of the window, resting his hands against the cool stone walls and searching for the threat outside that he figured Raphie had seen. He didn't even appreciate that Raphie had dashed across the cabin from the kitchen until he ducked under Griff's arm and grabbed the window latches, hauling them shut again with a startling bang.

Griff stared down at Raphie in shock. Raphie was gasping for air and trembling, his eyes glassy. "Sorry," Raphie whispered, scuttling back from the window and clutching his hands to his chest. "Sorry, I know it's so stupid. But Sparrow's never been outside alone in her life. She'd bolt and get lost. She's my best friend, the only friend I've had for years. I'd lose her out there, she'd be so scared, and I'd never forgive myself, and-"

He hiccuped back a sob, and Griff threw all his carefully measured plans out the (firmly closed) window. He closed the small gap between them and enveloped Raphie in his arms.

"Fuck, I didn't even think," he rasped, cupping the back of

Raphie's head and caressing little circles. "I'm a twat. You're totally right. It won't happen again."

Raphie's breaths were like the flutterings of frightened little bird's wings. But as Griff held him, he slowly calmed. "Of course," Raphie whispered. "Sorry. I just worry so much about her. I have to protect her from the world."

*And I have to protect you,* Griff thought sadly.

"You don't ever have to apologise for caring," Griff assured him. "Or for being scared. Your whole world has been turned upside down. It's my job to think of everything. I should have realised about the window. Now I won't forget, I promise."

Raphie sniffed and buried his head against Griff's shoulder, rubbing Griff's back. "Thank you," he mumbled, relief clear in those two words.

God damn it, Griff felt so *right* just holding Raphie like that. He wanted to never let him go.

Instead, he only held on to Raphie a little longer, allowing him time for his panic attack to ease. Having spent his life cooped up in a bloody penthouse, hidden away from the real world, he was bound to have some heightened anxieties about things. Knowing how much he loved his cat, it was natural that he'd be worried about her getting lost. Privately, Griff thought she almost certainly could fend for herself just fine in the wild and find her way home with no trouble, but Raphie's heart would be forever broken if they got separated.

"Oh, look," Griff said kindly, squeezing Raphie's side. "Sparrow knows you're upset." Indeed, she'd scampered up on the sofa arm near them, and was sitting back on her hind legs like a meerkat, letting her front paws drop like T-rex arms. When she saw the two men turn and give her their full attention, she gave Raphie a very cross *'merwarp!'*

Raphie chuckled wetly and rubbed his eyes. "I'm sorry,

baby girl," he said thickly, letting Griff go to scoop her up in his arms. "I'm being silly, aren't I?"

'Silly' was the last word Griff would use to describe Raphie, but he kept that to himself.

Instead, he continued to inspect the property, not just assessing the security of it for Raphie's sake, but also double-checking it was cat-proofed against Sparrow pulling a Houdini. Protecting Raphie's cat was another avenue Griff could safely channel his feelings towards Raphie without actually acting on them.

In the meantime, the cottage began smelling divine as Raphie pottered about the kitchen, listening to his music again and chatting away to Sparrow as he prepared his and Griff's dinner. When he fried fine strips of bacon in butter, Sparrow changed professions from escape artist to master thief, bobbing and weaving her way expertly past Raphie until she could snag any chunks of meat from the chopping board she could.

"Bad girl!" Raphie cried, swatting her away. His delighted and affectionate expression suggested to Griff that he didn't really mean it.

Griff almost fooled himself that he wasn't watching Raphie the whole time as he effortlessly moved around the kitchen, plucking ingredients from the shelves to make a smoky, spicy tomato sauce to go with the pasta he was cooking. But Raphie was so captivating when he was relaxed and at ease, Griff couldn't help it.

"Feel free to have a glass of wine, if you'd like," Griff said once he'd triple-checked everything he could. "Winston insisted."

Raphie bit his lip and grinned. "Really? I love red. Will you join me?"

As much as Griff would have very much enjoyed that, he

had to stay razor-sharp, for both Raphie's safety and to ensure his virtue was protected. No way was Griff going to be anything but crystal-clear right now.

"Sadly, I can't. But please, you go ahead." He almost added that seeing Raphie have a nice time was enough of a reward for him in that moment, but that would definitely have sent mixed signals, so he kept his mouth shut.

Instead, he made himself useful by laying the table for them, then cutting up and buttering the fresh crunchy loaf they'd picked up at the little shop. He couldn't remember the last time someone had cooked for him that wasn't in a restaurant, and even then, it was probably years since he'd been out for a nice dinner. That was an extravagance he could ill afford. So when Raphie placed the hot, delicious-smelling bowl of pasta in front of him, Griff felt a tiny bit overwhelmed. It was hard not to be touched that Raphie had done this, even with Griff reminding himself that Raphie was simply being practical and cooking for them both.

This wasn't a date.

Even when Raphie lit a couple of candles and plucked a rose from outside to drop in a small vase he found on one of the bookcases.

"I feel like I'm in Lady and the Tramp!" Raphie said with a giggle as he finally plopped onto his seat. "Oh, you didn't have to wait for me," he added, looking at Griff's untouched plate. "I get excited and distracted so easily." Illustrating his point, he suddenly jumped up again to fetch Sparrow's wet food, tipping it out from the packet and into a small bowl for her to have on the floor by his feet. "Right, sorry, I'm here now." He beamed at Griff from across the table.

Griff's heart overrode both his brain and his cock as they ached at Raphie's sweetness. "S'okay," he said genuinely, picking up his fork. "My mum always told me it was polite to wait for everyone to be seated. Especially the cook."

Raphie took a bite of food and moaned a little, so Griff followed suit. Wow. Yeah, Raphie knew a thing or two in the kitchen. The spaghetti dish was kind of simple but extremely tasty.

Raphie took a sip of wine, then licked his lips. "Your mum sounds nice," he said conversationally. "Are you guys close?"

Griff tried not to sigh too much. Usually, he'd shut down anyone who bothered to ask about his family – which wasn't often – but strangely, he found he wanted to tell Raphie about this stuff. Even if it was only the basics.

"We were," Griff said, sipping his water. "But…she passed away when I was in my early twenties. Cancer," he added stiffly.

Raphie swallowed, concern flooding his face. "I'm so sorry," he said hoarsely. He wasn't much younger than Griff had been when he'd lost his mum.

Griff shook his head and wound some more linguine around his fork, giving himself something to focus on. "It was about fifteen years ago now. The pain doesn't go away, exactly. But it's become duller, I guess. She was a lovely woman. Certainly always tried her best with me, even if we did butt heads from time to time."

"And your dad?" Raphie asked.

Griff laughed ruefully. "Let's just say he didn't have an elite hit squad at his disposal, but he did his best with his fists anyway." He managed a small smile at Raphie's sad expression, not wanting to dampen the mood too much. "Mum always did her best to take the brunt of it, though. She had her clever tricks to distract him or calm him down." *Not that she should have had to,* Griff thought bitterly. "Luckily, I haven't seen him for years. When I was big enough to help her, me and Mum got away from all that."

*And then she fucking got cancer and died,* Griff thought angrily. Sometimes, life sucked balls.

But this was Raphie's holiday, and Griff wasn't going to spoil it. "Now, my nan I thought was going to live forever, the old battle axe," he said with a laugh, making Raphie chuckle too, thankfully. "Oof, they don't make 'em that tough anywhere else other than the East End. A proper Bow woman, working down the market every day of her life except Christmas, and even then, she'd be off down the soup kitchen at the village hall by the afternoon, making sure no one went without a hot meal." He rubbed his chin and shook his head. "All the kids on the estate called her Nanny Christine, and she always had time for every single one of them."

He realised Raphie was smiling fondly at him, then he reached out and placed his hand over Griff's, giving it a squeeze. "Sounds like you come from a line of great women," he said sincerely. "I bet they'd be proud of you today."

Griff wasn't sure if that was true or not, but he wasn't strong enough to deny Raphie's words. Instead, he smiled back, then they shifted the conversation topic to something a little lighter as they finished their meal. Raphie was fascinated by Griff's upbringing in the thick of it in London, so Griff delighted him with stories of him and his mates being scallywags in their youth.

In turn, Raphie surprised Griff by telling him about some of the community projects he and his mum anonymously donated to every year to fund youth centres and communal gardens and the like. Even LGBT therapy schemes and retreats for vulnerable kids. In fact, that twenty-grand piece of paint-splattered art that Griff had turned his nose up at turned out to have been from a charity auction, and the artist themselves had come from an underprivileged background.

It was a good job Raphie's food was so good, otherwise Griff would have been stuck eating humble pie. He recalled his resentment upon seeing the penthouse for the first time, and silently took that judgement back. It was nice to know that Raphie and his mum hadn't been so removed from the city below them, after all.

After dinner, there was no denying they were both succumbing to exhaustion after such an eventful day. Griff insisted that Raphie take the first shower, having not had one at the bed and breakfast. Plus, even Griff with his trimmed hair could appreciate that it would take hours for Raphie to dry his locks with that small travel hairdryer he'd bought at the service station earlier. It was funny, in a way. The things Griff would never have considered before in terms of haircare were already becoming second nature to him. A bit like how he double-checked Sparrow's lead before taking her out for a short walk around the cabin, then triple-checked all the windows were still closed when they came back inside.

"So...I'll see you in the morning," Griff said awkwardly.

He'd had a shower in a fraction of the time Raphie had, but then hung around until Raphie had finished drying and braiding his hair for the night. They'd each picked their preferred bedroom, and Griff had already assured Raphie that he'd keep his door open all night.

There was nothing left to do but hit the hay, and yet...

There they were, both still standing around in the kitchen, looking at one another. Raphie was back in his panda pyjamas, and Griff was in some jogging bottoms he'd picked up as well as a T-shirt. This really shouldn't have been a sexy moment for either of them, so why the hell did it feel so charged?

Raphie nodded, stroking his plaited hair, which did nothing to help Griff's situation with his loose-fitting trousers. "Um, sure," said Raphie. "Sparrow will sleep wherever she wants. She'll probably roam around. Hopefully, you won't mistake her for an assassin if she walks on your head." He giggled nervously, but Griff shook his head.

"I'd never hurt her, I promise."

Raphie licked his lips, looking Griff up and down. "I know," he said softly. Then he blushed. "Okay, well, um… night!" He spun on his heels and scuttled away into his own room.

Griff sighed. "Night," he said gently, heading to his own bed.

He was completely shattered, ready to drop off as soon as his head hit the pillow.

So of course he ended up staring at the ceiling in the moonlight for an hour, completely wide awake. As much as his body was craving sleep, his mind was stuck on a loop, replaying all those moments he'd shared with Raphie that day. It was like his desire was a physical thing, a beast prowling around the room, swishing its tail.

God fucking damn it.

Griff gritted his teeth and balled his fists. There was nothing to be done but go to sleep. No other alternative. None. Nope.

Well…maybe he could just take another look around the cabin? Check everything was still shipshape. And it wouldn't hurt anyone to poke his head around Raphie's door and make sure he was still breathing. Right?

Griff couldn't take it any longer. He threw back the covers and marched across the room, yanking the already ajar door back…

Only to discover Raphie on the other side, his fist raised, about to knock.

For a few seconds, they just stared at each other. Raphie was the first to speak as he dropped his arm. "Hi," he said a little breathlessly, then he gulped. Griff tried very hard not to flick his eyes to Raphie's throat as he swallowed, but he failed. God, how was everything about this man so impossibly hot?

It didn't help that he was just wearing his damned panda pyjama bottoms, which he somehow managed to make hot as sin as they hung off his slim hips. Griff didn't know where the top half of the pyjamas had gone, and he didn't care.

"Hi," Griff croaked. "Are you… is everything okay?"

Raphie gulped again. "I was just standing here debating how much of a selfish wanker I'd be if I knocked and asked if you were totally, absolutely one-hundred per cent sure that you didn't want to share a bed. For safety reasons. And… um…other reasons…"

"Right…" Griff said slowly. "And? What d'you decide?"

Raphie bit his lip. "I don't know," he confessed. "You opened the door before I could."

His eyes trailed down Griff's body, and Griff could feel it like a physical caress. He may have been in joggers and a T-shirt, but in that moment, he felt naked and a little vulnerable. With Raphie, though, that was somehow a good thing.

Raphie cleared his throat. "And I suppose you were just getting a glass of water?" he asked.

Griff didn't miss the hope in his words. He licked his lips, ready to spin the lie he'd told himself about checking the cabin's security. "More…selfish wanker territory, actually," he admitted hoarsely.

For several long seconds, they just stared at each other, their chests rising and falling. Griff could feel the blood rushing down south as his skin tingled and his legs quivered.

"Raphie," he croaked, the plea clear in that one word to both of them.

Or, at least, that was what Griff assumed. Because before

he could draw another breath, Raphie launched into his arms, jumping up as Griff's hands automatically cupped his arse, hauling him up so Raphie could wrap his legs around Griff's waist. Their mouths crashed together in desperation, tongues and teeth clashing deliciously as Griff stumbled backwards, towards his bed.

# 12

# RAPHIE

OH FUCK. OH FUCK, OH FUCK, *OH FUCK.*

Raphie was in Griff's arms. They were kissing again, but this time…this time Raphie had a feeling there would be no knock on the door to interrupt them.

He was as hard as a rock, his cock pulsing as it rubbed against Griff's firm abs. It was hot as hell that Griff had just picked him up like he weighed nothing, but what was even hotter was the fact that between the frantic kissing, Raphie could tell that Griff was taking him to the bed.

Were they going to have sex?

Raphie was more desperate for that than he could even fathom. He'd been dreaming of this moment for years, and it didn't seem possible that now it could really be happening. But Raphie wasn't about to pinch himself to make sure. If this was a fantasy, he didn't care. He wanted to see it through to the end, regardless.

"Griff," he moaned as they tumbled on top of the mattress. Griff had apparently kicked back the covers when he'd got out of bed, and the sheets were warm from where he'd been lying. As dreamlike as this was, Raphie had also never felt so present in his body in his whole life. Griff's fingers dug into his back as he rolled them over, then Griff was crowding Raphie, looming over him and grinding his hips against Raphie's. Even through their clothes, the rub of their stiff cocks against each other was unbelievably hot, making Raphie cry out in desperation.

So of course Griff stopped immediately. "Raphie?" he asked in concern, brushing Raphie's hair back where some strands had come loose from his braid and were sticking to his forehead. "Are you all right?"

Raphie huffed and covered his eyes for a second, cursing but also loving Griff's deeply kind and caring nature.

"I'm bloody marvellous," he promised, managing to get a small laugh from Griff. He felt safe to look again. "I've just never done this before, so it's a bit overwhelming. But in a very, *very* good way that you should not stop – understood?"

Griff bit his lip and cupped the side of Raphie's jaw. In the moonlight, his beautiful brown eyes looked like dark pools as they flicked back and forth, questioning Raphie. "This is your first time with anyone, isn't it?" Griff asked in a low mumble.

Raphie squirmed, doing his best not to pant. "Yes," he said.

He felt like Griff had probably already guessed that from the fact that Raphie had lived up in a *tower* his whole life. However, it was also kind of sweet of him to double-check.

So long as it didn't hold them back now.

"I never thought it would be this good," Raphie whispered. "With someone like you, who I care about. I…I don't know what to think. Other than I want this so bad, Griff. I want to share this with you."

But Griff paused, his eyes narrowing. "Losing your virginity is a big deal," he said slowly. "I want this to be special for you. Are you sure-"

Raphie growled and slapped his hand over Griff's mouth

with a giggle. "I really, really like you, Griff. But you don't have to be all gentlemanly right now, even though, yeah, that's pretty hot too. Virginity is a social construct. As long as I'm enthusiastically consenting – *which I am* – that's all I ever cared about. Being with a nice guy, having fun. That's all I want. I'm not some fair maiden. I'm a horny-as-fuck twenty-one-year-old, desperate for his first dicking with a stupidly hot guy. Okay?"

Griff barked out a laugh as he dropped his head back away from Raphie's hand, snorting as he then peered back down at Raphie. "A social construct, huh?" Raphie nodded. "You read that on the internet, boffin?"

This time, Raphie didn't hold back on his squirming, writhing against Griff's hips and legs, running his hands up his solid chest, feeling every single muscled bump under his T-shirt. "I certainly did," he said playfully. "How sexy is that, huh?"

Griff growled, sending sparks straight to Raphie's already too tight cock. "Incredibly sexy, clever clogs," Griff said as he leaned down. Then he captured Raphie's mouth for a searing kiss. "I shouldn't be doing any of this," he muttered as he trailed his lips along Raphie's jaw, making him shudder from head to toe. "But fuck me, you're so hot I can't sodding fight it anymore."

Raphie laughed. "Hot, me? Yeah, okay," he said in amusement. He was a lot of things, but when compared to Griff, that was kind of ridiculous.

Except Griff suddenly broke off his kisses and burned his gaze into Raphie's, gripping the back of his head firmly. "Hot," he rasped, "as fuck. Mesmerising. Beautiful. Like no other man I've ever met. I know you've not been out in the world long, but trust me when I tell you that there's no one quite like you, Raphael d'Oro, and you are stunning. I'm lucky to even get one night with you."

Raphie stared at Griff, his mouth slightly open as he shivered, his skin running hot, then cold. How could he have been insecure earlier about what Griff really thought of him? With that answer, a person could develop an overinflated ego in no time.

Raphie managed to swallow, wetting his throat so he wouldn't croak. "Thank you," he whispered, trailing his fingers down Griff's heaving chest. He almost seemed angry, but Raphie hoped by now that he knew him better than that. He was…being passionate. Stubborn.

Raphie loved it.

"I'm lucky to have one night with you, too, Griff," he said, not breaking their gaze. "I need you to know that. I meant what I said about virginity, but this is also still incredibly special. I…I *really* like you, okay? And tonight is already better than I'd ever imagined it could be."

Griff just regarded him for a few moments, then licked his lips. "Thank you," he murmured, then captured Raphie's lips for a gentle, tender kiss.

Raphie wasn't sure at all that Griff wasn't still stuck on that stupid idea of Raphie falling for the first warm-blooded man to come his way. Did he seriously think Raphie hadn't had a couple of other bodyguards or members of staff who had turned his head? But none of them had come close to Griff. He was unique, with his kindness and *hotness.*

Raphie could work on convincing him of that later. Right now, they had more pressing matters.

Like the hard cock digging into Raphie's thigh, rubbing a wet patch through Griff's joggers and onto Raphie's pyjamas.

Holy fuck, they needed fewer clothes between them, *right now.*

Raphie had imagined this moment of getting naked with a man for the first time would hold great weight, and be almost terrifying. But as he started pulling at Griff's T-shirt,

Griff simply whipped it off in a flash before wriggling out of his joggers whilst Raphie kicked off his pyjamas.

Then…that was it. They were naked. And Raphie didn't feel scared as Griff lay back on top of him. He just felt exhilarated and free, his whole body on fire, like the best kind of electric shock was running through him. Griff's skin was scorching hot and damp as their bodies moved together, his muscles rippling and his many tattoos only just visible in the moonlight. He had a trail of thorns around his right bicep that Raphie was very keen to explore sometime later.

"What do you want, baby?" Griff murmured against Raphie's throat. As well as rolling his hips over Raphie's, he also pinched and squeezed one of Raphie's nipples, making it hard. Between that and the pet name, Raphie's mind short-circuited.

"I, uh, yes, Griff…*don't stop.*"

Griff chuckled. "Not stopping, I promise." He nibbled Raphie's ear. "But this is your moment, your fantasy. What have you been dreaming of?" He nuzzled their cheeks together, the stubble grazing deliciously together. "If you're going to insist on turning me into a ravisher of virgins, I want to do it right for you."

Raphie whimpered. "No other virgins, just me," he protested.

Griff laughed, loudly and freely, making Raphie's heart sing. "Look at that pout," Griff teased. He bit Raphie's lower lip and dragged it between his teeth. "Okay, I promise. No other virgins. Just you, okay?"

Raphie groaned, wondering if it was possible to come from just a little foreplay. "Okay," he whispered. He grabbed either side of Griff's face. "I so want you to fuck me, but I don't think I can last that long." He knew he was sounding needy, but that was because his need was fucking great. He *needed* Griff to make him come, and soon. "I want everything," he said desperately.

"You're really killing this old man, here," Griff grumbled with a laugh that resonated through Raphie's chest.

"Not old," Raphie said firmly.

Griff nipped and sucked at his collarbone, all the while still sliding their cocks together. "Fine. How about 'mature and experienced'? Someone who knows a thing or two about making a young thing like you feel fucking amazing?"

Raphie nodded frantically, his fingers scrabbling at Griff's back. "Yes, please, Griff. Anything. Everything."

"Can I suck you for a bit?" Griff asked, so serenely it almost made Raphie choke. Like Raphie hadn't been fantasising about getting a blow job since he'd discovered what one was. "I want to make you feel so good, Raphie."

Raphie nodded again, looking into Griff's eyes and gasping. "Y-yes," he managed to utter. "That sounds great. Please, thank you."

Griff snorted and kissed Raphie's lips affectionately. "Those manners are going to be the end of me," he said fondly. "I'll do a 'spiffing' job for you, okay?"

Raphie half-laughed, half-groaned as Griff kissed his way down his chest. He took a while to suck on both of Raphie's nipples, stroking Raphie's weeping cock with his calloused hand as he did. His pace was enough to keep Raphie hard, but not so he was in danger of coming any time soon.

"Fucking tease," Raphie said with a laugh, shaking and gasping. He ran his fingers through Griff's short, dark hair, watching obsessively as he kissed down Raphie's stomach, nuzzling his thatch of hair before finally, mercifully, licking a stripe up Raphie's straining length. "Holy fucking cocksucker!" Raphie shrieked. So much for manners.

Griff hummed fondly, kissing and licking Raphie's head like an ice lolly on a warm summer's day. Raphie was leaking and writhing, not sure exactly what he was chasing other than *more*. But Griff knew, slipping his lips over Raphie's tip, and wrapping his hand around the base to squeeze and stroke. Raphie's hips bucked, but Griff used his other hand to hold Raphie down. Somehow, that made it even better.

It was such a vast improvement over Raphie's hand. Wet and hot and *holy fuck* when Griff swallowed it was like Raphie's brains were trying to escape through his cock. Griff twisted his hand around the base and used his tongue along with his lips on the tip, and Raphie was babbling nonsense, tears running down either side of his face in pure pleasure.

But it was when Griff looked up through his dark eyelashes, his gaze meeting Raphie's, that he almost tipped over the edge. "G-Griff!" Raphie shouted in warning.

Griff squeezed the bottom of his shaft, hard, and came off the top half with a pop. "Do you want to come down my throat?" he asked, like he was offering Raphie some of the French chocolate they'd bought earlier. It was so dirty, but it was also ridiculously sweet. His expression was eager, but his demeanour was calm.

Raphie breathed deeply a couple of times. What *did* he want?

"I want this to last," he whispered. This was his first time having sex, with a man who honestly looked like some kind of god, or at least an action movie hero. He was also so kind and caring, and there was no guarantee Raphie would get another chance with him again. They'd both mentioned about only having one night.

Raphie was already panicking about it being over too quickly.

"Hey, hey," said Griff. He crawled quickly up Raphie's body and hugged him, kissing his cheek beside his ear. Immediately, Raphie felt himself calm. "I'm not going anywhere, okay? We have all night." He sighed and stroked

Raphie's sides as Raphie clung to him. "This may just be a 'social construct', but that doesn't mean I don't want it to be great for you."

"And great for you," Raphie mumbled. *Fuck*, he was overwhelmed.

Griff chuckled. "I'm not going to complain if it's great for me as well," he assured Raphie. He kissed his cheek again, then lifted himself back a little so they could see each other. His thumb rubbed reassuringly along Raphie's jaw, and the weight of his body over Raphie's was grounding.

Raphie sighed, lifting his hand to cup the side of Griff's face. "In theory, the 'social construct' thing made so much sense. But, uh, in practice..."

"It's bollocks?" Griff suggested with a grin.

Raphie slapped his arm lightly and huffed. "I still don't think I'm going to magically wake up a 'real' man tomorrow. But...there's a lot of feelings going on here." He licked his lips. "Because of you."

Griff's expression was kind before he gently kissed Raphie's lips. "Good," he said pointedly. "Lots of feelings is the way it should be. But if you want to stop – if it's too much-"

"No!" Raphie blurted, then he cleared his throat. Griff looked mildly startled. "No. I kind of want the opposite." He trailed his hand down Griff's neck and along his collarbone. "I want to make it last. Not, like, edging" -another thing he'd read about- "but not rushed. If, um, that's okay?"

Griff sighed affectionately and lifted Raphie's hand, kissing the palm, then placing it against his stubbly jaw to nuzzle against it. "Anything you want is okay. How about... some more foreplay, then we can frot? That way we can come together."

Raphie bit his lip. "Is that boring?"

Griff snorted. "With you, nothing is boring. I'd hope it

would feel fucking awesome, and we can take it nice and slow."

Raphie nodded, trying to weigh up every option. "If we're going to go slowly, should we just do anal, then?" he asked, his heartbeat picking up. Even just saying the word flooded him with nerves. Saying the words felt clunky, and he instantly wished he'd tried to word it sexier.

He was pretty sure Griff spotted that. He raised his eyebrow down at him. "There's nothing 'just' about that. Is that what you *want?*"

Half an hour ago, Raphie would have said that getting fucked into the mattress by Griff was absolutely what he'd wanted. But now...

"Maybe...maybe the foreplay stuff sounds nice?" he said, posing it as a question. He'd got into his head, and lost all confidence. He'd read a library's worth of smut, and imagined this moment for so long. Nothing compared to the real thing, though, and he was worrying he was ruining it. "But if we're only going to do this once, perhaps we should-"

"Raphie, no," Griff interrupted. "That's no reason to jump into anything. I...there are lots of reasons we shouldn't be doing this, mostly because I've thrown all professional conduct out of the window." He rolled his eyes and huffed. "But I'm not sure we can get that cat back in the bag now."

Raphie shook his head, trying not to get his hopes up too much, but also wanting to agree. "Can't close Pandora's Box."

Griff nibbled his lip, seeming visibly torn. In fact, it was almost like the other closed-off Griff was coming back.

Raphie couldn't have that. He surged up and caught Griff's lips for a needy kiss. "No bags," he whined playfully. "No boxes. Just me, and I'm very, *very* horny, okay?"

That seemed to break the tension, thank fuck. Griff chuckled and nuzzled Raphie's neck, kissing along his jaw before he looked him in the eye again.

"Okay," said Griff. "All I'm saying is there's no pressure either way, but don't think of this as your only chance. With me or anyone else. Let's just focus on having a good time tonight, and doing what makes us feel good *right now*, okay?"

Raphie slowly exhaled, feeling some of the pressure lift from him. "Yeah," he said softly, caressing the side of Griff's face. "That's a brilliant idea. Clever clogs," he added, feeling some of his playfulness come back.

Sure enough, Griff grinned. "I only have brilliant ideas, boffin," he said warmly, then he seized Raphie's mouth for a kiss. The fire was coming back to life between them, now they knew where they both stood. Griff hummed. "How do you feel about me rimming you?"

Raphie spluttered. Licking out his arsehole? Really? "Uh…" he said, unsurely. "Is it hygienic?"

Griff threw his head back and laughed. Then he brushed Raphie's damp hair back again. "So sweet," he murmured. "Yeah, it's just like a blow job. Besides, you had a shower like an hour ago, so I wouldn't worry about that." He waggled his eyebrows suggestively. "But it *feels* fucking awesome, and in my experience, it takes most guys a while to get the confidence to get good at it. What do you say? You want to let this old dog show you a new trick?"

Raphie hit Griff's arm again, this time with a bit more vehemence. "*Stop* calling yourself old, okay? I know you're joking, but you're hot and I'm not a baby." He bobbed his head. "At the same time, yes, please, Griff. Use your back catalogue of sex experience to impress me, please."

Griff snorted and rubbed their cocks together, sucking on Raphie's pulse point. "Lie on your front, and I'll do my best."

Raphie caught his lips for a kiss, then did as he was told, flipping over, then pressing the side of his face against the pillow. He was nervous and curious, his heart fluttering and his breath a little ragged. But ultimately, he trusted Griff.

Especially when his lover took his time pressing little kisses to the base of Raphie's spine and kneading the backs of his thighs. By the time Griff's hands and lips reached the globes of Raphie's arse, he felt like putty being shaped to Griff's will.

He moaned as Griff nudged Raphie's legs apart, making the bed dip as Griff shifted his position. Raphie's eyelids had drifted closed, so he didn't see exactly what Griff was doing down his end of the bed, but Raphie was so relaxed he was more than happy with whatever Griff decided to do.

But when he pulled Raphie's cheeks apart and blew gently on his hole, Raphie wasn't quite as prepared as he'd thought he'd be. He jerked and yelped, then groaned in embarrassment. "Sorry," he mumbled into the pillow as Griff laughed good-naturedly at him. "That was good. Um…do it again?"

"As you wish," he said with a warm chuckle. He kissed the curve of Raphie's bum and massaged the cheeks. The sensation of feeling air against his hole was a little strange, but Raphie was getting used to it.

So much so that when Griff blew against it again, Raphie shuddered and enjoyed the moment, rather than jumping out of his skin. "Oh, wow," he moaned, gripping the bed sheets. "Griff, that's – *fuck!*"

He took every preconception he'd ever had about rimming back. The second Griff's tongue licked Raphie's tight ring of muscle, it was as if his whole body burst into flames.

Griff hummed and kissed his hole, then licked again. "Nice?" he asked, his tone definitely teasing.

"*Uh-huh,*" Raphie garbled into the pillow. "Less talky-talk, more eaty-eat, please."

Griff laughed, but he was already holding Raphie's cheeks well apart, darting his tongue out for little licks. Then he dragged his tongue up the entire length of Raphie's crack, and Raphie rutted his cock against the mattress as its previous hardness began to return.

"You like that, gorgeous?" Griff asked, licking and kissing Raphie's most intimate area.

Raphie whimpered and nodded before he remembered that Griff couldn't see him. "Y-yeah," he stammered. "So good. Don't stop."

"I won't," Griff promised.

And he meant it.

The man had a serious talent. Raphie had absolutely no clue how long he lay there, grinding his hips against the mattress whilst Griff kissed and sucked and licked his hole loose. It was like a massage, but a hundred times better. Raphie was a puddle of quivering jelly by the time Griff began stroking his dripping wet hole with a lone finger, probing at the entrance.

"Yes, please," Raphie begged sleepily. He'd fingered himself plenty of times, and had even worked up the courage to order a couple of toys to be discreetly delivered to the penthouse in recent years. But those things were *nothing* compared to the feeling of Griff's thick finger penetrating him.

He probably only pushed inside an inch or so, but to Raphie, it felt huge and momentous. And fucking *delicious*. His own fingers were always at an odd angle, and the dildos he played with were generally room temperature at best and pretty rigid. Feeling Griff's hot finger moving inside him was like nothing else, and Raphie writhed against the bed, on the verge of sobbing.

"Yes, *yes*," he cried into the pillow, shaking and sweating. He'd never felt so alive.

Griff sucked and kissed Raphie's aching balls, licking along the strip of skin between them and his hole. "Do you still want to come together?" he asked, slowing his pulsing finger down.

Raphie took in several shaking breaths, blinking his eyes back open. It took him a second to process Griff's question. "Yes, oh, yes," he said, looking over his shoulder once his wits returned to him. "You're fucking gorgeous, you know that?" Raphie said almost reverently.

He looked between Griff's amused face and his red, shiny dick as Griff crawled up the bed and lay down beside him. Raphie licked his lips. He'd finally seen another man's cock in real life, and he was *not* disappointed. It was a little intimidating thinking about trying to fit that in his arse or even down his throat, but that didn't mean Raphie wasn't eager to try.

"Do you want to touch me?" Griff asked in a low rumble, rubbing Raphie's back soothingly. His words were the most delicious invitation. Raphie nodded, reaching out to run his fingers over the hot length, awestruck at the differences between his own cock and Griff's throbbing member. Griff shuddered and sucked in a breath. "That's it. Feels good."

Raphie rolled over onto his side so he could get a better angle, then caught Griff's lips for a kiss as he wrapped his hand more confidently around his cock. Griff moaned and hugged him closer, clearly liking what Raphie was doing.

But Raphie didn't want to stop there. He thought of how good Griff had made him feel, and he was desperate to not fuck up and prove to Griff that he could keep up with him. He didn't want to be a clumsy virgin who might get it all wrong.

But…he thought he'd be rubbish at learning sign language and badminton before he'd tried them, and he'd turned out to be pretty fucking awesome at both of those things. So how did he know he wasn't some sort of cocksucking protégée?

He could be a dick-gobbling champion in the making for all he knew.

"What are you giggling about?" Griff asked Raphie, stroking his head, clearly amused. Raphie stopped kissing down Griff's wiry happy trail and leaned his face against Griff's rough palm.

"How I'm going to be brilliant at my first blow job," he said with a grin.

Griff raised his eyebrows, smirking fondly. "Is that so, boffin? You study them on the internet?"

Raphie nodded. "Uh…but if there's anything in particular you like?" he probed.

Griff rubbed his thumb against Raphie's lower lip, sending thrills straight to Raphie's still hard cock. "Just wrap your lips over your teeth, then do whatever feels comfortable to you." He laughed softly. "It's pretty difficult to totally fuck up a blow job."

Raphie nodded. Then on impulse, he caught the tip of Griff's thumb with his tongue and sucked on it, looking Griff in the eyes as he did.

His lover groaned and bit his own lip. "Fuck, yeah, gorgeous. Like that. You're so impossibly beautiful."

Raphie was already pretty flushed, but he still felt more heat rise on his cheeks. He liked Griff calling him beautiful a *lot.*

Raphie had thought a great deal about what having a cock in his mouth would feel like, but he hadn't thought much about the taste. As he slipped his lips over the red-hot tip of Griff's length, the slippery pre-cum hit his tongue, as well as Griff's musk, such a primal masculine taste and smell that Raphie wanted nothing more than to drink it all in. But he inhaled a bit too eagerly as he was trying to swallow all of Griff down, and – mortifyingly – he ended up coughing and spluttering his way off again, his eyes watering.

"Hey, easy," Griff said tenderly, caressing the back of Raphie's head. "Take it slowly. There's no rush."

But Raphie huffed, determined to be good at this. So he tried again, copying what Griff had done to him. He only attempted to get the top third of the cock in his mouth, then he wrapped his hand around the rest and began to stroke.

Griff inhaled sharply through his teeth. "Oh, fuck, *yes*. Like that, gorgeous."

Knowing that Raphie was doing a good job and making Griff feel amazing was one of the biggest thrills of his life – and that included jumping off a bloody building yesterday morning. Griff gasped and swore as his hips bucked. For someone whose job it was to stay in control, Raphie got a huge thrill from feeling him lose it under his touch.

Raphie bobbed his head and sucked, almost forgetting to breathe through his nose. He was so hell-bent on doing this the best he could. Griff's cock felt *amazing* on his tongue. But it wasn't long before Griff was tugging on his braided hair.

"Raphie, Raphie," he gasped. He pulled on Raphie's arm, encouraging him back up the bed.

Worry flooded Raphie's body. "Did I do something wrong?"

"What? No!" Griff spluttered, getting Raphie to straddle his hips. "Too good. Come here. Kissing now. Come together. *Now*."

Oh…there was that bossy Griff that Raphie had loved so much before. Griff wasn't complaining about Raphie's performance. He was close to coming.

Raphie panted as he straddled Griff, lining up their cocks so Griff could start wanking them off together. Raphie whimpered and dug his fingers into Griff's tattooed chest, wondering if maybe they could do this again, but next time, Raphie would really ride Griff's hard, throbbing cock in his arse.

Not that this wasn't good. It was incredible, actually. "Griff…" Raphie whispered, feeling his own climax finally start to really crest.

"Let your hair down?" Griff grunted, his eyes wide and his face, neck, and chest all red and blotchy. "Please."

Raphie had done that. He'd undone this stunning, stand-offish man, bringing him to a climax that was consuming him.

Without needing to tear his eyes away from Griff's, Raphie reached behind himself and tugged the hairband free. Then he used both hands to shake all his hair out like Griff had requested, elongating his body as he rutted in time with Griff's jerking hand.

"Fuck *me*, you look like a merman," Griff gasped.

Raphie's hair was probably going to tangle up in seconds, but he didn't care. He was freer than he'd ever been in his whole *life*. Griff used his other hand to paw at Raphie's chest, then he wrapped it around the side of Raphie's neck. He pulled him down a little, so Raphie's hair fell like a curtain around them. They were in their own little world, and it was perfect.

Griff squeezed the side of Raphie's neck. Just like when he'd held Raphie's hip down, being held in place sent a thrill shooting through Raphie's whole body.

Literally. "Griff!" he warned as his orgasm peaked, but this time, Griff didn't stop.

"Come all over me, beautiful," he rasped, arching his back and speeding up his hand even faster. Raphie's cock felt so impossibly amazing against Griff's in his strong hand, he couldn't hold on any longer.

"*Griff!*" he cried as his climax surged through him. But as he began to spurt thick white ropes of cum, so did Griff. Griff gnashed his teeth and bellowed, his skin red and damp and utterly delicious. They mixed their mess on his hairy chest, dripping over Griff's hard abs and exquisite ink. Raphie felt wrung out. He'd *never* come that hard before. It was like he was made of fireworks.

Griff jerked and spurted a little longer, gasping underneath Raphie in an erotic display of manliness. Then he grappled for Raphie, tangling his hands in Raphie's hair and dragging him down for a tight hug against his sticky chest.

Raphie had been right. His hair was already a complete mess. But his heart was full to burst, and that was all that really mattered in that moment.

## 13

## GRIFF



*What have I done?*

Griff bit his lip, using a feather-light touch to brush some of Raphie's hair from where it was stuck to his forehead. He was dead asleep, which Griff couldn't blame him for. It was four o'clock in the morning, for heaven's sake. He didn't move a muscle as Griff carefully unstuck another couple of strands.

Maybe he was the worst kind of arsehole, but as Griff lay there in the pre-dawn light, his eyes travelling over his lover's peaceful form, he couldn't bring himself to regret a sodding thing.

He knew he'd had great sex before. Spectacular one-night stands and tender, mind-blowing moments with men he'd really loved. But nothing quite like what he'd just shared with Raphie.

As Griff lay there, captivated by something so simple as watching Raphie breathe, he was torn between trying to work out just what made this man so astonishingly unique, or just accepting his fate, which was that of a totally shafted bastard.

They had three days to get to Campanula. And as much as it hurt to acknowledge it, at that point, Raphie would in all likeliness ascend to the throne and into a whole new life. Griff could only hope to have the honour of his company until then.

And then he'd have to let him go.

Those were just the facts. There was no changing them. Raphie was a prince, and about to step into a completely different world where Griff couldn't follow him.

But for the next couple of days, it was just going to be the two of them. Griff had tried to fight this unbelievable chemistry between them. He really had. But ultimately it had been like trying to ask the moon not to shine. Raphie was a force of nature that Griff was utterly hopeless to resist.

And after their time together last night, he didn't want to. *Bloody hell.* It was as if Griff had been sleepwalking for decades, and Raphie had brought him back to life. With his earnest little speeches and heartfelt pleas of lust and painfully honest longing. Not to mention his brains and his smile and his big, welcoming heart.

Griff felt incredibly honoured to have been the first man to make love with him.

*But you won't be the last,* that nasty voice in the back of his head sneered. Griff was starting to think that voice would never be satisfied, no matter what.

Yes, okay. It was incredibly hurtful to think of someone else touching Raphie the way Griff had. But this was real life, not a fairy tale. There was no 'happily ever after' here. Griff was just a chapter in Raphie's life, and if he was very lucky, it would be one they could both cherish for years to come.

Griff had wanted tonight to be special for Raphie, and he hoped he'd achieved that. Raphie had certainly seemed content, and had passed out like a log mere seconds after Griff had cleaned them both up from the delicious mess they'd made. Griff had drifted off not long after, with Raphie in his arms, but he was never really off duty in situations like this, and it hadn't been long before he'd jerked awake.

Oh, who was he kidding? He'd never had a situation like *this* in his entire life. And now he'd put himself in an impossible predicament. Was he going to get careless making puppy dog eyes at Raphie? He'd never forgive himself if he allowed anything to happen to this incredible man.

Or…would it be like the Spartans of Ancient Greece? Where warriors were encouraged to sleep with each other so as to develop relationships and feelings, ensuring that they would protect each other on the battlefield far more than they would a mere comrade. Griff had always been intrigued by that concept, but he'd never fully understood it until now. What he felt for Raphie left him with no illusion as to just how far he'd go to protect him.

He'd die to save Raphie.

Griff swallowed as Raphie snuffled in his sleep. He was on his side, using Griff's arm as a pillow. The fact that Griff's hand had pins and needles should have been a warning sign that this was wishful thinking. Crossing a line and not only developing feelings for his client, but *acting* on them, was extremely dangerous. But Griff wasn't clever like Raphie was. He couldn't switch off his heart now.

Griff would be his warrior, and he knew for sure he'd do anything to keep him safe. He'd been trained to take a bullet for any client. Griff would throw himself in front of Raphie without a second thought. Not because it was his duty, though. But because he wanted to.

Griff sighed. "I'm so fucked," he grumbled. He laid his hand carefully on Raphie's chest, feeling his heart beat and his ribcage rise and fall. But he couldn't bring himself to be to mad about it.

Ever since he'd set foot inside that penthouse, it had been one impossible-to-predict scenario after another. Griff could drive himself insane trying to control everything over the next few days, or he could use all his energy on making sure Raphie had the best protection possible. And…just maybe… Griff could help Raphie explore his sexuality.

It probably wasn't ethical, but Griff could worry about that later. He was done fighting this pull between them for now.

He must have started dozing off. Because the next thing he knew he had four paws stomping all over his face. "Gah!" he gasped, immediately awake. Raphie was still curled up next to him on his arm, but luckily this was not an assassin come to kill them both.

Hopefully.

Sparrow sat on the bed and glared at Griff in the early morning light streaming around the curtains. Her tail swished angrily, and her purr was low, like a chainsaw.

Griff bit his lip. "I can explain," he whispered softly.

Sparrow sat up on her hind legs and let her front paws hang, her jade-blue eyes narrow and fixed on Griff as she tilted her head.

"No, seriously," Griff hissed. "I really like your dad, okay? I'm not taking advantage, I swear. I'll protect him."

The cat lowered her front paws back down, then flopped onto her side. Griff was almost tempted to pet her exposed belly with his free hand, but he wasn't that much of an idiot. He sensed there might have been a hint of a truce between them, however.

"He's a great person," Griff said sincerely to Sparrow. "But I suppose you know that already. I just wanted to say it out loud." He shook his head sadly. "I don't have anyone in my life who I can tell I've met an amazing man. Enby," he corrected with a little frown. Sparrow licked her nose and blinked at him. "See, he's teaching me things. Like about being nonbinary. He's funny and hot as sin and...oh Sparrow," he said heavily. "I have to remember this is only for a few days. After that, I'll have to let him go. I-"

He cleared his throat, which was suddenly tight.

"Will you look after him, then?" he asked. "Be the best guard kitty? He has a big heart, you see. He can't just give it away to any old arsehole." He pointed at his chest. "One's enough. You might need to remind him of that when I'm gone."

Sparrow narrowed her eyes at him. Then in an instant, she was up on her feet again, marching over the bed. She hopped up on the pillow and proceeded to stomp over Griff's head, down his face, then turned in a circle on his chest before curling up there.

Griff blinked at her face, mere inches away. She was flexing her paws, extending her sharp claws each time. Like she was saying to Griff 'You *better* not hurt him, or you'll have me to answer to'.

Griff sighed and risked petting between her ears. Surprisingly, she let him. "I'll do my best, I promise," he whispered.

"Who you talkin' to?" Raphie slurred. He yawned and rubbed his eyes, still mostly asleep.

"Just Sparrow," Griff said. He leaned over to cup the side of Raphie's face, gently kissing his forehead. "Go back to sleep, beautiful."

Raphie sighed and snuggled against him even closer. "Okay, Griff," he said happily.

Griff raised his eyebrow at Sparrow. "See?" he whispered. "I'm taking care of him already. Making sure he gets his eight hours."

Sparrow didn't look all that impressed. But she also didn't

seem interested in moving from Griff's chest any time soon. She glared at Griff for a few more moments, then closed her eyes and lowered her head onto her paws. Soon, her rhythmic purrs filled the room, lulling Griff back to sleep for another couple of hours.

He dreamed. The details slipped through the ether as soon as he tried to concentrate on them, but he knew he was in a busy crowd, trying to push through the opposite way to where everyone else was walking. He held Raphie's hand tightly, pulling him along behind him, but Raphie was struggling. The throng was trying to tear them apart…Griff lost his grip on Raphie's fingers…

He awoke with a start, gasping for air. The sun was fully risen, so once Griff had blinked the dream away, he could see he was alone, tangled in the rumpled sheets.

Hang on. Alone wasn't good.

Immediately, he flew out of bed naked and launched himself into the belly of the cabin…

…where Raphie was totally fine, dressed in his pyjamas, his hair in a messy ponytail, cooking bacon in a frying pan.

He spun around in shock just as Griff managed to grab a cushion from the sofa to hide his modesty. Still, Raphie burst out laughing, delight dancing in his eyes as he covered his mouth. "Good morning?" he said, raising a questioning eyebrow.

Griff cleared his throat. "You weren't there when I woke up. I, um, might have panicked."

"Aww. I was making you breakfast," Raphie said cheerfully, picking up a spatula and waving it around. Then he looked again at Griff who was still chewing his lip and willing his heartbeat to calm down. "Oh, shit," Raphie said, suddenly realising. "Did you think I'd been kidnapped or something?"

Griff shrugged. "That *is* my job," he mumbled. He felt silly for not smelling the bacon before he'd bolted out the door. Now he was fully awake, he realised the mouth-watering aroma was drifting through the whole cottage. But he'd been too afraid to even notice it.

All he'd registered was that Raphie had been gone.

A part of his brain had also irrationally thought that Raphie might have snuck out after their one-night stand. But this wasn't London, and Raphie wasn't a random hook-up. He wasn't going to abandon Griff in the middle of nowhere France.

But to see that he was actually cooking Griff breakfast in bed was a little too much. This guy was too pure for this world. What had Griff done to deserve to cross paths with him, even if only for a short time?

Raphie placed the spatula back down against the pan and made his way over to Griff. "I'm sorry I scared you," he said, slipping his arms around Griff's waist. He rested his head on Griff's chest as Griff wrapped his free arm around Raphie's back. His dishevelled hair was a pertinent reminder of their time together the night before, even if the rest of Raphie smelled like his shower gel. Griff kissed the top of his head.

"It's okay," Griff assured him. "I just worry about you, beautiful." He noticed that Raphie seemed to like that pet name above the others, and sure enough, he shuddered against Griff, a smile just visible on his face, which was tucked against Griff's shoulder.

"Thank you," Raphie said. Then he kissed Griff's naked pec.

Griff kind of loved how quickly they'd fallen into this physical intimacy. It was probably for the best, so they could make the most of the few days they had together and not dance around their feelings.

Their time together might be short, but at least it would be honest.

Raphie sighed and smiled up at Griff. "You hungry? I am, so I figured you'd be."

Griff nodded and hummed. "Starving," he agreed. "That smells amazing. Is that stuff we bought yesterday?"

"And a few extras from Winston's pantry," Raphie said happily. "It'll be a few more minutes."

"Do I have time for a quick shower?" Griff asked. He'd had a clean up the night before, but he wanted to be at his best for Raphie.

"Sure!" Raphie spun around and skipped back to the kitchen. "Shall we eat out here? It'll probably be easier than in bed, though less romantic," he mused.

Griff shook his head and tsked. "Out here is still plenty romantic, believe me. Um, thank you."

Raphie blushed, and Griff (and his modesty pillow) went to the bathroom for the world's fastest freshen-up. He didn't want to keep Raphie waiting after he'd gone to all that effort.

By the time Griff had gone through the shower and yanked his joggers and T-shirt from the night before back on, Raphie was just dishing up a mountain of food. Sparrow was winding around his feet, meowing impertinently. Her plan was obviously to either wail Raphie into submission, or trip him up so the bacon landed on the floor anyway. Wailing won out.

"Oh, you are so spoiled," Raphie chided as he dropped a small piece from his own plate down for her, but he sounded anything but cross.

He'd made himself and Griff bacon, scrambled eggs, buttery toast, and fried tomatoes, all topped off with baked beans he must have found in the cupboard. They hadn't had time to really discuss breakfast menu options the day before, but Griff would never have imagined them sharing a full English in a post-coital glow. As Raphie placed two mugs of tea in front of them and sat down, Griff reached over the table and took his hand, encouraging them to look at one another.

"Thank you," he said sincerely.

Raphie bit his lip as he smiled. "It's just breakfast," he said with a shrug.

But Griff shook his head. "Not just for breakfast. Last night was special. Thank you for trusting me." He really did feel like Raphie had given him a gift by sharing his first night of intimacy with him.

Raphie exhaled loudly and gave a shaky laugh. "Oh, thank *fuck,*" he said enthusiastically as he squeezed Griff's hand. "I was kind of terrified you were going to be all stiff about it and pretend it hadn't happened or say it couldn't happen again."

Griff lifted his hand to kiss Raphie's knuckles. "Let's skip all that bollocks, yeah? We only have a few days before you have to be in Campanula. Things will get complicated then, we both know that." *Because there's no way anyone will let me be with you once you're king,* Griff thought sadly, but he didn't let it show on his face. "Until then, I was hoping we could keep um…"

"Fucking?" Raphie asked excitedly.

Griff snorted. "I was going to say 'being close', you dirty thing."

Raphie smirked and kissed Griff's fingers before taking his hand back to dive into his breakfast. "All right, if you're going to insist on being all romantic," he grumbled. But he winked at Griff before sucking on the prongs of his fork, waggling his eyebrows suggestively.

"Oh, shit, I've created a monster," Griff pretended to gripe, but they both knew he didn't mean it.

Something relaxed in his chest as they ate breakfast and made easy conversation. It wasn't often life was kind to him, but he figured he could enjoy this turn of fate for a little while at least.

"So," he said, trying his best to sound like a bodyguard and not an anxious teen asking his first boyfriend out on a date. "Will you be able to see the council and the royal family as soon as we get to Campanula?"

Raphie gave him a thoughtful look as they began clearing up the table. "You know, that's a really good question. I actually don't think they'll all be gathered until the day of the coronation. It's summer, so the council is on holiday. We'll probably have to hang around literally until midday-ish on Friday before the ceremony in the evening."

Griff tried *incredibly* hard not to grin. He'd asked the question for *professional* reasons.

He wasn't fooling anyone, least of all himself. But if the logistics worked in their favour, he refused to feel guilty about it.

"I was thinking," he said as they washed and dried the dishes, keeping his eyes on his hands as they worked, "that we've got a few days' grace. Part of me wants to push on, but the truth is, we're safer here than anywhere else. We could keep on driving today and end up trying to find somewhere safe to hide out in Campanula for a day or two, risking being found out by the assassins whilst we're hanging around to see the council. Or we could stay here an extra day. I think we'd be better to rest up another night, then try and make the remainder of the drive in one go."

He peeked a look at Raphie, who raised his eyebrows. "Really?" he asked, sounding unsure, which of course made Griff unsure, because he was going *soft*.

"Only if you're okay with that," he mumbled. "We could probably find somewhere in Campanula to lie low, but it wouldn't be as secure as here."

Raphie beamed shyly at him. "Another day in this picturesque cabin with my hot, sexy man? Oh, no, how will I cope?"

Griff flicked soapsuds at him, trying to mask his relief, with the added bonus of making Raphie squeal deliciously. "Okay, then," Griff said with a nod. "That sounds like a good strategy. We don't want any nasty surprises in Campanula."

Raphie hummed, grinning like he probably knew precisely how full of shit Griff really was.

He cleared his throat. "So, what do you want to do today?" Griff asked. He wasn't very used to having time off. When he did, he usually went for a run, or had a beer and a frozen pizza in front of the TV. Unsurprisingly, Raphie had a much better idea than that.

"How about we spend the morning on the beach?" he suggested excitedly. "I know it's only a little lake one, but it's a million times better than my swimming pool. I mean, I *know* I was lucky to have my own rooftop pool," he added sheepishly. "I'm not that out of touch. But this is a *beach*. We could take some towels to lie on actual sand, and Winston has a collection of books we could maybe borrow from." He danced on his toes and cupped his hands together in anticipation of Griff's answer.

"Sounds brilliant," Griff said honestly.

He wasn't much of a reader, but he could check the sports news on his phone and just relax for a little while. Well, not relax. He was always on duty until Raphie was safe. There was no one to take shifts with here. But he very much liked the idea of the sun on his skin, and a happy Raphie by his side.

Winston's cabin was stocked with all kinds of useful things, like the sunscreen they discovered in the bathroom. They didn't have swimming trunks, but they'd each bought a pack of underwear at the supermarket and they both figured a pair of those would do. Raphie mercifully thought to use Winston's washing machine to clean the clothes that they'd been wearing over the past few days. That way, they'd be able to get to Campanula without having to start turning things inside out.

As she was sleeping in a patch of sun anyway, they decided to leave Sparrow safe inside the cabin rather than tether her lead outside and be worrying every second that she might break free. Again, Griff wasn't used to a cat needing so much protection from herself. On the estate where he grew up, cats just came and went as they pleased. But Griff believed Sparrow, as capable as she was, wouldn't want to get lost and separated from Raphie, so keeping her secure like she was used to was the best option.

Before long, Griff and Raphie were set up on the little sandy shore with the lake lapping near their feet, sparkling in the sunshine. It was Griff's favourite kind of weather. Warm, without being stiflingly hot.

He had expected Raphie to immediately sprawl out and lose himself in one of the books he'd found on the shelves. Instead, he sat up on his towel, retrieving a brightly coloured plastic thing from the bag of stuff he'd lugged outside. It was pink and spiky and moulded into a shape that fit perfectly in his palm. When he pulled the band out of his hair and slipped it over his wrist, Griff understood that it was a kind of brush without a handle.

Raphie swung his mane over his shoulder and began to work his way through the tangles at the base of his white-blond locks. Griff swallowed, watching in a mesmerised fashion. He recalled the way Raphie had shaken his hair loose at Griff's request as they'd frotted to completion the night before. He'd looked like an other-worldly creature. A merman, an elf, a sexy nymph hell-bent on driving Griff crazy.

For a while, Griff watched Raphie work. Raphie seemed so lost in his task, Griff wasn't sure if he was aware that Griff was observing him. But eventually, Griff's curiosity got the better of him.

He was obsessed with that bloody hair.

He licked his lips and peered at Raphie over his sunglasses so Raphie could see more of his face. "Could I try?" he eventually worked up the courage to ask.

Raphie stopped brushing and looked over at Griff with interest. "You want to brush my hair?" he asked, sounding hesitant.

Griff nodded. "Only if that's something you might like? My mum always said it was one of the nicest feelings. I did it a lot for her when she was sick."

It felt strange for him to bring up a memory of his mum in her last months and not have it stab him in the heart. But in fact, by sharing that little titbit about her, it made Griff feel like she and Raphie were able to become closer in a way. They'd never know each other, but in that moment, he couldn't help but feel like they almost did.

"Oh, that's lovely," Raphie said, touching Griff's knee with his fingertips and smiling fondly. "I'd be honoured if you wanted to have a go with my hair. That's sweet of you."

They moved around so Raphie was sat cross-legged in front of Griff, his hair falling behind his back again. Griff could see which bit on the right had been de-tangled already, so he carefully sectioned that side off, draping it over Raphie's shoulder. Then he started at the base of the next bit, like Raphie had done and his mum had taught him, and began to gently brush.

It was one of the most intimate things Griff had ever done. Raphie's little contented sighs as Griff patiently worked through the knots were like balm on Griff's soul. He almost felt like he fell into a trance as he worked the brush over and over, gently pulling down until the hair became smooth and he could move on to the next section. The only other sounds that filled the air were the rustling of the trees and the lapping of the water against the sand.

Griff interspersed his brushing with little touches to Raphie's skin. He grazed his fingertips or the back of his knuckles against Raphie's arms, sides, and thighs, each time eliciting a beautiful hum from Raphie. He swayed slightly as Griff worked, never flinching, even if Griff accidentally tugged an unexpected knot too hard.

When Griff had made sure Raphie's whole head was tangle-free, he laid it all down Raphie's back again and ran his hands over the locks a few times, feeling how the hair had warmed in the sunshine.

"Was that okay?" Griff asked.

Raphie sighed deeply. "Lovely. So lovely. Do you want to help me braid it?" he asked over his shoulder. He had a kind of serene, punch-drunk look on his face.

Griff smiled, ridiculously thrilled that he'd done a good job. He'd never tried anything like that with a lover before. The only thing he could vaguely compare it to was taking a shower together and washing his partner. But this was a hundred times better than that. Maybe because Raphie's hair was so unique to him. Or maybe because he'd appeared to respond so well to Griff's ministrations, but Griff was tingling all over. It was like he was floating on a cloud with Raphie, far away from all their problems.

"I don't know how to plait hair," he admitted. "Could you teach me?"

Raphie giggled. "Of course. I'm the boffin, remember?" He fluttered his eyelashes and looked at Griff with such affection it took Griff's breath away. "It's pretty simple when you get your head around it." He took a small section of hair, expertly splitting that into three more parts between his fingers. "You go over and under the middle strand, like this." His fingers were a blur as he magically created the plait out of nothing.

Griff chuckled. "And again in slow motion replay?"

Raphie ducked his head and smiled bashfully at him. "Okay. This time, for beginners."

He made several little braids through his hair until Griff felt like he got an idea of what to do. Raphie took those and somehow entwined them together into a crown-like arrangement, similar to how he'd been wearing it the morning Griff had met him. Then the two of them added several more through Raphie's locks. Raphie's were faster and neater, but Griff was still proud of the few he managed. It almost felt as if he was marking Raphie, like leaving a love bite.

Maybe his plaits would last until after he was gone?

He pushed away the bitter-sweet thought, focusing on the here and now. He and Raphie didn't have long, and if Griff was going to allow himself this dalliance, he didn't want to waste a minute of it.

Once there were a couple of dozen tiny plaits, Raphie got the rest of his hair and made it all one big braid, securing it with the hairband he still had around his wrist. As soon as it was neat and tidy, he sighed. "That's better," he declared, smiling at Griff. Then he managed to surprise Griff yet again by flopping down and dropping his head in Griff's lap. "Thank you."

Griff grunted, but he was also smiling. "You're welcome."

For a while, they stayed that way, basking in the sun like a pair of lizards. When it got too hot, Raphie went crashing into the lake, shrieking at how cold the water was but still jumping about in it all the same. Griff was only able to resist joining him for so long before he jogged in up to his waist as well. Raphie was trying not to get lake water on his hair, but that didn't stop them from splashing water at each other with increasing arousal clear on both sides from their tenting underwear. Eventually, Griff picked a squealing, breathless Raphie up to deposit him onto the towels so they could kiss and frot and come again.

It was bliss.

The rest of the day was spent snoozing and reading on the little beach or lounging inside the cabin. Sparrow came back to life in the evening, right around the time Raphie started making dinner, funnily enough. "No, no," he said, hastily snatching up some of her tinned food. "We only bought one packet of bacon. *This* is for you."

Griff would have bet money on her still getting her paws on at least a scrap of bacon before the evening was through.

He felt bad that Raphie was doing all the cooking, but the only things Griff knew how to prepare were basic and geared towards his high-protein diet designed for building muscle. Still, he insisted on joining Raphie in the kitchen this time to slice up onions and grate cheese. He was impressed that Raphie knew how to make quite different dishes from a similar stock of ingredients.

"It's all about the seasoning," he said proudly, stirring that evening's casserole. "Our cook, Phillipe, taught me that. He's so clever."

Griff figured a lot of people would have turned into spoiled twats with the kind of upbringing Raphie had experienced. Hell, he'd outright assumed Raphie was going to be a brat right up until the second he'd laid eyes on him. It just went to show what a kind heart Raphie had, one that was even more precious for how easily it could have been blackened by greed and riches.

After all, his dad had been so corrupted by wealth and

power, he'd had assassins set up in place to take Raphie out *after* his death, when he wasn't even around to benefit from Raphie's removal. There could have been a high chance that Raphie would turn out just like him.

His mum must be an amazing woman, not only to have passed on so many amazing traits, but to have raised such a wonderful son. It warmed Griff, thinking of the love he had for his own much-missed mum.

Griff wouldn't have believed he'd be capable of hating a man so much who he'd never meet, but the fury he felt towards the former king of Campanula was visceral. To him, Raphie had just been an illegitimate child, an unwanted bastard, who held the power to swoop in and take the throne away from the child the king had recognised and groomed to be his successor. He'd never know the way Raphie danced and sang along to the music he loved so much, or how he snuck little titbits of food to his beloved cat, or the adorable way he wriggled his fingers whilst he was making his mind up about something.

But Griff knew all those things. He'd know them long after he'd have to say goodbye to Raphie, too. In a way, he should perhaps be grateful that Raphie's dad was a psychotic nutjob who'd organised sub-par assassins to chase after his offspring. Otherwise Griff would never have had this opportunity to get to know Raphie.

To let him into his heart.

"What are you thinking?" Raphie asked from across the table where they'd sat down to eat.

Griff shook his head and pulled himself from his stupor, allowing a genuine smile onto his face. "Uh," he said bashfully. "That sometimes life can be shit, but you can get something great out of it when you least expect it."

Raphie studied him for a few seconds, a smile also

creeping onto his face. "Am I the something great?" he asked shyly.

Griff snorted, amused by him fishing for compliments. Like Griff had anything a *fraction* as amazing going on in his life as Raphie. "I dunno," he said, waving his fork around and glancing at the cabin. "This place is pretty sweet. I guess you're all right."

Raphie squeaked in indignation, then flicked a bit of onion at Griff, making them both laugh.

When Griff had managed to wipe the casserole from his eyebrow and kissed his troublesome lover across the table, he became serious for a second. "I *am* glad our paths crossed, even if it was under strange circumstances." *And just for a short time,* he added mentally. Despite them both knowing this was temporary, he didn't like saying that to Raphie. Like maybe if he didn't vocalise it, he could ignore that very pertinent fact.

Raphie smiled coyly down at his dinner. "I certainly didn't expect you," he said softly.

Griff bit his lip. Raphie *did* know this was temporary, right? Griff had been pretty clear, he thought. But if he hammered home the point any more, it might come across like he was trying to get rid of Raphie or something. That definitely wasn't his intention. But the sincerity in Raphie's words worried Griff a little.

He'd tackle that problem when it arose. Right now, Raphie had cooked another amazing meal, and Griff was feeling thoroughly spoiled after only twenty-four hours of domestication. "To surprises," he said, holding up his water glass to clink with Raphie's wine.

Raphie beamed, his serious expression replaced by mischief again. "To surprises," he agreed.

As it transpired, Griff was in for a couple more that evening.

Conversation was easy, as always with Mr Chatterbox, and they ate dinner slowly, Raphie enjoying his wine and Sparrow enjoying the leftovers. After washing the dishes, the two of them relocated outside onto the porch with mugs of tea, leaving Sparrow inside again, and watched the sun set over the tops of the pine trees. Everything was so new and exciting with Raphie, making Griff see things differently through his jaded eyes. Griff felt like once again he'd woken up from a hundred-year nap thanks to Raphie's pure delight at the world.

He'd have thought just sitting outside, talking about this and that, might be kind of dull for both of them. Griff was always working and Raphie came from bucketloads of money, after all. This wasn't what either of them were used to. But it was peaceful, making Griff feel calm and contented. Especially when they'd both placed their empty mugs on the floor, and he reached over to hold Raphie's hand, thrilled by how delighted that simple act made Raphie.

Dusk was settling in properly and the night-time critters were coming out in earnest to chirp and sing when Raphie turned to Griff where they were sat on the edge of the porch, their feet scuffing the grass below.

"So, can we have sex again?" he asked eagerly, apropos of nothing. "Anal, I mean. I bought supplies at that shop when you weren't looking."

Griff burst out laughing, taken completely by surprise. "Is that so?" he asked.

Raphie nodded, his eyes wide and his cheeks flushed as he smiled. He squeezed Griff's hand a little tighter, shifting closer. "I've read all about it, and I think I'm ready."

Griff sighed fondly, then cupped his free hand against the side of Raphie's face. "Never mind 'ready'. It's not something you have to get over and done with to reach the next level of gayness or something. It's about what you desire."

Just talking about sex was apparently enough to have Raphie panting again. Griff was more than happy to keep frotting and swapping hand and blow jobs, but Raphie's pupils were blown wide, and he was practically quivering in anticipation.

"I…I just want *more,*" he said breathlessly. "I want to try new things with you, Griff. *Dirty* things," he said in a conspiratorial tone that might have been funny if it hadn't been so damn endearing.

"Well," said Griff, not quite believing the words that were coming out of his mouth. "More is good, for sure. Would you like to top me?"

Raphie blinked at him. "Really?"

Griff shrugged. "If you want to." He hadn't offered that to anyone since his early twenties. He liked topping. It was usually the best way to remain in control of the situation, in his experience. But with Raphie, he felt like their dynamic would be there no matter what the position.

Raphie evidently had reservations, however.

He frowned, like he was working things through. "Doesn't the bigger man usually top?"

Griff grinned, caressing the side of Raphie's neck. "That sounds like another social construct to me," he teased gently.

Raphie blushed crimson. "Sorry, I-" he stuttered.

"Hey, no," Griff said, shaking his head. "*I'm* sorry. I'm being a twat. I just love hearing all the stuff you've read. But I guess, in real life, things can be a little different. Unexpected. Messier."

Raphie hummed and smiled. "I kind of like that they're messier," he said, running his hand over Griff's side in an almost ticklish way. "Otherwise, there might be nothing out here to surprise me."

"Yeah?" Griff asked. "Like what?"

Raphie blushed some more. "Like you."

Griff's heart skipped a beat. *Only for a few days,* he reminded himself sternly. This wasn't going to last. But while it did, he was bloody well going to make the most of it.

He nuzzled against Raphie's cheek and kissed his jaw. *"You* surprise me," he murmured.

Raphie giggled, his hands trailing over Griff's chest. When he was bold enough to rub Griff's nipples with his thumbs through his T-shirt, Griff groaned a little louder than he usually would. He nipped at Raphie's ear, showing how much he liked being played with like that.

Raphie was breathless already, and Griff loved it. "So… you like bottoming?" Raphie asked with a squeak.

Griff smiled at his sweet innocence. "I like having sex," he answered. "Some guys have strong preferences either way, and that's fine." He kissed Raphie's pretty lips and dragged the lower one through his teeth, making Raphie produce the most delicious moan. "You said you wanted to try everything. I quite liked the idea of me taking care of all the prep, and then just lying back and letting you go to town on my arse to see if you liked that."

By his hot and heavy breathing, and the way he was distractedly pawing at Griff's chest, Raphie liked that idea, apparently.

"Uh," he croaked with a nod. "Yeah, sure. That sounds, uh, really great. Thank you."

Griff laughed affectionately and kissed his mouth again. "Love those manners," he mumbled.

He knew he could prep himself pretty quickly. Besides, he kind of wanted to really feel Raphie pushing his way inside him, with a burn that would linger for days. So instead, Griff decided he'd focus on getting Raphie insanely turned on. Not only was he very confident that they'd both enjoy that, but he figured if Raphie was horny, he'd be more relaxed and eager to top.

Griff remembered being twenty-one, after all. That insatiable need to fuck any willing thing that moved. He was almost certain that when Raphie got his confidence up, he'd be just the same.

Time to go see if his theory was right.

# 14

## RAPHIE

HAVING BEEN HELD PRISONER BY CIRCUMSTANCES HIS WHOLE life, Raphie had always imagined he'd be fiercely independent in the real world, wanting to make all his decisions for himself. And that was true, to a certain extent.

But when it came to Griff guiding him through his new intimate experiences, Raphie was perfectly happy letting him take the wheel. Especially when he did that thing where he picked Raphie up and carried him to bed, like he was doing again now. It made Raphie feel like quivering jelly in his arms.

Griff hummed, kissing Raphie's pulse point as he held him close to his chest in a bridal carry. Raphie had his arms slung around Griff's solid neck, squirming at Griff's nips and kisses. "Griff," he moaned. He was a little nervous but mostly excited for what was to come.

They entered Raphie's bedroom and closed the door on an indignant Sparrow. She wasn't used to being separated from Raphie, but she'd soon get used to it. Right now, there was no way he wanted an audience, even if it was just a feline one.

Griff placed Raphie back on his feet, kissing his mouth hungrily. Having done it a couple of times now, Raphie didn't hesitate as they began undressing themselves and each other, hardly breaking their kissing as clothing started littering the floor. Raphie smiled against Griff's mouth, giggling a little from sheer happiness.

There had been many years when he'd genuinely worried if he'd even make a real connection with someone like this. It had seemed so impossible when he'd been locked in the penthouse for so long. But now here he was, with a shockingly gorgeous man, both tumbling into bed, naked and hard as rocks, their lengths bumping and leaking together as they rolled over the covers.

It had been easy for Raphie to think that despite his mum's wealth, he'd been pretty unlucky having to hide himself away from the whole world. But in that moment, he felt like the most blessed man alive in Griff's arms. They'd chosen Raphie's room for tonight, as that was where he'd stashed the supplies he'd surreptitiously bought the day before. At the time, he'd felt a mixture of pride and ridiculousness when he'd grabbed the condoms and lube, wondering if he was totally mistaken about himself and Griff. Now, he was insanely glad that he'd let his wishful thinking guide him.

He'd never have imagined that Griff would want to bottom, though. After getting past his initial shock, Raphie had to say that he was extremely turned on by this plan. Griff had promised him new experiences, and this certainly counted as that. The fact that Griff would trust him like this was kind of heady to Raphie. His cock throbbed at just the idea of being buried within Griff's arse. He wondered if it would feel as good as all the romance books he'd read made it out to be.

"Fuck, you're beautiful," Griff growled against Raphie's throat, rolling his body over Raphie's. "Taste so good."

Raphie hummed, remembering how awestruck he'd been by Griff's masculine scent when they'd first met, and how he'd just wanted to roll around in it like a cat in heat. And now he was. He inhaled deeply, nuzzling his face against Griff's chest, near his armpit, drinking in his musk. There was something so primal about the way they'd been having sex. Raphie wondered if it would be like that with all men.

Then he quickly shut down that line of thought. Picturing sex with anyone else made him feel sad and hollow, and made his cock want to wilt. It probably showed his lack of experience, but even just the idea of being with someone that wasn't Griff made his heart want to break.

Luckily, he didn't have to consider that for now. Raphie snapped his attention back to the present, in which Griff had opened the bottle of lube, and now had his hand behind his back. He moaned into Raphie's mouth, and Raphie realised he already had two fingers up his arse, stretching his hole out.

Stretching himself for Raphie's cock.

Raphie's breath hitched, but he refused to be nervous. Griff was doing all the hard work. All Raphie had to do when the time came was put on the condom and sink into Griff's thick, round arse. He trusted Griff to tell him what to do, like he had with giving head. Raphie just had to relax and enjoy himself.

He'd expected Griff to be busy for longer, but in the next moment, he was removing a condom packet from out of the box. "You need help?" Griff asked Raphie between sloppy kisses. Raphie's mouth was starting to go numb from so much unprecedented use, but he loved it. Just like he loved the feeling of plucking the foil packet from Griff's fingers, grinning against his lips.

"Nope," Raphie said proudly. "I've been practising. *A lot.*"

Griff groaned loudly. Raphie felt his eyes were watching him hungrily as he tore open the foil and wasted no time rolling the slippery condom down his straining length. "Yeah?" Griff rasped, his voice low and heavy with lust that drove Raphie wild. "I bet you spent hours getting yourself hard, playing with your cock, just so you could be the best at suiting up."

"Does it make you hot, thinking of me wanking for practice?" Raphie teased, running his sticky hands down Griff's arms.

"So fucking hot," Griff growled. He kissed Raphie roughly, then grabbed the lube to squirt all over his hand before grabbing Raphie's encased erection, jerking him off and slicking him up at the same time. "Are you going to stick this up my arse now? I want you to fuck me like a randy bunny rabbit."

Raphie snorted at the ridiculous comparison. "I'm not a *bunny,*" he said indignantly.

Griff was grinning against his mouth, though, still stroking Raphie's cock to keep him as hard as steel. "Little boffin bunny," he teased with such warm affection Raphie shuddered. "Let's see what you think about that virginity of yours when you're balls deep up to my taint, driving yourself wild inside my hole."

"Oh, my fucking god, Griff," Raphie stuttered, almost choking he was gasping so much. He was already so turned on, and they hadn't even tried to get his cock inside Griff's arse yet.

That was all about to change, though. Griff rolled them over so Raphie was suddenly on top of him. Then Griff let him go to hold his knees up to his shoulders, almost bending himself in two and exposing his hole, just for Raphie. "I'm ready for you, beautiful," he said between searing kisses on

Raphie's mouth. "Just push your way in. I want to feel you. You're so fucking gorgeous."

Raphie nodded, filled with confidence from Griff's encouragement. He shimmied down the bed, his breath hitching at the sight of Griff's red, straining cock, heavy hairy balls, and dark, wet hole, begging to be filled with Raphie's cock. He bit his lip, lining the tip up with Griff's entrance. Despite his prep, it still felt pretty tight as he began to push against the ring of muscle.

But holy fucking *shit* did it feel incredible. Raphie's cock had never been squeezed like this before. His hand utterly paled in comparison to the sensation of slowly sinking into that impossibly tight, hot hole, even through the condom. He gasped and gnashed his teeth as Griff groaned.

"That's it, beautiful," Griff said. He let his knees go as he wrapped his legs around Raphie's waist. With one hand, he cupped the side of Raphie's face, and with the other he held Raphie's hip. "Feels so good, just keep pushing."

Raphie nodded frantically, dripping with perspiration. Griff's body was slick too, and the room stank of their mixed musk. Raphie took deep breaths, not able to get enough of it. He sank further and further inside his lover until he couldn't go any deeper. Then he took a second to recover, trembling as he focused on staying upright and not collapsing on top of Griff.

"Perfect," Griff murmured, rubbing up and down Raphie's arms. "Take a minute. You feel incredible, baby. Move when you're ready."

Raphie grunted, dropping his head as he caught his breath, and his braid swung over his shoulder. "You're sure I'm not hurting you?" He'd read all about how bottoming kind of burned at first, especially when you weren't used to it. Griff said he hadn't done it in years.

But Griff shook his head and leaned up to kiss Raphie on

the mouth. "I love it. You feel amazing. If you're ready, I want you to fuck me. *Hard.*"

Raphie gulped, feeling like his dick swelled even more, although he was sure that couldn't be possible. He was so turned on he was on the verge of passing out. He had to keep reminding himself to breathe and make sure the oxygen was flowing to both his brain and his cock. "Fucking hell, Griff. Everyone kept saying sex was good, but this is the *tits.*"

Griff dropped his head back and laughed enthusiastically, making Raphie's heart clench in the best way. "Where are all those fancy manners now, little boffin?"

Raphie grinned as he gave an experimental roll of his hips. "Up your arse, with my cock," he teased playfully. Sure enough, the movement made Griff gasp and moan, the smile dropping from his face as Raphie made him feel amazing.

Griff's hands were so tight on Raphie's hips that Raphie was sure his fingertips were going to leave bruises. He kind of hoped they would.

"Fuck," growled Griff, screwing up his face. "I love you with manners *and* a dirty mouth. That's it, beautiful. Keep doing that."

Somewhere in the back of Raphie's mind, he noticed that Griff had said the L-word *again.* Of course he hadn't said that he loved Raphie himself, just things about him. But that part of Raphie's brain squirrelled away that little nugget to ponder over later.

Right now, he had some fucking to do.

He pulled his hips back and slammed his cock inside Griff again, making them both moan and pant. Then he did it again and again, picking up the pace, his heart beating like a steam engine as the delicious friction made his dick throb and his balls tingle, his climax starting to build.

"Yes, there, that's it!" Griff bellowed, his fingers digging in even harder.

Raphie could just about tell he was hitting the little nub deep inside Griff, tagging his prostate. Raphie had managed to find that inside himself with his toys, and from the look on Griff's face, it was even better getting pounded by a real, hot cock. Raphie went harder, loving watching Griff lose his mind as he writhed under Raphie.

Raphie braced one hand on Griff's chest, then wrapped his other hand around his thick cock. It was leaking so much precum, Raphie's hand glided perfectly over it, and he began to pump it in time to his thrusts. Griff bellowed, rutting his arse even more fervently against Raphie's length buried within him. Raphie bit his lip as his climax built, fast.

"Griff," he warned, not able to utter anything else.

But Griff understood him, nodding desperately. "Me too," he said with a gasp. "Nearly there, Raphie. Come in my arse!"

As if on command, Raphie went rigid as his balls emptied, his explosive release filling the condom as his cock throbbed inside Griff. Griff batted Raphie's frozen hand away so he could frantically stroke himself to completion as well, only taking a few seconds before he was shooting thick ropes all over his chest of milky-white cum.

Raphie blinked as they both panted, their cocks done spitting but still hard as the two of them looked at each other. They were a sweaty mess, but Raphie trailed his eyes over Griff's naked, tattooed, muscular body, thinking he'd never looked so perfect.

He rolled his hips one last time before his cock began to soften. *Mine,* he thought possessively.

Never mind Raphie not wanting to think about having sex with anyone else. He *definitely* didn't want to think about Griff fucking any other guys. Nuh-uh, nope. Not ever.

But as Raphie eased out and disposed of the condom, his high already beginning to fade, a tiny, horrible voice of logic wormed its way into the back of his mind. As Griff tugged him out of the bed and out towards the bathroom, a question formed in Raphie's head that he knew he'd been purposefully avoiding for days.

What would happen when they got to Campanula?

Nothing over the past few days had been like Raphie had anticipated it might be. He'd been in a kind of limbo since he'd learned about his birthright as a child, wondering if he'd even ascend to the throne of his home country or be denied by the powers that be. He'd researched Campanula obsessively online, picturing what it might be like to live in the minuscule European country.

But he'd never considered he'd have someone like Griff in the mix.

Hell, who was he kidding? There had never been anyone like Griff or any reason Raphie should have predicted such a complication. It was all very well them being here in their dreamy French cabin bubble, where they made spectacular love and ate home-cooked dinners together, but Raphie had studied royal protocol excessively.

There were a lot of rules about who royal family members were supposed to date and marry. Even more so for the reigning monarch. In fact, there hadn't been an unmarried king or queen to take the Campanula throne in more than a hundred and fifty years. If Raphie's claim was successful, where would that leave him and Griff?

Did Griff even see a future for them beyond this little slice of heaven they had here? He'd mentioned about just living in the moment, and Raphie was too afraid to ask.

He didn't want to spoil a good thing, though, especially when Griff had helped him into the quaint bathroom and pulled him under a hot shower. Now they were kissing and washing away the mess they'd made, but Raphie wasn't able to bask in his post-orgasmic glow like he really wanted to. Why couldn't his stupid brain shut up?

Unfortunately, Griff apparently noticed how quiet Raphie was being. "Hey," he said softly, using his thumb and index finger to tilt Raphie's head up to face him under the water stream. "Was that okay? I thought you enjoyed it."

Raphie spluttered, disbelieving that Griff could assume anything else. "Oh, I definitely enjoyed it." He fluttered his hands over his lover's muscular form, standing on his tiptoes to kiss his lips. "It was spectacular – incredible – amazing!"

Griff sighed and kissed him back, running his hands up and down Raphie's spine. "Good. I'm glad. Because I loved it. I know I said that it'd been a long time since I've done that with anyone, but I'm glad I tried it again with you."

Pride swelled in Raphie's chest. "I told you I'd be great at sex," he said, poking Griff's chest.

He was rewarded by Griff's rich laugh. "So you did, boffin," he said affectionately. "I didn't doubt you for a second. Now turn around and let me wash your hair."

"You're obsessed," Raphie teased, although secretly he was thrilled. More than that, he loved that Griff had a thing for his pride and joy.

Griff snorted. "Shut up and let me have my fetish," he said playfully.

Raphie sighed in contentment, relaxing as Griff gently undid all the braids they'd worked on by the lake, massaging the shampoo and conditioner through the locks. Ordinarily, Raphie wouldn't wash his hair nearly as much as he had these past few days. But he'd never stank of sex like this before. And he'd never had someone else obsessing over his hair like this either.

He felt another pang. If they were staying one more day at the cabin, he would have left it. But he was painfully aware that they had to get back on the road tomorrow, their fantasy bubble over after tonight. Raphie knew he shouldn't be greedy. He was lucky to have even this amount of time with Griff to himself. But his whole life, he been at the mercy of other people's whims, and it seemed cruel to have had this time, only for it be taken away from him so quickly.

But he couldn't change facts. He was the rightful heir of Campanula. Wheels were in motion for something much bigger than his first real-life crush, and he had to accept that.

Right?

There was also still a chance that his claim would be rejected or the assassins would catch up to them before they even made it across Europe. Two very cheery thoughts. But it proved to him that there was still so much uncertainty. He had no way of knowing how the next few days would go, just like he could have never predicted how the previous days would have panned out.

After a lifetime of routine, he was suddenly faced with so much uncertainty.

So what would happen if he started making some choices for himself? Why did he have to be at the whims of others? He had a mind of his own, not to mention wants and needs that he was perfectly entitled to ask for. He couldn't necessarily change Campanulan law or speak for how Griff was feeling. But Raphie knew that the way he cared for Griff was exceptional.

Raphie had the right to at least make that crystal-clear and do everything in his power to protect this blossoming, fragile thing between the two of them. Didn't he?

At that moment, Griff murmured that Raphie's hair was clean, so Raphie turned in the cramped bathtub and wrapped his arms around Griff's trunk-like waist, resting his head on his chest. "Thank you," he said with a sigh, not really talking about his hair.

Raphie made himself promise that he'd be grateful for any time they could spend together. But he also knew himself and how stubborn he could be. He was an only child *and* a prince to boot, so he had a thing about getting his own way.

When the time came, he knew he was going to fucking fight for Griff with every breath he had. Even if that meant taking on the whole of Campanula…

…or Griff's own stupid sense of nobility.

15

---

## GRIFF

WINSTON'S CABIN WAS SITUATED IN THE EAST OF FRANCE, NOT far from the Swiss border. So once Griff and Raphie had (reluctantly) packed up their things and convinced Sparrow back into the car, it hadn't been long before they were approaching another international border.

The further they got from the cabin and the bliss they'd experienced there, the more Griff's old doubts and insecurities were crawling back into his mind.

He would have given almost anything to have said 'fuck it all!' and simply stayed hidden away. The last couple of days had been the most perfect and serene he'd ever known. But how long could his and Raphie's bubble have really lasted, anyway? After a time, Raphie would surely become bored of nothing to do but have sex, especially once he realised that Griff wasn't much company. They might have had a lot of chemistry, but what did they really have in common? Raphie was way too smart for Griff with his education befitting a prince. Griff had barely finished school and didn't know much beyond his life in the East End.

He gripped the steering wheel, trying to accept the fact that they might not have been in Campanula yet, but the fantasy was already slipping away from them.

It was right for them to be back on track, heading towards the country where Raphie was destined to take the throne. *That* was his life. Not nestled away in the countryside with Griff.

No matter how much Griff was surprised to find he would have loved that.

He'd always been a city boy, born and bred in London. The suburbs, and especially the arse-end of nowhere countryside, had never really appealed to him. It was astonishing what difference forty-eight hours could make. After a couple of decades in a job that swayed violently between heart-stopping adrenaline and crushing boredom, with clients who more often than not either ignored Griff or resented his presence, his time playing house with Raphie had turned out to be an unexpected oasis of bliss.

Considering he'd spent so many years surrounded by people in one of the busiest, most densely populated cities in the world, Griff was starting to appreciate how detached from everything he'd really been. It had taken being stranded in a cabin with just one other person – a perfect, wonderful person – to make him realise that, and to understand that being connected didn't mean being in a crowd.

Apparently, all it could take was just that one person, if they were the right one.

That was dangerous thinking, though. Raphie wasn't Griff's anything. He didn't have the right to claim him as his own, no matter how much he was starting to want to. The further they got from the cabin, the more Griff could feel he was drifting apart from Raphie and back to reality. It fucking sucked, but that was just the way things were.

The threat they were facing was still very real, and all Griff had to protect Raphie with was a fire poker he'd lifted from Winston's fireplace. Their tactical delay had gifted them an extra day of safety in paradise. At the time that had felt like a blessing, but now Griff was wondering if that was just going to make it all the more difficult when he had to leave.

He couldn't afford to let his mind wander in that direction, so he dragged it back to focus on the road ahead. The Swiss-French border was nothing at all. One minute, they'd been driving down the A35 past the Basel-Mulhouse-Freiburg airport in Saint-Louis, the next they were in Switzerland, crossing over the River Rhine. Unbelievably, it would only take them three and a half hours, and then they'd be in Italy.

It was becoming very real to Griff how soon he'd have to prepare himself for letting Raphie go.

Forever.

During the small hours of the morning, where dangerous thoughts lived, Griff had wondered if he could stay in Campanula and be Raphie's secret lover, one who he didn't have to declare to the public. But Griff knew deep down there was no way he could live a life with one foot in a relationship with Raphie and one foot in the shadows. But that wouldn't be fair on either of them, whether Raphie knew that or not. Once Raphie stepped into his new life, Griff knew he'd have to walk away and never look back, for both their sakes.

And as he drove through the picturesque sights of Switzerland that morning, he knew this was the start of what a shattered heart was going to feel like.

He'd had a couple of break-ups before he'd sworn off relationships and dedicated himself to simple hook-ups. He remembered being sad and having to adjust to life without whoever he'd been dating. But it had never felt like this, he was sure. And Raphie was still right there by his side, for fuck's sake. How could Griff already be missing someone like a severed limb when they weren't even gone yet? But he could feel the gaping hole starting to grow in his heart and the desperate loss of this incredible man he couldn't have.

Griff wasn't sure if he could recover from this.

Sure, he'd go back to London and find something to do. But after Raphie, he was pretty certain that he was done with the whole private security sector. He couldn't imagine protecting anyone else after this, and he wasn't sure he even wanted to. The work that had once been thrilling and fulfilling didn't hold the same attraction to him now as he looked towards the future. It was crazy, but his heart was still back at that cabin, in the peaceful countryside. He was having wild thoughts, like how he could grow tomatoes and get a dog – but only if Sparrow would be okay with that.

He bit his tongue and gripped the steering wheel tighter. *No.* There would be no Sparrow. There would be no Raphie. Just Griff. And maybe a dog.

"You're quiet," Raphie said. Griff could hear it in just those two words. He was trying to sound casual, but there was tension in his voice. It hadn't gone unnoticed by him that Griff had woken up with the weight of the world on his shoulders.

Or maybe in his heart.

Griff mustered a smile, though, as he reached over and squeezed Raphie's knee, careful not to disturb Sparrow on his lap. "*Someone* wore me out last night," he said flirtatiously. "*And* this morning," he added, recalling their shared blow jobs with absolute fondness. His future might look bleak without Raphie in it, but Griff sure as hell was going to take some spectacular memories away with him.

One day, he hoped he'd be able to look back on them with affection instead of a harrowing sense of loss.

"Oh," said Raphie, blushing beautifully and squirming in his seat. "Okay, then. I thought you might be…I don't know… regretting things."

Griff scoffed, genuinely offended. "I don't regret a single moment of our time in that cabin, and that's the gospel truth."

He didn't now, and he never would. He knew he couldn't have Raphie for more than another day or so, but he would *always* cherish what they'd had, like a precious gift. He found Raphie's hand, entwined their fingers, then raised them so he could kiss the back of Raphie's hand.

"I hope what we shared was really special for you, beautiful," he said, warmth filling his chest. "Because I've been with a lot of men – and I'm not saying that to be harsh or whatever – I'm trying to give you perspective. Sex is sex. It's genuinely difficult to totally cock up, in my experience. But fuck my life, that was some next-level thing we shared, okay? Please don't be overthinking with that boffin brain of yours that I didn't like it or whatever. It was amazing. *You're* amazing. Got it?"

He glanced over to see Raphie's pink cheeks and slightly slack jaw. "I love it when you're bossy like that," he rasped, making Griff's balls tingle most unfairly. It took all his restraint he had not to swerve the car over to the hard shoulder of the motorway and have his wicked way with Raphie once more.

*Fuck.* Would they get the chance to be intimate again? They were due to arrive in the capital of Campanula by that evening. The deadline wasn't technically until tomorrow night. But as much as Griff hadn't wanted to hang around Campanula in case the assassins found them, they wanted to spend tonight somewhere close so they'd be ready to present

Raphie tomorrow morning. They might need a few extra hours in case anything derailed their plans again. Raphie quite rightly wanted to present himself to the royal household and parliament a few hours before the coronation ceremony.

He was about to ruffle a *lot* of feathers.

But did that mean Griff had held his perfect, naked body for the last time? More than that, in some bizarre twist, he wondered with even more pain if he'd brushed Raphie's hair for the last time. After their shower last night, they'd blow-dried his impressive mane before putting it in a simple single plait to sleep in. He didn't really look right this morning without all the teeny-tiny braids worked into the big one, and Griff's heart panged at how his fingers itched to be a part of that styling process again.

It was bonkers. He'd never in his whole life wanted to be a part of a lover's grooming regime. He'd never even really had an opinion on clothes and hair beyond whether or not the person in question was happy with how they looked. That had always been enough to make Griff happy, too. But with Raphie's hair, it was like Griff was becoming a part of Raphie's soul when he helped craft all those little braids. It was probably stupid. What the hell was wrong with Griff?

It was just hair, right?

Except…it was like Raphie's signature. Like the sound of his voice or his fingerprints. He told the world who he was with that hair, and selfishly, Griff supposed he liked the idea of Raphie announcing to all and sundry that Griff was a part of who he was, even if it was only through a couple of clumsily plaited braids.

He gave himself comfort by making a small promise to himself. Before he left Raphie's life forever, he'd plait one – just *one* – braid for him. Then it would be up to Raphie how long he wanted to keep that braid for. Griff could leave his lover with a sort of echo, a physical reminder of their time together.

But he couldn't keep up this miserable mood all day. He'd sworn to make the most of their last few hours, and he'd meant it. They'd left the cabin at the crack of dawn, and had crossed the French-Swiss border at around nine. They'd had toast, but that felt like forever ago.

He nudged Raphie's leg, getting him to turn down his beat-riddled pop music a fraction. "Do you want to look for somewhere to get a proper breakfast? I have a hankering for eggs."

He loved how Raphie's face lit up at the suggestion. It was no mystery to Griff that Raphie had loved their cosy time together just as much as he had. The idea of sharing another meal obviously warmed his heart as well.

"I'm on it," Raphie happily declared as he got his phone out.

Griff tried not to count down the hours they had left, or the meals they had left to share before Raphie's destiny would be changed by the council.

In theory, it was about twenty-four hours and four meals at most.

He hated it, but there was nothing he could do to change it.

---

THE DAY, predictably, passed way too fast. Even with Griff dawdling over both breakfast and lunch, not helped by the fact that he knew Raphie was dragging his feet too. They also stopped at several vista points, despite the fact that they could see the stunning views of the mountains from within the car whilst it was still in motion. Raphie kept insisting that Sparrow needed air, and Sparrow kept looking at him like she was calling him on his bullshit.

Griff didn't say anything, because he was a selfish bastard. He wanted to protect Raphie from the explosive political situation he was about to walk in to, as well as keep him by his side just that bit longer. So it was already getting close to dinner time by the time they travelled around the outskirts of Milan. Griff could tell by Raphie's body language that he was desperate to stop and have dinner there, despite the substantial breakfast and lunch they'd had in the motorway service stations.

Raphie would have plenty of time to visit all kinds of cities in his new life. It was too dangerous for them to go into a metropolis like that when they were so close to Campanula. So even though he felt like the bad guy, Griff ignored Raphie's hopeful looks and planned to get them something to eat once they crossed the border into Campanula. Even then, their best bet would be to grab a sandwich or something on the move, then hide away in some small hotel and hope the assassins didn't find them. They were too close to risk getting caught now.

Griff wished they could have a proper meal to say goodbye. Preferably one of Raphie's beautiful home-cooked ones over candlelight. But this was real life, not a fairy tale. There wasn't some magic ritual that was going to make his and Raphie's parting any easier, so he needed to let all his wishful thinking go.

To make things worse, there was also an added level of uncertainty around *when* Griff would finally leave Raphie for good. He knew as soon as he presented himself to the council, Griff couldn't be anything more to Raphie than a bodyguard. But when would Raphie actually be safe? When would he have a new security detail that he could really trust?

How long would Griff have to hang around in a torturous state of limbo, not being able to be with Raphie in any meaningful sense, but having to see him dangled in front of him like a steak before a starving man?

He'd just have to put on a brave face, and hope their parting wouldn't be a long drawn out affair. Except the universe didn't seem to be on their side. Griff knew they'd wasted some time earlier, but he wasn't feeling too guilty about it until they passed through the city of Bologna and suddenly found themselves at the mercy of flooding diversions. Just as they were getting close to Faenza, only one fucking hour from Campanula, Griff found himself being diverted onto more and more obscure roads, taking them southwest into the forest, and away from the border.

"There are no flood warnings on Google Maps," Griff grumbled, his gut uneasy as he jabbed at the phone app. "All the roads look open to me."

Raphie shrugged. "Maybe it just happened, and the internet hasn't caught up yet?" he suggested, sounding way too cheerful. "Maybe we'll just have to get to Campanula tomorrow morning instead. That won't be too terrible, will it?"

Griff frowned. Fucking hell. He hadn't wanted to have this conversation at all, stubbornly believing that Raphie was on the same page as him. But he had to face facts and be the bringer of bad news.

"Raphie," Griff said, aware that his voice was more of a warning tone than the warm one he'd intended. "You know we're nearly there. Then it's game on. You've been preparing for this for years, right? In case it ever happened that you had to challenge your right to the throne. Well, this is it. The moment isn't hypothetical anymore. We stayed an extra day in the cabin so we wouldn't be loitering in Campanula and I firmly believed we both deserved a fucking holiday. But we can't live in a fantasy bubble anymore. This is really happening."

Raphie blew a nervous raspberry. "I know that!" he said a little too high-pitched to be believed, especially when it came with a nervous giggle. "And I *am* prepared. This is the only way to protect me and Mum and stop those bloody assassins. And…yeah, it might mean I actually have to be king, too. That's just…whatever. But you'll still be there protecting me, right?"

"Of course," Griff said stiffly, not liking where this was going. His heart and stomach were in knots. They'd just passed *another* diversion sign, and it felt like they were the only car on the sodding road now. Evening was falling fast, and thunder rumbled overhead. Griff felt like it was very apt for his mood. "It's my job to keep you safe."

He could feel the pause growing more pregnant between them as he twisted and turned deeper into the forest. "Griff," Raphie said hesitantly, sending a fissure cracking through Griff's heart. "It's not just your *job*, right? You're not just going to vanish once we get to the palace?"

Griff shook his head. "I'll stay by your side until everything has been resolved with your claim to the throne."

"Yes, but," Raphie said, sitting up and getting visibly agitated in the passenger seat, "as my bodyguard or as my… friend?" It sounded like he struggled for the word, and Griff couldn't blame him.

"I'll always be your friend, Raphie," he said quietly, trying to ignore the new fissure lancing through his heart. "But I thought you understood that what we had…these incredible past few days…they won't work in the real world. You're about to be *king*. I'm just some fucking bit of rough from the East End, okay? I…it doesn't matter what we feel. You know there are certain protocols that have to be adhered to. Once you're safe…I can't stay with you."

Raphie scoffed, and it wasn't a nice sound. Griff didn't dare look at him, instead focusing on the dark road that was completely without streetlights. He'd feel nervous driving along here without having this soul-crushing conversation.

"Yeah, well, *when* I'm king, all those stupid protocols can fuck off out the window," Raphie said hotly. "I'll *change* the rules for you."

"For a man you just met who's twice your age?"

Griff hated asking the question. He fucking *loathed* himself for even saying the words out loud. Because he knew how strongly he felt for Raphie even after such a short time, despite their age gap. But Raphie needed a wake-up call. He needed to be doused with a cold bucket of water, even if Griff detested himself for being the one to do it. But there was no one else around to do the pouring.

It had been bad enough suffering through his own heart breaking. But in that moment, he swore he could feel Raphie's breaking too from the other side of the car.

"Right," he said bitterly. "Because I'm just a silly, sheltered virgin who doesn't know what the hell he's talking about."

"No!" Griff cried, almost – *almost* – tempted to give in and be foolish himself. But he'd sworn to protect Raphie at any cost.

Even that of his own ego and heart.

"No, Raphie," he said, struggling to remain calm as he navigated around yet another bend. Where the *hell* was this diversion taking them? "You are absolutely none of those things, and if the situation was different-"

But he didn't get to explain that if Raphie was under no obligation to Campanula's crown, that if he were free to be with whoever his heart desired, not who the state would approve of, Griff would be unworthy of such an honour, but he'd take it anyway. He didn't get to tell Raphie that he wasn't 'silly', but that he was *extraordinary*. He didn't even get to open his mouth.

Because in the blink of an eye, both the front tyres of the car blew out with a deafening BANG, and Griff totally lost control of the wheel as they careened into the pitch-black forest at full speed.

# 16

## RAPHIE

ALL OF RAPHIE'S ANGER AND ANXIETY OVER GRIFF LEAVING was wiped away in a flash by the pure fear that consumed him. He couldn't process what was happening as the car lurched, swerving off the road, feeling like it left his stomach behind them on the tarmac.

They plunged through the trees, branches smacking against the windscreen like arms flailing and trying to grab at them. Raphie let out some kind of yell, but Griff made no sound other than maybe a grunt or two as he wrestled with the steering wheel and stamped on the brakes, somehow managing to slow them down without smashing into any of the tree trunks.

Eventually, the car bumped against a mound of earth and came to a halt. Raphie's heart was slamming against his ribcage like a wild animal, fighting for release, and nausea rolled through him, threatening to make him throw up.

Sparrow was clearly scared to death, and had leaped from Raphie's lap up onto his shoulder, digging her claws through his T-shirt, scratching his skin. Her eyes were impossibly wide as she crouched as close as she could to Raphie, a low, menacing purr vibrating through her and against Raphie's shoulder.

"It's okay," he whispered to her, petting her back awkwardly. "It's okay, baby girl. You're okay. We're okay. G-Griff. What happened?"

Griff slowly dragged his hand over his chin, his calloused palm audibly scraping against his stubble. Raphie had just been on the verge of hating him for giving up so easily on what they had, for abandoning Raphie for the bullshit sense of duty Raphie had feared would hold him back.

But none of that mattered now, not when the shit had hit the fan.

Raphie looked at the man he'd fallen hard for and silently begged him to be okay. To tell Raphie it was going to be *okay*.

"Are you hurt?" Raphie whispered.

That snapped Griff from his reverie. He shook his head and inhaled sharply, blinking several times. "I'm fine. Are you injured at all?"

Raphie shook his head. "I'm not hurt, but I'm kind of freaking out," he admitted. "Did we blow a tyre, or…?"

Griff shook his head again and looked around. But they were surrounded by darkness. "We need to exit the vehicle, *now*. Make sure Sparrow is secure on her lead, get the backpack on your front with her inside, and then we move. Got it?"

Raphie nodded as he reached for the bag by his feet. "We're just going to leave the car here?" he asked as he coaxed Sparrow into the top half of the rucksack, but she was spooked and didn't want to comply.

Griff had told him to still make sure all his essentials were in the backpack he'd brought from London, in case they had to leave the rest. The new clothes were reminders of their time together, though, and Raphie didn't want to abandon them. But Griff's expression was grim as he snapped his seat belt loose and exited the car, looking around.

"Yes, we're leaving the car here," he said tersely.

Raphie didn't need to be told that they were under attack again.

"Sparrow, baby, please," he begged. But she was terrified and squirming. She didn't mean to, but she was scratching Raphie's hands and arms. After a few more seconds, he gave up and decided to keep her in his arms for now. When she calmed down, he'd get her safely in the bag. For now, they needed to move.

So he slung his rucksack over his back and got out of the car. Now that Griff had killed the engine, Raphie could appreciate how still and quiet the forest was. He gulped as goose bumps flurried over his skin. A quick glance at the front tyres told him they were both completely shredded, and the back ones weren't much better.

"What did that?" Raphie whispered.

"Stinger," Griff grunted quietly.

His expression was stony in the dim moonlight as he quietly popped the boot and retrieved the fire poker they'd taken from Winston's cabin. Raphie hadn't actually thought they'd *need* the iron rod for protection, but now he wasn't so sure.

"It's a row of connected nails thrown across the road," Griff continued to explain as he closed the boot again with a soft click. Raphie's eyes were adjusting to the gloom, but the tree canopy was blocking most of the moonlight. Griff didn't stop scanning the tree line as he moved to Raphie's side, wrapping his arm around his back as they hurried further into the woods. "It means whoever did it is probably close. They must have set up the fake flood diversions to funnel us into their trap. I'm such an *idiot*. But you're going to be okay, Raphie. I promise. Just do exactly as I say, and-"

He suddenly went rigid, his eyes bugging out as his back arched, his jaw clamped together. "Griff?" Raphie cried, forgetting to be quiet as he watched helplessly as Griff let go of him and crashed to the ground. *"Griff!"* Raphie screamed, dropping to his knees as Griff jerked and shuddered on the dirt and dried leaves of the forest floor.

Raphie was still clutching Sparrow to his chest as she panicked too and dug her claws into his skin. With his free hand, he attempted to shake Griff's shoulder. He had absolutely no idea what was happening to him. Was he having a seizure? Raphie was so terrified he was watching his lover die that it took him a few seconds to realise that two bits of metal were sticking out of Griff's shoulder blade.

"What the-" he stammered.

He'd been so wrapped up with terror over what was happening to Griff, he hadn't even heard the two pairs of feet as they approached. But he certainly noticed the torch beam that suddenly came to life and shone in his face, obliterating his night vision. He cried out, screwing up his eyes and flinging his free arm up. The shock made him jerk backwards, landing on his arse.

"Well, look what we have here, Bob," a smug female voice declared in a cockney accent.

Raphie ripped his arm back down in horror to see two figures looming over him and Griff. Mercifully, Griff stopped jerking in that moment and gasped for air. Raphie belatedly realised he'd been tasered, and the man who was holding the gun must have finally released the trigger to stop stunning him. The metal prongs were connected to his gun with thin coils of copper that Raphie could just make out in the torchlight coming from the guy's other hand.

Raphie wanted to cry, not just from fear. He was so fucking furious that this prick had hurt the man he cared so desperately for. But he was helpless. Griff had been holding the poker, but he'd dropped it with the shock and now it was lost to the shadows. Raphie could hardly see the two people behind the light beyond their outlines which were looming over him and Griff.

"Raphie," Griff rasped, blinking and trying to sit up. *"Run."*

The other figure was a woman, the one who had spoken before. "No, Raphie, *stay*," she said in mock concern, then cackled. "Fuckin' hell, you two have been a right ball ache to catch up with. You stay right where you are, got it?"

To Raphie's horror, she pulled out a huge knife from a sheath on her belt, the metal glinting wickedly in the moonlight. He hugged Sparrow even tighter to his chest, feeling her heart racing as fear threatened to paralyse him.

What the hell was she planning on doing with that serrated blade?

"You're the idiots who used too many smoke grenades, aren't you?" Griff grunted. His face was covered with sweat, but he'd managed to half-sit up.

"No, we're the idiots who finally caught you," the man, Bob, said proudly, shocking Griff again.

"No!" Raphie yelled, but mercifully it only lasted a few seconds this time. It was enough for Griff to slump back on the ground again, though.

The woman rolled her eyes. "We're not any kind of idiots, Bob," she snapped mulishly. They were both in their fifties, Raphie would have guessed as his eyes tried to adjust. It was hard with the torch swinging around. Although they were dressed in heavy black clothes, he could tell they were both stocky, their brown hair going grey, with matching square jaws. Siblings, he'd guess.

He didn't really care. He wanted to punch them both for hurting Griff. "Leave him alone!" he demanded, adrenaline and desperation giving him false confidence. "It's me you want, not him!"

"Raphie, no," Griff pleaded weakly. His hands were balled into fists, and he laboured to breathe, but he still turned his face up to the siblings and snarled. "If you touch him, I will kill you both. Got it?"

Bob laughed and kicked Griff in the stomach, hard. Raphie could have sworn he felt the blow himself as he cried out, tears spilling from his eyes.

"Oh my fuckin' god, Betty," Bob crowed. "I fink they're bum boys! Fuckin' queers!"

The woman, Betty, sneered at Raphie, pointing the tip of her extremely sharp knife at him. Raphie's insides rinsed cold as his vision became laser focused on that deadly point. "Who knows what this one is," Betty scoffed. "Boy or girl? Are you a fuckin' princess? Did Daddy make a mistake?"

"Ten years," Bob griped, kicking Griff again and giving him a shock. Raphie was unable to stop the sob from escaping his throat as Griff yelled and shook, the Taser's rapid *clack-clack-clack* slicing through his heart. How had everything gone wrong *so* fast? "Ten fuckin' years," Bob continued to rant, "we've been hangin' around, waitin' for some old codger in a country we've never heard of to finally croak. We were *retired!* But then all these other fuckers came out the woodwork, tryna take the job that's rightfully ours, and who the fuck would turn down seven million quid, hey?"

He stopped the Taser, and Griff groaned, his body still twitching. "It…won't be any…use to you…when I kill you," he rasped.

That made the siblings laugh. "You know, we were gonna let you go," Betty gloated at Griff. "Seemed a shame to bump off someone so hot. But if you're a fuckin' cocksucker, I think we might just make the princess here watch you kick the bucket. Give him a fond final memory."

"*No!*" Raphie pleaded. He tried to scramble to his feet, but he was suddenly faced with the knife-point almost touching his nose, and he froze. "H-he's just my bodyguard. He's married. Got kids. Please let him go."

But even as he tried his best to lie, Bob grabbed Griff's hair to yank him up and punch him across the jaw with a sickening crunch. Raphie shrieked, and Sparrow scrambled against him. He'd never felt so petrified, so helpless, so *infuriated* in his life.

"Just your bodyguard?" Bob asked, giving Griff another shock as he collapsed. "Sure, poofter."

"You know what?" Raphie spat out, so desperate to stop them hurting Griff that he'd veered into reckless. "If he doesn't kill you, I will. My father is *dead!* He can't pay you anymore!"

"Is he fuckin' serious?" Betty demanded of Bob. "We know that, you twat. The contract *activated* when he died. We just 'ave to prove we've snuffed you out. Then dearest Daddy's accountant presses the magic button, and we fuck off to the Cayman Islands for the rest of our lives."

"What do you reckon, Bets?" Bob asked, jutting his chin towards Raphie. "You wanna bother taking the whole head for proof or just a finger?"

Griff bellowed and swung wildly, taking Bob by surprise as he surged to his feet. Raphie's heart leaped into his mouth as the two men grappled, and Griff smacked the Taser out of Bob's hand. For a second, Raphie dared to hope...

...then Griff got spun around by Bob's punch to his cheek, turning him right into Betty, who blasted his face with pepper spray.

Griff and Raphie both screamed as Griff's hands flew up to his eyes, tears already streaming down his face. Betty grabbed his shoulders and kneed him brutally in the gut, then shoved him back onto the ground.

"Stay *down*," she barked, waving her knife between Griff and Raphie. "You are ruinin' my fuckin' fun. You are not gettin' out of this alive, either of you. So just pack it in and stop getting' on my fuckin' nerves. Right, this is how it's gonna happen, Bob. You deal with Mr Macho Poofter, and I'll take Mr Pretty Princess."

Bob grinned savagely, pulling a set of knuckle-dusters from one of his pockets. "I think I'll go slowly. Beat the shit out of him until Pretty Princess don't even recognise him. Or...wait – do you think he'd *enjoy* that?" he asked with disdain.

"No," Raphie whimpered with a sob, and Sparrow hissed. "Stop it!"

Griff's eyelids were bright red and swollen shut and he was struggling to breathe. Mud was soaking through Raphie's jeans against his knees, and his backpack felt like it weighed a ton. He wished he was big and tough. He wished he could outsmart them. This couldn't be the end for him and Griff. It just *couldn't*.

All he could do was keep begging. "Please don't hurt him, *please*."

Betty laughed nastily, stalking back to Raphie. He should have tried to get to his feet whilst he had the chance. What was wrong with him? But now that huge hunting knife was back in his face. "Perfect, Bob. Then I'll think of sumin' fun to do with this little freak. But first, I think I want a trophy. You're not going to need all that hair after you're dead, are you, princess? I reckon you'd really hate it if I cut it off, though."

Several things happened at once.

"*NO!*" Griff roared, thrashing blindly. Betty lunged for Raphie's hair, even as he tried to scramble away, seizing him by the base of his neck. And Sparrow finally decided she'd had enough.

With a twist of her body, she leaped from Raphie's arms, bolting into the darkness. It was only in that second did Raphie realise her lead had slipped free of his hand.

She vanished.

*"SPARROW!"* he screamed, scrabbling to his feet, flailing wildly. *"SPARROW, NO!"* Betty still had his hair, though, yanking him back.

"What the fuck are you doin'?" she cried.

"Raphie, run!" Griff yelled, grappling with Bob before he put Griff down again with the Taser.

Raphie was trying to. If he sprinted, he could maybe find Sparrow still. She couldn't get lost. She *couldn't.* She needed him. *"SPARROW!"* he screamed through his frantic sobs. He clawed and twisted, trying to get free, get to Griff, rescue his baby, *anything.* He and Betty stumbled and spun around, and suddenly white-hot pain took his breath away. Betty's knife sliced through his forearm, spraying blood everywhere.

Raphie barely registered the injury before Bob charged him, tackling him around his waist. "Listen here, you little shit…" he growled.

"Get OFF me!" Raphie yelled, still lashing out with all his limbs and arching his back against the hold, horror fuelling his fight. "Griff!"

And as if by magic, Griff was there. He'd pulled the Taser darts from his shoulder, and he snarled like a wild animal in the second it took Raphie to look up at him.

He crashed into Raphie, Betty, and Bob like a bowling ball scattering all nine pins. They went slamming into the forest floor, and Raphie couldn't help but cry out in pain as he fell on his arm. Bob's torch went flying, making them all almost as blind as Griff in the dark woods. But Griff wasn't letting that stop him. As Raphie scrambled backwards, he could see

Griff's shadowy figure going berserk, punching and kicking the shit out of the siblings.

Of course, they were giving as good as they got, and they could also still vaguely see. Thank fuck Betty appeared to have dropped her knife in the kerfuffle, but she and Bob outnumbered Griff two to one. Despite their age, they were still vicious, and Bob had those knuckle-dusters.

Raphie had to *do* something. Maybe he could find Betty's knife. He had no idea if he could stab a person, but with Griff's life on the line, he was willing to find out. Or…

…or that wasn't the only weapon that had dropped to the ground.

Raphie spun around, lurching for the torch, then searching frantically for the fire poker. It took him maybe twenty seconds, which felt like an eternity with the fight happening behind him. As soon as he saw the glint of metal, he didn't hesitate. The poker was cold and heavy in his hand, but adrenaline gave him strength despite his right arm dripping with blood. He snatched up the rod and charged into the fray, whirling it around and cracking Bob over the head with it.

Bob stumbled backwards, pinwheeling in the wildly swinging torchlight from Raphie's other hand. Before he could recover, Raphie beat him again and again. *"Stop! Hurting! My! Griff!"* he spat, punctuating every word with a smack of the poker. Bob had his arms out, trying to protect himself, but his knuckle dusters were useless against Raphie's poker and unbridled rage.

With a final burst of energy, he swung the metal poker with everything he had at Bob's head. The older man whirled on his feet like a spinning top, crashing to the ground.

He didn't get back up again.

Heaving for breath, Raphie turned around back towards

Griff and Betty, brandishing the poker and flashing the torch so he could see them.

Unfortunately, his guts dropped into his feet as he realised Griff was on his knees and Betty was stood behind him. She had one hand fisted through his hair, and the other was pressing the knife so hard to his throat it was already bleeding.

"No," Raphie whispered. He'd lost his beloved cat. He *wasn't* going to lose Griff as well.

Betty grinned, her teeth stained red and her eyes wide and wild. "I thought you might like to watch me gut him, Princess," she hissed maliciously.

"Raphie?" Griff croaked. His eyes were even puffier, completely blinding him, and his breath shallow and ragged. Raphie guessed that was how Betty had been able to overpower him. Fucking pepper spray. *No, no, no! This wasn't fair!*

"I'm here, baby," Raphie said desperately. He took a step forwards, but there was no way he'd be able to get to Griff in time. "It's going to be okay," he said anyway. Because it *had* to be. He couldn't live in this world, knowing Griff wasn't in it.

"Raphie, *run,*" he begged, even as Betty tugged his hair and exposed even more of his throat. "I'll be fine. You have to get away!"

"No, Griff," Raphie sobbed.

"GO!" he bellowed.

Raphie shook his head, stamping his foot as tears streamed down his face. "I'm not leaving you, Griff! *I love you!*"

Betty gagged. "Oh, shut the fuck up, you fuckin'-"

But she didn't get the chance to insult them again. Because out of the shadows came flying a hissing ball of ginger fury. Sparrow emerged from one of the tree branches above, landing on Betty's face, wailing and scratching at her eyes.

Betty screamed as Raphie gasped, not able to believe what he was seeing. The knife slipped away from Griff's throat just an inch, but it was all he needed. In a flash, his hands grabbed Betty's wrist, twisting it and sending the knife flying as in a blur. Sparrow took that as her cue to jump clear as Griff flipped Betty over his head, onto her back on the ground, winding her and rendering her immobile for a second. It was long enough. Griff groped for her face with his hands before landing a punch that sent a crack resonating through the forest and almost snapping her head clean off.

Like her brother, she didn't get up after that.

For a moment, Raphie just stared. Then he gasped a lungful of air and dropped to his knees as he began to sob. Sparrow raced to him, her sparkly pink lead flashing in the torchlight still shining from where Raphie clutched it in his hand. He dropped the poker, though, so he could scoop up his precious baby, still not truly believing that she'd come back to them.

Griff was still on his knees, shaking and panting. When Raphie's legs felt like they could support him again, he stumbled over to him, flinging his arms around him with Sparrow wrapped around his shoulders.

"It's okay," Raphie whispered hoarsely as Griff hugged him tightly with both arms. "Sparrow saved us. They're both out cold. We're safe now. We're okay."

"Good kitty," Griff said weakly, kissing Raphie's neck. "She's brave, just like her daddy."

"Oh, Griff," Raphie gasped again, crying in earnest. He didn't feel brave at all. He felt utterly shattered.

As they clung to each other, thunder rumbled overhead. Raphie gasped as the heavens opened, cold rain drenching them in seconds.

Raphie wasn't sure how they were going to make it through the night.

He just knew they had to move before the siblings woke up or any more assassins found them. With Griff still blind, there was no one else to get them out of there other than Raphie.

So he helped the man he loved to stand and did exactly that.

# 17

# GRIFF

Raphie had managed to keep his backpack on during the fight, and it was waterproof. It hadn't been too hard to convince Sparrow to hide inside it after her ordeal, so at least she and Raphie's essentials were mostly dry.

Or so Raphie had said, because Griff still couldn't see.

There weren't many things in life that scared Griff. He wasn't keen on heights, that was for bloody sure. But even jumping off that damned penthouse roof was preferable to the suffocating darkness he'd been enduring for the last hour.

He was doing everything he could to hide his fear from Raphie, now that the immediate threat from the assassins had passed. But Griff had never known terror like when he'd been blind and realising that Raphie was about to die, and that didn't just vanish in an instant. Not to mention that now they were moving through the rain-soaked, uneven terrain of the forest, and Griff's heart stopped every time he stumbled on the mud or slick tree roots. Not because he might fall. Raphie was propping him up too tightly for that. But because he was running on empty and every unexpected sound or movement could have been more assassins come to finish the job.

Griff was shivering, both from the cold of the rain and the residual adrenaline that kept reminding him how close Raphie had come to dying. And himself, he knew. But the thought of Raphie being taken from him was far scarier than losing his own life.

Raphie was destined to be king of Campanula and was going to change the world. But more than that, he was a bright light of goodness, a pure soul. He deserved to be protected, and that was what Griff intended to do.

He tried to peel his eyes open again, but they were stubbornly swollen shut still. He needed to recover soon, but there was nothing he could do to speed up the healing process. The helpless feeling didn't help with the fear that was gnashing at his chest.

At least with the fist fight, he'd been able to hear which direction it had been to throw himself back into it. And then it had been sheer luck that he'd landed any punches at all without being able to see. But he'd been fuelled by adrenaline and rage. Now that was fading, Griff couldn't hide from the pain on his face, nor the panic-inducing fact that he was still as blind as a bat.

At least the rain felt good on his swollen, burning face. The pepper spray had caused him difficulty breathing, too, but that paled in comparison to the last hour Griff had spent totally unable to see, letting Raphie guide them through the forest and the rain. Griff was supposed to be protecting *Raphie*, not the other way around. Griff's condition was slowing them both down as they fumbled their way through the mud and slippery tree roots, the cold downpour beating noisily on the leaves and branches and puddles around them. He felt helpless and angry that he'd failed so badly in his duty.

But more than that, he was afraid. And he couldn't let Raphie know it, because he still had to do his best to protect Raphie, and that meant supporting him whist he tried to get them both back to civilisation.

Ever since he'd become large enough to defend himself and his mum, Griff's power was in knowing he was the biggest, toughest guy in the room, the one with the sharpest eye and the quickest reflexes. But without his sight, his strength meant fuck all. So how was he supposed to keep Raphie safe?

Griff couldn't distinguish between any sounds over the pounding rain that was rustling thousands of leaves. Mud squelched and twigs snapped under their feet, and Griff's heart hadn't stopped pounding since the wheels on the car had blown. Between the blood pulsing through his ears and the immediate forest noises, Griff was driving himself crazy straining for anything that could alert him that anyone else was following them or about to attack.

If someone snuck up on them now, all the brute force in the world wouldn't do him and Raphie any good if Griff didn't know where to punch. Griff was frightened that he'd lose Raphie after all. It had come so close with the murder siblings, but what if Mr Morning Star or Wannabe Ninja showed up? Griff might have scoffed at their ineptitude before, but all it would take would be one lucky shot, and it would be all over.

Griff was trying to make peace with walking away from Raphie for his own good. But that would only be if he knew Raphie was alive and well in the world, moving on with his life.

But just now, Raphie had almost died. He could still die.

Griff really did lose his breath when he thought about that too long and hard. There was absolutely no way he would ever forgive himself if he'd lost Raphie. Life just wouldn't be worth living.

Raphie had been patiently leading Griff between the trees, one arm wrapped around Griff's waist, the other intermittently using his phone to navigate them towards the town of Forli without getting it too wet. But now he brought them to a halt and ran his hands along Griff's arms.

"Hey, hey," Raphie said over the pouring rain. He placed his palm over Griff's pounding heart. "Are you feeling worse? Griff, talk to me. What's happening?"

Griff realised he was short of breath and trembling. *Fuck.* He'd been trying so hard to keep everything concealed but it had spilled over anyway. He was a mess.

Raphie would be safer without him.

"I'm slowing you down," he grunted. He wished he could see Raphie's expression, but he knew from his training that the pepper spray would last at least another hour. Thankfully, the rain was good for one thing, as it was constantly washing the chemicals from Griff's eyes. Hopefully, that might mean he could see a little sooner.

But until then, he was a liability.

"It's fine-" Raphie began, but Griff interrupted him.

"You should go ahead. Run for it. Get to civilisation and safety. I'll catch up when my eyes are less useless."

Raphie hit him.

Not hard. Just a slap to the arm. But Griff still flinched in shock.

"*Stop* it!" Raphie spat crossly. Griff heard him stamp his foot. "I am not leaving you to save my own skin. That would make me a really terrible person! You don't think so little of me, do you?"

Griff's shoulders slumped. "No," he mumbled. "You're basically the best person I've ever met. But, Raphie, I'm endangering you by slowing you down!"

"You're the reason I'm alive, Griff," Raphie said in a kinder tone, rubbing Griff's arms. "We're making good progress, okay? We just have to keep moving." There was a pause that made Griff anxious. "Once we get to the town and your eyes are better, I...I understand if you want to part ways-"

"No!" Griff barked, startling himself with his own intensity. He dugs his fingers into Raphie's arms, biting his lip. He kept trying to open his eyes in frustration, but it was as if they were welded shut. "I'm not leaving your side until I know you're safe at the palace and the assassins have been taken care of. But it's my job to keep you safe, and right now-"

It was Raphie's turn to interrupt Griff. "Right now," he said firmly, "I feel ten times safer being with you than I would alone, and besides, I just *like* you, okay? I know I've lived a sheltered life, but I was under the impression that friends stood by each other. And you're...well, you're more than a friend. So...shut up. I'm not abandoning you."

Griff gave a weak laugh, some of the tension between them washing away in the rain. "Okay," he mumbled. "You make a good point. I just wish I could see that you're okay," he said thickly, dragging Raphie into a hug. He sniffed and rested his cheek against the top of Raphie's wet head. His skin was freezing, so Griff took a moment to just try and warm him up with his body heat. "That bitch said she was going to hurt you...*and* she almost cut your hair off."

Raphie sighed against him and dug his fingers into his back. "But she *didn't*," he said emphatically, taking one of Griff's hands and placing it on his braid. "I promise. Feel that? But my hair doesn't matter. *You* matter. I thought she was going to...she almost..."

He choked back a sob, and Griff knew he was thinking about that knife against Griff's throat. It still stung where she'd dug the blade in, but honestly it was nothing compared to his burning eyes, so Griff didn't really care.

"I'm fine," he lied. Well, what he meant was that physically, he'd eventually be okay.

His head was a wreck. He was completely discombobulated at losing his sight and fretting over what could be lurking in the woods. He was pre-emptively heartbroken at the idea of walking away from Raphie. And adding to that were three words Raphie had screamed when Griff was begging him to leave him behind and save himself.

*I love you!*

Griff knew Raphie had been panicking and afraid, but he couldn't shake how much he wanted from the bottom of his heart for those words to be true.

Did Raphie really love him? Did Griff love him back? How could he possibly tell after only a few days?

The jagged hole in his chest at the mere thought of losing Raphie suggested that this wasn't just a fling. It had never been about only the sex between them. It was about how Griff couldn't bear to be apart from this incredible young man who'd come crashing into his life. In the end, it came down to the fact that Griff hadn't realised how incomplete he was until Raphie had made him whole.

And now he had to let him go all over again.

He wasn't sure how long they stood there embracing in the rain, but when Raphie's teeth started chattering, Griff roused from his reverie. "Come on," he insisted. Body heat was no substitute for actually getting dry. Besides, their talk might have made him feel a little better, but he was still anxious about being tracked down again. He fumbled his hands up Raphie's body to cradle his face and gently kiss him. "We need to find civilisation and get you out of the rain. Not to mention patched up properly. I can feel that bandage you put on your arm."

Raphie sniffed. "It's really not that deep a cut. I didn't want to worry you," he mumbled, sounding guilty.

Griff chuckled ruefully. "Too late for that, beautiful."

Raphie caressed the side of Griff's face. "Are your eyes any better?" he asked.

"A little," Griff said, giving up trying to get Raphie to stop fussing over him. "I still can't see, but they're burning less."

"Well, I can't really see either, so we're even," Raphie said weakly as they started carefully walking again. "There's a smaller town that's closer than Forli," Raphie announced over the rain. "Castrocaro Terme. It's pretty tiny, but it has shops and a big hotel. Shall we aim for there to spend the night?"

Griff wrestled with himself for a second. He'd been clinging to the hope that they might be able to make their way to the Forli train station and still get tickets to Campanula tonight. But it had to be getting late, he was in pain and exhausted, and they were exposed out in the forest like this. Their priority had to be to get dry and then get some sleep. Besides, maybe in a small town, they'd be safer from the other assassins.

"Sounds like a good plan," he said as Raphie carefully helped him stumble around a bush. "The sooner we get out of the rain, the better."

"Agreed," said Raphie heavily.

Griff had told him not to use the torch and just navigate by moonlight, although they'd brought the torch with them just in case. If only *not* to leave it with the siblings. It was too risky to be shining it around, though, in case any of the other assassins were lurking around. They'd also tied up Betty and Bob so they hopefully couldn't follow after them.

The situation was so bad that Griff had actually considered using that knife on them. But that wasn't his nature. He wasn't a killer, and he didn't want Raphie to see him do that. They'd alerted the authorities anonymously, so Griff just had to hope the Italian police found the siblings before they escaped.

His and Raphie's only concern now was getting to the town and bunking down somewhere relatively safe. This was exactly why they'd factored in extra time before tomorrow night's council meeting. Raphie could still make it in time, so long as there weren't any more complications.

They couldn't present Raphie to the palace in this dishevelled state, however, so they'd find a low-key hotel, grab some supplies, and tend to their wounds.

Both the physical and metaphorical ones.

Griff couldn't believe Raphie had almost died thinking that he didn't care desperately for him. That he wouldn't do anything for them to be together if there wasn't a *throne* keeping them apart. Telling Raphie they couldn't be together had felt like the right thing to do in the car, but after that attack, Griff wasn't sure he had the strength to keep his hands off Raphie, not until he absolutely had to.

Raphie would understand when they talked about it calmly and logically. Griff couldn't do anything to keep them together once Raphie became king, but he would do everything to ensure that Raphie understood what he meant to him.

Griff knew what he had to do. But he was aware that he wasn't having much success making peace with that.

*If.* If Raphie became king. One of the many unfortunate side effects of being temporarily blinded was that Griff had even less to distract him from his thoughts without his vision.

His guts twisted as they continued to shuffle over the uneven forest floor. Raphie might have been the legitimate heir to the throne in Campanulan law, but Griff would bet money on people seeing him as a usurper. There was a chance that his claim would be rejected.

And then what? Would Raphie be allowed to fade back into obscurity? Griff doubted it, otherwise they wouldn't be on this modern-day quest in the first place. The assassins wouldn't stop. *Fuck.* The council might accuse Raphie of treason or something, and throw him in *jail.*

Griff wouldn't let that happen. He'd keep him safe.

A tiny part of him wanted to hope for that outcome, but that was beyond selfish and Griff squashed the thought angrily. He *wouldn't* wish a life for Raphie on the run, constantly in danger, just so they might be able to stay together. No, Raphie deserved to be happy and free, even if that meant being without Griff.

Especially after a life spent cooped up in that penthouse. Raphie deserved *everything,* and Griff wanted to make sure he got it. Thank fuck Sparrow had come back to him. Griff had never heard a more haunting sound in his life than the way Raphie had screamed for his beloved cat. She'd been his best friend when he'd had no one, and Griff would have hunted through the whole damn forest to try and reunite them. Luckily, she was as smart as she was brave, and had made her re-entrance at the perfect time.

In almost two decades of private security, Griff would never have thought he'd owe his life to a cat. But if it had to be any cat, he was glad it was Sparrow.

"That's it," Raphie murmured as they picked their way through what felt like another patch of fat, slippery tree roots. "You're doing great, Griff. I don't think it's long now according to my phone. Just keep hold of me."

Griff swallowed a lump in his throat, then pressed a kiss on top of Raphie's hair. "I'd be dead without you," he said truthfully. Either from Betty's knife or from exposure getting stranded in the woods at night in the rain.

"Don't say things like that," Raphie told him softly, squeezing his side. "We're fine, that's all that matters. *And* I got to experience a forest for the first time. I mean, I wish it had been under completely different circumstances, but it does smell amazing."

Griff chuckled. "That's my little boffin, always seeing the silver lining."

Raphie hummed. Griff probably didn't have the right to call him his, but in that moment, he was. So Griff was going to enjoy it whilst it lasted.

They kept walking, with Raphie never letting Griff go as he murmured instructions to guide him through the woods. A couple of times they stopped so Raphie could check that Sparrow was doing okay in the bag. Griff loved Raphie's compassionate nature. It would be so easy to focus on their own predicament right now, but Raphie had to know that his cat was okay.

Apparently, she was perfectly happy each time they stopped under a particularly dense bit of canopy. In fact, Raphie described her expression every time he opened the bag as 'what the hell are you doing disturbing me?' That made Griff smile in spite of all his worries.

Every time they stopped, he rubbed rainwater as aggressively as he could against his eyes, making sure they were getting washed thoroughly. Mercifully, the burn was subsiding and he even felt like he was getting a little movement back in the lids.

"It felt like they hated us more because they worked out we were gay," Raphie said, suddenly, after their latest stop. "They...they were *disgusted* by us."

Griff repressed the anger that threatened to flare inside him. Raphie didn't need his wrath right now. He needed his comfort. But there was no doubt Raphie's first – extremely vicious – brush with homophobia was playing on his mind, and probably would for a while. *Fuckers,* Griff thought savagely towards the siblings. He kind of wished he'd beaten the crap out of them a bit more.

"Yeah," he said sadly. "There are some really shitty people out in the world. I'm sorry you had to run into it so soon. But…well, fuck 'em." Raphie laughed, sounding surprised, but Griff shook his head and kissed his wet hair. "Seriously. Always do your best to stay safe, but don't pay people like that any attention. They're pathetic and so, so small." He grinned, despite everything, and squeezed Raphie's side. "Not clever boffins like you."

Raphie laughed with a little more conviction this time. "I am a 'woke Zoomer', after all," he said proudly. Griff wasn't sure what that meant, but if Raphie was less sad, then that was okay.

They trudged on, Griff's alertness and fear like a fourth member of their party. But Raphie had a way of soothing him just by being close. Not to mention that the better Griff's eyes got, the more his anxiety dramatically reduced.

"Oh!" he cried suddenly, stopping and gripping Raphie's hand. "I can see blurs." He could hardly peel his eyelids open more than a crack, but it was progress that left him feeling not quite so useless for the first time in hours.

Raphie made a joyful sound, kissing Griff's cheeks and lips. "Just in time. We're getting close to the village. Can you tell the trees are thinning out?"

As night had fallen, Griff couldn't say that he was able to distinguish between the blurs all that much just yet, but over the next ten minutes his eyes rapidly improved. He cracked them open more and more, until he was able to see stars through the branches above, and ahead, where the woods stopped and a field started. Artificial lights danced in the distance, and Griff couldn't remember seeing a more beautiful sight with his poor, tired eyes.

Well, aside from Raphie, of course.

"There only seems to be one hotel in this place," Raphie said as they approached the field. "So I just booked us a room there. I hope that's okay?"

"That's amazing, thank you," said Griff, kissing Raphie affectionately on top of his soaking head. "They don't do room service, do they?"

"I'm already looking at the menu," Raphie said, kissing his cheek, then wiping the rain off his phone screen. "Looks like they specialise in wood-fired pizza."

"Order one of everything," Griff said, only half-joking.

There looked to be a main road that they could walk along, and after the past couple of hours stumbling blindly through mud and over tree roots, it felt like bliss for Griff's feet and back to get to the tarmac. Griff couldn't lie. After getting zapped fuck knows how many times by that bloody Taser, then walking for over two hours in the rain, he was very much ready for a bed.

Especially if it had Raphie in it.

He knew he should probably wrestle with himself some more over that, but fuck it. They'd almost died, and this might be the last night they had together. In fact, it almost certainly would be. So Griff figured if Raphie wanted to sleep in his arms, he'd be more than okay with that plan.

Griff had been expecting a small collection of houses and maybe a few businesses from how Raphie had described the size of the town on the map. Like one of the small suburbs between London and towns in Essex he'd travelled through. Perhaps with a supermarket and petrol station.

As they approached and the lights got brighter, Griff could finally see that what they'd found was a hamlet that surrounded an honest-to-god medieval castle on top of a hill. The buildings were eclectic: some looked hundreds of years old, some from the sixties, and some, like the hotel

Griff and Raphie were approaching, were ultra-sleek and modern.

"Wow," said Griff, his worries momentarily forgotten as his head spun around. He made the most of what he could see through the rain with the help of the hotel's fancy up-lighting, old street lamps, and the architectural lighting illuminating the historical building. The castle felt like it was watching over the whole town, protecting the people.

"I thought it was a small hotel," Raphie said worriedly as they got closer. "I wanted to help us keep a low profile."

"Don't you dare apologise," Griff said firmly. "After what we just went through, we deserve some surprise luxury. We'll pay for the booking in cash and hopefully get some peace overnight."

He wanted to give Raphie that so badly. He wanted to wrap him up in cotton wool and just hide him away from the world. It had been difficult for Griff whilst he'd been walking and still blinded not to picture their cabin back in the French countryside. He'd been bitterly wishing they'd never left, but now he felt like things maybe weren't *so* terrible.

Raphie had to get to Campanula, there was no two ways about it. And seeing as they were almost there, this was the perfect place to recuperate after their terrifying ordeal.

"Oh, look," said Raphie, stopping and pointing to one of the shops on the high street they were walking down. "That shop has a pharmacy. Let's stop and get some supplies."

Griff was aware he probably looked mildly disturbing, but they absolutely needed some more first aid. So he followed Raphie inside the small supermarket, the quaint bell tinkling as they came dripping inside. Sure enough, the woman behind the till gasped and let out a string of concerned words in fast Italian, gesturing wildly to Griff and Raphie as they entered her store.

But Raphie was calm as he spoke back to her in what

sounded to Griff like flawless Italian, waving his open palms at her like he was soothing a horse. The woman clutched at her blouse, her eyes wide with alarm, but then she spoke some more to Raphie and moved from behind the counter. She beckoned to them as she walked into the shop.

"I convinced her that we'd already called the police about our 'mugging'," Raphie said, the quotation marks clear in his voice. No one needed to know it had been a murder attempt, not until they got Raphie to Campanula. "Which, I mean, technically we did. She seems placated, but only if she can show us what first aid stuff to buy."

"Fine by me," Griff said, shaking his head. He'd feel pretty confident in what they'd need to pick up in a Boots back home, but all the packaging was unfamiliar here. He respected Raphie's skill with the language, but Griff appreciated a local's advice, too.

Once they'd got a whole basket's worth of medical supplies, cat food, and snacks, they also picked up an umbrella to take to the till. As they were already drenched, it didn't make all that much of a difference as they hurried with their new purchases to the hotel, but at least they'd have a brolly for tomorrow.

They walked up a curving pathway through immaculately kept grass towards a red canopy over the glass-fronted entrance. Griff felt himself sag with physical relief at the prospect of being in the warm and dry, and really hoped they'd be safe here for the night.

He might not be so strict on his no-killing rule if anyone interrupted his last chance to sleep with Raphie in his arms.

The lobby was mercifully devoid of people as they entered, but Griff and Raphie started splattering rainwater noisily on the marble floor as soon as they entered, drawing the attention of the receptionist. His face dropped and he started flapping his hands as he ran around the desk.

*"Italiano? Deutsche? Français? English?"* he rattled off like a machine gun as he practically sprinted to Griff and Raphie.

"English!" Griff latched on to immediately. He knew Raphie would take care of them, but Griff was feeling pretty useless. *He* was the bodyguard here, so if he could understand what was being said, he might feel like he was regaining a little of his control.

"My goodness, sirs," the receptionist cried as he came to a halt in front of them and clapped his hands. He was slim with dark hair and oval glasses that he peered over to inspect the mess that was Griff's and Raphie's appearance with proper scrutiny. "Is everything okay?"

Griff nodded, and hugged Raphie to his side. "We've had a tough evening, but we're fine now." *Hopefully,* he added to himself. "We'd really just like to check in and order some room service."

"The booking is under Michael Caine," Raphie said, to the receptionist. He gave Griff a small smile, presumably to convey that, yes, he'd used the name of the star of the original Italian Job on purpose, after their conversation about films what felt like years ago. Griff loved that he'd continued the tradition they'd started in Dover of using movie-related aliases.

The receptionist waved his hands and jogged back to his computer. "Of course, of course. My name is Angelo. Let me see what I can…ah! Yes. Let me upgrade you. I am very sad to see a lovely couple such as yourselves in such a state. I hope this might help. Yes, excellent. We have a suite. Will you allow me to book this room, and send up a complimentary gift basket?"

Griff stared, speechless. After the violent attack they'd endured that had undoubtedly been made worse by their attacker's homophobia, to be welcomed as a couple was like a balm. "T-thank you so much," he managed to utter. It was difficult to not remember the bed and breakfast owner, Bev, who had also mistaken them for a couple.

This time, Griff didn't hold himself back.

He kissed the top of Raphie's head and hugged him close, smiling at the receptionist. "A little pampering would go a long way, I think."

Angelo blew a raspberry. "A little? No. Give me ten minutes." He was typing furiously on his computer. "Here are your key cards. Please, get settled. You can order dinner through the phone service, and I will also add a complimentary wake-up service with breakfast, the works. I expect to see you as new men in the morning, yes?"

Raphie smiled at Griff, making Griff's heart melt. It was true. A little kindness went a long way. "Thank you," said Raphie. "We promise. New men tomorrow."

Angelo waved them off. "Leave those clothes outside to be laundered. You will find bathrobes in the suite. Your sad time is over, only relaxing now. Understood?"

Griff smiled weakly as he turned Raphie towards the lifts. "Got it," he said with a salute. He waited until they were in the left before he cupped Raphie's face to look him in the eyes. "And that's another thing about the world," he murmured gently, pressing a chaste kiss to Raphie's lips. "For every evil arsehole, you'll hopefully find a good Samaritan like that."

"He was so *kind*," Raphie said with a sniff.

Griff smiled and wiped away the tear that fell. "Just like you," he said warmly.

Angelo didn't disappoint them. The room was huge with tasteful light wooden flooring, olive-coloured walls, dark wooden furnishings, and modern art prints hanging up. The bed was almost as big as Griff's whole living room, with a dining room set by the balcony doors, and a sunken bath in the marble bathroom.

"Bugger me sideways," Griff said with an exhale, scraping his hand over his face. If they couldn't recover in here, they'd be hard-pressed to do so anywhere.

A knock at the door put him on alert, but a quick look through the spyhole showed him it was a bellhop with their – *enormous* – gift basket. Griff was still cautious as he opened the door to accept it, but all was as it seemed.

Raphie let out an orgasmic groan as he skipped over. He'd already freed Sparrow from the bag to let her explore her new surroundings – but she scooted under the bed and didn't seem interested in coming out again. Griff hoped they wouldn't get in trouble for having her in there after Angelo had been so nice, but honestly in that moment, he was too tired to care. Especially when Raphie's face lit up at their surprise goodies. *All* that mattered was that they were here and safe. They'd just leave a whopping tip for housekeeping.

"Chocolates," Raphie began announcing as he looked through the basket, "fruit, sparkling water, sparkling *wine,* bubble bath, a little platter with biscuits with cheese *and* meats, coffee pods for the machine, tea, milk, cream, oh, *Griff...*Let me run you a bubble bath for your poor muscles."

Griff's heart ached. He absolutely did not deserve this ray of sunshine.

It was time he did his bloody job.

"No," he growled, batting Raphie's hands away and doing his best to loom despite feeling like crap. Sure enough, Raphie's breath hitched and his eyes dilated as he looked up at Griff, giving Griff a much-needed boost of adrenaline as his cock stirred in his wet trousers. "It's *my* job to look after *you.* Come here."

Raphie broke into the sweetest smile. "Okay, Griff," he said softly.

Griff gently took Raphie's arm and began peeling back the bandage Raphie had thrown on from his rucksack's basic first aid kit. Raphie hissed quietly as he exposed the cut from Betty's knife. To be fair, it was shallow. But it was long, almost the whole length of the inside of his forearm, and the skin around it was red and angry looking. Not so much that Griff worried it was infected, but it was clearly hurting.

Without speaking, he found the painkillers they'd bought so they could both take some. Then he began carefully undressing them both so they could get into the sunken bath that Griff got running with the hottest water as they could stand. Griff would wash the wound in there, as well as his own, then they could see about ordering some food.

He felt like if he kept the evening broken down to small, manageable tasks, he could cope. No thinking about tomorrow.

So of course Raphie piped up as soon as they were submerged into the blissful water. Griff had his back to the side and Raphie between his legs, his back pressed up to Griff's chest so Griff could hold him tightly. The steam filled the room and their lungs, the bubble bath smelling like sweet roses.

"Griff…" Raphie said tentatively, half-glancing over his shoulder at him.

"Yes, beautiful?" Griff replied, because he was fucking hopeless.

Raphie chewed his lip, then looked up at him properly with his gorgeous forest-green eyes. "Please don't leave. Not if you don't want to. Don't feel you have to. We'll find a way, I promise."

A lump rose in Griff's throat. He hugged Raphie close to him, kissing his hair which was once again wet, but this time also clean of dirt and twigs. "I don't *want* to leave. Not even a little bit. I'd do anything to stay close to you, Raphie. But…"

"But you think when I become king, you can't stay?" Raphie frowned and fixed Griff with a stern look. "We have no idea what's going to happen. Why can't you just wait and see what happens?"

*Because I'm trying to brace myself for a shattered heart,* Griff thought bitterly. *Because I don't know how I'll survive letting you go.*

Saying that out loud would just make everything worse, though. He honestly didn't see an outcome where Raphie claimed his birthright – and therefore saved himself from those damned assassins – and Griff would be seen as an acceptable partner for him. Raphie would already have so many obstacles to people taking him seriously as the former king's illegitimate son. Griff wouldn't complicate that by adding a scruffy, wholly unsuitable lover to the mix. Campanula was crying out for strong leadership after decades of the old selfish, incompetent king steering them into the gutter. Raphie needed to succeed for his people. It was a tiny nation, but that was still hundreds of thousands of people.

Griff couldn't risk getting in the way of any of that.

But after their ordeal, he also couldn't be so harsh to Raphie with the truth in that moment.

"I – I don't want to make promises I can't keep," he said, caressing the side of Raphie's face as their gazes searched each other. "But I will swear to stay by your side as long as I can."

He knew that almost certainly meant until the council meeting tomorrow afternoon, probably the small coronation ceremony, and maybe until Raphie was settled with his new team. Griff didn't really want to think about it.

But for a fleeting second, his heart took flight, and he imagined if that could be *forever.* He had honestly never felt like this about anyone, and it didn't matter that he and Raphie had only known each other a few days or that Griff was older. If anything, those things worked in their favour as far as Griff was concerned. He *loved* that Raphie was wide-eyed and innocent, and there was no denying Griff's heart by trying to dissuade it with logic.

This was love.

He swallowed the lump in his throat as they shared a tender kiss. Griff was glad his eyes were still a little swollen. Hopefully, if Raphie noticed they were wet, Griff could brush it off as the residual effect of the pepper spray.

What bollocks was this that the man he finally fell in love with after all these years was the one he couldn't have?

Griff made the choice to switch his brain off, losing himself in physical sensation. He refused to spend any more energy worrying over what he couldn't change. He could control the here and now, and that meant Raphie's comfort and safety.

And pleasure.

The kiss deepened naturally between them, and Raphie twisted in the deep bath until they were face-to-face, reaching against each other beneath the water. Raphie clung to him, like a nymph to a rock, kissing and biting at Griff's lips, moaning as they stroked each other's hard lengths.

It wasn't the first time that Griff had faced a near-death experience and needed to get off once the shock had faded. Adrenaline did that to you. But in the past, it had always been anonymous hook-ups. Often pretty fucking kinky ones, but the rush faded as soon as the orgasm had and the guy had vanished out the door.

But with Raphie it was far simpler, far more intense.

It felt like mere moments before they climaxed in the bath. The comedown, on the other hand, was slow and peaceful as they tenderly washed each other, getting rid of any physical residue from everything that had transpired in the forest. Griff got to wash Raphie's hair again, and took his time massaging his scalp with the conditioner to really relax him.

Once they were dry (including Raphie's hair with the surprisingly good hotel dryer), Griff made sure Raphie's arm was properly bandaged as well as patching up his own many cuts and bruises. Raphie insisted on being the one to put the plaster over the Taser welts on Griff's shoulder, an angry pout on his face the whole time that Griff found so endearing it almost made him well up again.

But then the bathrobes were dropped to the floor, and Griff had Raphie splayed over the bed, his hair fanned over the pillows, worshipping every inch of his perfect creamy skin with his mouth and fingers. He took his time, like he had that first night, sucking and kissing and licking every intimate part of Raphie, and not just his hard cock and deliciously warm and musky hole. Griff kissed the insides of his elbows, the backs of his knees, the dips of his throat and collarbones, until Raphie was a weeping, pleading, beautiful mess. Only then did Griff lie his whole body on top of Raphie, pinning him down and making him feel completely safe and secure. Their cocks were in his hand, and they thrust until the world fell down around them and all that was left was their afterglow.

Griff didn't need anything else.

It was only in the morning, when they unhappily rose with the wakeup call Angelo had organised, did reality come crashing back down on them. Griff was mollified when the wakeup came with an insane amount of breakfast. They never did get around to ordering all those pizzas the night before, so between them, they demolished the runny eggs, tangy cheese, salty meats, buttery croissants, and everything else that came with a full continental.

It was at that point that Raphie unfurled the newspaper that had come with their food, and choked at the front page.

It was all in Italian, so Griff had no idea what it said until Raphie stopped coughing. Eyes wide and watering, he turned to Griff.

"It's about Campanula," he whispered.

Griff swallowed his mouthful with a swig of coffee, cold dread washing through him. "And?"

Raphie licked his lips. He'd gone as white as a sheet. "And it's not a council meeting and small coronation tonight after all."

Griff rested his hand on Raphie's knee through his dressing gown. "So?" he asked, not sure if he wanted to hear the answer.

Raphie took a deep breath. "So they're skipping protocol and not bothering with the council meeting. Princess Alessa will be crowned tonight in front of close to a thousand people...at a full royal coronation ball."

He licked his lips and stared at Griff.

"We're too late."

# 18

# RAPHIE

"*GRIFF...*" RAPHIE WAS COMPLETELY UNSURE AND overwhelmed as he stared at his reflection in the full-length mirror in the tailors' they'd found in Forli. "This is *never* going to work."

Griff had practically been chewing a hole in his lower lip all morning, but in that moment, he turned on a dazzling smile. He looked up at Raphie from where he'd been glued to his phone, sorting out all their logistics to get to Campanula and into the palace, shaking his head and beaming.

"It'll be *fine*," he insisted. "Winston has a man on the inside. He and your mum have been planning all kinds of eventualities for years, in case your dad did what he did."

He couldn't say too much in front of the tailors in case they spoke any English, but he was right and Raphie knew it. Raphie's mum had warned him years ago that one day he might need to return to Campanula, and she and Winston had done all they could to help prepare for any scenario they could think of.

Still, there was a difference between getting into the

building and Raphie gaining access to the council and what remained of the royal family to plead his case.

But a *ball.* No one had ever said anything about a ball. It was always supposed to have been the council meeting followed by a low-key coronation ceremony, *then* a grand affair when Alessa turned eighteen.

In actual fact, the meeting was purely ceremonial, a tradition that was just for show. Like how a new prime minister in the UK couldn't technically create a new government until they'd asked the queen's permission. It was just pomp, but every single prime minister did it. If that meeting was disregarded, it would raise questions, much like skipping the gathering of the council was causing Raphie concern now. Were they trying to hide something?

Or maybe as far as the council were concerned, Princess Alessa was the only option for their monarch, so why hang around for the proper ceremony until she was eighteen? Maybe they just really loved throwing balls?

Ordinarily, Raphie would keep up to date with world news every day, paying particular attention to Campanula. But ever since they'd been on the run and Griff had come into his life, he'd been in a bubble. Thank goodness the hotel had sent them up a newspaper that morning, and that it had been a local one concerned with the state affairs of Raphie's nearby home country. Once more, he and Griff had been ripped from their cosy bubble of luxury like they had from the French cabin, catapulted again into panic mode as they caught the train from Castrocaro Terme to Forlì and prepared to cross the border into Campanula.

But first they had to buy a stupid suit, because Raphie couldn't possibly walk into a royal ball in his jeans. He would have probably needed to purchase new clothes to face the council regardless, but a ball was next level. Raphie had no idea what to expect outside of what he'd seen in fiction. He was totally and completely out of his depth.

Thank goodness Griff was still with him. But even after their talk last night, Raphie's anxiety was constantly simmering away that he was going to up and leave at any second. No matter what Raphie said, Griff seemed totally convinced that he wasn't good enough to be with a king. How could he not see how incredible he was? It was giving Raphie a stomach ache.

At least he still had Sparrow. After the fright she'd given Raphie when she'd bolted, his heart squeezed every time he looked at her, realising how close he'd come to losing her forever. She was laid down contentedly in the changing room now, alternating between watching Raphie and snoozing.

Raphie gritted his teeth and closed his eyes. It was all too much. He knew his priority should have been everything around claiming his right to the throne, stopping the assassins, and working out how to start steering his country in a better direction. But those were all such huge, possibly insurmountable tasks.

Griff was right in front of Raphie, and it was him Raphie wanted beyond anything else. That probably showed his immaturity, but he couldn't help it. His heart was set. Griff had shown him the world, literally, but Raphie didn't want any of it if he couldn't have Griff by his side.

And the whole thing was all the more complicated by how clearly conflicted Griff was. One minute he was worshipping Raphie, showing him things he'd never dreamed of with their bodies, but also cherishing his heart. Like how right now he was putting on a show of confidence for Raphie, despite almost certainly being just as apprehensive about what they had to accomplish this evening, just to make Raphie feel better. But then the next minute, he was talking about leaving again, and Raphie wasn't sure how much more his heart could take.

For now, though, Raphie clung to Griff's confidence, even if it was slightly false.

"Our aliases are on the guest list for tonight," Griff continued, nodding, "and there's a design agency printing our invites on the down low in Campanula as we speak. Winston may be in a bunker, but that man knows how to get shit done." He laughed. "I think I would have liked having him as a boss."

There it was again – that implication he'd be leaving at some point. Raphie tried to ignore it. He was having trouble breathing anyway, and he didn't want to start shaking and get pricked by the tailors, who were fitting him up for a suit at incredibly short notice. They were like Cinderella's mice, all working their arses off so Raphie could make it to the ball.

But what was the point? The council had already made up their minds. His little half-sister was going to be crowned tonight. Sure, she was only twelve years old and would undoubtedly be a puppet of the same people who had supported their father for the past two decades, but there was no more time to petition. They'd changed the rules and picked the king's successor early. Raphie didn't stand a chance. Why show his face when it would be better to just hide himself and his mum away for the rest of their lives and hope the assassins never found them? Or that they got bored and abandoned their mission?

Of course, that would mean spending the rest of his life cooped up, just like his whole life had been until now...but maybe if Griff came with him, it wouldn't be so bad? Would it?

Raphie's stomach flipped, and he almost got himself stuck with a pin. In his heart of hearts, he knew that he never wanted to be a prisoner again for as long as he lived, and he certainly didn't want to do that to Griff. But what could they possibly hope to achieve from crashing tonight's ball? Shattering a little girl's dreams and embarrassing her? Getting arrested for treason? Showing his face so the assassins lying in wait could put a throwing star in it?

So many fun options.

And then this *suit*. Raphie was really trying to be an adult about this, but he'd never felt so uncomfortable in his whole life. He bit his lip and glanced at his reflection again, looking hurriedly away before the tears he was peering through could fall. He'd never even tried on a suit before, and now he was starting to understand why he'd never felt the need.

Growing up, he'd worn whatever he'd wanted. His mum had never batted an eyelid so long as he was happy and comfortable. But this thing he was being caged in felt like an alien that had slithered over his body and was slowly forming a solid, suffocating shell with every stitch the well-meaning and obviously talented tailors were making.

"I'm s-so sorry," he managed to stutter in Italian. "But could we take a break for a minute? I know, I know!" he cried at the head tailor Edmundo's immediately aghast face. "You're on a deadline. But just one minute, please?"

The team weren't happy, but they exited the private dressing room, leaving Raphie alone with Griff. "What's going on?" Griff asked gently, stepping closer to Raphie.

"I don't think I can crash this ball," he said shakily. "And I certainly don't think I can do it in *this*." He held out his arms, showing off the deep purple blazer, black trousers, white shirt, and black bow tie they'd picked out. It had all looked amazing on the hangers, but when Raphie looked at himself in the mirror, seeing his slim frame and braided long blond hair, he felt like he was going to be sick.

Griff immediately locked his phone screen and dropped it into his trouser pocket. It had taken mere minutes to fit him in a classic black suit. He was the picture of masculinity and looked so good Raphie had praised himself for not getting hard just looking at him. That was until his own strangeness had overwhelmed him, making him feel like a ghost wearing the wrong person's skin.

But Griff stepped up to the plinth where Raphie had been trying his best to stand still for the fitting, placing his hands on Raphie's arms. It was only then did Raphie realise how much he was trembling, and how close to passing out he felt.

"Beautiful, no," Griff said. "I thought you wanted this. We're going to get you in front of everyone who matters before the princess is crowned. They deserve to hear your case, and we *have* to neutralise the contracts your dad set up with those assassins. What are you afraid of? Talk to me."

Raphie laughed ruefully. "About tonight? Everything. Right now?" He managed to glance around Griff at the mirror for less than a second before nausea rolled over him. "Like there's something seriously fucking wrong with me. Men are *hot* in suits. You look like a wet dream. Why do I want to cry and recoil when I look at myself?"

Griff rubbed Raphie's arms for a second. Then he kissed him. Then he rubbed his arms again, his eyes darting around as he chewed his lip. Raphie's heart was ready to combust on the spot. Griff obviously didn't know what was wrong any more than Raphie did, but it looked like he was trying his hardest to find a solution regardless.

If there had been any doubt before, Raphie knew in that moment that he loved Griffin Thompson.

Griff exhaled and nodded. "How about a dress?" he asked brightly.

Raphie might have been sheltered, but he knew that it wasn't 'normal' for men to wear dresses. So he knew it had taken a lot for a tough, East End guy like Griff to not only come to that suggestion by himself, but to be genuinely chuffed that he had. From his expression, he was only thinking that he might have helped Raphie. He wasn't freaking out that the man he was sleeping with might want to wear a dress to a *very* public event.

Yup. Definitely love.

Raphie smiled and placed a hand on Griff's smooth cheek. He'd shaved that morning and looked quite dapper. "Thank you," he said sincerely. "I love wearing floaty summer dresses, but that doesn't feel right for the ball either. It's..." He dropped his hand and clenched his jaw in frustration. "It's like I can't breathe."

Griff hooked his index finger in the bow tie, then yanked, undoing it with one firm tug that made Raphie's cock pulse. Then he flicked the top button of Raphie's shirt open and stepped back down from the plinth with that assertive energy that really did make Raphie hard in his fancy suit trousers.

"How's that?" Griff asked.

*Take me now!* Raphie wanted to yell. Instead, he looked back at his reflection...and it felt like the first breath he'd taken in an hour.

"*Yes,*" he said emphatically. He inhaled deeply and snatched the bow tie through the collar of the shirt, ripping it free and smiling. He looked at Griff, the icky feeling starting to fade. Not completely, but it was much better. "Yes. Thank you. I much prefer that."

Griff gave him a firm look. "You have to feel perfect, beautiful," he said gravely. "This is your battle armour. Trust me. You have to feel like a million quid, or this won't work." He looked intensely along Raphie's body. "Why don't you let your hair down and imagine you've got a bunch of braids in it like usual?"

Raphie gulped. He really wanted to do that, but...

"Yeah, I'd like to, but kings don't look like that," he said dismissively with a shaky laugh.

If he thought Griff had stepped onto the plinth with conviction before, the way he came face-to-face with Raphie in that moment was enough to topple cities, to end wars.

He loomed over Raphie, placing his hands on his shoulders, and drilling his dark brown eyes so forcefully into Raphie, it was like another physical touch. A *strong* one.

"You, Raphael d'Oro," he said in a growl that made Raphie's whole body shudder, *"are* a king. You're a warrior. With that hair, you are Legolas of the woodland realm. You are Geralt of Rivia. You are Daenerys Stormborn of House Targaryen, Mother of Very Brave Cats." Raphie had to laugh, despite his fear and now raging erection, held down by only the expert tailoring he'd been subjected to. "Take your hair out and show me your royalty."

Raphie watched him with wide eyes as he stepped back down, not daring to breathe. He blinked, double-checked he hadn't come in his boxers, then hurriedly reached back to pull the hairband free and shake his simple plait loose.

Griff bit his lip, his eyes blown and all over Raphie like he was performing a striptease. "Your Highness," he murmured.

Raphie half-gasped, half-laughed. "Okay, this is better," he admitted enthusiastically. He studied his reflection again. "But I don't know if it's missing something?"

He looked over to catch Griff adjusting the bulge in his trousers. Griff didn't apologise or look abashed. He just licked his lips and cleared his throat. "Shall we call Edmundo back in, then? Maybe you could give him an updated briefing?"

Raphie tore his eyes away from Griff to reconsider the mirror. The suit was beautiful, really. The plum jacket was a fine crushed velvet, and the black trousers fit like a glove. Raphie liked his neckline now the bowtie was gone, but as he touched the dip in his throat, it was like something was missing. Then his eyes travelled down his whole silhouette.

"I just feel like it needs more...*flow*," he said eventually. "Does that make sense?"

Griff arched an eyebrow at him. "Can you say that in Italian?" Raphie nodded. "Well then, let's get Edmundo back in, and you can tell him."

The team were relieved to re-enter the small room, eagerly recommencing their pinning. Raphie felt awkward explaining what he meant about flow to Edmundo, but the head tailor listened thoughtfully.

"You want something with a little more femininity to it?" he asked. Raphie didn't hear any judgement in his words, he was simply thinking out loud.

"Uh, yes, I guess so?" Raphie answered. "But I don't know what."

Edmundo snapped his fingers as his eyes lit up. "I have an idea. Two, actually! One moment, please."

Griff raised his eyebrows at Raphie as Edmundo bustled out of the room. "He's going to try something," Raphie said in English with a careful shrug. It seemed like most of the pinning was finished now, though, so he could see what the finished suit would more or less look like. It was good. Raphie still wasn't a hundred per cent comfortable, but having his hair loose and down definitely helped.

"You look gorgeous," Griff murmured. His eyes had been blazing with lust before, but now they were soft and full of...

Affection was probably the safest word to use. Raphie could hope for love, but he had to remember that Griff had been with a lot of men before Raphie. As much as Raphie would protest that he knew his own mind and feelings, there was a grain of truth to the fact that Griff was his first, and that held a lot of weight. Maybe it was puppy love or the real deal, but either way, Raphie didn't want to put too much pressure on Griff when he was already trying to convince him to just *stay*.

He wished they didn't have this ticking clock hanging over their heads. If Raphie were a normal guy, he'd just be able to date Griff and see if they fell in love naturally.

Instead they had less than six hours to get ready for a ball that would – one way or another – change their lives forever.

"Okay!" Edmundo announced as he re-entered the room. His colleagues stepped back from Raphie, who was eyeing up what Edmundo had in his arms. He couldn't really see more than a lot of material – dove grey wool on one side, black silk on the other.

Edmundo came to a halt behind Raphie on the plinth, then shook out the garment with a flourish. Raphie gasped.

It was a cape.

It had a collar and buttons, like a winter coat, but no sleeves. Just slits where his arms could go through. Edmundo grinned as he draped it over Raphie's shoulders, both of them staring at his reflection.

It was exactly what had been missing. Raphie went from feeling like he was going to crawl out of his own skin, to standing tall as if he were king of the whole world.

Maybe…just maybe…he could face being king of Campanula.

"It's perfect," he rasped in Italian, hot tears pooling in his eyes for entirely different reasons this time. He'd never felt so powerful before – all from adding one bit of fabric.

Edmundo grinned smugly. "I know," he said happily.

Raphie turned to Griff, who was beaming at him. "What do you think?" Raphie asked excitedly in English.

"I love it," Griff admitted. "But I love what it's done to your face even more. I can tell you're happy, comfortable."

Raphie nodded and bit his lip. Now, it was as if he couldn't take his eyes off his reflection.

Edmundo held up a finger, then produced some kind of silver chain that was a few inches long from his pocket. There was a silver rose on each end of the length. "May I try something?" he asked over Raphie's shoulder, their eyes meeting in the reflection. Raphie nodded, so Edmundo came and stood in front of him.

Raphie bristled as he redid the top button of the shirt. But then he pressed the roses, which Raphie realised were on studs, like earrings, into the collar points. The chain hung in a U shape between them, almost like a necklace.

Raphie studied the effect carefully. It definitely didn't give him the same stifling reaction that the bowtie had. Even though there was the same pressure against his throat, Raphie didn't feel suffocated, and the bling was just the right balance between masculine and feminine.

"Amazing," he said, shaking his head, not quite able to believe the change. "Yes, perfect. You're a genius, Edmundo."

Edmundo was still grinning as he brushed his hands together and stepped back from the plinth. "I know," he said again with a wink. "Now! Let's get this suit off you to make the amendments and get you to the ball on time."

Nerves flared once more in Raphie's belly, but as he took in his reflection again, he felt just the tiniest bit less afraid.

Griff was right. *Now* he would be dressed for battle.

19

RAPHIE

It probably would have been fine if Raphie could have gone straight to the ball and faced the council. But waiting for battle was no fun, as he soon found out.

From the time they left the tailors' to when they arrived in Campanula was a complete and utter blur. It was as if as soon as he took his fancy outfit off to travel, his precious new-found confidence started slipping through his fingers like water, and the panic started creeping back in. Raphie was extremely grateful to have Griff guiding him every step of the way as they finally crossed the border into the tiny country Raphie was born in.

His whole life had been in theory. He'd spent years studying Campanulan culture, language, and history. He knew the floor plans of the palace pretty much by heart. He'd practised his speech to the council with his mum for the last couple of years.

And now all of that was worth absolutely bollocks-all in the real world.

He had to keep it together. His life depended on it, as did his mum's, and probably Griff's and Winston's now. He owed it to the people of Campanula to at least *try* and fix the mess his estranged father had made of the country. But it was extremely difficult not to feel like a fraud.

Luckily, Griff had gone into bossy mode, steering Raphie everywhere they went, and (with the help of Raphie translating) buying their train tickets and navigating the taxi once they reached Campanula. Griff and Winston had coordinated efforts to book them a hotel room to get ready in later, and for their counterfeit ball tickets to be couriered directly to their door.

A week ago, Raphie had done nothing but dream of what it might be like out in the real world. Now nothing seemed real anymore, and he was sailing too fast through the hours that brought him closer to his destiny. It didn't feel like liberation, though. He felt like he was a criminal biding their time before facing the gallows.

Part of him wished he'd stayed at home. No matter how confident he'd felt wearing his suit before, he couldn't possibly manage being king. He hadn't been able to even order fish and chips. How could he run a country?

What the hell had he been thinking?

And yet, if he'd stayed home and they'd never been attacked by the assassins, he would never have become this close with Griff. No matter how uncertain their future was, Raphie wouldn't trade that for anything.

Griff was the only solid thing that grounded him throughout the frantic day. Griff had guided him with a firm hand on the small of his back through the small town of Castrocaro Terme and on to the train to Forli, where – after the suit-fitting – they changed to get their connection into the heart of Campanula. As they took a taxi from that train station to their hotel, Raphie hugged his backpack to his front, Sparrow secure inside, Griff's sturdy hand resting on his thigh the whole time. Griff's touch was like an anchor, keeping Raphie from floating away.

The suit and cape had absolutely helped him feel less terrified about going to the palace to stake his claim. But confidence could only take Raphie so far. There were a hundred different variables and things could go wrong almost every which way. It was impossible to stop his mind from whirling.

That was until Griff dragged him onto the hotel bed and drove Raphie out of his mind with his skilled mouth and lips and tongue and hands. The rest of the world always fell away entirely when Raphie was overwhelmed by the feel of Griff's hot, rock-hard cock – this time sliding between Raphie's clamped thighs until Griff spilled everywhere, the potent smell of his musk filling the air. By the time Raphie came with a yell down Griff's throat, he was boneless and blissed out, then Griff steered him into the shower to clean him off, ensuring the distracting euphoria would last as long as possible.

It wasn't until they were both dressed and Raphie's hair had been styled to perfection did Raphie's writhing nerves reappear in his guts. He studied his reflection, touching the many braids woven into his locks, wondering if there was any way they'd get a happy ending tonight.

Would Campanula accept Raphie as their king? Would they let him *try* and save their failing economy, education, and healthcare after his corrupted father had done his best to destroy them?

And more importantly, selfishly speaking, would Griff stay? He seemed completely convinced that he wasn't good enough to be with a king, and Raphie didn't know how to persuade him otherwise.

First things first, they needed to get into the ball.

Apparently, Winston had insisted that it was more

important to arrive at the palace in an appropriate manner so they wouldn't risk causing suspicion, rather than maintaining their low profile. Therefore, he'd booked Raphie and Griff a limousine to chauffeur them. There was a chance a last-minute booking would attract the interest of any of the assassins in Campanula on the lookout for them, but that was just a risk they had to take. If they arrived in a bog-standard taxi, everyone was sure to notice.

In fact, as they made their way onto the royal grounds, Raphie began to wonder if a horse and carriage wouldn't be out of place. He leaned so he could stare out of his closed and tinted window at the impressive rectangular building they were crawling closer to in the long procession of cars they'd joined. Even though evening was falling and the glass was slightly darkened, Raphie could tell that the palace was a buttercup yellow, four stories high, with at least fifteen windows across each floor, and the turrets at either end rose up even higher with bell towers.

Raphie had studied images of the palace for hours. That was nothing compared to seeing it in person, even in in the fading daylight.

Raphie gulped. Was that supposed to be his *home?* He knew he'd lived his life in the clouds up until last week, surrounded by luxuries, but the penthouse seemed so small and intimate in comparison to this mammoth, historical place.

The trail of cars moved slowly down the driveway, giving Raphie plenty of time to begin panicking again, even in his magnificent new outfit and after Griff had done his best to utterly relax him. Raphie bit his lip and fussed with the lapel of the cape and the cufflinks by his wrists, trying to imagine the very worst outcome of the evening.

He'd be accused of treason and thrown in jail. The assassins would succeed and kill him and Griff. *No.* The very worst outcome would be if Raphie lived and Griff *didn't*. Their attack in the forest had proved that. So long as Griff lived, Raphie could deal with anything. He'd find a way to make it through and keep them together.

If that was what Griff wanted.

"Breathe," Griff murmured, pulling Raphie from his reverie as he squeezed Raphie's hand. Raphie glanced over, managing a tiny smile for Griff as he inhaled deeply.

"Sorry," he said sheepishly.

Griff shook his head. "No need to apologise. You've got this. You look amazing, and you have every right to be here. Whatever happens tonight, you can be proud of yourself that you tried to do the right thing for you, your mum, and your people."

"Fuck," Raphie said shakily. "You make it sound so noble when you put it like that. I feel like I'm just rolling with the punches, going with the flow. Putting one foot in front of the other because I literally don't know what else to do."

Griff smiled, lifting Raphie's hand to kiss the back of it. "You're following your destiny," Griff said warmly. "Remember, this mess is all your father's doing. You're just trying to unravel it. And no matter what, I'll be right here, by your side. Okay?"

Raphie nodded mutely, his gaze sliding beyond Griff and out along the grounds. The front driveway had two lanes either side of three long, rectangular ponds that led up to the front of the palace. On the outside of each road, there were immaculate gardens with hedges trimmed into eloquent topiary swirls. It was stunning, but Raphie could only appreciate it in an abstract way. His thoughts were circling like water around a drain.

*How long will you be by my side?* he wanted to ask. Griff had told Raphie that if it weren't for his pesky royal title, he'd be with him…but Raphie had no real-world experience to trust if that was really true.

He closed his eyes and inhaled again, feeling Griff's hand against his own, strong and steady. *First things first.* He dug deep for the confidence he'd felt at the tailors' in his new suit, then tried to picture a *best*-case scenario. He saw himself striding into the ball, facing down the council members (who, in his imagination, were all conveniently sat at one long table, like a judge's panel) and announcing his birthright. They'd thank him for his time, but assure him that they were in safe hands with the princess and her regent. Oh, and that the assassins had been called off. He could go home to London now, with Griff by his side.

Easy-peasy.

Except…was that what he really wanted? To go back to the way things were? *Could* he even do that? He'd changed so much at his core since last week. He felt like a totally different person now. There was certainly no way he was going back to hiding up a tower for the rest of his life.

*Just get through the door,* he told himself.

Luckily, they'd been able to leave Sparrow in the hotel room with the 'Do Not Disturb' sign on the door, so that was one less thing to worry about as their limousine inched closer to the front of the driveway. Raphie would probably have nightmares for weeks about her almost escape. But right now, she was probably curled up on the hotel bed, blissfully unaware of what Raphie was about to face.

"Hey," Griff murmured, cupping Raphie's face and encouraging him to look Griff in the eyes. "You've got this…*Your Highness.*"

Raphie giggled nervously, but he bloody loved Griff calling him that. With the partition up between them and the driver, Raphie felt safe for Griff to say that out loud…he also felt confident enough to kiss his lover deeply, feeling braver by the second.

For now, Griff was by his side, and Raphie had never felt more magnificent as the car finally came to a halt. The doors were opened for them, and Raphie exited onto a red carpet under a flurry of camera flashes. Journalists called out to him in Italian and the slight variation of Italian that Campanula used, asking who he was. Raphie ignored all of them, as they were going to take their photos one way or another.

Instead, he waited for Griff to come around the car. He offered Raphie his arm, and Raphie held it firmly as they walked towards the grand entrance together. Raphie smiled and nodded as the questions about his identity got louder, but otherwise, he didn't interact with any of the press.

They'd know who he was soon enough, he was sure.

His heart was in his mouth as Griff handed over their invitations, but they passed with only a brief inspection. Whoever Winston's contact was, they had obviously done a good enough job with their forgery, and Raphie got a small moment of respite to breathe as they entered the impressive foyer.

Raphie swallowed as his eyes darted around, attempting to absorb every detail as fast as possible. Again, photos did no justice to seeing it in person. There was a sweeping marble staircase that led off to the right. Portraits, gilded mirrors, family crests, and decorative swords were mounted on the intricately painted walls, china vases stood on plinths, and a round chandelier made from cut glass and yellow gold hung from the very high ceiling.

This was his family's legacy.

He'd poured over history books, learning of the kings and queens who'd come before him and his father, but it had never honestly felt truly real. But as he walked by several portraits of his kin who had lived hundreds of years before him, he couldn't help but be awestruck.

Even if they kicked him out, he was glad he'd seen some of his heritage in person.

He'd spent so long trying to distance himself from his despicable father, especially since knowing he'd put a hit out on Raphie upon his death. Raphie didn't want to be anything like him. His evil ways had shaped Raphie's whole life, forcing his mum to flee Campanula with him as a baby, keeping him hidden away in that penthouse, and now trying to have him murdered.

But this was who he *was.* He had royal blood, there was no escaping that. But for the first time in his life, he wasn't sure he wanted to. Looking around at the glorious palace, he felt important for the first time in his life. Like he was part of something bigger and better than just himself.

It suddenly struck him that he also felt like that with Griff.

That seemed like too big a thought to comprehend in that moment, so Raphie left it to really analyse later. All he knew in that moment was the comparison didn't feel wrong.

In fact, Griff's affection towards him felt exactly as important as a grand royal legacy.

*Later,* Raphie told himself.

They followed the stream of people who were making their way left, and Raphie tried not to feel claustrophobic as the throng became more of a crush the closer they got to a large set of open double doors. He clung to Griff, concentrating on his breathing. He'd made it through the streets of London, the underground, and the crowd on the ferry, so he could make it through this and into what had to be the ballroom. Once they'd entered, there had to be more space.

Right?

"I'm here," Griff murmured, caressing the top of Raphie's hand which was resting on the crook of Griff's arm. "Keep your eyes open. See anyone we know yet?"

Raphie had spent years studying the members of the Campanula council, not to mention the royal family themselves. On their train journeys that morning, Raphie had walked Griff through the current key players' photographs so he'd have a chance of helping Raphie out.

Of course, that probably should have been something they'd worked on over the past few days, but they'd been... busy. Besides, Raphie was self-aware enough to admit that he'd been trying to ignore anything outside of his and Griff's blissful love-nest bubble, but now he kind of wished they'd done a little more homework. It was one thing to recognise someone from a promotional photograph you'd had time to get familiar with. It was something else entirely to try and recognise the same person in extravagant formalwear, in the flickering lights of real candles in the ballroom, with hundreds of people competing to be heard over the din of the room.

Raphie exhaled as they were announced (as Andrew Hathaway and Julian Andrews, because apparently Griff wasn't done with their movie in-joke aliases yet), looking around as they walked arm-in-arm down the stairs. The ballroom was busy, but not as crammed as the hallway had been with people queuing to get inside. Raphie was glad, although now they had a new problem.

People kept turning to look at them.

His mouth went dry as he dropped his gaze to the carpeted floor. "They know we shouldn't be here," he whispered to Griff, his fear rising.

They couldn't recognise him. Raphie and his mum had done their best to make sure Raphie had never been photographed, aside from for his passports. But the ball guests were definitely paying an unusual amount of attention to Griff and Raphie.

But Griff leaned over, murmuring into his ear. "They're looking because they've never seen anyone as stunning as you. Stand proud, beautiful."

Raphie's breath hitched as Griff pressed the briefest kiss just behind Raphie's ear, but it was enough to stir a fire in his belly. He lifted his gaze and rolled his shoulders back. Griff was right. He had to present himself with poise and dignity when they found the members of the council. He had to *show* them he was the future king, not just tell them.

The top of his list to find was the premier, who was Campanula's equivalent of prime minister. A shrewd man by the name of Mancini, he was a staunch conservative and had been a firm supporter of Raphie's late father. Raphie was particularly nervous about pleading his case to him, but it had to be done. There was thankfully also the chancellor, who was a more liberal environmentalist, and the home minister, who'd been campaigning for socio-economic reform in Campanula for years. They both made Raphie slightly less apprehensive.

But then, there was the biggest obstacle of them all.

The princess.

Raphie's eyes were drawn to the young girl who was sitting with her mother at the head of the room. They were raised on a plinth, sitting on chairs that weren't quite thrones, but had aspirations to be. Both mother's and daughter's hands rested on the carved wooden arms, the backs covered in rich pink velvet. The queen and princess surveyed the guests of the ball, their expressions difficult to decipher. They just looked poised and mildly interested, but Raphie assumed there had to be more going on than that.

The raspberry-coloured drapes hanging either side of the floor-to-ceiling windows matched the throne chairs almost exactly, but the carpets and walls were a striking mix of mint green and cream. Opulent chandeliers hung above them, and the air was warm from the number of guests already mingling together. Scents of hot, savoury hors d'oeuvres drifted through the crowd, as well as wafts of countless perfumes and aftershaves.

Raphie looked at the small princess again. This was her *home.* Raphie wasn't just here to challenge her right to the throne. He was here to turn her whole world upside down, not entirely dissimilar from the way his life had been blown apart by the assassins in the penthouse. Did that make him the bad guy? If he became king, would she and her mother be okay to share their home with him? It was every bit as much Princess Alessa's birthright as it was Raphie's.

It was yet another worry to add to his already turbulent mind.

Griff's head jerked suddenly to one of the windows, breaking Raphie from his reverie. "What?" he asked, immediately on alert.

For a second, Griff frowned. Then he shook his head. "I thought I saw…never mind." He smiled down at Raphie. "It's hard not to jump at every little movement, which is difficult in a busy place like this."

Raphie nodded, understanding. "I'm okay with you being vigilant, though," he said, chewing his lip and looking around. "You've got a good track record of saving our lives."

Griff hummed, his eyes still scanning the room as he held on to Raphie tightly. Raphie leaned into him and tried to ignore the people hovering around him, clearly intrigued by someone they didn't know and keen for an introduction.

"Have you pinpointed any council members yet?" Griff asked Raphie, his low rumbling voice somehow able to drown out everyone else's chatter. "How do you want to go about this?"

Raphie shook his head. "Not yet, but I think we should-"

"Would you like some Prosecco, gentlemen?" a waiter asked, spinning around and offering them a tray filled with glittering drinks flutes.

It was only as Raphie smiled and reached for one did he realise that the waiter had spoken in English, with a very posh accent.

Several things happened at once.

Raphie recognised the man's handsome face as the assassin who had almost got them with a morning star back at the penthouse, the one who'd apparently tried to attack them at the bed and breakfast.

Griff lunged forwards, slapping the whole tray upwards. Prosecco flew into the air as the twirling glasses arched up then down towards the carpet.

The gun in the man's hand – a real fucking *gun* – fired with a silencer. But Griff had shoved the assassin's arm up when he'd sent the tray flying, so the bullet hit somewhere near the ceiling. That was about the same time as people started yelling and screaming in shock as they were doused in sparkling wine, not even noticing the gun yet.

Raphie would have apologised to them, but he was too busy staring as Griff and the assassin whirled to confront one another. Griff landed the first punch and knocked the gun from his hand. Mr Morning Star retaliated immediately, though, and then the crowd was far more concerned by the fight that was breaking out rather than the sprinkling of Prosecco they'd received.

Raphie stepped backwards...into a hand that wrapped around his shoulder and a knife that pressed to the base of his spine.

"We meet again, Princess," Bob's nasty voice growled in Raphie's ear.

# 20

# RAPHIE

Raphie didn't hesitate. Adrenaline was already pumping through him, and the attack in the forest was still fresh in his mind. He stamped as hard as he could on Bob's foot and elbowed him in the gut, breaking free and lurching forwards. Bob cried out, but Raphie pinwheeled his arms and managed to put several feet between them.

"Griff! Be careful!" he cried. "Bob's here, too!"

Griff waved him off, dodging a blow from Mr Morning Star, then managing a swipe at his legs. "It's okay. I've got this. Run!"

Unfortunately, the crowd was hastily edging backwards, forming a circle around the brawling Griff and Mr Morning Star. Shouts were ringing out for security, who Raphie had no doubt were making their way through the throng, as well as several people yelling at the two men to stop fighting. Raphie ran to the other side of the circle that had formed by the jostling crowd, turning back and locking eyes with Bob as he glared with malice.

Bob arched an eyebrow smugly, and Raphie's stomach dropped. If he wasn't desperate to chase Raphie, there had to be a reason. Why would he have grabbed him in the first place, then not make chase now?

Griff was a blur, still trading blows with the other assassin, but as he sent the guy sprawling on the floor, he was able to take a second to wipe the blood from his lip and frantically look around.

"Raphie! I said get out of here! Find security!"

From the sounds of it, security was almost on top of them, but Raphie had no idea if they would help them or arrest them along with the assassins. People were yelling at him now, asking what was going on in a variety of languages. An older woman in a fur stole was beating Mr Morning Star with her sparkling clutch bag as he scrambled to his feet...

...and he promptly lunged for Raphie.

With a bellow, Griff sprinted for Mr Morning Star, just as Bob threw himself back into the fight as well. But at that moment, Raphie was yanked backwards into the throng. The last thing he saw was the flash of Bob's knife in the candlelight as he raised it...aiming for Griff's back.

"*NO!*" Raphie roared, scrambling against whoever was pulling him away. But they wrapped their arm around his neck and dug what unmistakably felt like the barrel of another gun into his side.

There was such a din from the yelling, pushing crowd, no one was paying too much attention to Raphie as he fought and twisted. He wasn't even that surprised when he finally caught a glimpse of his assailant and realised it was Betty, also dressed in a simple black suit like her brother. In fact, Raphie realised that she had a palace security badge attached to the breast pocket of her jacket. That was why Bob hadn't chased him. He knew his sister had been waiting to pounce.

"Unlike those fucking morons," Betty hissed into his ear, "I plan on getting out of this place very much alive and definitely not arrested. So be a good little princess and come with me quietly."

"Oh, yeah, sure," said Raphie sarcastically. If that *was* what she wanted, he was willing to bet that she wouldn't shoot him in front of all these people. *"Griff!"* he yelled wildly. *"Betty has a gun!"*

Enough people spoke English that the crowd immediately parted around them…creating a natural gangway for the ninja from the boat to summersault down into. She pulled out a pair of nunchucks as she squared off with Raphie and Betty, Betty still with the gun jammed against Raphie's ribs.

"Are you kidding me?" Raphie cried. Were there any more of the assassins from the penthouse here? Were they going to fight it out here in front of all these people to see who managed to kill him first?

"You have foiled my plans for the last time, Elizabeth-san!" Wannabe Ninja screeched.

Betty scoffed. "Did you seriously just jump down from behind the *curtains?* How long have you been hiding there?"

"Give me the boy and I'll let you live!" Wannabe Ninja yelled, flicking the nunchucks in a figure of eight in front of her. The two women began circling one another, not taking their eyes off each other, with Raphie in between them.

"Get off me!" Griff bellowed from somewhere, and panic made Raphie kick back into action like he'd been doused with a cold bucket of water. Griff had both Bob and Mr Morning Star to fend off.

"Griff!" Raphie screamed over the chaos that the ballroom had become.

He wrestled against Betty's hold on him, scrambling to get free. In that moment, Wannabe Ninja lunged for them, pulling Betty's attention away from Raphie for a split-second. Raphie arched his body, smashing the back of his head into Betty's nose, meaning he could slip free just as the wailing ninja collided into Betty, sending them both sprawling onto the floor. Betty's gun went skittering from her hand, through the feet of the crowd.

Raphie was completely turned around as the throng moved like a hive of angry bees. "Griff! Where are you?" he yelled over the several languages being shouted through the air.

But the desperate call of "Raphie!" told him where to go.

"I'm coming, Griff!" he bellowed back. Betty and Wannabe Ninja were still grappling, and Raphie made the most of their distraction.

His heart was pounding as he whipped his cape and changed direction. He stumbled into the space where Griff was fending off Bob and Mr Morning Star. He gasped as he saw Griff spin Bob by the lapels of his jacket into Mr Morning Star, sending both assassins careening backwards to the floor.

"Griff!" Raphie cried as he threw himself into his lover's arms, trying to pull him away from the fight. "Are you okay? They're everywhere!"

"I know," Griff grunted, kissing the top of Raphie's head. "I'm okay. You?"

"I'm fine – *watch out!*"

They spun as Bob lunged for Mr Morning Star's gun, which had been abandoned on the floor until now, probably being kicked around by the ever-moving horde of ball guests. But now Bob seized it triumphantly, lifting to aim it at Raphie's head. Griff grabbed Raphie, putting himself between Raphie and the gun as Raphie screamed...

He wasn't the only one.

*"Enough!"* a shrill voice rang out.

It was so commanding, all the voices around Raphie and Griff hushed. Raphie expected to hear a shot ring out from the gun, but when he peeked around Griff, he saw that several real securities officers had piled on top of Bob, obviously recognising his uniform as a fake. Yet more officers were tackling Mr Morning Star, and the gun and the knife had been kicked away from them both, but Raphie's stomach dropped as four guards also approached Raphie and Griff.

They were all brandishing Tasers, and Raphie didn't hesitate. He was in front of Griff with his arms thrown wide before he'd even realised what he was doing. "Don't hurt him!" he pleaded in Campanulan, his chest heaving. "We mean no harm! I can explain! Just don't hurt Griff!"

Griff moved in a flash, wrapping his arm around Raphie and holding the other hand out placatingly towards the security officers. "I'm supposed to be protecting *you*, remember?" he grumbled. "We didn't start the fight, I swear," he said louder to the guards in English. So Raphie repeated his words in Campanulan.

There was a beat where the security guards paused…then they all looked to the right.

Where twelve-year-old Princess Alessa had just stamped her foot, rage blatant on her young face. "What's the meaning of this?" she cried. Her mother, Queen Ismerelda, was standing behind her with a look of shock and concern.

Rather than run away from the ruckus, they had pushed their way into it. Raphie was surprised, to say the least. He realised it must have been the princess's voice that had stopped the fighting, and he had to admit he was impressed. It appeared she had quite a backbone.

"If you can explain why you have disrupted my ball and endangered my guests, then please do so. Right now," Alessa demanded in loud, clear English. She might have looked like a doll in her purple ballgown and with the tiara on her flowing golden hair. However, there was a fire in her eyes that Raphie had to admit he was impressed by for someone so young.

Raphie swallowed, flooded by nerves once again. Of all the ways he'd pictured this moment, he couldn't have imagined a more disastrous turn of events. He nervously brushed his hands down his front as more security guards emerged, dragging the disarmed Betty and Wannabe Ninja with them, both angry-looking and in handcuffs as they were deposited onto the carpet. The crowd parted wider, creating more of a circle.

Everyone was looking between Raphie and Alessa.

"Oh, fuck," Raphie whispered under his breath.

Griff's strong hand squeezed his shoulder. "Take a breath. You've got this," he murmured reassuringly.

Raphie licked his lips and nodded, brushing his hair back off his shoulders and stepping forwards. He was fully aware of the hundreds of pairs of eyes on him. He'd barely met fifty people in his whole life until last week, and now he had the attention of an entire ballroom.

He did his best not to tremble.

"Okay, yes, right," he said with a short bow towards the two women, keeping eye contact with the princess. He took a breath and tried to steady his racing heart. "Your Highness. M-my name is Raphael d'Oro. My mother is Annabella d'Oro, and my father was…well, the truth is he was King Tommaso. Who, as you know, was…well…your father, too."

So much for poised and dignified.

"The papers, Raphie," Griff murmured as Alessa's eyes grew wide, and a murmur ran through the crowd.

"Oh, yes!" Raphie cried in relief. He fumbled in his trouser pocket for the envelope there. It was crumpled, but still sealed. It had been in the bottom of his rucksack before getting stuffed into his pocket, after all. "I have my birth certificate, DNA paternity results, and written testimonials."

Everyone was still staring at him, but now they were open-mouthed. "I promise I'm not a lunatic," he whispered.

Alessa looked over her shoulder at her mother. The girl's hair was long and white-blonde, unmistakably similar to Raphie's. "I beg your pardon," she said, turning back to Raphie. "But what exactly are you saying?"

Raphie licked his lips and glanced at Griff for support. One solitary nod was all he needed. He smiled gratefully at Griff, then looked back at the princess and queen, aware that all four assassins were still wriggling furiously on the carpet, and everyone else in the ballroom was staring at him.

"I'm saying," Raphie began as he adjusted the cape on his shoulders, "that I am King Tommaso's oldest child, and therefore the legal heir to the Campanulan throne. Which is why he sent *this lot,*" he spat out, jerking his thumb at the assassins, "to track me down and kill me after he died two weeks ago." He swallowed, his nerves reaching a peak as the envelope quivered in his shaky hands. "He wanted to make sure I would never be king."

Alessa shook her head. "No, sorry. If you're my half-brother, where have you been all this time? Hidden under a rock?"

"More like up a tower," Griff said. His tone was warm as he placed a hand on Raphie's shoulder and stepped closer, but Raphie didn't dare look back at him. If he did, there was a strong chance he'd throw himself into Griff's arms and cry, so he kept his focus on Alessa and her mum. But Griff's hand felt strong, like an anchor, giving Raphie courage.

"That's right," Raphie agreed. "My mother gave birth to me in secret here in Campanula, then fled to London where she kept me hidden my entire life. My friend, Griff, is part of my private security team. He's the one who got me across Europe." Raphie hoped Griff didn't mind being called his friend in that moment. It seemed simplest, given the circumstances. "We'd hoped to make it in time to present my case to the council in the meeting that should have taken place this afternoon. We had no idea there would be a ball," he added sheepishly.

"Why did you hide?" Alessa asked with a frown.

Raphie shook his head ruefully. "Because my mother knew as soon as my father found out I existed, he would try and take me from her, to either kill or corrupt me."

"This is preposterous!" a voice rang out in Campanulan. Raphie turned to see a stuffy old man with grey hair and ruddy cheeks push his way through to the front of the crowd.

It was the premier, Mancini.

He brandished his fist. "How *dare* you accuse our beloved king of such nonsense! A child out of wedlock? Attempted murder? You disrespectful whelp! Not that you understand me, I'm sure. You upstart, English, fa-"

"Actually," Raphie interrupted in Campanulan. He'd heard quite enough homophobic slurs for the time being. "I was born here and speak the language perfectly. I'm sorry to shatter your illusions of my late father, but I'm almost certain he arranged contracts with all these people over a decade ago. They've been trying to kill me for a week." He smiled sweetly at Mancini. "Although I'm sure you have *no* idea what I'm talking about, do you?"

From the flicker of fear across Mancini's face, Raphie's suspicions were confirmed. The premier was just as corrupt as Raphie and his mum had always suspected.

"Well, I don't know what you're talkin' about," Betty cried in indignation. "Do you, Bob?"

"Haven't the foggiest," yelled Bob. "Ridiculous! I demand to see a lawyer!"

"I am not with them," mumbled Mr Morning Star.

"Ah, fuck it," groused Wannabe Ninja in a South London

accent, completely different to the fake mystic voice she'd been using up until now. The guards had pulled her face mask off, so her words rang out clearly. "This was a last hurrah, anyway. I've been happily doing landscape gardening for years. This was all a bit of an inconvenience. Everything the kid is saying is true."

"*Shut up!*" Bob and Betty screeched in horror together.

"Uh, okay. Thank you," said Raphie uncertainly. The last thing he'd been expecting was a testimonial from one of his pursuers. Wannabe Ninja nodded at him with a strange kind of smile. Almost like she respected Raphie in that moment.

He turned back to Alessa. He figured he wasn't going to get much support from Mancini, just as he'd suspected. His best bet was to address the princess directly.

"Your Highness," he said solemnly, in English once more so as not to exclude Griff and many of the other guests. He offered out the papers in his hand. "I'm so sorry to crash your coronation ball. This wasn't what I planned, believe me. But our late father's goons have been chasing us all the way from London."

Alessa looked to one of the security guards who gave off an air of extra authority, suggesting he was possibly in charge, and he took the papers from Raphie.

"Find Bianchi from the legal office," he said quietly in Campanulan to one of his lackeys. "We need to verify this immediately." The lackey nodded and disappeared into the crowd. Raphie gulped, hoping his credentials were as up to par as his mum had promised.

"So," Alessa said slowly. "You're here to take the throne from me?"

Raphie threw his palms up and shook his head. "Honestly...I don't know," he said, exhaling heavily. "I was happy to stay in London, I really was. But then Tommaso-"

*"His Royal Highness,"* Mancini interjected angrily. Raphie ignored him.

"My late father, Tommaso, organised to have me and my mum *murdered,* so I was forced to show my hand. I knew claiming my title might be the only way to dissolve the hits put out on us, but also…" He bit his lip. There was no going back now. "It *is* my birthright. I am the rightful heir to the throne, and…well, I've been training for this my whole life. I want to do my duty to my country."

Alessa's eyebrows rose. "I see," she said. But she didn't sound upset. More like she was thinking through Raphie's words.

But the premier wasn't done blustering. "This is a disgusting accusation," he said, again in Campanulan, proving that he *understood* English, but just refused to speak it. "Our beloved king would never do such a thing. That you would even suggest it speaks greatly of your low moral character!" He turned to Alessa and gave her a simpering smile. "Don't listen to the silly man, Your Highness. He's obviously not well to be speaking so poorly of your dearly beloved late father."

But the princess narrowed her eyes. "I am no longer a child, so you will not speak to me as such, Premier. And we all knew my father was a bit of a bastard."

Raphie choked, and he wasn't the only one. Numerous people in the crowd gasped and let out nervous laughs. The older woman in the fur sole waved her glittery clutch by her head. "Well said, Your Highness," she said somewhat gleefully.

Mancini had gone all red and blotchy. He opened his mouth a couple of times, then took a breath as if to launch into another tirade. But Alessa lifted her hand. "Be quiet. I'm talking to my half-brother. If that's what he is?"

Raphie hadn't noticed, but a man had appeared beside the

head of security. Presumably, this was Bianchi, as he was pouring over Raphie's birth certificate. "It certainly *looks* legitimate at first glance," said the lawyer, scratching his head. "Obviously, we'll have to investigate further to prove they aren't forgeries."

"Understood." Alessa hummed, giving Raphie a shrewd look. "So…you say my – our – father paid these people to… eliminate you from the picture?" she said slowly and uncertainly.

"Yup," said Wannabe Ninja said cheerfully. "The contracts were set up about ten years ago. Or was it closer to fifteen, now, Betty?"

"I said shut *up,* you moron!" Betty hissed incredulously.

Alessa frowned and looked between the assassins and Raphie, whilst Raphie's heart fluttered in his chest. He still had no idea which way this was going to go. Alessa chewed her lip. "Can anyone prove this? All we have so far is your word and some documents that will need verifying."

Raphie opened his mouth. Honestly, he didn't have much more than the documents and his mother's account of the king's behaviour and general character. Proof beyond that might be a little trickier to come by.

"Uh…" A timid-looking man in thick black glasses and a tweed suit that was just a little too big for him stepped through the crowd, raising his hand.

"Yes?" said Alessa in confusion.

"Hi," said the timid man. "Sorry, uh. Yes. I'm not sure if this counts as evidence, *per se.* But my name is Gabriel Lastra. I'm part of Minister Rossi's office." That was the finance minister, Raphie recalled. "Or, at least, I was," Lastra continued. "He vanished a week ago, along with a couple of other ministers, as I'm sure you're aware, Premier."

He nervously licked his lips as Raphie's eyebrows rose. The other rats had fled the ship already? Maybe *that* was the real reason the council meeting had been forgone. The corrupt members had already vanished, and it was just Mancini left with his trousers down. Raphie's heart sped up. If the council was no longer riddled with corruption, maybe this wouldn't end with him in a foreign jail cell for the rest of his life.

Lastra cleared his throat at the vicious look Mancini threw him. But he wasn't backing down, apparently. "There have been several huge discrepancies in the budget that we've been trying to work through in Rossi's absence."

"Rossi, that's him," said Wannabe Ninja with a click of her fingers. "He was the one who told us the game was on, and promised to set up a bank account in the Cayman Islands for whoever offed the boy first."

"What is *wrong* with you?" Bob demanded. "Shut the fuck up!"

The ninja shrugged. "I'm bored now the fun's over. Besides, you know we're all going to jail, and I have *no* trouble spilling my guts for a lighter sentence."

"Trying to kill Raphie was *not* fun," Griff growled menacingly.

Wannabe Ninja chuckled. "Sure it was, handsome."

"Premier Mancini," the queen snapped, breaking her silence. The premier looked sheepishly at her. "Is this true, about Rossi and the others? They helped my late husband try and hurt this poor boy?"

Raphie was surprised by the compassion in her voice as she raised her hand to indicate him.

Mancini straightened his cuffs and cleared his throat. He was sweating profusely.

"We have…had trouble locating Rossi, yes," he admitted, this time in English. "I was unaware anyone else was, uh, missing, though. And, um, I can't speak to the other accusations, but…well, that truly is a disgrace, if so. Um…"

Alessa looked up at her mother. "We can freeze those accounts, yes?" She looked to Lastra. "Yes?"

Lastra nodded enthusiastically. "Absolutely. You just need to give the order."

The princess bit her lip. "But...I haven't been crowned yet, and our law is very clear." Her gaze met Raphie's. "The eldest child is heir, whether born in or out of wedlock."

Mancini got some of his puff back. "Your Highness," he spluttered. "You can't be serious! He is an outsider! He has not been trained. He is...well, just *look* at him."

Raphie refused to flush, even with the shame that rushed through him. But he remembered Griff's red-hot eyes on him, telling him he was fucking royalty, and straightened his cape again. He was meant to be here. *He was born for this.*

"I can assure you that I have trained my whole life for the possibility that I might have to assert my right to the throne one day," he said calmly. "It brings me no joy to come out of hiding and cause chaos. I wouldn't have had to if my father had just left me alone. I couldn't think of any other way to stop the assassins, though."

"Yes, I can see that," said Ismerelda, not unkindly. "But now we are in a bind. Our law is clear. You are the heir, no matter how inexperienced."

"Like *I'm* more experienced," said Alessa with an eye roll as she folded her arms. "No one questioned me when it seemed like I was the only option. What's the difference between me and Raphael, Mr Mancini?"

Mancini ground his teeth. "Your Highness," he said with an ingratiating bow. "You are *clearly* of royal breeding. Your mother is nobility. We have no idea who this person's mother is," he added scathingly, waving a hand at Raphie. "He clearly has very little breeding at all."

*Fuck.* Raphie almost didn't care that Mancini was insulting him. But that was *exactly* Griff's argument why they couldn't be together. That to be with royalty, you had to be of a certain social calibre. Raphie thought that was preposterous, but if that was what the country's premier thought, did he and Griff stand a chance?

"Kindly stop referring to my half-brother's mother as if she were a horse, Mr Mancini," said Alessa snootily. Raphie did his best not to twitch his lips with a smile. "I don't care who his mum is, and neither does the law. If my father is also his father, that puts him first in line."

"I don't claim to come here and know what's best, though," said Raphie hastily, waving his hands. "If I ascended to the throne, I would need advisers to help me steer Campanula back on the right path, particularly with regards to the economy."

"Oh!" the geeky finance guy, Lastra, said excitedly, practically vibrating, unable to contain himself. Raphie blinked at him, unsure as to why he was so happy. But then he continued speaking. "Oh, yes. I like him very much. Bravo! Yes, please. Let's do that."

"The economy *is* in shambles," the older woman with the glittery clutch and fur stole grumbled. Many around her made noises of agreement.

"Okay, everyone, *shush*," demanded Alessa, stamping her foot again in a very bratty manner befitting a princess, which Raphie had to say he quite enjoyed. She *was* still twelve, after all. "None of you are listening properly. Mr d'Oro." Raphie nodded at her. "Are you saying *I don't have to be the queen?*"

She stared at him earnestly with saucer-like eyes. Her mother bit her lip, looking like she was holding her breath. Raphie glanced back at Griff, who gave him an encouraging nod. Mancini looked like he was ready to explode.

Raphie took a shaky breath. "I don't know," he said softly. "I am prepared to be king. That is what the law says…but…"

"What is it?" Alessa said, lurching forwards, clutching her

hands to her chest. "Because whatever it is, we'll fix it. I don't want to be queen. Neither does Mamma. It made Papa a *terrible* person. I'm sure you and your mother know that. I don't want it, please – please take it from me."

"Your Highness?" spluttered Mancini in horror. "We cannot possibly know if this English *boy*" -he clearly said the word with speculation, reminding Raphie of Betty and Bob's 'princess' taunts- "won't just run our nation into the ground! We don't know anything about him!"

Queen Ismerelda touched her hand delicately to the jewels around her neck and tilted her head as she looked at Raphie. Raphie gulped and tried not to fidget.

"He stepped in front of this man," she said thoughtfully, glancing at Griff, then back to Raphie. "His bodyguard, who is much larger than him. He begged us not to hurt him. I believe that shows an immeasurable deal of compassion."

Raphie blinked, a lump in his throat as he turned back to Griff. Griff gave him a sad smile. *Fuck.* Raphie still didn't know what to do, or how Griff truly felt.

"Thank you," Raphie said softly, turning back to Ismerelda. "I appreciate that."

She gave him a nod. "What is your hesitation? If this is indeed your birthright?"

She turned towards Bianchi, the lawyer, who had been talking on the phone as he continued scrutinising Raphie's documents. He blinked, realising his queen was looking at him. He glanced at his phone. "It's all checking out so far at the Registry of Births and Deaths," he said, sounding bemused. "This young man is, by all accounts, King Tommaso's eldest son, born to an Annabella d'Oro, twenty-one-years ago."

A rumble of intrigue passed through the crowd. Raphie kind of wished they could have done this in private, but this ballroom was filled with some of the most important people in Campanula. If they were on Raphie's side…well, that had to be a good thing, didn't it?

"Are you prepared to be king, Raphael?" Alessa asked, her voice full of hope and her eyes wide as she clenched her small hands.

Raphie licked his lips and took a deep breath. He hadn't come this far to be anything less than honest. "I am. It's my duty. But…I want the freedom to be with the person of my choosing. To be *myself*," he added pointedly, catching Mancini's eye. "I know Campanula has strict ideas of what kings and queens should look like, of who they should marry, like most monarchies still do. I…I would want to challenge that."

There. He'd done it. Whatever the consequences now, he knew he'd tried.

"Are you gay?" Alessa asked in an excited whisper. "Because I thought you might be." She danced on her toes. "Father would have *really* hated that! How excellent!"

Hope bubbled in Raphie's chest. His eyes stung with tears, but he wasn't sure yet if they were joyful. This was a very delicate moment. "Uh, yes," he said as loudly and clearly as he could. He'd never had any intention of living in the closet once he'd escaped his sheltered life. However, it was still pretty scary coming out to an entire roomful of people. But he cleared his throat and decided not to leave any doubt. "Yes, I'm gay. And, um, nonbinary. I know I might not look like a traditional king, but I would do my utmost to perform my duties to the very best of my abilities. But I won't cut my hair."

"It *is* even longer than mine," Alessa agreed, sounding awe-inspired as the ballroom filled with murmurs again. "Amazing."

"My goodness," said the old lady with the sparkly clutch

bag, peering over her glasses. "That's one for the history books, isn't it?"

"Of course he's gay," snarled Mancini, jabbing a hand towards Raphie. Raphie couldn't help but flinch at the sheer hatred radiating off him. "Campanula deserves *strong* leadership. This…this…*sissy* couldn't possibly be the one to deliver it! The rest of Europe will laugh at us!"

Try as he might, Raphie couldn't stop the lump from rising in his throat or his eyes from burning. This was one of his worst fears, come to life. He was being rejected and ridiculed for the way he looked and the man he loved. For the way he'd simply been *born.* How could he ever have thought he'd be good enough? The world rejected people like him who didn't look and act like a *real* man. He should have never come here. He felt smaller than he could have ever imagined.

Then he felt Griff's hand slip over his shoulder.

"You're wrong," Griff said loudly and clearly to Mancini. "Europe – the whole world – *needs* someone like Raphie. He is a good, kind, intelligent person who will do everything in his power to look after his country." He jutted his chin out defiantly at the premier. "Whether other nations are ready to accept him or not."

If Mancini were a cartoon, he'd have had steam coming out of his ears. Princess Alessa was positively shining with excitement.

But it was neither of them who spoke.

"On behalf of the United Kingdom of Great Britain and Northern Ireland," a new voice resonated through the room, "as well as the Commonwealth of Nations, Raphael d'Oro will be accepted as King of Campanula."

Raphie's head turned to see who had emerged from the throng to champion him, unable to believe his eyes.

Prince James of England was as gorgeous as he looked on

TV. He wore a navy military dress uniform with a red stripe running down each side. Shiny medals with colourful ribbons hung from his breast pocket, and an actual sword dangled from his hip. Mr Morning Star immediately ogled the antique weapon with wide eyes from his undignified position on the floor.

Standing proudly beside James was his husband, Theodore Glass, in a classic three-piece suit and a look of pure delight in his eyes. He swirled the Prosecco in the glass he was holding delicately between his fingers, clearly having fun.

They both beamed warmly at Raphie as Raphie's jaw hit the floor. "T-thank you, Your Highness," Raphie managed to utter.

"Hi, James! Hi, Theo!" Alessa waved from the other side of the circle of people. "How are all your dogs and swans?"

The men smiled and shared an affectionate look with each other. "Very well, Your Highness, thank you," said James, inclining his head.

"Still causing trouble," added Theo with a grin.

"Excellent," said Alessa, sounding proud.

"On a personal note," Prince James continued, turning back to Raphie with a wry smile, "I would like to also say, *bravo*, Raphael. You've endured a lot, but you're still here. I look forward to dinner with you and your sister in the near future." He glanced at Griff. "And perhaps your friend, as well?"

"W-what," spluttered Mancini, finally rediscovering his voice and gesturing wildly towards James. "This can't...that doesn't count! He's not even in *line* for the British throne!"

"I speak on behalf of my whole family, I assure you, Mr Mancini," said Prince James calmly. Half a smile tugged at his mouth. "Including my grandmother."

"I think that settles it, don't you, Mamma?" said Princess

Alessa, glancing at the queen before grinning at Raphie. "Campanula is grateful to have your family's support, Prince James." She clapped her hands. "And now we will have its first gay king! Or…queer monarch. That's a more inclusive term all around, isn't it?" she asked Raphie excitedly.

"Y-yes, it is," he assured her, warmth spreading through his chest. "Thank you."

Griff leaned in to murmur in Raphie's ear. "Another woke Zoomer boffin," he said with both warm affection as well as disbelief. "God help me."

"You'll get used to it," said Raphie with a breathless laugh, overwhelmed by too many emotions. Relief, pride, and incredulity all mixed together.

Theo Glass winked at him. "King Raphael!" he cried out in his distinctly Essex accent, raising his Prosecco glass.

Premier Mancini looked like he was going to try and protest one last time, but an icy glare from Queen Ismerelda silenced him.

"King Raphael!" Princess Alessa agreed, throwing up some dab arms.

"King Raphael!" bellowed the old lady, waving her glittery clutch in the air. Several other people were nodding, and then someone started to clap.

Before Raphie knew what was happening, the applause was spreading throughout the hall, and people began chanting, *"King Raphael! King Raphael!"* He could feel his eyebrows crawling up his forehead as his heart threatened to beat out of his chest. Were these people really *that* supportive of him?

"Fucking queers," Bob sneered from where he was sat on the carpet.

The older lady smacked him over the head with her clutch.

Ismerelda ignored him. Instead, she beamed at Raphie. "I

believe that means you have the support of the people, too," she said gently as the applause died down. "So…is the young man in question the one you were determined to protect with your own life?"

She moved her gaze to Griff over Raphie's shoulder. Apprehensively, Raphie turned to face Griff, anxious tears pooling in his eyes and his heart beating like a train.

This was the moment he'd been most afraid of.

If Griff could be with Raphie freely, with nothing to hold them back…*would* he?

"Yes," Raphie whispered, his eyes locked with Griff's brown ones. Griff was tense, his arms by his side, unmoving. "This is him. He's not royalty or nobility, but he's a good, kind man, and…"

*And I love him.*

"And if he wants to be with me, I want that, too."

"Oh my god, this is killing me!" Alessa hissed. When Raphie glanced back at her, she was dancing on her toes again, her fists bunched up by her head. "Bodyguard man! Do you want to be his royal boyfriend or not? I ship it! I stan it!"

Griff licked his lips. "I don't know what those words mean, but…" He reached forward and took Raphie's hands in his own. The older lady gasped. Alessa squealed. "But I do know that I would go to the ends of the earth to be with Raphie, the man – the *enby* I love. If you'll allow me."

"WOOHOO!" Alessa cried, punching the air. "My half-sibling has a boyfriend! This is awesome!"

"Bravo," said Prince James again as he nodded, warmth radiating from him and his husband.

Raphie was too stunned to speak. He was almost too afraid to.

Almost.

"You love me? Really?" he whispered.

Griff sighed as he nodded. "Pretty much since the moment I met you, beautiful."

"Okay, so, *now* will you be king?" Alessa asked impatiently. "Now that we've all approved of your hot boyfriend?"

"*Alessa,*" the queen admonished, and Mancini made another noise that clearly stated he wasn't approving anything in a hurry, but Raphie didn't care. If Griff loved him and wanted to be with him, there was nothing he couldn't do.

He stepped up to Griff, cupping the side of his face and leaning in close.

"Yes, I'll be king," he said, then pressed his lips to Griff's. "And I come with my very own knight in shining armour."

"Bloody right, you do," said Griff before kissing him back.

EPILOGUE

GRIFF – ONE WEEK LATER

"ACCORDING TO CAMPANULAN LAW," RAPHIE ANNOUNCED AS he came to join Griff on the balcony, "if we were to get married, you'd get the title of duke. 'Duke Griffin.'" He waved his hands around like a music conductor. "I think that has a nice ring to it, don't you?"

Griff smiled, moving from where he'd been leaning on the railing, and sat down at the small table that was situated on the balcony. They had a spectacular view of the palace grounds from the suite they'd been graciously allocated by Princess Alessa and her mum. The sun was shining, and birds were chirping. In the distance, the rest of the city could be seen, but the lush green royal gardens made Griff feel like he was in an oasis.

It felt like something out of a fairy tale. But Griff was starting to get used to that now.

After the spectacular kerfuffle at the ball, neither Raphie and Griff were quite sure how things were going to pan out. But as it transpired, Alessa really liked being royal without the pressure of actually ruling, and had graciously stepped aside just like she'd promised to have Raphie crowned right there at the ball in her place.

It had been one of the proudest moments of his life watching Raphie ascend to his birthright, knowing that they loved each other. That they were *allowed* to love each other. With the blessings of both the Campanulan and British royal families, Griff had finally been able to give in to his heart's desire and admit that wild horses couldn't drag him from Raphie's side.

And now here they were, living in Raphie's ancestral home in a kind of luxury Griff could never have previously imagined.

Even though relations had seemed stable, Griff would never have expected Alessa and Ismerelda to absolutely insist that Raphie and Griff move into their own suite right away. It seemed a bit ridiculous to call such a grand palace a home, but that was what it was to the princess and queen, and they'd opened it up to Raphie and Griff without question.

What was possibly even crazier was that Griff had accepted without a moment's pause. In the real world, moving in with a boyfriend after a week would seem like madness. But this was Griff and Raphie's fairy tale, and Griff had absolutely no interest in going back to London. In fact, he had no interest in being anywhere Raphie wasn't.

Their suite was already feeling more like home than any place Griff had lived in his whole life.

"That's the third time you've tried to casually bring up marriage in a week," Griff said fondly. Raphie came skipping up to him, looking delectable in just a pair of lilac silk pyjama bottoms. His hair was braided neatly down his back.

Griff had plans to mess it up again, he didn't mind admitting.

His cock stirred under his fancy dressing gown just

thinking about it. It had been a hell of a week. They hadn't been so exhausted as to not to have sex…a *lot* of sex, but every time had been pretty quick and dirty. Not that there was anything wrong with that, but now they had a morning off, Griff had a whole lot of slow and luxurious plans he was keen to act on.

"I don't know what you're talking about," Raphie said innocently as he dropped sideways onto Griff's lap and flung his arms around his neck. His little fib was undermined by the grin on his face and the way he waggled his eyebrows. "It was simply a fact I learned that *happens* to pertain to marriage of two men, something that's never happened with a Campanulan king before, but now if it does, the powers that be have settled on a dukedom for any potential husband of mine. Isn't that fascinating? I'm *learning*."

"Of course you are, my clever boffin," said Griff warmly.

He placed his coffee down, then ran his hands up and down Raphie's bare back, feeling how his skin was warm from the sun. They both very much suited the Campanulan weather and pace-of-life so far, and London was already feeling like a faraway memory even only after a couple of weeks away.

As the law was on their side, it had been relatively simple to crown Raphie instead of Alessa last week, and they'd spent every day since getting used to their crazy new life. Griff didn't mind. As soon as Queen Ismerelda had told Griff he could be with Raphie, nothing else mattered. Griff would learn every custom and do anything that was asked of him with patience and grace. All that mattered was that he was there with Raphie and would be for as long as Raphie would have him.

Griff did kind of hope that would be forever, but it was still fun to tease Raphie about his not-so-subtle proposal hints.

"One week as king and it's already going to your head,

bossy boffin," he said with a dramatic sigh, shaking his head. "What if I don't want to be a duke? What if I want to be a marquis or a lord? Hmm?"

Raphie brushed his fingers along Griff's cheek and kissed him tenderly. "You can be whatever you want, my love."

Griff grumbled and tickled Raphie's side. "It's no fun if you're going to get all mushy about it."

Raphie giggled and squirmed. "Tough! I'm the king, and if I want to be a brat about it to my *boyfriend,* that's what I'll do!"

Griff growled, his cock throbbing from their affectionate teasing and Raphie's solid weight on his lap. "Is that so, Your Highness?"

Raphie groaned, kissing Griff harder and grinding his backside against Griff's legs. "Say it again," he whispered.

"Do we still have the morning off, *Your Highness?*" Griff asked, kissing Raphie's neck. He hummed and stroked his hand along Raphie's thigh, where he was obviously tenting his silky pyjama bottoms.

Annabella and Winston were due to arrive at the palace that afternoon. With the assassins safely in custody, Raphie's mum and head of security were free and safe to come out to visit Raphie for the first time since his coronation. Although Griff suspected Winston wasn't coming in an official security capacity as much he was as Annabella's other half. He had to admit the thought warmed him. They would stay for a couple of weeks, but then head back to London.

It had been an emotional call from Raphie to his mum after they'd been able to escape the ball. Annabella had stayed up late to find out how everything had gone, wanting to hear it from her son first and not the international press. Griff had held Raphie's hand as both d'Oros had cried on either end of the phone with relief and happiness. After twenty-one years, their ordeal was finally over. They were free, with no more secrets to hide.

Annabella had kept switching absently between English and Campanulan as she'd sobbed down the phone, but Griff had been able to gather that she was incredibly proud of Raphie.

Griff knew the feeling.

Three weeks ago, he'd never left his penthouse. Today, he was a true *king*.

Annabella had wanted to fly out to Campanula immediately, but Raphie had convinced her to hold off. He'd had a feeling that he was going to have to hit the ground running with his new duties, especially overseeing the appointment of several new council members, not to mention all the dignitaries he had to meet and greet. It had been a real whirlwind, but Griff had been by his side every step of the way.

And thanks to their new official royal tailor (Edmundo, of course), he'd even been able to look the part. Someone worthy of being with a king. Slowly, the voice in his head that had been so eager to tell Griff that he wasn't good enough for Raphie and never would be was growing fainter and fainter. Griff knew he had a lot of insecurities to wrestle with, but he'd do anything to be with Raphie, plain and simple.

Until Annabella and Winston arrived, Griff and Raphie had been given their first proper break since the royal ball. The staff had been given strict instructions not to disturb them unless there was a global catastrophe.

And Griff intended to make the most of it.

Raphie nodded. "Yep. The whole morning. I'm all yours," he said breathlessly. "Whatever will you do with me?"

Griff growled and stood up, scooping Raphie in his arms as he giggled and squirmed. "Whatever I like," he said, loving how that made Raphie shiver against him. "I'm the boss, now."

Raphie nodded again, his face buried in the crook of Griff's neck as they made their way to the bedroom, his fingers digging into Griff's back. "Oh, *Griff*," he moaned wantonly. "Tell me what you want."

Griff kissed along Raphie's collarbone as he crossed the threshold into the bedroom – *their* bedroom. Griff had never shared a bedroom before. He had to admit, so far, he was loving it.

Griff knew he'd never have to worry about paying his bills or going hungry again, but more than that, he loved knowing that no matter what craziness waited for them outside the door, he and Raphie had their sanctuary back, like they'd found in the French cottage, a blissful little bubble that was all theirs.

And Sparrow's, of course.

"Oh, no. Off you go," Griff said, shooing the ginger cat from the bed.

It had taken Raphie a lot to trust Griff in allowing Sparrow to roam freely through the palace and its grounds. She'd been by his side since she was a kitten, and Raphie was terrified that something might happen to her. But in the end, he'd realised that she needed her freedom as well, and she'd be perfectly safe here at the palace. After a couple of days, Griff could tell that Raphie was starting to relax and trust that she'd always come home, ignoring all the fancy baskets and hammocks that Raphie had bought for her.

Because her favourite place to sleep was his and Griff's bed, naturally.

Most of the time, Griff had to admit he loved having the scary furball close, and Raphie obviously cherished having her near. But right now, her daddies needed their special alone time.

Desperately.

Raphie dropped his head back and laughed as Sparrow gave them an impertinent meow, swished her tail, and hopped down from the bed.

"Sorry, baby," Raphie said with a giggle as Griff shut the door on her. However, he lost his mirth as soon as Griff turned his molten gaze back on him, and deposited him onto the mattress of the four-poster bed.

"Are you really that sorry?" Griff asked as he crawled over his lover.

Raphie shook his head, his eyes transfixed on Griff, his mouth hanging open until he gulped. "No," he rasped. He leaned up to capture Griff's lips for a kiss. "Oh, Griff. It's been days. I'm ready to explode."

Griff snorted as he reached down to squeeze Raphie's hard length through his pyjamas, making him gasp. It had maybe been thirty-six hours at most, but Griff sympathised. That did feel like an eternity for them. Griff usually took every opportunity to pleasure Raphie with his hands and his mouth, and Raphie had even topped him again the other night.

But Griff knew what he wanted now, and he was pretty sure Raphie was desperate for it, too.

"You still hung up on virginity being a social construct?" Griff teased.

Raphie scoffed and bit Griff's lower lip. "I literally don't give a fuck about anything other than getting you naked and coming all over you, Griff Thompson."

It was Griff's turn to shiver as he nuzzled their noses and cheeks together. Raphie was freshly shaved and smelled like honey and citrus, and Griff was ready to devour him.

"Well, I want to come *in* you, Raphael d'Oro. I want your arse cherry. I want to fuck you, knowing no one else ever has, and they never fucking will."

Raphie stilled, staring at Griff as he gulped. "Oh, wow," he whispered. He bit his lip and shoved his hand between them, pushing his silk bottoms down and squeezing the base of his throbbing, dripping cock *hard*. "S-sorry. I was about two seconds away from coming. *Jesus*, Griff. Yes! Hurry up and fucking *ravage* me. I've been wanting this so badly."

Griff growled as he pulled Raphie's pyjama bottoms all the way off and discarded his own robe, leaving them both gloriously naked. "Anything for you, beautiful," he murmured against Raphie's chest, trailing kisses until he found a nipple to suck and nibble. Raphie writhed under him, his hands tugging on Griff's hair.

Which reminded Griff of that mess he wanted to make.

He came off the swollen, shiny nipple and slipped his hand behind Raphie's neck, pulling his golden braid over his shoulder. "I want your hair loose," he said. Of course, he could have simply pulled the tie out himself, but he knew they'd both enjoy it more with Raphie following his demand.

Sure enough, Raphie panted shallow breaths, his pupils blown with lust as he hastily ripped out the band then began shaking out his plait. He leaned upwards, running both hands over his head, then flopping back down with his astonishing hair pooled around him like an angel.

It still hurt Griff to remember Raphie in the Italian tailors', telling him that 'kings don't look like this'. So far there had been minimum fuss over Raphie's appearance, with it being mostly miserable old men protesting. Everyone else was mesmerised by their new king's ethereal look, which Griff didn't find surprising at all.

But he was the only one who got to see Raphael d'Oro like this. Completely open and beautiful and pliant, waiting for Griff to fulfil his every desire.

"Your Highness," he murmured reverently, brushing the backs of his fingers along Raphie's jaw and down his neck.

Raphie bit his lip and whimpered, his hands resting on Griff's biceps as he breathed shakily.

"How do you want me?" he asked.

Griff couldn't help the lopsided grin that pulled at his mouth. "Fuck, I want you every way I can think of. It's all your fault. I haven't been this sex mad since I was your age."

"Good," Raphie said wickedly, squirming suggestively under Griff. "This boffin needs a lot of educating, remember? Teach me your sinful ways, baby."

Griff moaned and kissed Raphie's perfect, pretty mouth, wrapping his hand around both their cocks. "I love you, Raphie," he said for the hundredth time since the ball. The words still hadn't lost their shine, though. "I can't imagine a life without you in it."

Raphie gasped and trembled at Griff's touch, but there was still a playfulness in his eyes. "Then you'll be my duke, won't you?"

Griff snorted and bit his naughty king's lip. "Yes, I'll be your bloody duke – *someday*. Can we just focus on the outrageous fuck-fest we're about to have? This is an important, life changing moment of getting a dick up your arse for the first time."

Raphie cackled with laughter, kissing along Griff's jaw. "Fucking hell, I want you so badly, Griff. I love your cock. I want you to spear me with it. Rearrange my insides."

"You minx," Griff rasped, his dick so hard he had to take a few breaths to calm down. "I'm going to blow my load before I get anywhere near your arse if you keep that up."

Raphie batted his eyelashes innocently. "Sorry," he said, not sounding sorry at all.

Griff scoffed as he reached for his bedside cabinet, where he'd already stashed a healthy amount of supplies. They'd used the lube several times already that week, but this felt different as he drizzled it onto his fingers then moved down the bed.

He wanted Raphie to remember this time for the rest of his life.

Raphie wailed and gnashed his teeth deliciously as Griff swallowed his cock all the way down to the root and pushed his middle finger inside his tight, hot hole. Griff wanted to make sure Raphie was thoroughly prepared for his first time, and didn't mind taking his time stretching his lover out, ready to claim him.

But he also didn't want Raphie to come too early, so once he managed to get three fingers inside him, Griff pulled his mouth off Raphie's cock, moving down to eat out his hole for a little while. It was more to tease him than anything else, as he was already pretty stretched. Griff kneaded Raphie's cheeks, keeping them parted as he worked. When he finally came off, Raphie's thighs were trembling, and his hands were flopped by his head, on top of his fanned-out hair. His eyes were closed, and he was breathing shallowly like a little bird.

He was stunning.

Griff wiped the back of his hand over his mouth and crawled up the bed to kiss and nuzzle Raphie's cheek. "Wake up, Sleeping Beauty," he said playfully.

"Not sleeping," Raphie slurred, blinking his forest-green eyes open and focusing on Griff. "Good, Griff. So, so good."

Griff smiled and pressed their lips together. "Do you still want me inside you? Do you feel able?"

Raphie nodded, his enthusiasm clear as he came back to his senses. But then he glanced down to where Griff had lost a lot of his stiffness whilst he'd been tending to Raphie's delicious hole. "Oh," said Raphie sweetly, reaching out and wrapping his slim fingers around Griff's cock. "You need a little help first, though."

Griff grinned, enjoying the feel of Raphie's hand on him,

but wanting something else. "I do. How about you lie back and let me feed you?"

Raphie hummed and bit his lip, letting Griff's member go immediately. "Yummy," he whispered, licking his lips provocatively. "Are you going to fuck my face and then my hole?"

That half-fixed Griff's flagging erection there and then. He groaned and kissed Raphie's already swollen lips roughly. "You're bloody right, I am."

"Such a commanding duke I have," Raphie purred as Griff crawled up his body. "Come and service your king, Sir Griffin."

"Am I a duke or a knight? Make up your mind," Griff teased.

"It's my fantasy," said Raphie, looking lustfully through his eyelashes at Griff's approaching cock. "You can be whatever I want."

"Well, in *my* fantasy," said Griff, pretending to be menacing as he angled his throbbing length past Raphie's lips, "there's less chit-chat, and more sucking. That's it. Take it all, beautiful."

Raphie moaned, swallowing Griff down perfectly and grabbing Griff's arse cheeks with a slap. Griff jerked slightly, loving the little sting that gave him. But then he was grinding down, sliding his length along Raphie's tongue and throat. It would be so tempting to come like this. He was close enough to climaxing. But he only allowed Raphie to blow him for as long as it took to get painfully hard again, which took no time at all. Then he was pulling free, amused by Raphie's pout and disappointed whine.

"Ah-ah. None of that, Your Highness," Griff said. He tapped Raphie's full, red lips with a finger, then rolled onto his back. "You promised me your sweet virgin hole, and I want it all. Let me watch you lube up your arse and my cock, then lower yourself down onto me. Ride me like a noble steed."

That had Raphie giggling as he scrambled to do as he was told. And then he was back in Griff's favourite position, leaning over him with his curtains of beautiful hair hanging around them as he got the right angle and began slowly impaling himself on Griff's slick, pulsing shaft. As wonderful as their bubble was in their royal suite, this was utter perfection. Griff's whole world was reduced to Raphie, with nothing to concern him beyond his long, golden locks, which protected them both from the rest of the world.

He ran his hands up Raphie's chest to cup the side of his neck on one side and his jaw on the other. "I love you, Raphie," he said with as much sincerity as he possessed. "I can't believe how much my life has changed because of you. You're my *everything*." He gasped as Raphie forced his way a little further down his cock. "You're my king and country, and you do know someday I'll be your duke for all the world to see."

Raphie shuddered as he bottomed out, then promptly attacked Griff's mouth for a searing kiss. "You're my everything too, Griff. I love you so much. I'm so glad it was you. It'll only ever be you."

Griff hugged him tightly as they kissed, allowing Raphie time to adjust to the intrusion in his body. But soon he was moaning and rolling his hips, seeking further gratification.

Griff gave it to him.

He moved his hands down, gripping Raphie's hips, hard. He wanted to leave bruises from his fingers, like two constellations of stars. Raphie equally grappled with Griff's shoulders and chest, scratching and digging his fingers in to try and get purchase as he rode Griff's cock hard and fast. Griff knew when he tagged Raphie's prostate, as he dropped his head backwards and wailed, making his hair cascade like a waterfall down his back. The air was filled with their musk and grunts of pleasure and the frantic slapping of skin.

Griff let go of one of Raphie's hips and began wanking him off. "Come all over me," he rasped, "like you promised. I'm all yours."

*"Griff!"* Raphie bellowed, coming spectacularly on command all over Griff's chest, his muscles clenching around Griff's cock and tipping him over the edge. Griff arched his back and cried out, hugging Raphie to him as they both trembled, chasing their orgasms to completion. A few shuddery gasps later, Raphie collapsed on top of Griff, trembling and clinging to Griff like a life raft.

Griff gently kissed his forehead and moved his hair out of the way so he could see all of Raphie's flushed, beautiful face. "Was that good?" he asked. He personally thought it had been spectacular, but it was more important that Raphie had enjoyed it.

Raphie panted and swallowed, looking at Griff for a few seconds before he managed to nod. "Amazing," he said hoarsely. "Incredible. Everything I could have dreamed of."

Griff smiled, surprised to realise a couple of tears were in the corner of his eyes. He didn't fight them as they fell, though. It was okay to be emotional.

His life had been so drab, so hollow, so meaningless. And then he'd met this human ray of sunshine, and everything had changed. It had been a wild ride, but now they had forever to explore together.

"You're my dream," he said between leisurely kisses as he softened inside Raphie, in no rush to part.

Raphie sighed happily. "I used to feel like my world was so small, with so few people in it. Now I have you, and you're my whole world, and it doesn't feel small in the slightest. It feels like infinity."

"You and your marriage proposals," Griff grumbled,

tickling Raphie's side, making him squeal. "Can't you wait and let me do some romantic bollocks and at least *try* and surprise you?"

Raphie hummed, kissing him sweetly. "You surprise me every day," he said warmly. "And I think you know I waited my whole life for you to rescue me from that tower, Griff Thompson. I can wait a little longer for some romantic bollocks."

Griff laughed, hugging him close. He hoped it would always be like this, with happy, hopeful Raphie making sure grumpy Griff never came back for too long. And in return, Griff would protect and care for Raphie for the rest of their days.

This was what happily ever after felt like. And Griff was never letting it go.

---

THANK you for reading Raphie and Griff's story, I hope you enjoyed it! If you want to read the story of Prince James and his Essex boy, Theo, please check out my Cinderella adaptation, <u>A Right Royal Affair</u>.

For more contemporary MM fairy tale adaptations by Helen Juliet, please check out the links below for eBook, paperback, and audio!

<u>Thorn in His Side</u> – Beauty and the Beast

<u>Sweet Tooth</u> – Hansel and Gretel

<u>Rise and Shine</u> – Sleeping Beauty (short story)

---

TO KEEP up with all my latest news, enter giveaways, read WIP teasers, and have the opportunity to get ARCs of new releases, please join my Facebook group, <u>Helen's Jewels</u>.

For more Helen Juliet books, please visit www.helenjuliet.com

For more books and freebie shorts from my American pen name, HJ Welch, please go to www.hjwelch.com.

***

Thank you to my team!

Cover Design: Cate Ashwood

Beta Reading: Amy Pittel

Editing: Meg Cooper

Proof Reading: Tanja Ongkiehong

General Awesomeness: Cheesebags (Ed, Amelia, and Conrad), Mummy, Hubby, and the magnificent fur babies, Arya and Tyrion. They could totally take down an assassin, too. Right after they've had a nap…

Joshua is determined to bring joy to Darius's life again, and Darius refuses to let Joshua hide his sweetness from the world any longer. Over time, it becomes clear that despite their differences, their hearts are drawing closer together. But can happiness ever be possible for a rose and a thorn when Darius's father will go to any lengths to see his deadly game through?

*Thorn in His Side is a steamy, standalone MM romance novel featuring tender bubble baths, a stubborn but loyal horse, thunder storms, enough healing touches to mend any broken heart, and a guaranteed HEA with absolutely no cliffhanger.*

**Click here to get the Thorn in His Side eBook**

**Click here to get the Thorn in His Side audio**

event savvy to throw a fundraiser ball in a secluded castle. All James has to do is behave himself around the sassy twink. But soon the chemistry between them is too strong to resist.

Their lives are too different and there's no chance James can come out as the first Prince of the United Kingdom with a boyfriend. But James knows if he doesn't show Theo how much he means to him, he'll lose him forever. Can love conquer all? Or is that something just for fairy tales?

*A Right Royal Affair is a steamy, standalone MM romance novel featuring a pack of unruly royal terriers, a romantic ball, feisty swans, a wicked step-father and a guaranteed HEA with absolutely no cliffhanger.*

**Click here to get the A Right Royal Affair eBook**

**Click here to get the A Right Royal Affair audio**

magical reunion, and Hans is feeling more lost than ever. Could Chester be enough to guide him back to true love?

*Sweet Tooth is a steamy, standalone MM romance novel featuring a scrumptious sweet shop, slow dancing to Elton John, an explosive family dinner, a loyal puppy, a very naughty use for candy canes, and a guaranteed HEA with absolutely no cliffhanger.*

**Click here to get the Sweet Tooth eBook**

**Sweet Tooth audio, coming soon!**

Rise and Shine

Luca feels like he's been asleep for a hundred years, but really it was just one bad night. He awakes in a room he's never seen before with a note from a mysterious stranger who seems to have come to his rescue.

Before he can sneak out, he finds himself face to face with his gorgeous knight in shining armour. It turns out that Ryan saved him from more than just a bad hangover. In a day that feels like a dream, Luca and Ryan discover their attraction, but as a simple tailor and a club bouncer, they're completely opposite. Could this really be true love?

*Rise and Shine is a 17K word steamy, standalone MM romance novella featuring a match-making Labrador, too much pizza, just the right amount of sofa snuggles, and a guaranteed HEA with absolutely no cliffhanger. Please note this story was previously released as a free giveaway. No content has been changed.*

**Click here to get the Rise and Shine eBook**

**Coming Soon: Rise and Shine audio**

# ABOUT THE AUTHOR

Helen Juliet is a contemporary MM romance author living in London with her husband and two balls of fluff that occasionally pretend to be cats. She began writing at an early age, later honing her craft online in the world of fanfiction on sites like Wattpad. Fifteen years and over a million words later, she sought out original MM novels to read. By the end of 2016 she had written her first book of her own, and in 2017 she achieved her lifelong dream of becoming a fulltime author.

Helen also writes contemporary American MM romance as HJ Welch.

You can contact Helen Juliet via social media:

Newsletter (with FREE original stories) – https://www.subscribepage.com/helenjuliet

Website – www.helenjuliet.com

Facebook Group – Helen's Jewels

Facebook Page – @helenjulietauthor

Instagram – @helenjwrites

Twitter – @helenjwrites

9 781838 124052